TREBIZOND

TREBIZOND

N J HOLMES

Matador
9 Priory Business Park,
Wistow Road, Kibworth Beauchamp,
Leicestershire. LE8 0RX
Tel: (+44) 116 279 2299
Fax: (+44) 116 279 2277
Email: books@troubador.co.uk
Web: www.troubador.co.uk/matador

ISBN 9781783060092

British Library Cataloguing in Publication Data.
A catalogue record for this book is available from the British Library.

Typeset by Troubador Publishing Ltd, Leicester, UK
Printed and bound in the UK by TJ International, Padstow, Cornwall

Matador is an imprint of Troubador Publishing Ltd

For Sarah

CONTENTS

BYZANTIN

KINGDOM OF
HUNGARY

Danube

PECHENEGS

DALMATIA

ADRIATIC SEA

NORMANS

BULGARIA ● Sardica

MACEDONIA

Adrianople ●

Constantin

Bari ●

Thessalonica ●

AEGEAN
SEA

ARABS

Sn

● Syracuse

Rh

Crete

MEDITERRANEAN SE

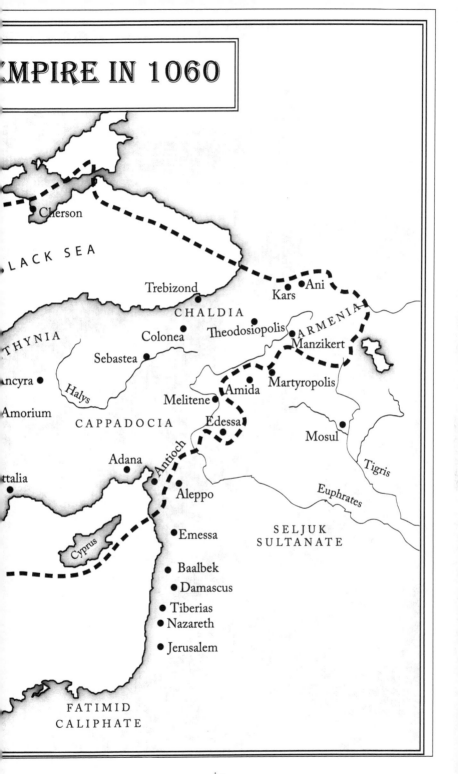

EMPIRE IN 1060

Cherson

BLACK SEA

Trebizond

Kars

Ani

CHALDIA

Colonea

Theodosiopolis

ARMENIA

Manzikert

BITHYNIA

Sebastea

Ancyra

Halys

Melitene

Amida

Martyropolis

Amorium

CAPPADOCIA

Edessa

Mosul

Adana

Antioch

Tigris

Attalia

Aleppo

Euphrates

Cyprus

Emessa

SELJUK
SULTANATE

Baalbek

Damascus

Tiberias

Nazareth

Jerusalem

FATIMID
CALIPHATE

THE WARS O
106'

Constantinople

Dokeia
1071

An

Nicaea

Sangarius

Halys

Dorylaeum

Ancyra

Cotyaeum

Amorium
1068

Smyrna

Iconium
1069

Chonae
1070

Ac
10

MEDITERRANEAN SEA

0   100   200 miles
0   100   200 km

ROMANUS DIOGENES
1072

Neocaesarea
1068

Trebizond

Kars
Araxes
Ani

Theodosiopolis

Sebastea

Tephrice
1068

Manzikert
1071

Khilat

Khoi

Caesarea
1067

Larissa
1069

Melitene
Tigris

Balesh
Martyropolis

manicea

Amida

Edessa
1068

Mosul

Euphrates

och Hierapolis
1068

SELJUK SULTANATE

Aleppo

	Major Battle
	City Sacked by Afsin
	City Sacked by Turks
	Byzantine Frontier

The Byzantines are a forgotten people. They called themselves Romans. In reality they were Greeks who saw themselves as the heirs of the Roman Caesars. When the Dark Ages enveloped Europe, they were the sole lantern bearers from a distant and glorious past.

Their disciplined and iron-clad armies, a legacy of the Roman Legions, ensured their survival. By the eleventh century, they were still the greatest power in Europe. Their Empire extended from Syria to the Danube.

It was in these years that a new enemy appeared from the Asian steppes. They were nomadic horsemen called the Turks. Descendants of the Huns, they would shatter the conventions of warfare. First, they subjugated the Persians and Arabs. Now Byzantium lay in their path.

The course of history was about to be changed, not just for Byzantium but for the whole of Europe.

PROLOGUE

They came from the East. Turkish horsemen riding fast through the long grass that rose and fell like the waves of the sea. The clouds scudded across the blue sky. Behind them the early morning sun was rising like an arc of fire, burning on the horizon.

Antonius Kamaterus looked out at the Turks from the dark stone ramparts of the fort. He could hear a menacing beating of drums and saw the riders breaking up into smaller groups. By the saints, there must be over a thousand of them, he thought to himself.

Antonius was the commander of the Roman garrison in the Armenian border-land of Tayk, and as he watched the Turks, he cursed that he was here, in this desolate edge of the world, trapped by its snow-capped mountains.

He thought of his wife and small daughter in Constantinople. At least they were safe in his parents' house. He raised his eyes upwards, thinking of the great face of Christ in the dome of the Cathedral of Haghia Sophia in Constantinople, and murmured a prayer that he would see them again.

"Is the gate fully secure?" he called down to his men as they lifted the last heavy wooden beams into place. Telling his second-in-command, Himerius, to keep watching the Turks, he turned and ran down the wooden steps that led from the wall to the gate. Two heavy wooden beams ran across it, reinforced by two more beams embedded in the ground and propped up against it. It was the best they could do.

Then Antonius ran back up the steps to the walls and disappeared into the fort's single tower, sited beside the gate. He climbed up the ladder that took him to the top, just one floor above the wall. His archers were waiting. There were about thirty of them, some armed with crossbows. From the top of the tower they had the gate well covered.

"Get ready for an attack any moment," he told the officer in charge of the archers. "Keep your heads down and cover the gate."

He had about two hundred foot soldiers spread along the walls, well armed with chainmail coats, large round shields, swords and spears. He climbed down the ladder to the top of the wall and ran along it, telling his men to prepare for battle.

"They're only raiders, we can hold them off," he told his soldiers but he knew his confidence sounded false.

By the time he was back on the section of wall above the gate, the Turks were cantering in small groups around the fort. He wondered where they would strike first.

The fort was sited on top of a hill. On one side was a steep drop while on the other sides the ground fell away gently, perfect for the Turks to manoeuvre their horses. Several groups of Turks began to move closer to the side where the gate and tower stood.

"Get ready to shoot!" Antonius called to the archers at the top of the tower.

Suddenly, a group of Turks made a break towards the section of wall where Antonius was. The archers leant over the crenellations and shot at the riders. Most of the arrows went wide but a crossbow bolt found its mark in one of the Turkish horses which stumbled and fell, throwing its rider.

Then before they reached the wall, the Turks suddenly stopped and turned. Antonius felt a sense of relief. Were they retreating? But as they turned, they raised their bows and a hail of arrows flew towards the Roman archers in the tower.

Although the Turks were shooting from horseback, they shot with astonishing accuracy from powerful, recurved bows, and a hail of iron-tipped arrows smashed into the Roman archers. There were screams and a man pitched headfirst from the tower. Antonius glanced back to see another group of them loosing their arrows at the tower as they turned. He'd heard about the Turks' skill at archery but he hadn't expected this devastation.

Grabbing a large round infantry shield for protection, he ran along the wall into the tower and climbed up the ladder. When he raised his head through the opening, he felt an arrow whistle close to his head. He ducked down and waited for a few seconds. Then holding his shield up, he leapt through the opening and onto the floor of the ramparts.

He was shocked by what he saw. The surviving archers were huddled behind the crenellations, not daring to shoot back. On the floor were a dozen dead and wounded. Some were screaming in pain, others trying to drag themselves to safety.

"Help me move the wounded!" he shouted at the archers but none of them moved. Just then another barrage of arrows rained down on them. Antonius crouched behind his shield as arrows thudded into it. One of them broke through the shield's metal cover and lodged itself in the wooden frame, its barbed iron head sticking out and grazing his leg. Ducking down, he leapt behind the stone ramparts.

Then, peering down at the gate, he saw a group of Turks carrying a long pine tree, sharpened to a point. They were surrounded on either side by horsemen who milled around in front of the walls, so contemptuous were they of the Roman archers, and poured a hail of arrows onto the tower and walls.

Antonius stared and his fear grew. The Turks had defeated his archers and there was no way of stopping the battering ram. He could only think of one thing to do. He waited for the next barrage of arrows to pass and scrambled to the ladder and down to the wall. He ran along it, crouching down, as arrows hissed past. As he went, he told his men to gather at the gate. Many of them were wounded or dead, hit by the arrows. Ahead of them, he saw his second-in-command, Himerius, sprawled on the walkway. He stopped and leant down to roll him over. His glazed eyes stared up at him. An arrow was embedded deep into his neck and blood seeped from his mouth.

"May God receive you in heaven, my friend," he murmured and continued along the wall, telling his men to go to the gate. As he went, he could hear the Turkish battering ram start to hammer on the gates.

Antonius gathered his men in front of the gate and they crouched behind their shields for protection from the murderous rain of arrows. He told them that when the gate buckled they could hold the Turks in the gateway. They had heavier armour than the Turks and they could beat them in hand-to-hand combat. The Turks could ride and shoot but on foot they could be beaten. He told them to crowd behind the gate and when it buckled to force their way through and form a shield wall.

They waited and the arrows kept falling. Every so often there would be a scream or angry cursing as an arrow found its mark. The gate shuddered painfully and the wood started to fracture and Antonius knew it wouldn't be long.

Then with a great crack the gates buckled open and the battering ram burst through. Antonius and his men were pushed back by the impact of the gates but he called out the battle-cry and they pressed forward, hacking at the Turks on foot. Antonius was in the front rank and he drove a spear through the chest of the first Turk who fell to his knees, clutching it. The Romans hacked down a few more but the bearers of the battering ram didn't fight back and fled, dropping it in the gateway.

"Hold the gate!" Antonius shouted out and the Romans stopped and didn't pursue the fleeing Turks. Then the arrows came again and there were so many of them that it seemed as if they darkened the skies. Men fell all around Antonius, arrows even piercing helmets and chainmail.

"Form the shield wall!" Antonius called out, and the Romans crouched behind their large round shields.

Then the arrows stopped.

Antonius dared to peer round his shield.

He gasped in horror at what he saw. It was not infantry that were charging towards them but horsemen and horsemen that were possessed by the devil. He glimpsed the savage faces of the Turks bearing down on him, spears thrust forward and heavy iron maces and swords held aloft. He called out to his men.

"Hold firm!"

But the impact of the Turkish charge was devastating. Their horses were fiery and trampled and kicked at the Romans as their riders ran their spears into the men in the front rank and drove their horses onwards, slashing and hammering with maces and swords at the soldiers behind.

Within seconds the Turkish cavalry had broken the shield wall and ridden deep into the mass of Roman infantry. As more and more horsemen ploughed into them, the Romans were flung aside or trampled underfoot.

Antonius himself had been knocked down in the first impact. As the horses rode over him, he found he could not stand. His right leg had been broken. In desperation he tried to drag his shattered leg across the ground. But he felt the pounding of the Turkish hooves all around him and lay still. He stared around him and all he could see was a mass of Turkish horsemen. His own men seemed to have disappeared, swept away into nothing.

Then a horseman stopped beside him. Antonius tried to raise himself, holding his shield up. He looked up, and for a second he saw a Turk in a gilded helmet and wearing finely wrought chainmail. He knew this must be their warlord. He saw eyes of steel looking down at him and he felt a weapon fly at his head from out of nowhere. Then he saw no more.

The Turk took a spear from one of his men and drove it into Antonius's severed head as it lay by his body. He lifted it up and held it aloft.

The warlord's name was Afsin.

PART I

SAILING TO TREBIZOND

April 1060

In those days, no walk of life was spared its tears and lamentation. Cities were wiped out, lands ravaged, all the territories of Rome were stained with blood. Some died miserably, pierced by arrow or lance; others were driven from their homes or carried off as prisoners of war. Dread seized on all as they hurried to seek refuge from impending disaster in caves, forests, mountains and hills. There they loudly bewailed the fate of their friends, mourned the loss of sons or grieved for their daughters; one wept for a brother, another for a nephew killed before his time and like women they shed bitter tears.

Anna Comnena, The Alexiad

I

It was Easter and the bells rang out in the great cathedral of St Chrysokephalos in Trebizond. They echoed crisply in the blue sky as a cool breeze from the sea spread through the city on that bright spring morning in 1060.

The chill of winter was fading and the spring sunlight beckoned to the inhabitants of this Greek city on the edge of the Euxine Sea, first founded by Greek colonists more than fifteen hundred years ago, and now part of an Empire that still called itself Roman and which had survived the collapse of its western half long ago.

The city spread inland from the harbour to its ancient citadel, climbing up a sloping table of ground that rose above steep rocky precipices on each side, with tall crenellated walls fiercely encircling it. The Greeks who had first founded it chose the site for its defensive position and called it Trapezus, meaning table in Greek. A sea of red clay roof tiles, punctuated by the domes of churches, lay within the city's walls which crossed twice to divide it into three fortified towns: the harbour, the middle town and the citadel, making the city appear as one huge fortification. Visitors, be they friend or foe, were not surprised to learn, as they gazed at the light-coloured stone walls, that no enemy had ever taken the city.

The Bishop had just finished his sermon, urging his congregation to pray to God each day for salvation from the Turks who had been sent to plague the Empire in punishment of the sinners amongst them. If only the citizens of Melitene and Sebastea, so horribly sacked by the Turks, had heeded the words of the Patriarch in Constantinople to pray for deliverance, then surely their destruction would have been prevented by the all-powerful lord. And now the Turks were besieging Edessa and Antioch in northern Syria with only the colossal ancient walls of both cities enabling them to survive. He added that God had blessed Trebizond with similar defences, built in times long forgotten, which would save them from the Turks if the Lord so wished.

He asked them to recite the Lord's Prayer and pray for God's forgiveness.

Then just as the congregation was dispersing, shouts rang out from the lower town by the harbour. Ships had been sighted. The townspeople flocked to the harbour, forgetting their preparations for lunch. They were not frightened, for the Turks had no naval power and the imperial fleet had always commanded the waterways and had many times defeated the longships of the Rus from the north.

They stared with excitement at a number of large boats, warships with oars and merchantmen equipped only with sails, still distant specks on the horizon, coming closer. Some of the crowd said that they knew who was in the boats. It was the commander of the Danube army, the Vestarch Romanus Diogenes, fresh from his victory over the Pechenegs in the Western Themes, as the provinces were called. They said that Alexius Gabras, the Count of Trebizond and Chaldia, had called a great meeting of the nobles of all the Eastern Themes to raise an army to fight the Turks.

The city rose steeply from the harbour to its citadel, affording a good view of the sea and, as the crowd chattered, pairs of eyes from all over the city watched the approaching fleet.

And no one watched more intently than Theodore Gabras, the Count's third son, who gazed from a window high in one of the towers of his father's castle in the citadel. He was sixteen years old, quite tall and with a strong build, but what was most striking about him were his hazel-coloured eyes which had a sensibility that decried the arrogance of his class.

Theodore was similar but also different from his two older brothers. Like them, he loved to hunt and to sail but whereas much of their enjoyment seemed to involve showing off about their exploits, he didn't feel the need to assert himself in this way. He was naturally kind and considerate, especially to those less fortunate than himself, and the arrogance and occasional brutality that his family exhibited as they governed the Theme of Chaldia was distasteful to him and sometimes made him feel isolated from them.

Yet, his sensitivity did not make him in any way weak or ineffective. In fact, he was one of the most determined and hardy of young men although this showed itself in his independent spirit rather than rough behaviour. He loved to escape from life at the castle, either riding fast into the pinewood forests that covered the steep mountainsides outside Trebizond, or sailing along the coastline to the fishing villages. Often he would go with his friends but sometimes he just enjoyed setting off on his own adventure.

He also had a clarity of mind and honesty of opinion that would get him into arguments with his brothers and parents. He could not lie and he would not flatter people with false comments or agreement. Many times this led to blows with his older brothers but he enjoyed this conflict when he felt that he was in the right.

His parents viewed him sympathetically. Since he would not inherit his father's title and wealth, they welcomed his independence and energy as signs that he would be able to succeed in establishing himself in the world outside Trebizond.

With girls he was inexperienced for his age, although this was certainly not for lack of interest. However, he would not use his status as a means of seducing girls of a lower social position, as his brothers routinely did. He was repelled by their frequent liaisons with serving girls or daughters of the wealthier merchants. His behaviour earned him the respect of his two sisters and they reassured him that he would meet someone from a good family in due course. Nevertheless, Trebizond was in a far-flung corner of the Empire and travel to it was difficult over the tall mountains, so that what visitors they had normally came by boat and were few in number. As he watched the fleet approach the city, he could not help but hope that these great nobles were also bringing their families, including their daughters, with them.

When the fleet finally docked in the harbour, the city was invaded, but not by a brutal enemy force, only by the multitude of excited guests, the newly arrived passengers from the boats. And Theodore's hopes, together with those of his two older brothers, were met when he saw whole families disembark from the boats.

Preparations were afoot for a great feast that night and the castle within the citadel was bustling with activity. Servants ran this way and that. An amphora of wine was smashed in the courtyard of the castle. Angry shouting ensued. The guests were shown to their rooms, and on a staircase Theodore passed a rather forbidding looking man and wife, clearly important members of the aristocracy, but from where he did not know, and after bowing deeply to them, he looked up and saw a girl of his own age, presumably their daughter.

Without thinking he stopped and turned to address her

father, asking if they needed any help. He rapidly introduced himself and the father smiled and looked less forbidding, explaining that he was John Taronites, the Count of the Anatolikon Theme. Then, as Theodore had hoped, he introduced his daughter. Her name was Eirene.

The moment Theodore saw her he knew that there was something special about her. Any man would have been attracted to her beautiful brown eyes and slim, striking figure but what captivated him above all was her demeanour. He sensed a natural, honest confidence and cleverness that would find few equals. And standing there in front of her, he felt embarrassed for he couldn't think of anything clever or amusing to say.

"You've travelled far. You must be tired." He tried to smile as if he had said something witty but it only made him cringe with embarrassment.

She answered simply and directly, "Yes, but we were lucky. The sea was calm."

That afternoon, Theodore could think of nothing but Eirene. He longed to see her again although he told himself that it was absurd to fall for her. Why should she be interested in him? Not only was he a poor marriage prospect, being a third son unable to inherit his father's title and power, but she had also shown no interest in him when they had met. Yet he couldn't stop thinking that he had just one more chance to see her at the feast that evening.

At last evening came, and Theodore joined his family in the great hall of the castle where banqueting tables were set out to form a hollow square. The finest food and wine was laid out: roast lamb with honey and oregano, seafood of all shapes and sizes cooked in the purest olive oil, and the most expensive fruit and wines. They were served in beautifully decorated plates and bowls, their shiny glazes covering bright colours of blue, green and yellow, illuminating vivid depictions

7

of octopuses, fish and scenes of harvesting and hunting.

The men and women were strictly separated, although the father of a family could introduce his wife and daughters to other families. Theodore looked everywhere for Eirene but could not see her. His heart sank. She was not there. He cursed himself for allowing his hopes to grow, and couldn't bring himself to smile as he was introduced to the many new faces.

But finally he found her. She was there, among the last of the throng of guests being introduced by his father. He bowed to her and when he lifted his head their eyes met. She smiled at him but no more than she might do to anyone. He so wanted to say something to her that would make her laugh but he couldn't think of anything and just mumbled a greeting.

Still numb from his sense that he would not speak with her again, he was next introduced to Andronicus Ducas, the Emperor's nephew. Andronicus was a few years older than Theodore and he was an amazingly tall young man renowned for his intelligence, good looks and skills at horsemanship and swordplay. He was said to have distinguished himself on the battlefield, fighting the Pechenegs the year before.

"Delighted to meet you," Andronicus said. He smiled at Theodore who felt flattered to be addressed in such a gracious manner by someone so universally admired. "Trebizond is a beautiful city; you are lucky to live here. I look forward to hunting in the pine forests."

Theodore felt embarrassed about his provincial background and answered politely and turned away.

A few minutes later, he saw Andronicus talking to Eirene. He was chatting and laughing with her. She seemed to enjoy his company. His eldest brother, seeing Theodore looking at Eirene, jabbed his elbow into his ribs and laughed.

"Don't raise your hopes with her. Didn't you know that

she's going to be betrothed to Andronicus? Apparently, he's besotted with her. Her family talk about nothing else. What a match!"

Theodore slipped outside onto a terrace in the cool night air. There was a superb view over the harbour. He looked at the fishing boats moored to wooden jetties. Some were rowing out into the dark sea with candles lit in glass bowls. What a fool he had been to fall for her, he thought. He knew that compared with Andronicus, he was nothing. Forget her completely, he told himself as he stared grimly at the dots of light on the black water, and he stood up straight and turned on his heel like a soldier on the parade ground and returned to the party.

Later, when the feast was in full swing and the air was filled with chatter and the sound of music from harps and recorders, he saw Andronicus trip over a half-grown dog that was scavenging under the dining tables. The animal had seen something and bolted across Andronicus' path just as he was walking to speak to someone. Andronicus tripped and staggered forward, with his arms outstretched and steadied himself just in time to avoid falling. He knew he had looked foolish. His normal relaxed smile disappeared.

He looked for the dog which had found the discarded chicken leg that had caught its attention and was lying on the ground, gnawing it. He went and gave the animal a savage kick that sent it running away, squealing with pain and surprise. But Andronicus had not finished. Theodore saw him follow the dog into a corner of the hall where it sat, cowering, as he approached it.

Theodore did not think about what he was doing. He saw the animal's face. It was a hunting dog, a few months old, and not wise to the ways of the world. Its brown eyes were terrified and it shivered and whimpered with fear as Andronicus approached it. Theodore rose from his place and, ignored by the throng of chattering and laughing people, he rushed to Andronicus's side.

"My lord, he's only a puppy. Spare him."

Andronicus turned round, surprised to be interrupted. His look alarmed Theodore. There was no anger in it but there was something strange.

"I don't like a disobedient dog." And he took his leg back, about to give the animal a kick that would probably have sent it to its maker.

Theodore grabbed his arm and pulled him back.

"Leave him alone!"

Andronicus turned around and said softly: "Get off me. Who do you think you are?"

Theodore let go of Andronicus. The puppy's terrified eyes looked up, expecting its end at any moment.

"I won't let you kick it," Theodore heard himself saying, as he put himself inbetween Andronicus and the puppy, and immediately regretted it. What on earth did he think he was doing, saying this to the Emperor's nephew? Suddenly, footsteps rang out and a woman's voice said:

"I want the dog. I'll take him. Give him to me."

It was Eirene. Andronicus was speechless. He looked at his betrothed and then again at Theodore. Then his smile returned.

"Of course, but for one as beautiful as you, this dog is a poor gift indeed. Let him have it since he has such a liking for the animal." Andronicus laughed, and taking Eirene's hand, he led her past Theodore and back towards the feast. But just as they left him, Eirene stopped and turned.

"Xenophon would have had a name for your dog," she said mysteriously.

Theodore looked on in silence, unsure what to say. Andronicus was pretending to ignore the exchange and looked the other way.

"Why Xenophon?" Theodore asked, wondering vaguely

if she meant the soldier and writer from ancient times.

"Because he loved dogs. And he fought bullies. And he came here to Trebizond. You must know that. Call him Actis."

Theodore bowed, puzzled by her remark, and lifting his head he saw Eirene looking straight at him. She smiled before looking away quickly. Andronicus pretended not to be listening. Then Theodore left them and went to pick up the puppy which wagged his tail and reached up to lick his face. Both of them had never felt happier.

The chatter and music of the feast resumed and then there was dancing. The men and women danced in separate lines facing each other but separated by a large enough gap to prevent any physical contact. Dancing was discouraged by the church as unseemly but it was nevertheless the highlight of every feast. Each age group danced in turn and, when Theodore stood up, he was pleased to see Eirene do the same. She moved towards him until they were facing each other, dancing the steps they knew by heart, without being able to touch but smiling triumphantly at each other. When they finished dancing, her eyes met his and she smiled in a knowing way so that when he returned to the table, his heart was pounding.

Later, when a performance by a troupe of Cretan acrobats engrossed everyone's attention, Theodore saw Eirene get up from her table and walk towards the tall lancet windows at the back of the hall, overlooking the sea. She glanced in his direction, and seeing this, Theodore stood up carefully so as not to be noticed, and strode casually over to her, hoping no-one would notice. But he need not have worried since all the eyes in the hall were transfixed on a goblet of wine as it was passed to a Cretan standing on top of a human pyramid, four people high.

"How's your dog?" she asked him with a mischievous look.

"Happy he's still alive."

Suddenly she looked deathly serious.

"I hate Andronicus," she whispered to him. "Mama wants me to marry him so that we can join the imperial family but I'd kill myself before marrying him."

"Will you marry me?" Theodore asked, for they were the only words he could think of.

"Yes," she said. "Ask your parents quickly. Ask them tonight. I'll persuade my father to accept. I can always get him to do what I want."

She took his hands in hers and he put his arms around her and their lips met. They kissed like children at first, and then passion took hold of both of them, and they held each other tightly and kissed like lovers. If anyone had seen them, it would have been a flogging for him and a nunnery for her for such shocking behaviour, but fortunately for them all eyes were still fixed on the Cretan who this time was juggling with three apples, the goblet of wine on his head.

Eirene knew it was only a matter of seconds before someone saw them, so she pushed Theodore away.

"Quickly. We mustn't be seen. Ask your parents. I'll get a servant to send you a message in the morning."

Theodore returned to his table in a daze. But little did he know that for him the events of that evening had only just begun.

II

Theodore's sister stared at him, her female intuition sensing that something was up. But he ignored her and his brothers and sat staring at the Cretan acrobats as they cleared their stage props away. The highlight of the evening was still to come and the sense of festivity in the great hall was turning to nervous expectation.

For everyone in the gathering knew that a rebellion against the Emperor might be announced that evening. The Emperor, Constantine Ducas, Andronicus' uncle, was hated more now than ever before. The powerful nobles of the Eastern Themes wanted action to be taken against the Turks. But Constantine opposed the mustering of the thematic armies precisely because he thought they could be turned against him. He had even disbanded the Armenian army that guarded the frontier against the Turks and now the Turks were pillaging the countryside with horrific brutality. The Eastern nobles wanted an Emperor who would lead an army against the Turks, and that man was Romanus Diogenes, the Count of the Cappadocian Theme and the most successful general in the Empire. Would it be tonight that he raised his standard to march against Constantine?

Theodore glanced up at his father, as he rose to his feet and banged the table. The chattering throng of people fell silent.

His father began by thanking the guests for travelling so far to Trebizond. He said that the Empire was in great danger. The Turks were overrunning Armenia and the Emperor Constantine had done nothing to stop them. Indeed, he had actually helped the Turks by disbanding much of the Armenian thematic army, preferring to have Armenian gold instead of military service. By doing this he had condemned to death the soldiers in the frontier forts who had been overwhelmed by the Turks. Now the Turks had taken control of most of Armenia. Only the main cities with strong walls and citadels still held out: Manzikert in the South, Ani and Kars in the North. But how much longer could they hold out for? Was Constantine sending an army to save Armenia? No. And where would the Turks attack next? The answer lay with the slaughter in Melitene and Sebastea. Our women raped, our children killed!

Theodore's father paused. What he had said about the Emperor was treasonable. His audience waited. Was now the moment when he would raise a rebellion and call on them to march on Constantinople to depose him?

Theodore's father lowered his voice and spoke very calmly. No, he didn't want a civil war. No, he didn't want to march on Constantinople. If they did that, would there be any soldiers left to fight the Turks? He wanted peace but he wanted the Emperor to listen to the demands of the Eastern Themes for an army to be raised to defend the frontier. Would he lead this petition to the Emperor? No, there was someone a thousand times more able and better suited to do this than him.

Theodore's father gestured at the man sitting next to him who rose to his feet, smiling. It was Romanus Diogenes. It was he who would approach the Emperor, Theodore's father said, for he was already the greatest soldier the Empire had, the man to whom the Emperor was indebted for his victory over the Pechenegs in Bulgaria.

There was rapturous applause. Romanus held out his hands, thanking them and asking for silence. He was every inch the soldier. Tall, strong and handsome, he smiled at the great assembly with a firm look of confidence in his eyes.

"First, let me say that I have sworn an oath of allegiance to the Emperor. We are not here today to raise rebellion. Just the opposite. We are here to help the Emperor to defend his Empire. Now I ask you, the leaders of the Eastern Themes, to support me in petitioning the Emperor to raise an army here in the East to fight the Turks. This can only be done by replacing taxation with military service as existed in the old days. Our people used to pay their taxes through service to the Emperor's standards. And those armies raised here in the Themes saved the Empire from the Arabs in the old days. Today, it is only our soldiers who can defeat the Turks. The Emperor's mercenaries are too few and untrustworthy, as we know from what happened to the army he sent to Armenia two years ago. Those mercenaries fled before the Turks and our cities were sacked."

The men among the guests rose to their feet and applauded loudly. He smiled at them confidently and held out his hand for silence.

"I have one more important thing to say! We are not alone in the Eastern Themes in understanding the threat of the Turks. Here beside me is a member of the Imperial family, the Emperor's nephew, Andronicus Ducas."

Andronicus rose to his feet beside Romanus who put his hand on his shoulder in a brotherly fashion.

"Andronicus has been the commander of the Scholae regiment, my best soldiers, in the Pecheneg wars. He has fought valiantly by my side. He has suffered the hardship of war with us. He is not only my most trusted officer but he is also my friend and he has promised to help me persuade his uncle, the Emperor, to fight the Turks."

Again there was wild applause and the men in the gathering rose to their feet and banged the tables in front of them. Andronicus surveyed his audience, smiling indulgently at them.

"My lords and ladies, it is an honour for me to have the trust of Romanus, my commander and the most talented general in the Empire. Let me tell you that I will not rest until I have persuaded my uncle, the Emperor, to help you defend your lands from the Turks. I regard it as my personal mission to help you!"

But as the applause broke out again, a man suddenly leapt forward from one of the tables to Andronicus's right. It happened so fast that most of the guests were not even aware of it but Theodore had a clear view from where he was sitting.

He saw a tall man with long black hair that fell in curls around his shoulders. His face was deeply tanned so that the whites of his eyes appeared even more prominent; eyes that flashed with anger. In his right hand he seemed to carry a dagger. He flung himself at Andronicus and slashed at him with the weapon. Andronicus shouted out in pain. The man had wounded him. There was a scuffle. Romanus seemed to be fending the man off, protecting Andronicus. The man fled.

"Guards, seize him!" Theodore's father shouted out.

But Theodore saw the man rush through the doorway and escape his pursuers. The crowd stared in shock, unsure what had actually happened.

Andronicus staggered to his feet. His eyes stared at the assembled crowd. He looked shaken.

"It's only a scratch," he spoke hoarsely, holding his arm which was red with blood. "Don't worry about me. We have more important things to attend to."

Theodore's father spoke loudly and clearly, his voice echoing in the silent hall, still frozen with shock: "My lord, I beg your forgiveness for this outrage on your honour. I assure you we will hunt down this murderous madman."

"Please excuse me while I have my wound bound," Andronicus said grimly. "But I will be back, and let the party continue!" he added heroically, smiling at his audience.

The guests broke into loud applause.

Andronicus forced himself to smile and bowed his head graciously, but Theodore, who like everyone else in the room had been gripped by the spectacle, thought there was something more than just shock that stayed in his expression. There was just a trace of guilt.

Theodore's father went around reassuring the guests, and it was not long before the genial atmosphere returned. There were no more speeches but when the women retired, the men remained to discuss further the petition they would bring to the Emperor.

But the guards did not return with the man. He had escaped.

In the early hours of the next day, Theodore retired to the room that he was sharing with his brothers, his own room having been given to guests. He had drunk a fair amount of wine and immediately fell asleep, dreaming of Eirene.

A few hours later he was woken by his full bladder, having drunk his fill of water to avoid a hangover, and staggered out of the room and down the spiral stairwell to the latrines, which were sited on the ground floor of the castle.

His mind was still fuzzy from the wine and the excitement of meeting Eirene. Leaning against the stone to steady himself, he trod carefully down the steps of the spiral stairwell. He met no one but he had a strange sense that he was being watched.

Then, when he'd relieved himself and was making his way back up the staircase, a figure jumped out of the shadows and put a strong, muscular arm around his neck and he felt the sharp point of a dagger held against his back.

"Tell me how to get out of here or I'll kill you," a voice whispered in his ear with the tinge of an Armenian accent. He could smell the sweat from the man's body. It made him want to retch.

"What? Who are you?" Theodore stammered in shock. He tried to turn his head to see who the man was but the arm around his throat was too tight for him to move his head.

"Just tell me how to get out of here. Show me the way."

"I will. Let go of my neck. I can't breathe."

The knife seemed to stick more forcefully into Theodore's back as the arm around his neck relaxed.

"If you run, I'll kill you," the man spoke with quiet grimness.

Theodore didn't doubt what he said. But he couldn't think of how to get out of the castle. The main gates were normally manned at night.

"Where do you want to go? To the port?" He asked lamely.

"No. Just get me out of the town. Is there any way where we won't be noticed?"

"No." Theodore honestly couldn't think of a way out which wouldn't be guarded.

"If you can't think of anywhere, I'll kill you."

Theodore's fear was replaced with anger and frustration.

"I can only tell you the truth."

Suddenly the point of the knife in Theodore's back vanished.

"I've seen enough bloodshed," the man said wearily. "If there's no way out, I'll let you go."

Theodore turned round. It was the same man who had attacked Andronicus. He was tall and Theodore had to lift his head to look at his face. He saw dark eyes staring down at him. He noticed that he wore a leather jerkin that was untied at his throat, and on the front of it there was embroidered a complex pattern of coiled serpents that suggested it was a garment of noble lineage. There was something soulful about his eyes that made Theodore feel sorry for him.

"Was it you who attacked Andronicus?"

The man looked at him in silence, before he said slowly:

"Yes, it was. My name is Ashot, Prince Ashot of the Bagratids. Andronicus betrayed us. He lied to us. He said that the Emperor would defend Armenia. But he tricked us..." There was a long pause and Ashot fell silent as he looked away from Theodore, as if he was unable to say what had happened.

So, he was Armenian. Theodore's first instinct was to distrust him. Armenians were regarded as untrustworthy foreigners by most Romans. Although they were Christian, the Armenian church had retained practices condemned by the patriarch in Constantinople as heretical, and the Armenians had resisted Roman rule until recently.

He knew his life would be at risk if he helped Ashot. But he also hated Andronicus.

Suddenly, he remembered the old tunnel. How stupid of him to forget it! It was an ancient construction and no longer used. It ran from the basement in the castle through the rock to open in a ravine to the east of the city walls. He wondered if the entrance in the basement would be locked since the last time he'd heard of anyone using it was more than five years ago.

"Come with me. There might be a way we can use. I can't promise anything but it's worth trying," he whispered. He clearly looked sincere as Ashot merely nodded his head and followed him.

The spiral stairwell descended into the basement, and since it was the middle of the night they met no one. Theodore took one of the burning torches with them, and there was also a full moon in a cloudless sky that night so that, as they made their way to the bottom of the stairwell, it was lit by a ghostly light shining through the tall unglazed windows.

But the basement itself was pitch black and Theodore had to hold the torch high to cast enough light to find the entrance to the tunnel. They found that it was covered with a heavy sheet of iron but it was not bolted down as Theodore had feared, and delighted with this, he and Ashot managed to slide it away.

Theodore told Ashot not to be afraid of the darkness in the tunnel. He said he had used it several times although it was a criminal offence for anyone to venture along it without his father's permission.

The tunnel itself was about ten feet tall and six feet wide at its largest, but narrower in some parts, since it was a natural fissure through the rock, hollowed out in some places to make it accessible throughout its full length. Theodore told Ashot that his father thought it had been part of an ancient temple where the castle now stood.

As they passed, Theodore glanced down and saw a beautiful mosaic pattern under his feet. He stopped for a second and lowered the torch. It was a picture of an ancient warrior with a round shield held up and a spear thrust forward. Beside it was a huge porphyry disc with Greek letters inlaid into it. He read the word: Xenophon. Then he remembered Eirene's words to him. Xenophon came to Trebizond. Why? He wished he could remember. But he thought of her, not Xenophon, as he rushed forward.

Theodore led Ashot, reassuring him in the darkness, until they could see the streaks of moonlight ahead of them, shining through a heavy iron grille that blocked off the exit. Ashot ran up to the grille, eager to make his escape.

"How can we break through this?" he asked Theodore.

"We can't. But there is another way. Follow me."

Theodore led Ashot down a narrow passageway to their

right, which shrank until it was only a couple of feet wide and tall.

Ashot looked confounded.

"Is this a trick after all?"

"No, I promise you it's possible to get through it. I did it as a boy."

"But I'm not a boy. You lead the way."

Leaving the torch spluttering on the ground, Theodore knelt on his hands and knees and crawled into the aperture. The memories of when he'd done this as a boy returned. The first time he'd been terrified. He called quietly to Ashot, telling him not to be afraid.

"How long is it?" Ashot gasped.

"Not long, I promise you."

After five minutes of crawling in the dark, slithering their way through the narrow gap in the rock, with Ashot breathing hard and Theodore calling out encouragement to him, Theodore reached the end. But it was blocked with vegetation.

He panicked for a moment, fearing that he wouldn't be able to push the roots and earth away. He felt mice and spiders fleeing from him. He pushed and pushed and clawed his fingers into the dense knotty web of roots. Finally, the vegetation gave way. He glimpsed the ghostly blue moonlight and felt the chill air as he slipped to the ground.

Ashot scrambled after him, and panting from his exertions, he knelt on the ground.

"Thank you friend. May I know your name?"

When Theodore had told him, he continued:

"I owe you my life. I lied my way into the castle. One day I will kill that traitor, Andronicus. I nearly killed him last night but Romanus stood in my way and I wouldn't harm him. You must tell your father to rebel against the Emperor. For the Turks are coming and I know what will happen when they come. I have lost everything. I once had a family."

Ashot paused. He swallowed hard and continued.

"Whatever happens, don't trust Andronicus. Whatever they say, the Emperor and Andronicus would prefer to see the Eastern Themes lost to the Turks than have anyone oppose them. Remember that."

And then he was gone, into the moonlit fields. In the distance dogs barked. Theodore stared after him, wondering what had happened to him in Armenia, and then suddenly realised he must get back to the castle before someone discovered that the metal cover to the tunnel had been moved.

But it was all right. No one had discovered their trail. Theodore returned through the narrow tunnel, picked up the burnt out torch, and crept back to his bedroom to lie wide-awake, his heart pounding, as his brothers snored in their sleep.

The next day the bright morning sun made Theodore's tired eyes ache. He looked at his hands which were still stained with earth from scrabbling through the tunnel, his fingernails black with dirt.

His mind was dizzy with everything that had happened. The image of Ashot's haggard face and the look of suffering in his eyes kept appearing like an apparition in his mind. But there was only one person that mattered to him: Eirene. Would she send him a message? How could she arrange it? He knew that the punishment would be severe if she was caught. He thought of Andronicus and his stomach churned at both the insult he had given him the night before and the prospect of challenging him for Eirene's hand in marriage.

Halfway through the morning, just as he was beginning to wonder whether the events of the previous night had all been a wild fantasy in his deranged mind, a tall young soldier from the Excubiti cavalry regiment, a few years older than him, called out to him as he was crossing the castle courtyard.

"Young sir, will you come here please?"

Theodore stopped and turned to face the man who gave him a wide, slightly mischievous smile, and said:

"I am Eirene's brother. I have this message for you."

He handed Theodore a parchment, carefully folded so as to conceal its contents, smiled again and left him.

Theodore turned and quickly got the parchment under his leather tunic. He wanted to be alone to read it and walked straight out of the castle down to the harbour. He went to sit on the harbour wall, and holding his breath, for he feared that she would say that she had decided to reject him, he opened the folded pages.

He stared at her handwriting, struck by how beautiful it was, as he read:

Dearest Theodore,

I have spoken with my father this morning and asked his permission to marry you. At first he did not agree but I explained to him that your family is a noble one, worthy of his consideration, even if it is unlikely that you will become count due to the rights of your older brothers. He likes your father and holds him in high regard. I also said that I will never marry Andronicus and that if I cannot marry you, I will not marry at all, and will spend the rest of my days in a nunnery. At first he was cross, but then he started to laugh and said that, although I would bitterly disappoint my mother, he would give me his permission. I know that he does not care for the Ducas family and regards Andronicus suspiciously. He will now wait to hear from your own father. I think he is afraid of my mother's reaction, and I am also a little afraid of what Andronicus will do, for I know that he is a brute, which is why I despise him so much.

At midday, I will try to be at the well in the courtyard. Be there if you can so that I can at least see my future husband in daylight!

Your own Eirene

Theodore put the parchment down. He breathed out slowly. He felt more alive than he had ever done in his life and jumped to his feet, smiling like an idiot, and rushed back to the castle.

He went straightaway and asked his father, who seemed surprised at first and then congratulated him on securing such a good match. A marriage union with the Taronites family was a good achievement, he said, smiling and thinking how much better Theodore was than his eldest brother, who had got a merchant's daughter pregnant which caused a scandal that had taken months and a fair amount of money to settle.

At midday, Theodore went to the courtyard, and after waiting for a long time, he suddenly saw Eirene emerge through the doorway. He looked at her as she scanned the people for sight of him. In the daylight, she seemed even more beautiful than when he had last seen her. He stood up and walked slowly towards her. She turned and smiled at him. And her smile said more than any written word.

III

Ashot walked alone along the dusty path in the gathering gloom of nightfall. He was tired and hungry after weeks of travelling, east from Trebizond and then climbing high into the Anatolian plateau. He had left behind him the Roman fortified town of Theodosiopolis which guarded the Armenian frontier, and then continued his trek into Armenia itself, his homeland.

Where was he going and why? He asked himself this question over and over again. For he knew that the answer made no sense. He was returning home to his lands north of the city of Manzikert. But his home no longer existed.

He wandered away from the path up to the highest rocky outcrop that he could see, somewhere where he would have a vantage point over any possible enemies, be they local brigands or the Turks themselves.

The evening was cold, although the spring days were becoming warmer, and he lit a fire and sat beside it warming his hands. He ate a meal of bread and olives that he had bought in Theodosiopolis with his last bronze coin.

Then he pitched his shallow tent and lay beneath it, wrapped in a sheepskin blanket. He didn't want to sleep for he was afraid of waking up the next morning. He dreaded the next day, for what remained of his old life was waiting for him.

But he was so tired that sheer exhaustion overcame his attempts to stave off sleep. He fell into a deep slumber in which he knew that he only had a limited amount of time to savour the life he had once known before it ended. He begged and begged that it would not end but he knew it was slipping away from him until suddenly he woke up. It was dark outside and he wondered how early it was in the morning.

The air outside his small tent was ice cold but he was still warm under his sheepskin blanket. He rolled onto his back and stared up at the top of the tent, inches above his head. He thought of Theodore, the young man who had saved him. What punishment would he have suffered if he had been caught? How brave he had been to help him.

And then he thought of Andronicus sitting there so smugly, the man who had betrayed him. He thought back to their first meeting.

It had been in Constantinople, when he and a group of Armenian nobles had travelled there to see the Emperor Constantine. They wanted to ask him to restore the Armenian army which had been disbanded more than ten years ago to pay taxes to the Roman emperor instead of doing military service. The Emperor had greeted them civilly enough. He had listened to their argument.

They had explained that there were insufficient troops to man the frontier forts. Only the great walled cities of Manzikert, Ani and Kars had strong enough garrisons to defend themselves. A few years earlier, the garrison of Manzikert had survived a month-long siege by the Turks. Peace had returned to Armenia but Ashot and his fellow noblemen knew that it would only be temporary. They had to rebuild the Armenian army before the Turks struck again. They told the Emperor that a strong Armenian army would defend the Roman Themes from Turkish attack. He had nothing to fear from rebuilding the Armenian army and everything to gain.

So, Constantine had listened and said that he would help. He would send his nephew, Andronicus Ducas, with them to Armenia to rebuild the army. He would dispense with the taxation and Andronicus would help them to reorganise and train the regiments that had been disbanded.

Triumphant, they returned down the military road from Constantinople, past Dorylaeum, the military supply centre and arsenal for the Eastern Themes, which Constantine had almost closed down, and finally, after two months of travel, they had reached Manzikert.

That night there had been a feast. Andronicus had spoken with Ashot:

"Tomorrow, we will start work. We will send out a proclamation declaring that taxation is no longer due but that military service must now be performed as in the old days. You may then return to your homes and tell your people."

And then Andronicus had struck.

Ashot and his fellow nobles had left their weapons behind, and with their senses dulled by wine, Andronicus had surrounded them with the Roman garrison soldiers, telling them that they would be arrested for treason. In the chaos that ensued, as some of the Armenians resisted the Romans and were cut down by swords and axes, Ashot had escaped. He knew every part of the castle of Manzikert well, for he had spent his youth playing there when the castle had belonged to his uncle. He had escaped through a window that led to a stretch of wall beneath the main tower, low enough for him to scramble down and then escape into the town, where he had hidden at a blacksmith's who his family had once made rich.

But he knew he had to get out of Manzikert quickly. His home was a small castle and he had about thirty men-at-arms, just enough to defend it against a small raiding party but nothing more. Would Andronicus try to attack his family? As he lay there under the canvas, he couldn't bring himself to remember any more. But today he would face those memories again. For the last time.

When dawn broke, he roused himself and ate more of his bread, and packed away his belongings. He put on his chainmail coat and sat staring at his sword. What good was this weapon now?

He stood up, preparing himself as if for battle, and started his descent into the valley where his home had once been. The familiar contours of the land came into view, and he felt as if he was travelling back in time, but with each step his sense of dread grew, for he knew that the past had been real and that he could not change it.

Finally, he looked up and saw a tower standing proudly at the top of the hill. He stopped and stared at it. It was his home. His castle.

He walked slowly up the hill until he could see the rest of it. The tower stood within a walled enclosure, within which there were several buildings, the largest of which was a stone-built hall, its roof collapsed and its great wooden beams blackened with fire, the rafters broken and sticking out like the ribs of a dead animal.

He stared at it for a long time, mesmerised by the sight, waiting for the memories to return, the horror to begin. He walked through the gateway, past the blackened gates that had been torched, and up to the hall. He touched its stone, the only part of it that had not been destroyed. Then his head was filled with the images that tortured him every night.

He had been too late. Andronicus's men had got there days ahead of him. They had killed the dogs first. When he found them, their bodies lay far from his house, crows eating their flesh. The labourers' cottages were next. Burned out shells. Corpses lying in the road, stiffened mouths open with silent screams, hands clawing the ground.

Then the castle. He gripped the stone hard as the memories invaded his mind. His men dead at the gates and walls, their bodies stripped and robbed of what possessions they had. The blackened timbers of the hall little changed from what he saw today. Inside, his wife raped and dead. His children, two sons and two daughters, clubbed to death. His eldest son, only ten years old, lay covered in blood, glazed eyes staring upwards, a hunting spear in his hand. He had done more than his father to defend them.

He had buried his family. Then he had fled to the woods, unable to find the strength to do anything else. He had fallen ill and wished that he had died but much to his disappointment he had survived. A goatherd had found him and taken pity on him, giving him bread and water and shelter. But his despair only grew.

He had wanted only one thing. Revenge on Andronicus. He returned to Manzikert, planning to kill him. There he learned that Andronicus had gone to Trebizond. He resolved to find him there and have his revenge. But he had failed yet again.

He knelt beside the stone entrance to his house. His mind was now full of the memories of his family as they had been when they were alive. Suddenly, he decided that he would end his life there and then. At least he could join his family, unavenged as they were. He drew his knife from its scabbard and raised the point to his throat. One strong thrust and the point would go straight through. He gripped the handle.

PART II

THE WOLVES FROM
THE SEA OF GRASS

August 1068

*After the Emperor died, the Turks again overran the East and came
close to Mesopotamia, attacking the Roman legions encamped near
Melitene. When the barbarians came upon them, they made their
stand along the river. The barbarians, with their long-range bowmen,
easily devastated them from afar. Positioned over them on the riverbanks
they fired down upon the Romans and wreaked havoc on them,
compelling them to flee. In the flight that followed, many Romans fell
in battle. The barbarians passed as far as Caesarea, destroying
everything in their way. They descended upon the holy shrine of the
famous saint Basil and ravaged everything, seizing the holy relics and
even breaking open the saint's coffin.*

Michael Attaleiates, The Histories

IV

It happened so quickly, and so utterly changed his life. Forever.

At first it had seemed to be a fairly ordinary, if frustrating, day in the hot summer of 1068. With the priest, and a dozen or so farmers, Theodore Gabras had been trying to free the wheel of the great watermill which was blocked by a branch that had fallen in the thunderstorms of the week before. The morning sun was starting to rise in the sky and it blinded them with its brightness and sapped their energy with its heat.

Theodore was now twenty-three years old. He and Eirene had got married, much to her mother's disappointment, and they had left Trebizond and bought a small estate in the countryside in the south of the Theme of Chaldia. Although they led a simple life, farming and bringing up their growing young family, without the grandeur or comfort of either's parental homes, for both of them the last seven years had been the happiest of their lives.

Theodore's rank placed him among an elite that was normally viewed with a mixture of awe and resentment by the ordinary people. But he was an exception, popular with the local farmers and traders, who often called upon him to help when the tax collectors came or the harvest needed to be gathered in quickly ahead of a storm. Now, they hoped he would be able to get the mill working again.

Holding the rope, Theodore leaned his weight against it and told them to pull. Sweat dripped from his face and ran down his neck into his linen tunic. He and five others took hold of the rope that was tied to one of the broad wooden blades of the wheel. One last attempt, Theodore thought to himself. They waited for his command to pull.

The rope went taut. Twelve hands felt it cutting into their skin. Then suddenly there was a cracking sound and the weight of the rope disappeared into nothing. They fell to the ground and jumped to their feet to see if it had worked. But no, the blade they were pulling had snapped in two.

"It's a bad omen," the priest said solemnly, peering grimly at the branch that was embedded frustratingly beyond their reach at the bottom of the watermill's wheel. "God is punishing the sinners among us."

Then, just after he had said these words, one of the farmers pointed across the plain to a black pall of smoke far in the distance.

No one's attention was more intense than Theodore's. He knew exactly where the smoke was rising from. It came from the direction of his estate and lands which lay hidden behind a small hill. He thought of Eirene and his two small sons. He had left them that morning, eating their breakfast. His older son was feeding their dog with pieces of bread with honey on them, dropping them on the floor. "Dogs don't eat honey," he had said a bit too crossly. Now his mind was seized with dread. The Turks had never reached Chaldia but last summer they had broken through the frontier defences and sacked Caesarea, two hundred and fifty miles to the south. In Chaldia, they had all thought they were safe. Until now.

One of the farmers that lived closest to him, Nicephorus

Metius, looked at him and as their eyes met both knew what the other was thinking.

Theodore spoke quickly: "I must go. Will anyone come with me?" But nobody moved.

"Nicephorus, will you come with me?" Theodore asked as he moved towards the horses that were tethered to the railing in front of the water-mill. He knew that Nicephorus' farm was next to his and therefore could be in as much danger.

Nicephorus looked unsure. "We have no weapons!" he said, following Theodore to the tethered horses.

"No matter…" said Theodore, reaching the horses and starting to untie his own.

The group of farmers stood in silence until the priest said in a tight, frightened voice: "Theodore, we will ride to Neocaesarea to tell the garrison… who will come with me?"

As several of the farmers answered that they would go with him, Theodore and Nicephorus mounted their horses and turned towards the road. But no one offered to go with them. Their lands were not close enough to Theodore's to be in such direct peril. Theodore did not care. His mind only had one picture in it: his son's expression as he had looked up at him.

Dust and sand were scattered by their horses' hooves as they rode away, and as they started to gallop they could not speak because of the noise and the wind blowing in their faces. Their eyes were fixed into the distance, peering at the smoke that still rose into the air.

It took ten minutes to reach the edge of his estate. As they drew near Theodore's fear made his limbs stiff and his fingers clumsy. Smoke billowed in thick clouds into the vast empty blue sky. There was no sign of life.

Then, as they got closer, Theodore heard the faint sound of barking. Turning the corner of the road and galloping along the last stretch leading to his house, his eyes scouring the land for a sign of the attackers, his house finally came into view. It was ablaze while the outhouses were intact. He pulled his horse up and stared, unable to speak or think. Then suddenly he heard the barking. It had been there all the time but his mind had blanked it out. Was it his dog, Actis?

His jumped from his horse, which backed away from the blazing house. He remembered that Eirene normally left Actis in a room at the back of the house. He ran round to find that the back of the house was as yet undamaged by the fire but the back door was locked and he had no key. He hurled himself against the door and its hinges broke under his weight.

Inside, he found Actis frenzied but unharmed. He knelt down and hugged the big hunting dog, who licked his face. Was this all that was left of his family? They rushed back to Nicephorus who was waiting for them. Theodore looked at Nicephorus. He didn't want to say anything. The crime was too awful to talk about. There was silence apart from the flames crackling and hissing as they rose into the roof, engulfing the house and causing thick black smoke to billow out of the first floor windows, filling the air with a hot acrid taste which made them choke so that they stumbled back towards the road.

They looked around. The farm buildings were empty as the Turks had taken the livestock. There were smashed amphorae in the farmyard and red wine stained the ground like blood. The small smithy which they used to repair their farm tools was smoking. Someone had been working it and the Turks had used its flames to burn the house down.

Theodore turned his face away from the heat and ran along the road which the attackers must have taken, looking for any signs of his family. As he turned the corner, he stopped and stared.

He saw a body sprawled in the road. His stomach churned with fear. He couldn't move. It must be one of his family. Then he recognised the clothes. He knew they belonged to his foreman, Michael. He felt a heady sense of relief and rushed to the body. He knelt down and rolled it over. What was left of Michael's face was a bloody wreckage, with one side smashed in by some heavy object. Theodore felt nausea rising in his stomach. One of Michael's eyes was intact and it looked up at him, glazed and lifeless. Theodore stood up. The air was hot but more oppressive was the silence surrounding these terrible crimes. He wanted to call out to God, asking what he had done to deserve this.

They searched everywhere for more bodies but to Theodore's huge relief they found none. Turning to Nicephorus he mumbled: "Turks. They must have gone past the border fortresses. Like with Caesarea." Nicephorus nodded.

"Will you come with me?" Theodore asked. "They must have taken my family. They can't have gone far. They might still be alive." He dared not think what had happened to them.

"We can't!" snapped Nicephorus. "We have no weapons and they're miles ahead of us; let's go to the garrison at Neocaesarea and get help."

"Too late! It will be too late!" Theodore implored him. "They might be heading back to Syria through the Tall Gates." The Tall Gates were the only route that the Turks could take through the mountains back to Syria without travelling two hundred miles south to the next pass.

Theodore remembered the story of how at the time of the last invasion of the Theme by the Arabs, a hundred and fifty years ago, there had been a battle at the Tall Gates as the Romans had ambushed the retreating Arabs by rolling boulders down onto them as they passed below. Maybe the boulders will still be there, he thought.

Nicephorus put his hand on Theodore's shoulder, saying firmly: "Come. Let's go to my farm and plan what to do. One of my servants can ride to the garrison at Neocaesarea. We still may be able to find their tracks and follow them…"

"I think we should go to the Tall Gates," Theodore urged him. "If we climb to the top of the pass we can see for miles all around us. We might be able to see where they are."

Theodore did not mention that he hoped they would find the boulders there that had been rolled down on the Arabs centuries before.

So, they rode, with Actis following, to Nicephorus' farm, where they were met by his servants who were getting ready to flee to the woods, for word had spread quickly that Turks were in the area. Nicephorus ordered one of them to Neocaesarea and then asked John, his bailiff who was a big burly man, to come with them in pursuit of the Turks. They armed themselves with what swords, spears and bows and arrows they could find but were dismally aware that these were more hunting weapons than weapons of war.

And then, without pausing, they set off for the Tall Gates.

Later that afternoon, Theodore's heart was pounding as he scrambled up the steep slope to the summit of the Tall Gates. His hands and knees were gashed and bleeding from the sharp rocks. He looked behind him. Their horses looked like ants in the distance down on the flat ground, where they had left them tethered to trees. Beyond the horses, the mountain sloped down to the wide plain below, its harsh rocky contours softened by the occasional tree or sun-baked vegetation. The air was hot and heavy as if it too had been scorched by the sun.

He called to his two companions, telling them that they were nearly there. Their grimy, sweaty faces looked up at him as they heaved themselves up, grasping at the rocks, almost on all fours, so steep was the incline. Nicephorus looked up at him, his teeth white within his brown face. Theodore felt a twinge of guilt. Was he wrong to bring them on this quest? They were good farmers and neighbours. Yet they were not soldiers. Nor was he.

The top of the mountain was now close. He knew that the pass lay beneath them. He remembered its vertiginous drop although he had only seen it from below. The sheer walls of stone were unforgettable. They flanked a cavernous gorge, flat enough at the bottom for an army to march along. Directly beneath them, its steep walls narrowed to only a few dozen feet across.

He was sure the Turks must be heading towards it. Once they were at the top they would know.

He reached the top, panting for breath. Sweat streamed down his face so that he had to rub his eyes to see clearly. He found himself on a wide plateau and a hundred yards ahead of him he could see the gorge dropping into the abyss below. He ran to it and crouched by the edge. Normally he would have been nervous, for he had a poor head for heights, but now he did not care. He had no fear any more. The stone walls of the gorge dropped terrifyingly down into the pass below. He tore his eyes away and stared into the distance.

Now he could see to the other side of the mountain. Ahead of him the plain stretched away towards a river. Near it the brown jagged landscape turned into a verdant terrain of crops and pasture. Then in the far distance, beside a bend in the river, he could see a dark shadow on the ground. It looked as though it might be a mass of insects. He stared until his eyes ached. The shadow was moving away from the river across the barren rocks towards him.

He knew what it was. The shadow was a huge host of horsemen and others on foot. They were heading across the flat plain towards the pass beneath them. He imagined his family among them, tear-stained faces wide-eyed with panic.

Nicephorus and John arrived at his side. Theodore pointed to the boulders left there by their ancestors from the Arab wars. He had been right. Two dozen large stones leant against each other, untouched for a hundred years, and unchanged except for some dry, parched grass that grew in the gaps between them on the arid ground. They had been chiselled so that they were rounded.

"These will do," he said. "So long as they know that we can roll these down on top of them, they won't risk going through. They'll have to find another route through the mountains. They'll have to go a hundred miles to the south."

Theodore could see that his companions wanted to turn and run. He felt desperately sorry for them. He should let them go. He should let them return to their farm. Yet he was also excited and pleased with himself to find these stones. He spoke to them earnestly, looking into their eyes.

"There must be soldiers following these raiders. They must be close behind. If we can hold them here, we could save our people. My family must be there. Please, please do this for me!"

Nicephorus stayed motionless for a minute, his face troubled and careworn, his eyes searching for an answer.

"Alright," he said. "But even if your family is there, there's no point in throwing away your life as well. We'll roll the boulders down but if they try to attack us up here then we must go. We can't stay and fight them. We'll take the path back to our horses and go. We can't hold them here."

They rushed to the boulders to see if they could manoeuvre them into position. They had to cut down branches to use as levers to roll them towards the edge of the abyss. Their ancestors would have had ropes and equipment to move them into position but these had long since crumbled to dust. Covered in sweat and gasping for breath, they struggled to move them towards the edge.

They could see the Turks were getting closer. They worked frenziedly, with the wind knocked out of their chests from the exertion of moving the boulders. They stopped when they had moved two of them into position.

Suddenly, they could hear voices in the pass below. Theodore hoped it was only an advance party reconnoitring the pass to see if it was safe. He waved to his companions to keep their heads down. They must not be seen. They lay on the ground, motionless, stifling their breathing.

Eventually they heard the sound of hooves departing. The Turks were going.

They lay against the boulders, looking at each other in silence. Theodore told them they needed to move two more stones at least. They were quicker this time, knowing better how to roll the stones.

"I will go to the edge by the thorn bushes over there," Theodore said, breathing hard. "When I can see them returning, I will give the signal to you and John to push the first boulder. Then I will join you to push the others."

Nicephorus nodded. There was fear in John's eyes. He did not want to be there. Theodore's dog, Actis, lay still, his eyes following every movement, alert to the gravity of the situation.

Theodore had no fear any more. He could only think of his family as he had last seen them, playing and laughing.

When they heard the Turks returning, Theodore crept forward. They must have decided that the pass was safe to go through. They could hear the sound of hooves and the harsh dialect of the Turks as they spoke. They waited.

The seconds lasted forever.

Theodore impatiently lifted his head above the stone to look down into the pass. He glimpsed a mass of Turkish riders below. He had never seen Turks before. The men looked small and sinewy with long black hair flowing over their shoulders. He was surprised by how small their horses were, some not much bigger than ponies. He saw their famous bows and quivers hanging from their backs. It was said they could shoot a man from a hundred yards as they rode. He raised his hand and shouted: "Now!"

Theodore and John hurled themselves against the first boulder, pushing it with their wooden staves, driving it to the edge of the gorge. It got stuck in a hole and they could not move it. But Nicephorus came running to them and threw himself against it with his bare hands as they lifted it up with their sticks. It moved and they pushed it to the edge of the ravine until they were perilously close to falling themselves. Then it fell. The weight they had been pushing disappeared into nothingness as the boulder fell over the edge. They started to run back to the other boulders, oblivious to the shouts and noise from deep in the gorge.

The other boulders were smaller. They pushed the second more quickly than the first and it too crashed down into the pass. They heard the Turks shouting, their horses neighing in panic and hooves clattering. They rolled the last two, which were the smallest, over the edge and collapsed on the ground, their hearts pounding.

Theodore had just enough energy left to stagger to the edge and peer down into the depths below. The Turks had gone. He could see a pony struggling to stand in the ravine below. It kicked its legs and rolled on the ground but its back was probably broken. Beside it lay the bodies of half a dozen Turks and their ponies, motionless or struggling to move, like the debris from a shipwreck brought in by the tide.

He shouted to the others: "They're going back. We've beaten them!" His mind was giddy with triumph.

Nicephorus came to join him, still panting, and said: "We

must go. They'll come up here and then we're finished."

"No!" said Theodore. "We're safest here. We can hold them even if they come up here. We have the high ground. They will have to climb up here if they want to attack us." He pointed to the edge of the cliff overhanging the pass. There was no way to get to the top from the pass except along a narrow ledge that wound its way up circuitously and came out in front of them. They were well placed to shoot arrows at anyone that appeared from it.

"If we stay here we can stop them from going through the pass and then they'll leave to find another route back to Syria."

His eyes were wild and Nicephorus grabbed his shoulders and shouted: "Are you mad? We must go."

"My family are down there with them. I can't leave. We can stop them here. They'll leave and look for another route. Then the Emperor might be able to catch them. Please, please will you do this for me?" Theodore begged Nicephorus, grasping his arm and looking imploringly into his eyes. Nicephorus turned away from him but he didn't leave.

They peered down into the gorge. They could see that it was now crowded with Turks.

Theodore pointed to where the path opened out in front of them, as he said quite calmly: "Do you see where the path comes out? They can only go in single file there. We can pick them off with arrows as they come out. Please, believe me, we can do it."

Theodore turned to run to pick up the hunting bows and arrows they had brought with them.

"Quickly," he said. "Take these." He handed them the bows, arrows, swords and axes they had brought with them. They obeyed him although Nicephorus and John looked pale with fear.

"We'll go behind those rocks. We can shoot at them over the top. Quickly, or they'll be here!" he begged them.

They lay in wait as the minutes passed like hours. Nicephorus knew that he had missed his chance. It was too late to retreat back down the other path. John's hands were trembling as he strung an arrow. Theodore looked at him with pity, doubting that he would be able to fight. He felt more calm and collected than he had ever been in his life. He strung his first arrow.

"Wait until they come round and then shoot," Theodore said in a hushed voice.

The first Turk appeared, moving slowly because of the sheer drop on his left. He was a veteran in his thirties. He looked around him apprehensively, curious to see who it was that had rolled the boulders down. There were no signs of Roman soldiers and he hoped that whoever it was had fled. At worst he thought they would find some desperate peasants. But then he suddenly saw three men stand up from behind the rock ahead of him and heard a dog barking furiously.

The three of them shot their arrows. Both John's and Nicephorus' went hopelessly wide as their shaking hands could not hold their aim. Theodore had no fear and he shot his arrow straight. He watched as the arrow flew towards the Turk, desperately hoping that it would strike the man down. He hated him more than anyone else in the world. But the arrow only struck his shield.

Another Turk ran past the first one, holding his small round shield up to protect him. Moving quickly, Theodore restrung his bow and shot again. His aim was less good this time and his arrow went wide. Nicephorus had restrung his bow and shot at the same Turk; his aim was good but again the arrow glanced harmlessly off the Turk's shield. Behind him, half a dozen Turks were now sprinting towards them. Theodore's plan had failed.

Nicephorus grabbed Theodore's arm just as he was about

to shoot again at the Turk and shouted: "Back down to the horses. Come now!"

Theodore dropped his bow and arrow and let himself be led by Nicephorus. The Turks were running towards them, shouting and waving their swords and clubs. John had already fled. Nicephorus turned to run after him and Theodore followed with Actis beside him.

They raced back towards the steep rocky scrubland from where they had come. Their horses were tethered down on the flat at the bottom, but three of the Turks were ahead of the others and gaining on them.

Then John stumbled and fell to the ground in front of Theodore and Nicephorus. Theodore nearly tripped over him. Both he and Nicephorus stopped themselves and turned around just as the Turks closed in on him. John scrambled to his feet but one of the Turks lunged at him with a heavy iron mace and smashed his skull with one blow.

Another Turk drove a spear into Nicephorus's side while a third one slashed at him with his sword, gashing open his throat. He never uttered a word as he toppled backwards.

Theodore was surrounded by the three Turks. He parried the sword blows of one of them but another was about to drive a spear into his unprotected side when Actis, who had been barking furiously, leapt at the man. The Turk hadn't expected this attack and he couldn't stop the dog's jaws closing on his right hand, crushing bone and tendons and causing him to scream. The Turks around Theodore rushed to his rescue, one of them sticking his sword into the dog's flank but the animal still had the strength to turn and leap up at him. The man lost his footing and fell to the ground. It gave Theodore just enough time to turn and run.

He ran to the steep slope which they had climbed earlier but he lost his footing on the stony surface and slid down, covering himself in cuts and bruises. He slid into a large rock and hauled himself to his feet before running down towards the flat land at the bottom. The Turks seemed to have given up pursuing him and when he reached the flat, he stopped, staring ahead of him.

He saw soldiers. But he didn't recognise who they were. They were foreign and looked strange to him. At least they weren't Turks, he thought. There were about thirty of them, some on horseback, others on foot leading their horses. They wore heavy chainmail coats and carried large round shields, brightly decorated with dragons and serpents. They carried long swords, spears and massive axes, the like of which he had never seen before. Many of them had long blond hair. They must be Franks or Normans, he thought, his mind too numb to be surprised. With a sense of relief, he assumed they were the Emperor's mercenary soldiers. He knew that the army had many. He shouted at them in Greek: "The Turks are in the pass! We can stop them. Please come with me!"

Their commander looked at the top of the hill from which he had rolled down. Theodore could see it was now crowded with Turks. The commander shook his head at Theodore and shouted orders in a tongue which Theodore didn't understand, and his soldiers started to back away, turning their horses around. Some arrows thudded into the ground around them as the Turks shot at them from the high ground and the soldiers raised their shields in defence.

Theodore turned to go back. He suddenly realised he was responsible for the futile deaths of Nicephorus and John and felt overwhelmed with guilt. He must atone for their deaths with his own. He would die fighting the Turks even if these soldiers would not. But the commander rode up to him and, holding up his shield to protect them from the arrows that hissed past them, he put his hand out to Theodore and said in surprisingly clear Greek:

"Come with me. Quickly!"

He freed a stirrup for him to put his sound foot into and raise himself up onto his horse. Then he and the other soldiers rode away out into the plain beyond the mountain, leaving the Turks behind them.

They stopped after a quarter of an hour, when they had put enough distance between them and the Turks. Theodore begged the commander to return to the pass. He fell to his feet and implored him:

"Please, please go back. My family might be alive. I held the Turks in the pass. We can still stop them. You are cowards if you won't go back."

The commander was a tall, strong man with long blond hair flowing over his shoulders. He had a scar across his left cheek. His blue eyes were alert, always looking around, as if the enemy was about to jump out from behind every rock they passed. His right hand was normally resting on his sword handle, the pommel of which was beautifully moulded into a fierce sea serpent, but when Theodore called him a coward, he raised his hand from his sword and grabbed Theodore's shoulder in an iron grip.

"Don't ever say that again or it will be your last word, my friend, believe me."

He smiled.

"But you are no coward and I like that."

Then his face became graver.

"There is no way we can fight those Turks. We are too few in number."

In any case, he told him, they must return to camp with the news that they had found the Turks. The Emperor was camped only a day's ride away, trying to hunt them down.

Theodore rode, sitting behind the commander, until they decided to stop overnight and finish their journey to the Emperor's camp the next day. Theodore explained who he was and the commander, whose name was Ragnar Arneson, told him that he was the commander of the Varangian guard, which was one of the Emperor's elite guards regiments made up only of Northmen, and his eyes shone with pride when he said that the Emperor himself would speak with him and listen to his advice. He said that he and his men came from a land thousands of miles away in the North and had spent a few years in the land of the Romans.

That night they camped on a craggy hill. Ragnar posted lookouts at vantage points on all sides in case there were Turks roaming nearby. The Varangians chatted and laughed. They were excited that they'd tracked the Turks down. They seemed to like the prospect of a fight. Ragnar was the only Varangian who spoke Greek reasonably well and he seemed to like Theodore. He came and slapped him on the back and congratulated him on fighting the Turks by himself. After they had eaten, and while the Varangians were busy pitching their tents and tending to their horses, Theodore sat alone by the camp fire. His mind was racked with guilt about the deaths of Nicephorus and John who had died for nothing, and with dread about the fate of his family. He stared searching into the fire as if it might tell him something. He watched the yellow and blue flames rise and fall. God had deserted him. He wondered what pain Eirene and his sons had suffered. They must have been through horrors that no women or children should go through. His eyes filled with tears. If they were dead, he prayed that the end had come quickly.

V

Eirene closed the back door of the house, leaving Actis, their dog, looking disconsolately at her. She was rushing because they were late to set off to the market in Katoryaka. The morning was not going well. She realised she had forgotten to tell her husband where they were going, and only just remembered to instruct Michael, the foreman, to tell him when he came back from mending the watermill. Her two sons were playing at the front of their farmhouse and she called to them to come straightaway.

Zoe, their maid, was holding the horses that were harnessed to their cart and, as Eirene and her children jumped into it, they turned and waved goodbye to Michael who smiled at them and shouted: "Be good, Gregory! Look after your mother!"

The journey was uncomfortable with the cart's wheels clattering along the uneven road surface. It used to be one of the main ancient Roman roads which connected the provinces of the Empire together, and many centuries ago it had been carefully built of stone and mortar. Today, it was a rough track but still used by the descendants of those that had built it, who still spoke Greek and who still lived busy lives in the cities and towns of their ancestors, among the great ancient buildings that were now mainly churches or had been turned into fortifications.

Constantine, Eirene's younger son, was playing the fool, pushing his elder brother, Gregory who, as serious as ever, was counting the coins his mother had given him. Zoe sat between them to stop the quarrelling and, after what seemed like an eternity, they reached Katoryaka, which was a village with a square in front of the church of the patron saint of the village, St Mokius. Although this had been long forgotten, it was in origin a pagan temple and its impressive façade of six Corinthian pillars dated back to the days of the successor kings to Alexander the Great. Already the square was bustling with activity as the local farmers set up their stalls and herded their livestock into pens.

It was still quite early in the morning and the market had not yet begun in earnest. The farmers used coins to pay for some of the goods but much of the produce and livestock were simply exchanged according to the needs of their respective owners. The sport was in bartering and all the farmers prided themselves on their skill at driving a good bargain.

The general good humour of the market was infectious, with people excited to hear the latest gossip. Snacks were sold from stalls: brightly coloured glazed bowls contained olives, bread, fruit and roasted pieces of meat, deliciously flavoured with honey and herbs. There was a wine stall near the church and some of the farmers were already sipping wine from glazed brown mugs and talking about the war with the Turks. The Emperor was somewhere nearby, one of them said, with the army he had brought from Constantinople to fight the Turks in Armenia. At least we're safe here, said another, with the fortresses at Theodosiopolis and Melitene well manned, his son had told him, who was in the garrison at Theodosiopolis.

Eirene was hoping to see the priest of the church, Michael

Choniates. She looked around the market stalls for any sight of him but she only saw the busy faces of the farmers and merchants as they chatted, laughed and scowled at each other. She took the children and Zoe to the church and there, in front of its six ancient pillars, she finally found Michael talking to one of the villagers.

"Eirene, how good to see you!" Michael said, looking round to see her. He introduced the villager to her and patted the boys on their heads as they looked around dejectedly, bored with grown-up conversation.

"Have you heard anything about the Emperor's army?" Eirene asked Michael. "Apparently, it's now quite close."

Michael said that a merchant had told him it was a formidable force, thousands strong, and heading towards Neocaesarea.

"Our army makes me more worried than I am about the Turks," Eirene said with a glum smile. "You know what happened when they tried to billet a regiment on our village last year. Their officer was an absolute scoundrel. Theodore nearly had a fight with him. I can't imagine what it will be like with a large army."

"I've already told my parishioners to keep their livestock in at night," Michael said. "Once the army is close, there will be some looting. It's impossible to stop. But I hope that the Emperor's presence will help to keep order. He's a professional soldier and respectful of the law I hear."

Michael paused before continuing: "But let's not worry ourselves today. God will protect those that pray to him."

They were still talking when suddenly, from the other side of the village, they heard shouting. Most people around them ignored it but then some farmers came running into the square in front of the church shouting: "Turks! Run for it!"

People looked up in amazement from their stalls. At first, there was disbelief. Then there was panic. They began to run.

Mugs and amphorae were knocked over and smashed. Eirene stood still, holding her children and too surprised to do anything.

And then they appeared: the wolves from the sea of grass. On the far side of the square several horsemen cantered towards them along the road. They slowed down and looked around them as the villagers fled towards the church. No-one had seen anything like them before. Their faces were brown and weather-beaten, with long black hair, moustaches and pointed beards, and they rode small tough horses.

One of the farmers, who had been too shocked to move from his stall, stumbled out in front of these horsemen and raised his arms in the air, pleading for his life. A Turk leaned over his saddle and dealt him a crunching blow to his head with a metal-clad club so that he spun forward to the ground.

Michael was the first to utter a word.

"We must get everyone into the church," he said. "God will save us. Quickly, let's open the doors!" He rushed to the main gates and heaved the heavy oak doors open.

Almost everyone in the square was running towards the church. Michael ushered them in through the gates. The villagers streamed in. Eirene pushed her children ahead of her. The Turks were not rushing to head them off, preferring instead to inspect the stalls that had been abandoned. Laughing to each other, they picked up the goods and produce. One of them poured a jug of red wine into his mouth and shrieked with laughter as it overflowed down his chin and onto his rough woollen clothing.

Inside the church a sizeable crowd had gathered and the shouts to close the gates intensified. The church was semi-fortified and could be defended. As the last stragglers ran through the gates, several men picked up the heavy wooden beam that secured it and dropped it into place. Michael jumped onto a bench and shouted to the assembly: "Pile the furniture in front of the gates. God will save us!"

Eirene went to Michael's side, near the main gates, with her children and Zoe. They waited, listening to the harsh shouts and commands of the Turks outside. They looked at each other in silence, too shocked to speak. Then there was a colossal crash that made the gates shudder and splinter. The Turks were going to batter it down.

Eirene knew that the gates would not last long. She looked at her children and Zoe. Gregory looked up at her. His eyes were wide open with terror. There was no escape.

Michael turned to her and said:

"God will save us!"

Then he called to the mass of people in the same authoritative voice that he used when preaching to them on Sundays and holy days:

"God will save us! I beseech you to kneel before the altar and pray for our salvation!" And he started to recite the Lord's Prayer.

Our Father, who art in heaven, hallowed be thy name.
Thy Kingdom come, thy will be done, on earth as it is in heaven.
Give us this day our daily bread.
And forgive us our trespasses, as we forgive those who trespass
    against us.
And lead us not into temptation, but deliver us from evil.
For thine is the kingdom, the power and the glory.
For ever and ever. Amen.

The mass of kneeling villagers followed his lead, praying quietly at first but their courage grew when they heard the sound of their own voices, until they were shouting the prayer as loudly as they could.

Michael gestured to Eirene to come with him up to the main gates which splintered and shuddered every time the Turkish battering ram hit them.

He paused for a few seconds in his chant of the prayer and said breathlessly to Eirene: "You must lead them praying while I meet the enemy. God will hear us and spare us."

Eirene stared at him, open-mouthed. His face looked absolutely determined. He had already turned his back on her before she could say anything. The chanting of the prayer was starting to falter without Michael's lead and, as she saw him start to clear the benches they had placed in front of the gates, she filled her lungs and shouted the holy words.

None of the villagers dared to look behind them at the gates although they heard the sound of a loud splintering crash each time the Turkish battering ram hit it. Their eyes were fixed on the altar at the front of the church and their chanting rose to a crescendo as Michael stood in front of the gates, ready to meet the Turks.

Eirene watched as the gates finally gave way and were forced open. The bright light caused her to blink. In jumped several Turks, dropping their makeshift battering ram. They looked at Michael in amazement as he stood before them making the sign of the cross and calling out to them: "In God's name, do us no harm!"

Michael stood facing the Turks. He felt strangely uplifted, placing himself in the hands of a God that he knew had the power to intervene in human affairs. He spoke loudly and confidently to them, as though they would listen to a reasonable request: "Spare the lives of these good people. They have done you no harm."

The Turks, who had at first stared at him incredulously, now started to laugh. They could see the villagers still kneeling with their backs to them and chanting, and they shouted with laughter. One of them gave Michael a push. He staggered back, which made them laugh even more.

Steadying himself, Michael gazed at the Turks in front of him. He felt quite calm and a bit light-headed. He closed his eyes and imagined the saints painted in his church. Their long hair flowed from heads hallowed in gold with one of them bearing, like Christ, a crown of thorns.

"Save my people for they have done no wrong," Michael pleaded to the saints in his imagination. He knew they had the power to save them but their eyes only looked at him mournfully, and he saw blood trickling from their crowns of thorns.

The Turks' anger was roused by Michael's hopeless bravery. A massive Turk stepped forward, his scarred face glowering at Michael. Red wine had stained his beard and leather jerkin.

Michael felt his shoulders being grasped by the angry hands of this Turk. He was forced to his knees. He opened his eyes. His vision of the saints had gone but he felt that God was close to him and he didn't flinch. Dismayed by this courage, the Turk pulled his head forward painfully by the hair, exposing his neck, and raised his sword above his head.

The villagers continued their chanting as Eirene watched the sword cut cleanly through Michael's neck. The giant Turk roared with laughter as the head rolled to the ground and blood spurted from the severed arteries. Eirene wanted to shout but she stifled it back with sobbing gulps.

Then the Turk looked up from Michael's headless body to where Eirene stood. She felt his eyes falling on her like those of a wild dog. For a second they looked at each other in silence. Then the Turk bellowed out at her in a drunken rage and strode forward, pushing the other smaller Turks out of the way. She knew that this was the end. But just as he was about to seize her, a loud, clear command shouted in Turkish made the Turk stop and look behind him at a horseman who had suddenly appeared in the entrance of the church.

Eirene also looked up at the rider. She could see that he was important for he wore rich clothes, and his metal helmet and chainmail jerkin were edged with gold. He looked a powerfully built man and beneath his helmet, she could see eyes that were hard and cold as steel. He rode his horse into the church and leaned down and struck the giant Turk across the face, shouting some rebuke which caused the man to kneel down and hold up his hands in supplication. Meanwhile, Eirene started to plead. She said she had money and would pay for their release.

But the Turkish emir was not listening to her. Indeed he had no idea what she was saying for he could only understand a few words of Greek. Instead, he gazed at her beautiful dark eyes which stared unblinking, defiantly looking up at him, braver than those of any man he had seen. He touched the shoulders of the kneeling Turk this time in a forgiving fashion, calling him Ulan, and told him to round the Romans up but to spare their lives. Ulan jumped to his feet, pleased to do his master's bidding and took Eirene's arm gently as if it was a child's. She protested and shaking his grip off, she led him to the villagers as if she was bringing in a tamed wild beast.

The Turkish emir watched. His name was Afsin, the greatest of the Turkish warlords.

VI

The Varangians had given Theodore a horse and they rode towards the Emperor's camp.

Ragnar rode beside him, relaxed and laughing in the early morning sun, his horse burdened with the weight of a Viking's war equipment, a great axe and a long, straight sword, a round shield decorated with a raven's head and his chainmail coat slung behind his saddle. He seemed to have taken a liking to Theodore and he chatted incessantly as they rode together.

He told him that a Turkish warband led by Afsin, the most dangerous and brutal of the Turkish emirs, had attacked Neocaesarea at night taking the garrison completely by surprise. It was only a few hundred strong and had been cut down within minutes. The townspeople had fled in all directions but most had been rounded up and led away. A large number, including all those who had resisted, had been killed. Those that had escaped capture or death had either been able to flee into the countryside or had found hiding places in the town, some of them in the underground sewers, a legacy of its ancient heritage which had long since fallen into disuse. The Turks had destroyed and burned the city, looting the great church of St Demetrius, and smashing into pieces the remains of its patron saint, which pilgrims had travelled to see and worship for centuries.

Theodore was shocked. He knew Neocaesarea well since not only was it the closest city to where he lived but it was also the second city after Trebizond in Chaldia.

"Our job is to catch Afsin," Ragnar said. "Once we've got him, the other Turks will be too scared to attack us. It's lucky for you that your Emperor Constantine died." Ragnar burst out laughing when he said Constantine's name. The old Emperor had died barely a year ago.

"He was an old woman," Ragnar sneered. "He couldn't even hold a sword without hurting himself. But the new Emperor, Romanus, is a real soldier. Your father and the Eastern nobles backed him to be Emperor. Even the old women in the senate couldn't stop him being crowned. Now the Turks are going to get such a beating," he laughed. "And we're going to give it to them."

"But not all the Ducas family are bad," he added. "Andronicus Ducas couldn't be more different from Constantine. A real soldier. Utterly brutal on the battlefield. Romanus loves him."

Theodore shuddered when he heard Andronicus's name. So, he'd survived and prospered. The memories of that evening in Trebizond when he'd first seen Andronicus came back. And he remembered Ashot's warning.

Theodore asked him where he came from. Ragnar said that he and his men were adventurers from a land far in the north thousands of miles away. He said they called themselves Northmen and they were proud not to be Svees or Danes who had kingdoms to the south and east of them.

"Our winters are cold. There is snow so deep that you could drown in it," Ragnar laughed. "So that is why we like to travel south to these warmer climates!"

Theodore had heard of these Northmen, known as Varangians, or Vikings to some, who served in the Varangian guard. He was curious to find out more and he asked

Ragnar why he had travelled so far to the land of the Romans.

"A long time ago our king came here to lead the Varangians and fight for the Romans. His name was Harald Hardrade. He came here long before he was made king and returned with wealth the like of which we had never seen before. He told us about the great city of Constantinople. He said that giants had made it when the world was born and that it had buildings that stood taller and vaster than was possible to build today because they were held together by ancient magic."

Ragnar's face became grimmer as he recalled the past. "Harald was the greatest King we ever had. Every year he led us to fight somewhere. Mostly, it was against the Danes. We sacked their towns and took their women. When they begged us for peace, Harald led us to conquer England. That is a fat land full of gold and pretty women. But the English ambushed us at a place called Stamford Bridge. Harald was killed and his son, Olav, made peace with the English. But I wouldn't go back to Northway with Olav. We'd never been defeated before and I couldn't go back to my wife and sons with the disgrace of defeat. So, we turned our longship east to go to Constantinople and find our fortune like Harald had done."

"How did you get to Constantinople?" Theodore asked.

"We sailed east past our homeland and the lands of the Danes, until we reached the great Svee kingdoms in the Slav lands, for the Svees had made the Slavs into their slaves. We paid tribute to the Svees to sail down the great rivers past the cities of Novgorod and Kiev, until we reached the Pecheneg lands above the Euxine Sea. We paid the Pechenegs to let us sail into the Euxine Sea and then on to Constantinople. There we met the Emperor, Constantine Ducas, and joined the Varangian Guard just as Harald had done. I fought in the

Pecheneg wars with Romanus, and when he was made Emperor, he made me commander of the Varangians, just as Harald had been."

"What about your wife and your sons? Don't you miss them?" Theodore asked of this wild man.

"No, there are plenty of women here and when I go back to Northway I will take back nearly as much gold as Harald did. Then our defeat will be avenged. I would prefer to die in battle than return home empty-handed."

"What if your wife thinks you're dead and finds another man?" Theodore asked, immediately regretting that he had asked such a question.

Ragnar showed no sign of taking offence. "I would kill them both when I return," he said simply.

When they reached the army's encampment, Theodore was amazed at the size of the army. He had never seen so many soldiers in one place before. They were encamped in a horseshoe-shaped bend beside a river, with a wooden palisade on the land side while the river formed a natural defence on the other side. In one corner of the camp was a huge compound for horses, fenced off and with more horses than Theodore had ever seen in his life, most of them either tied to railings or hobbled with their back legs tied with strips of leather and rope.

When they passed through the gates, they were surrounded by a din of voices, the neighing of horses and clanging of iron. Smoke and smells of cooking wafted in the air. Theodore rode with Ragnar along the main path to the centre of the camp. There seemed to be soldiers of every race here. The gates were guarded by heavily armoured infantrymen, who Theodore recognised as Armenians, wearing chainmail coats and carrying long, straight swords. Although they had originally been farmers and craftsmen, many had lost their families and livelihoods in the war with the Turks, and they were now full-time soldiers, dour and tough and dependent on the Emperor's pay.

Ahead of them were lines of tents in the centre of the camp which looked smart and well ordered, but all around them, and spread out over a great area, was a chaotic mass of shabby tents and open fires, with thousands of poorly equipped, dishevelled infantry soldiers cooking, eating and lounging around. Theodore knew that these were the levies from the Themes, mainly farmers like his neighbours, obliged to perform military service for the Emperor. In days long ago, they had prided themselves on their military skills and formed the backbone of the army.

But now he was shocked to see that they were like an army of beggars. Some of the officers had chainmail coats and swords but their men were lucky to have an axe as their principal weapon. Many just had spears, scythes or long hunting daggers. Hardly any had armour other than a shield from the government arsenal. Like every Roman, Theodore knew by heart the legendary stories of the hero of the thematic armies of old, a great warrior called Diogenes Akritas, who saved princesses and killed Arab warlords. The epic stories were retold over and over again on feast days and by camp-fires. What would he have thought of this motley remnant of those once great armies, Theodore wondered, as they rode towards the Emperor's tent in the centre of the camp.

However, as they approached the centre of the camp, they met very different soldiers. Ragnar nodded to the commander of a group of cavalrymen as they passed, proud looking men, riding big chargers and heavily armoured with both chain-mail coats and lamellar armour plating over their arms and legs. Theodore knew that they were from one of the regiments of full-time, professional soldiers called the Tagmata and stationed in Constantinople. But there were only two regiments of them left, the Scholae and the Excubiti, for the Ducas family had come to rely more and more on mercenaries. The Tagmata were the elite of the army and Theodore had even considered joining them, for they were mainly recruited from the younger sons of noblemen, like him, who had no title to inherit and must make their way in the world. Their equipment was of the highest quality and often passed down from generation to generation. They carried kite-shaped shields that the Normans had copied. Their favourite weapon was the heavy, jagged-edged mace since one swing of it could deal a bone-crunching blow to your enemy. They also carried two swords, a long straight sword and a curved scimitar, both carried on the same side.

Theodore also saw some Normans, who he had only seen a few times in his life before. They looked like the Varangians, many with blue eyes and blond hair. But unlike the Varangians they rode horses, sitting upright in their saddles and holding long spears.

As they approached the Emperor's tent, Theodore was astonished to see people that looked like Turks! His alarmed expression made Ragnar laugh.

"Don't worry, they're our friends. They're not Turks. They're Pechenegs. They worship the Emperor. He defeated them and now they work for him. They're the best scouts in the world. They ride as silently as ghosts and they shoot arrows on horseback as deadly as the Turks."

When they reached the Emperor's tent, which was a huge structure with richly embroidered fabrics of bright colours patterned with golden thread, Theodore wondered what this new Emperor, Romanus Diogenes, would be like. He had seen him just that one time in Trebizond when he had first met Eirene. But that was long before Romanus had become Emperor. He remembered when his father told him that Romanus had been proclaimed Emperor in Constantinople and was going to bring an army to defeat the Turks in Armenia. He had scarcely seen him look happier. He had told him they would now be safe. How wrong he had been.

They waited for maybe thirty minutes outside the tent. Ragnar spoke to the guards.

"He doesn't usually keep me waiting," Ragnar said proudly.

Finally, when they were allowed into the tent, they saw Romanus standing by a large round table strewn with maps. He lifted his head from the maps to look at them. He was a tall man, over six feet, and powerfully built. He looked every inch the soldier, just as when Theodore had first seen him in Trebizond.

But what shocked Theodore most was the sight of another man, standing beside him. It was Andronicus Ducas. Theodore recognised him instantly. He was little changed from that evening in Trebizond: tall and confident, the years had aged him only a little and his chainmail coat made him look even more formidable.

"What did you find?" Romanus looked eagerly at Ragnar.

"We've found one of the warbands. A few thousand strong. It could be Afsin. But they got through a pass in the mountains. They're probably heading back towards Syria." Ragnar said, in his simple but clear Greek.

"Were they close enough to Neocaesarea to be the ones that attacked it?"

"I think so," Ragnar replied. "They could have done it."

"Who is he?" Romanus looked directly at Theodore.

Ragnar spoke first: "This man tried to stop them! He's a hero, my lord, or mad. He was at the top of the pass rolling boulders down onto the Turks and holding them off with hunting bows. We rescued him."

Then Theodore spoke as he bowed: "My lord, my name is Theodore Gabras. My father is Alexius Gabras, the Count of Chaldia. My family were taken by the Turks."

Romanus's expression changed completely. A cloud seemed to pass over his face. He frowned.

"I have bad news for you. Prepare yourself for the worst."

Theodore immediately thought of his family. An image of their dead and abused bodies hung in front of his vision. His stomach churned with dread.

"I am sorry to tell you this but your father is dead. Your mother too. And how many brothers did you have? Two died with your father in Neocaesarea. They had travelled there from Trebizond to meet me. The Turks caught them by surprise. They attacked in the night. It was a massacre. The Empire has lost a great man and I have lost a friend."

Theodore stood perfectly still when he was told this news. He didn't feel the anguish that had gripped him in his search for Eirene and his children. Instead he felt a sense of emptiness. He thought of his father; his mother; his brothers. He couldn't believe that they were all dead. And he had thought that they were the safest of everyone, behind the impregnable walls of Trebizond.

"You had no other brothers?" Romanus asked sombrely. Theodore shook his head.

"And so now you are the Count of Chaldia. I give you my blessing, Theodore." Romanus gestured to Andronicus. "You will report to Andronicus, my commander of the Eastern Themes."

Andronicus bowed. He had eyed Theodore impassively up to now, showing no sign of any recollection of their last meeting.

"Count Gabras, I am honoured to have you reporting to me. I am truly sorry about your parents and brothers."

"Now tell me everything you know about this warband that went through the pass," Romanus continued hurriedly, giving Theodore no time for grief.

Theodore told them about the raid on his home and the

fight in the pass. Romanus listened in silence and then he said: "There are several bands of Turks raiding us at the moment. The one you found is probably the one led by Afsin. We've chased him all the way from Syria. He sacked Caesarea last year. I want to put his head on a spear in the centre of the hippodrome."

The four of them gathered around the great table as Romanus pointed to the different routes he thought Afsin's band could be taking. They all agreed that Afsin's route would almost certainly be east towards Syria with his plunder. Romanus said he would get the Pecheneg scouts to reconnoitre all the passes through the mountains. Ragnar added that the captives they had with them would slow Afsin down, so that they had a better chance of catching him.

As Theodore and Ragnar were leaving the Emperor's tent, Andronicus went up to Theodore who braced himself, fearing that he would mention Eirene and the events of that evening in Trebizond.

"My deepest sympathies for the loss of your parents and brothers. As for your family, I hope God has protected them and will deliver them back to you."

His concern chilled Theodore. He bowed his head and murmured:

"I will not give up searching for them."

Andronicus put his hand on Theodore's shoulder.

"I will pray for them."

VII

Eirene, Zoe and the children left Katoryaka behind them, deserted except for the dead bodies sprawled in the dust.

They were travelling in a cart which was a special privilege compared with the other prisoners who were stumbling on foot, exhausted and still in a state of shock. No one knew where they were going. The Turks were bad tempered and violent. If they took a dislike to one of the captives, or to anyone who was slow because of weakness or fatigue, then they would pull them aside and cut them down with a sword or club.

Zoe was terrified of the leering Turks and could only mumble that they were all going to die or worse, as the cart shook and bounced along the rough track.

"Don't give up," Eirene tried to comfort her. "We're still alive."

Just then Afsin rode past with his bodyguard, Ulan. He could not help looking at Eirene and seeing this, the Turk who was guarding her, smirked. Afsin saw this and a scowl spread across his face. He instantly spurred his horse over to the man and struck him a hard blow across the face. The man was nearly knocked off the cart and cowered, begging forgiveness. Still scowling, Afsin rode on to the head of the column. After that the guard treated Eirene with more deference and caution, so that she felt bold enough to ask for food and water.

Later in the afternoon, Eirene realised that they were heading towards the Tall Gates, the narrow ravine that led through the mountains. When they reached them, the Turks made them wait. Eirene knew that it would be easy to defend the ravine and she started to hope that someone might be there. She thought of Theodore, and prayed that he was there with soldiers. But she knew that the garrison at Neocaesarea was too far away to have made it to the ravine by now.

Then they heard shouting and horses neighing. What was happening?

The lines of Roman captives looked up, daring to hope. Their Turkish guards raised their horse whips and cracked them and the Romans looked down at the ground quickly.

They waited in the hot sun, hoping. But there was no more noise from the Tall Gates. Frowns returned to their faces. Then at last, the Turks told them to move on. When they reached the ravine, they saw dead horses pushed to one side. Then two spears planted in the ground, and on each was a man's head.

Eirene gasped as she recognised Nicephorus's impaled head. She covered her children's eyes. Tears filled her eyes as she blinked them away. What hope did they have now?

As they travelled into the evening, there was no sign of life in the vast, flat, rocky landscape that stretched away far into the distance ahead of them. The mountains behind them started to recede into the background, taking Eirene's last hopes with them.

What would happen now? Eirene thought frantically about all the possibilities. Would the garrisons at Melitene, Theodosiopolis, Neocaesarea and other places be able to intercept them? Was the Emperor's army any closer to arriving? Where was Theodore? She kept thinking of Nicephorus's impaled head. Had Theodore been at the ravine with him? She felt bitter that Theodore had not saved them.

He hadn't even been there to protect them. But she knew that wasn't his fault. And then her bitterness turned to tears when she thought that Theodore might be dead too.

She was horrified by the plight of the prisoners taken at Katoryaka. At first, Afsin's clemency had saved them as if the priest, Michael's, prayers had been answered. But by the end of the day barely half of them were left alive. Most of them had been brutally killed by the Turks either for being too slow on the forced march which was set at a fast pace, or too old or ugly to be sold as slaves, or there was some hint of arrogance or rebellion in their expression which offended their captors.

She knew that she couldn't rely on being rescued. Afsin's warband was a large force, about three thousand strong, and would only be stopped by a similarly-sized Roman unit. She knew that there was only way to keep her family alive. Afsin had clearly taken a liking to her. And even though she came from one of the most noble families in the Empire, now she must use that to her advantage.

That night they camped on a hilltop, with lookouts posted in the high places around them. Afsin sat in his tent deep in thought. He knew that they must leave quickly. The Romans would be pursuing them and the Emperor's army was close by. They had been lucky to sack Neocaesarea so easily and he knew how fickle luck was.

But there was something unknown to all but a select few of his followers. Afsin was in almost as desperate a situation as Eirene. Although he was renowned as a great warlord, he was in fact a fugitive. His raid into Roman territory had been done to escape from the death sentence passed on him by Alp Arslan, the mighty Seljuk Sultan.

His crime had been committed when he and his followers had been living in the captured Roman city of Ani in Armenia. One of Alp Arslan's hajibs, a Turk called Gemushtegin, had arrived with orders from the Sultan. The man had told him to bring his warband to join the Sultan's army fighting in Syria. Afsin had never liked this man who had been awarded a high rank by Alp Arslan at his court and had become arrogant, preferring to live like an Arab courtier. He regularly mocked the Turkish emirs for their lack of etiquette and manners but that day he had gone too far. When Afsin had said he was reluctant to leave, he had insulted him in front of his own men, calling him a goatherd from the Sea of Grass who was honoured to be a servant of the Sultan. That night, in a fit of drunken rage, Afsin had had him murdered in his room in the citadel, cutting his tongue out before they tortured him to death. The next day he had led his Turkomans into Roman territory to pillage and plunder.

Now what could he do? He knew his men wanted to return to Syria with their plunder and prisoners. But he couldn't go back to face Alp Arslan. He dreaded the thought of what punishment would be meted out to him. Alp Arslan was famed for his brutality and his skill as an archer. He would have any emir that disobeyed him killed, and normally he performed the execution himself.

His only hope would be to offer him all the plunder they had taken and all the information he had gathered about the Roman defences, the location of fortresses, troop sizes and the roads and routes within Roman territory. But even then he knew that it might not be enough.

No, he wanted to stay in Roman territory and strike again. And this time it would be the city that he had heard was the richest of all in this region. It would be Trebizond.

That evening, he called a council of his twelve head men. He told them that the greatest prize of all now lay before them: the city of Trebizond on the Euxine Sea coast, renowned for its wealth. The Romans wouldn't be expecting an attack there, he told them, since they would assume they wanted to head straight back to Syria with their plunder. They would ride north into the mountains and past the fortress at Theodosiopolis and then down onto the plain by the sea and to Trebizond.

At first they looked sullen. It was too far away and the Emperor's army was said to be nearby, according to some of the captives they had taken. Then Afsin told them that it was a particularly wealthy city. They also knew that he was no fool and that what he told them stood a good chance of being true.

Afsin said that they must kill their prisoners so that they could move quickly to take Trebizond. It had been a mistake to take them. But they could take any of the women they liked the look of. They agreed. This would be their last attack before winter and the one that would make them so wealthy they would have the Arab emirs of Aleppo, Mosul and even Baghdad grovelling at their feet.

Yet as Afsin left his head men, he wasn't thinking of Trebizond. There was something else that dominated his mind. It was Eirene. Ever since he had first seen her, he couldn't stop thinking about her. His women meant nothing to him now. Not even the dark-eyed Armenian girl who was his favourite.

After the meeting, Afsin called Eirene to see him. He had given strict instructions for her to be treated with respect. She stood before him with her hands tied together in front of her. She was indeed one of the most beautiful women he had ever seen. Tall and well proportioned with flowing dark hair, her beautiful brown eyes watched him with disdain. Transfixed, he stared at her. He knew he wanted her more than he had wanted any other woman.

She stood trembling slightly, prepared for humiliation and perhaps death at his hands. Looking away from him, she closed her eyes and waited.

VIII

They had found the Turks. When Theodore was summoned to the imperial tent, he found Pecheneg scouts with Romanus and Andronicus, poring over the great map spread out on his table. The Pechenegs had found a large band of Turkish raiders, maybe Afsin's warband or maybe another, some two to three thousand strong, heading east into the mountains carrying prisoners and plunder. They were about twenty miles from the camp. If they set off immediately they might catch them up by midday.

Romanus was a whirlwind of activity. He called for his best cavalry, the Scholae regiment, the light Pecheneg cavalry and the Norman knights led by their leader called Crispin. He wanted a fast-moving cavalry force that could catch up with the Turks and lure them into a pitched battle. He also decided to take the Varangians, since, although they fought on foot, this company of Vikings had their own horses to carry them, and Romanus knew that they would fight to the last man rather than retreat. He left the thematic soldiers behind since they were mainly infantry and would be too slow to pursue the Turks.

As they set off, Romanus gave Andronicus command of Crispin and the Normans.

The force was some two thousand strong. Although they

might be outnumbered by the Turks, Romanus was confident that if he could corner them in a pitched battle, each one of his heavily armoured soldiers would be worth at least two or three Turks.

To Theodore's huge surprise, Romanus summoned him when they set off. To ride with the Emperor was an extraordinary honour, and Theodore felt apprehensive as he approached this man for he knew from Ragnar how quick tempered he could be. But Romanus seemed to have developed a liking for him and, as they rode together, he talked to him in an amiable way. Romanus told him that his plan was to use the Pecheneg mercenaries to trick the Turks into pursuing them with a feigned retreat and then ambush them with his heavily armed soldiers. He explained that he had used similar tactics when he defeated the Pechenegs in Bulgaria. Now his main worry was the lack of cohesion within his heterogeneous army.

"I don't trust these Norman knights," Romanus confided in him. "They are proud and only want to seize land for themselves. But until we can build up our own forces I have to use them."

As Romanus talked to him, Theodore's mind was racked by the thought of the horrors that had befallen Eirene and his children. Were they dead, or prisoners of the warband they were pursuing?

Shortly after midday, Pecheneg riders rode up to Romanus and told him that the Turks were nearby. They were following the ancient Roman road through the Taurus mountains. Romanus was pleased. He rode with the Pechenegs, his veteran eyes scouring the countryside for the best place to mount an ambush until he found it a little further ahead in a wooded valley, away from the main road, with enough trees to provide cover for an ambush.

Romanus hastily called a council of war in the woods. He

strode up and down before his commanders. His dour expression had returned and he barked out orders to them, telling them his plan, without the slightest indication that he wanted their views.

"I've sent the Pechenegs to lure the Turks back to this place where we will be waiting for them. Ragnar, you will assemble the Varangians in a shield wall hidden in the woods at the end of the valley. When the Pechenegs return, you will come out of the woods and the Turks will charge you, thinking you are few enough in number to beat."

Romanus then turned to Michael Alyattes, commander of the Scholae regiment of heavy cavalry.

"Michael, you and your men will be hidden in these woods with me. When the Turks make contact with Ragnar we will charge them in the flank."

Then he turned to Crispin, commander of the Normans.

"You, Crispin, are my reserve force. You will ride over to the other side of the valley and if we need you, we will blow the imperial horn three times as the signal for you to charge the Turks from the other flank."

Theodore was standing next to Andronicus.

"My lord Andronicus," Romanus spoke in a much softer tone to his second-in-command. "I ask you to go with Crispin. And Count Theodore, you will report to Andronicus."

Romanus stood back, surveying them.

"Do I make myself clear, gentlemen? Very well. We have no time for the priest's blessing. Take up your positions immediately. I pray the Pechenegs have found the Turks. May God bring us victory."

Theodore rode with Andronicus, Crispin and the Normans. They crossed the valley and dismounted, hidden in the trees. The Normans held their horses, and stood talking grimly. The atmosphere was tense. They looked out from under the cover of the trees into the empty valley, which now looked deserted, Ragnar having hidden his men at the far end, while Romanus and the Scholae were concealed from view on the other side. Andronicus spoke with Crispin in a furtive way as if he did not want to be overheard. Theodore felt there was something slightly conspiratorial in their conversation but mainly he just felt out of place. He was no soldier. He fumbled to adjust his sword strap. He had been given the standard equipment of the Scholae: a long cavalry sword, chainmail coat and a kite-shaped shield. The Normans were checking their equipment and talking sombrely among themselves.

Theodore went to sit on a fallen tree. His mind was racked with dread about what the Turks had done to his family. He could not bear it any longer and paced up and down, staring at the ground. Andronicus went up to him and spoke kindly.

"Count Gabras, when we charge, you have my permission to stay behind. There is no shame in this. You have just joined the army and the Emperor told me you have little military training. Your family has died at the hands of the Turks. Spare yourself at least."

Andronicus left Theodore and went to inspect the Normans. To give them something to do, Crispin, had ordered them to form a battle line. But they waited for a long time. Too long for the Normans who dismounted and sat talking or playing with dice. The Pechenegs had left several hours ago. Everyone was getting impatient. Tension was building. The midday sky was starting to descend into the west.

Theodore sat prodding at the ground with a stick, playing with the ants as they scurried about in their purposeful way. He could say no more to Andronicus and the Normans. Then, suddenly, faintly in the distance, he heard the sound of hooves pounding and men yelling. The Normans jumped to their feet. Theodore rushed to the front of the trees. It was the Pechenegs. They were streaming back, racing at full speed on their small horses. They galloped along the course of the dried out stream in the middle of the valley, and straight towards the trees where the Varangians were hiding. Then the Turks came into sight. A large force, maybe a thousand strong. They were waving their swords and clubs as they chased the Pechenegs.

The Pechenegs slowed as they reached the woodland at the end of the valley. Suddenly out of the woods the Varangians rushed forward on foot to form a shield wall, several men deep, stretching from one side of the valley to the other. They allowed the Pechenegs to ride through the shield wall to safety.

The Turks were astonished to see the wall of brightly coloured shields emerge from the woods. But they did not check their speed for they thought they must be some Roman levies and they had little respect for the Roman soldiers they had met. However, as those at the front closed in on the wall of shields, behind the shield emblems of sea serpents and ravens, they saw tall men with long blond hair and with great axes, and suddenly they were afraid for they knew that these warriors were not of any kind they had met before. As they charged towards the shield wall, holding their swords and spears high into the air, they forgot their war cry so overawed were they by the terrifying baying of the Varangians, shouting the name of Odin and with trumpets blowing in deep, menacing tones. With dread the Turks at the front realised that these were not the peasant soldiers they were used to meeting.

As the Turks crashed into the Varangians, the sound of splintering shields, the piercing shrieks of horses and the shouts and cries of men, echoed across the valley. Theodore watched from the woods, expecting to see the shield wall swept aside. But the brightly coloured shields of the Varangians remained steady, stemming the Turkish onslaught. The front of the Turkish horde compressed against the shield wall in a dense mass of broken horses and warriors. The Varangians pushed forward, heaving their great shields into the Turks and swinging their axes over their heads. Ragnar was delirious with excitement. In his eyes the Turks had become the hated English, and he was avenging the defeat they had inflicted on Harald Hadrada. He urged his men on, crying out: "For Harald and Northway!" and the Turks shrank back and started to flee.

Theodore jumped to his feet in excitement and just stopped himself from shouting out aloud. He felt intensely proud of Ragnar and his men. And then as the Varangians broke the Turks and turned them to flight, two mighty horn blasts sounded from the other side of the valley and the Scholae charged into the left flank of the main body of Turks. Riding horses much bigger and more heavily armoured than the Turkish ponies, they easily pushed the first Turks they met aside. Theodore saw a Roman cavalryman colliding with a Turkish pony and rider, the pony flung to the ground and trampled under the hooves of the heavy charger while its rider brought his heavy iron mace down on the unseated Turk as he struggled to rise to his feet.

Theodore ran to Andronicus and Crispin. Andronicus was watching the action closely. Crispin gave orders to his men to mount their horses and prepare themselves.

Theodore hauled himself into his saddle beside Andronicus who looked at him and smiled.

"Remember my advice, Count. Don't throw your life away."

The Normans waited in a battle line, two horsemen deep. There were three hundred of them and their chargers were nervous, pawing the ground and shaking their heads.

Theodore waited anxiously for the sound of the three horn blasts calling the Normans to charge. It did not come. For five minutes the Roman cavalry and the Varangians pushed the Turks back and it looked as if victory was theirs. But then another great force of Turks appeared in the valley, much larger than the first, for it was the rest of the raiding party, and it numbered well over a thousand. Their comrades fled into their ranks and the new Turks looked angry and eager to avenge their defeat. They spurred their horses forward towards the Romans and Varangians.

Then came the sound Theodore had been waiting for. Three horn blasts, loud and clear, ringing across the valley. Theodore looked up at Andronicus who seemed not to have noticed it.

"My lord, we must charge!" he cried.

Andronicus spoke calmly, looking him straight in the eye.

"The Emperor is winning, is he not? I would not want to claim his victory from him. I think we should wait a little longer."

Theodore was stunned. He stared at Andronicus, in disbelief.

"But my lord, the Emperor was clear that three horn blasts were the signal for us to charge."

"I have no memory of that, Count Gabras. You misheard him I think."

Theodore gulped back his incredulity and spurred his horse towards Crispin, who was as impassive as Andronicus.

"The Emperor has given the order for you to charge," he said desperately.

Crispin turned to him and said in simple, broken Greek: "Andronicus my commander not you."

Theodore stared at Crispin and then back towards Andronicus. He was too shocked to know what to do. Then he realised that Andronicus's treachery suited Crispin well, since he could wait to see who would win between the Emperor and the Turks, perhaps with a view to taking on the weakened winner and taking all the plunder for himself. He remembered what Romanus had said to him about his distrust of the Norman mercenaries.

And as they watched the battle fiercely raging before them, the advantage seemed to be passing to the Turks. The lines of Roman cavalry began to break up under the sheer weight of Turkish numbers for they were outnumbered more than two to one. And the Turks were angry and wanted to avenge their dead brothers. Theodore saw them jumping off their ponies and hurling themselves at the Romans with their swords and daggers. They would dart under the large Roman horses and stab them in their stomachs or slash at their heads and flanks.

"The Emperor needs you now!" Theodore yelled at Andronicus and Crispin. "You have sworn allegiance to him and you receive his pay and will share in the plunder."

But they ignored him.

Instead of confronting them further, Theodore pulled his horse round to face the line of Normans. Their eyes watched him from behind their nose guards as he said: "If you charge now, the Turks are at your mercy. Their plunder is yours."

Few of the Normans understood the Greek words he spoke but nevertheless it was clear what he meant.

The Normans looked at the mass of horses and men battling in the plain. The Varangian shield wall remained steady as the Turks threw themselves against it in vain but the Roman cavalry was in disarray and taking heavy casualties. They knew the Varangians would be well rewarded if they won the battle. They looked at Theodore who had taken his sword out of its scabbard and was waving it in his hand. They had come to fight and they could see it would be an easy victory for they could take the Turks by surprise. Most of them were also utterly unaware of the deal that Andronicus and Crispin had struck and, while Theodore was unknown to them, he was at least a Roman officer and he was urging them to charge. A few of them trotted forward towards Theodore and then the whole line of Normans started to move. Theodore raised his sword into the air and cried out to them as he dug his spurs into his horse and trotted forward out of the woods.

Now Crispin had no choice and he rushed to the front of his men. Andronicus followed behind him. The Norman cavalry emerged out of the woods, all three hundred of them, in battle order.

Theodore dug his spurs deep into his horse and galloped straight at the Turkish flank, shouting at the top of his voice. He felt strangely unafraid of death, just as he had been in the fight at the Tall Gates. Death would be so much easier than life: the coward's choice, he thought, as he galloped at full stretch towards the enemy, shouting out some warcry, in fact it was "Ragnar" that he called out, but he did not know it. Behind him the Normans followed.

The Turks did not see them until it was too late. They were fighting the Romans in a chaotic battle with many on both sides unhorsed and fighting hand to hand. Romanus himself had even galloped into the thick of the battle and was shouting and rallying his men. Only the Varangian shield wall was in good order, steadily moving forward and pushing the Turks back.

Theodore felt the sun and the wind on his face as he galloped. Straight in front of him, a handful of Turks had turned and noticed the charging Normans. Theodore was ahead of the Normans but their horses caught him up and he was part of the mass of cavalry as it crashed into the Turks, scything them down just as the first Roman charge had done. The Norman charge was renowned for its ferocity, and the long spears which the Normans tucked fast under their arms, knocked many Turks clean off their horses, splintering their small round shields as they held them up in defence. Dozens of Turks were ridden down by the Normans and as the rest of the Turkish cavalry looked round to face them, they panicked, seeing that they had enemies on all sides except for one, and they started to break and flee back towards the mountain pass.

Theodore was at the front of the Norman charge and the Norman spears cut down most of the Turks in his way. He slashed out with his sword and hit a Turk that was turning to flee but he went past him so quickly that he did not know what damage he had done. As the Norman charge was slowed by the mass of Turks, so Theodore found himself facing a dark-skinned Turk, who looked at him desperately as he turned his horse to retreat. Theodore thrust his sword at the man and it hit his small, wooden shield. The man responded by swinging an iron mace at Theodore's head, which was only just caught by Theodore's shield, as he raised it high. The force of the blow nearly unhorsed him but he felt his anger well up in him and, shouting, he spurred his horse right up to the man and smashed his heavy shield into the man's side. But the Turk was a skilled rider and held on as he moved out of Theodore's reach.

All the Turks were in flight now and to his right, Theodore saw the standard of the Scholae, a tall purple pennant with a white cross, coming towards him. Panting with exertion, he spurred his horse towards it. A large group of Scholae came towards him and he saw Romanus and his commanders, looking exhausted and covered in blood. He rose up to them, calling out until they looked in his direction and Romanus himself saw him.

"What took you so long?" Romanus called out to him through the din of battle.

Theodore rode up to him.

"Andronicus," he answered, breathing hard. "He wanted to see you defeated."

"How dare you say that!" said Romanus, his look of triumph replaced with an angry frown.

Then a large body of Turks, retreating from the Varangians, flung themselves against them. Theodore turned and struck one with his sword but it glanced off the Turk's shield and he dropped it, exposing his unshielded arm as the Turk raised his club. A crunching blow hit him on the side of the head. Suddenly everything went silent. Before his eyes the mass of men and horses seemed to move in slow motion as he looked up into the bright glare of the sun. Then there was darkness.

IX

Eirene kept her eyes shut. She was expecting Afsin to seize her and force her into some degrading sexual act. She waited to feel his hands on her breasts and body as he ripped her clothes off. She tensed herself for the horror that was about to be committed.

But Afsin only stood looking at her. Normally, the women he captured would beg for mercy. Sometimes, they would cry. But seldom did he feel pity for them. He thought they were lucky to be alive and should show their gratitude to him. He would take them if they pleased him and give them to his men if they didn't. Yet now he felt uncomfortable in front of this woman that he wanted so much. Never in his life had he seen such courage from a woman as when Eirene had stood, facing Ulan. Never had he seen such a beautiful face so defiant.

Eirene opened her eyes to see Afsin watching her. What was he thinking, she wondered? What cruel humiliation was he planning? Tears came to her eyes and she bowed her head and sobbed into her arm as it covered her face.

For the first time, Afsin was moved by a woman's tears. He longed to say something to her but he knew no Greek, so instead he said in Turkish:

"You have more courage than most men I know."

Then he turned and went to sit on a wooden chair that had been plundered from a church. It was for a bishop and it had gold and ivory inlaid into it. He sat and looked thoughtfully at Eirene. He wanted her so much and yet he could not bring himself to take her against her will.

The tears stopped and she looked at him through eyes that were red with pain. Suddenly, she thought that she had repelled him with her sobbing and a new fear came into her mind: he would kill her or let the ordinary soldiers rape her. She dropped to her knees and looked directly at him, with her hands grasped together in front of her as if in prayer.

"Please don't harm my children," she begged him.

She spoke Greek that he couldn't understand. He didn't care for he knew he would not harm her, whatever she said. He stood up and went to the entrance of his tent and shouted to a guard in Turkish that she couldn't understand:

"I want this woman well looked after. Her children and servant as well. If anyone mistreats them, they'll have me to answer to. Understand?"

The guard nodded.

"Now, get them a tent! And give them all the food and water they want."

Afsin nodded to Eirene to go with the guard who presumed her privileged treatment was due to ransom money that could be obtained for her, or simply that she was to be a new addition to his collection of women back in Mosul. Whatever it was, he knew Afsin's wishes were not to be questioned.

As Eirene left, she turned to Afsin and said thank you, almost in a whisper. In return, he smiled at her.

Afsin sat alone in his tent. What was he doing, he thought to himself? He should have taken her then and there. He knew he wanted her more than anything else. What was the matter with him, he wondered? He flung himself down in the bishop's chair and stared vacantly at his weapons hanging from the central pole of his tent.

The flap of his tent opened and his servant put his head through cautiously, unsure of his master's mood, and asked if he wanted food brought to him. Afsin nodded. The man left. Afsin continued to stare into the space around him. But his vision was not empty. It was filled with his memory of Eirene's face. Those beautiful brown eyes, her delicate aquiline nose, the curve of her chin. Her face was perfection itself. And the look of courage in her eyes.

That night as they camped under clear, cold skies, Eirene noticed that the guard who Afsin had struck was increasingly wary of her, now that Afsin's feelings for her had begun to be known. She knew this was her only chance and she must use it quickly.

That evening she made a plan for their escape and told it to Zoe and her children.

When the middle of the night came, Zoe and her children lay beside the cart pretending to be asleep, as Eirene had told them to do. The camp was silent. Only their guard was awake, occasionally pacing up and down beside their cart to prevent himself from falling asleep. He was tired and irritable.

When Eirene gave him the signal, Gregory, her eldest son, lay on the ground and started to groan. He clutched his stomach and brought his legs up to his chest, writhing in agony. Eirene went to the guard. She spoke to him but he just looked at Gregory with a tired, disdainful stare. He wasn't going to do anything. Eirene pointed at Gregory and then towards the other side of the camp where Afsin's tent was. Although she spoke only a few words of Turkish, she made it clear to the guard with her gestures and expressions that she would tell Afsin of his neglect. She raised her hand and pushed him, firmly but not violently, to express her irritation.

This infuriated him and he struck her a blow that sent her reeling to the ground.

Eirene sat, tasting blood on her cut lips. It was exactly what she had wanted him to do. The guard realised he had gone too far. Fear spread over his face. He wanted to make amends. He gestured towards the physician's tent, the man who tried to heal their war wounds and illnesses with bandages and Arab ointments. He told her to wait there and he would return.

The moment he was gone, Eirene seized her chance. She knew that the other camp guards had become lazy and normally slept at their posts, so confident were they that the Romans would not attack. They broke into a run towards the edge of the camp. There were no guards alert enough to see them in this section of the camp. The only sound was from their feet on the dry sandy soil, and the only signs of movement were their black forms moving stealthily, with their breath smoking in the cold night air. It was a moonless night and the darkness was like a blanket under which they were hidden.

They reached the perimeter of the camp, beyond which tall hills rose steeply into the black night. They climbed up the rocky scrubland with both adults helping the two children. Within a few minutes they had reached a plateau from which they looked down onto the dark silent camp. Facing them was a tall craggy hill leading into the mountains and they started to climb its steep slope. Eirene led them as they bent down, scrabbling to hold on to the rocks and stones to prevent them from slipping.

Suddenly they froze. They could hear steps behind them. Eirene turned. She could just see a black silhouette moving rapidly towards them. It must be the guard pursuing them. He would soon catch them up. She urged them on and they climbed up to a narrow goat-trail with a steep drop on one side. She told Zoe to hurry on with the children. She would meet their pursuer here. She turned, picking up a stone in desperation as her only weapon.

Eirene crouched down watching the black figure as best she could in the dark. The figure was searching, looking this way and that. But he seemed to be alone. She hoped that he would decide to pursue a different route from the one which they had taken. But theirs was the obvious way to go and their pursuer was on their trail and getting closer and closer.

Like a rodent sniffing out its way, the figure found their path and scrambled across the steep slope towards the ledge where Eirene was. She hid behind a boulder. She waited, listening to the footsteps and the forced breathing and muttering of whoever it was. She waited to spring out and surprise him.

She jumped out in front of the figure. It was the guard. His face lit up with triumph when he saw her. But out of Eirene's hand flew the stone she had been holding. It caught the man on the side of the face and stunned him. He clutched his face, and she ran at him trying to push him over the ledge and down the steep slope but he grabbed onto the side of the rock. He did not fall.

Eirene stopped and started to back away along the ledge. She had lost the power of surprise. She had no weapon in her hands as he drew his sword. Then as he started to move towards her, his face snarling with triumph, there was the sound of a heavy stone thudding into his face. He grunted and lost his footing and slipped down the steep slope. There was nothing to break his fall as he rolled to the bottom, several hundred feet below them, and lay still. Eirene turned to see Zoe behind her. She had thrown the stone. Eirene told her to run. They disappeared into the darkness of the night.

Eirene led them by the light of the moon through the hills, following what tracks they could find, and by dawn they were far away and exhausted. As the sun rose and the cold of the night gave way to another day of burning heat, Eirene knew that they must keep going and only rest at midday when the heat was at its height. She scanned the horizon for any sign of pursuit but could see no one. They ate most of the food they had taken and set off again. By midday they found a rocky outcrop where they had some shade from the overpowering heat of the sun. There was still no sign of the Turks pursuing them and it was just possible that their escape had passed unnoticed until later in the morning. Comforted by this thought they relaxed a little and in no time all four of them were asleep.

When Eirene awoke she panicked. She saw by the sun's position in the sky that it was now late afternoon. She hastily roused Zoe and the two children, who were bleary-eyed with sleep and could only stumble forward, as Eirene persuaded them to get going again. There was still no sign of any pursuers but they needed to put as much distance between themselves and the Turkish camp as possible.

Yet Eirene had no idea of the direction that they were heading in. They walked through a barren, mountainous and rocky landscape. She hoped that she was not leading them round and round in circles and that somehow they would find help and shelter even if only from a goatherd or a peasant farmer. Soon they would have no more food. But Eirene banished this thought from her mind, and told her children and Zoe to keep going, as she lied to them that soon they would find a village she knew of. The four of them trudged wearily onwards.

It was in the early evening that they saw horses far away across the hills winding their way down through the rocks and steep slopes. Eirene nearly cried out with despair. Although they were far in the distance she knew that they were Turks. She could tell by the way they moved that they were riding the small Turkish horses. She said to Zoe: "We must move faster! Do you see them? They're behind us. Don't talk too loudly. The children mustn't hear us. They'll be too scared to move."

They started to run. If only they could get beyond the next hill, thought Eirene, they might not be visible to the horsemen. But as they climbed the hill she knew that they were painfully conspicuous. The horsemen must have seen them because they started to move faster and in their direction.

They panted and sweated as they climbed the hill. Gregory was pulling his younger brother, Constantine, who was struggling to keep going. Eirene started to panic. The horsemen were getting closer. They must move more quickly. She picked Constantine up in her arms. He was heavy but she was desperate and she hauled him up the slope. They had no idea what was on the other side. The horsemen were still some way off but they were gaining on them.

They made it to the top of the hill and staggered past the boulders and sparse vegetation to look down into the valley below. Eirene stopped in astonishment. Before them was a small encampment. The people looked dishevelled and weary and they had piled up their possessions in carts in a defensive circle around their tents. Eirene imagined that they were Roman farmers fleeing from the Turks. They ran down the slope towards the camp and as they drew near she shouted out to them.

The first people they saw looked up in astonishment and fear. Eirene gestured behind her. On the brow of a hill some way in the distance, the group of horsemen was visible.

"The Turks are coming!" she called out as she ran down the hill to the farmers.

At first, only a handful of farmers turned to look at her. Then when they heard her words, they panicked and the encampment turned into chaos as men, women and children rushed to grab their belongings and flee.

"There aren't many of them. It's better to fight them than to flee." Eirene shouted at them desperately. "The Turks will hunt you down if you run away."

Eirene had seen her father many times on the parade ground drilling the thematic levy and she knew how he and the officers shouted out commands. She faced the frightened group of farmers and told them to gather their weapons. They hesitated for a few seconds but when she repeated her command in an authoritative voice, they obeyed this noblewoman for they could see that it was too late to flee.

She told them that there was no time to do anything other than to drag the carts as close together as possible to form a tighter defensive circle. All of those without bows she positioned evenly around the circle. She told the bowmen to plant a good supply of arrows in the ground beside them so they could fire rapidly at the Turks. She told the women to keep the children in the tents away from the fighting.

Then the Turks suddenly appeared on the brow of the hill, black forms silhouetted against the blue sky. The farmers looked at them grimly. The Turks stopped. They were surprised to see this group of peasants and their carts, ready to meet them, or so it seemed.

The Turks waited, discussing what to do. The farmers braced themselves behind their carts, stringing their bows.

Then the Turkish leader spurred his horse forward and the others followed him down into the valley. As they approached the ring of carts, they drew out their swords and lifted up their maces and clubs. They thought it would be easy to teach these peasants a lesson. But suddenly the air was filled with arrows. Most of them went wide but some thudded into the Turks and their horses. A heavily set Turk looked in amazement at the shaft of an arrow protruding from his chest before he lurched forward clutching it and fell from his horse. The arrows continued to fall, and the Turkish leader spurred his horse forward, calling his men to follow him as he charged the ring of carts. The Turks were angry, and their leader jumped from his horse and climbed onto a cart. His shield had caught several arrows and he nimbly sidestepped a thrusting spear as he brought his long sword down on the farmer facing him.

Eirene rushed forward, a long hunting dagger in her hand. The Turkish leader, a tall man with long black hair and a wolfskin cloak held at his throat by a golden brooch, stopped to face her. He hesitated as he looked at her, struck by both the beauty of her dark eyes staring intensely at him, and the sudden realisation that she must be the woman he had been instructed to recapture. He knew of Afsin's rumoured infatuation with her and that he would pay dearly for any harm that should befall her. These thoughts caused him to lower his sword as though he could reach out and grab her. Eirene, sensing the confusion in the Turk's mind, seized her chance. Driven by her instinct to protect her family more than herself, she planted the hunting dagger deep in the man's chest. He staggered back, realising his mistake and cursing his own folly as he tasted blood in his mouth. His vision was beginning to blur as a farmer beside him drove his spear into his side, pushing him sideways to the ground.

The other Turks, seeing their leader killed, started to back off. There were only ten of them left and they faced about fifty of these Roman peasants, too many even for these hardened warriors. They backed away from the carts, holding their small round shields up to ward off the farmers' arrows. The farmers kept up a steady stream of arrows as the Turks retreated. When they had ridden far enough away into the distance, Eirene told the farmers to move quickly. The Turks would be back with reinforcements, she said. They needed to abandon their heavier baggage, only taking their lightest and fastest carts with the minimum amount of their possessions.

They set off, carrying the wounded and the bodies of the two farmers killed in the fight. Eirene led them. She knew that they had to get to a place of safety beyond Afsin's reach. So, they headed west away from the Turks and towards the Iris river and the great bridge over it, which led to Amaseia, the largest Roman fort in the area.

They travelled for two days and nights until they reached the safety of the bridge which was guarded by a strong force of thematic soldiers. They were exhausted and they could barely pitch their tents and light fires before they fell asleep. To her delight, the soldiers told Eirene that the Emperor had arrived with a great army and was hunting the Turks down. Eirene smiled and kissed her children and Zoe. She felt triumphant. They had escaped and now she prayed for one thing only: that Theodore too was alive and safe.

X

When Theodore awoke, he felt as if he was returning from the land of the dead. He had been knocked unconscious in the battle and his head was heavy with a painful wound.

At first he panicked when the memories of the battle returned to him. He thought he was still on the battlefield and he reached for his sword, knocking over the table and smashing the bowl of water that was on it. The room swayed before him as though he was drunk. But Ragnar came in and helped him back to bed and explained that they were in Sebasteia. They had won the battle, killing many Turks and capturing most of the rest. Romanus had executed half of the prisoners, he said, and had sent their heads back to Constantinople.

"But did you find Eirene?" Theodore asked, wide-eyed and shaking.

"No, we did not," Ragnar answered in a matter-of-fact way. "The Turks had very few prisoners and they were not from Chaldia. I do not think it was the same raiding party that took your family and sacked Neoceaserea. They seem to have escaped."

Theodore sat back too stunned to say anything. The room was starting to steady itself before his eyes. But the anguish of worrying about his family made him want to be alone. He closed his eyes.

Later that day Theodore was summoned to see Romanus.

He still felt drowsy from the blow to his head, and Ragnar's news had shattered what little hope he had left. When he entered the Emperor's tent, Romanus looked up at him intently and, as he paced up and down in front of the great table in the middle of the tent, strewn with maps and wax tablets, he said:

"Tell me why Crispin did not obey my orders. Tell me the truth about Andronicus and Crispin."

Theodore told him exactly what had happened, and as he told him, Romanus became angrier and angrier. When Theodore had finished, he turned to face him and slammed his fist on the table.

"You lie, Count. Andronicus is a loyal ally of mine. How dare you suggest otherwise? Andronicus has told me the truth. Crispin is the traitor. He left it until the last moment to attack. He wanted to see me defeated so that he could set up his own kingdom here. I have never trusted the Normans and Crispin will pay dearly for this. "

"My lord, I can only tell you what I saw. Neither Crispin nor Andronicus wanted to charge. Crispin was a traitor but so was Andronicus."

"I do not believe you, Theodore. Andronicus was my most loyal commander in the Pecheneg wars."

"My lord, I promise that I tell you the truth." Theodore still regarded the Emperor as his benefactor and he spoke openly and frankly. "In the Pecheneg wars, Andronicus's uncle, Constantine, was Emperor. Now that you are Emperor, he may have other motives."

"What you don't know is that I owe my life to Andronicus," Romanus glowered at Theodore. "He saved me from the Pechenegs. It was in the war along the Danube. I had advanced too far and was surrounded. He led the charge that saved me. Why would he want to betray me now?"

There was a long pause. Theodore wondered whether he had made a mistake. Perhaps Andronicus had genuinely misunderstood the instructions given to him? Then he remembered what Ashot had said about him. No, he was a traitor.

"My lord, I can't change what I saw with my own eyes." Theodore tried to sound as reasonable as possible.

When Theodore said this, Romanus exploded in a fit of rage.

"How dare you! You have gone too far, Theodore. I will settle this matter now."

And he called the guards to get Andronicus.

When Andronicus entered the tent with Ragnar, he looked at Theodore without a trace of guilt or any emotion other than pity.

"This man believes you betrayed me," he said, pointing at Theodore.

Andronicus stood silently for a moment. He nodded his head sombrely and said:

"My lord, I think I know the reason for the Count's allegation against me. His wife was in love with me and wanted to marry me. She made a fool of herself. He is jealous and has always held a grudge against me. Also remember that he has no understanding of warfare and I suspect the events of the last few days have affected his mind. He is just confused and distraught. I ask you to forgive him. He fought bravely in the battle for one so inexperienced in war."

"Forgive him? For such treachery! My friend, you are far too generous to this fool. I will have him imprisoned for treason!"

But before he could say anything further, Ragnar turned to the Emperor.

"He is a brave man, my lord. He is confused and has made a mistake as we all know. But I also know that he is loyal to you. It is wrong to treat him like this!"

Ragnar was as volatile and impetuous as Romanus himself, and something about Theodore's courage and his desperate plight, appealed to the Viking's sense of honour.

"Ragnar, you will do as I command. Take him away. He will be tried for treason." Romanus spoke curtly.

"In that case, my lord, I ask you to release me from my oath of loyalty."

And so saying, Ragnar took his sword from its scabbard and knelt before Romanus, turning the blade's handle to him as a request to release him.

Romanus stared at Ragnar. He was angry but he knew how much he owed to Ragnar who had effectively won the battle for him. He also liked Ragnar more than any of his generals and respected his views on tactics.

"You take him then. He can join your regiment. But he is stripped of his title. From now on, he will be one of your men."

Romanus dismissed them and called Andronicus to the table to discuss the army's next movements. Theodore did not look behind him as he left. His head was spinning. He knew that he had made a terrible mistake to tell Romanus the truth. He even began to doubt his own memory. Had Ashot's words against Andronicus all that time ago poisoned his own judgement? He cursed him as he walked away in a daze.

A few days later, Ragnar and Theodore watched Romanus lead the bulk of the army south to the great city of Antioch to secure the Empire's southern frontier against the Arabs of northern Syria who had captured the city of Artah, taking advantage of the disruption to the Roman defences caused by the Turkish raids. Crispin's Normans were in disgrace and had been sent to garrison Armenia. Romanus had decided to leave Ragnar and Andronicus to guard the Euphrates crossings against any further Turkish attacks. He left Andronicus as commander-in- chief.

In the days afterwards, Ragnar looked after Theodore. He gave him command of ten men but treated him as a friend rather than a junior officer, and the two of them would go to the parade ground where Ragnar taught Theodore how to fight.

"My friend, you may have courage but you need to learn a few tricks with the sword or your life will be short." Ragnar chuckled. "So let's use wooden swords to start with and I'll teach you how to fight. Our Roman friends have plenty of wooden swords although we would only use them to teach children." He smiled broadly at Theodore, as he might do to a favourite child.

They got the wooden swords and Ragnar taught Theodore how the Northmen fight. Theodore had been a decent swordsman as a boy but he knew that he had no battle experience, and would be no match for veteran soldiers like the Varangians or the Scholae, or the Turks.

Ragnar told him that a good swordsman not only has lightning reactions and always makes a riposte immediately after parrying his opponent's attack but he also needs to surprise him with something unexpected like a punch from his shield. His own favourite tactic was to duck down and swing his sword at his opponent's legs. He told Theodore that people always forget to protect their legs and feet. If you catch someone's legs or ankles with your sword you can disable them or throw them off balance much more easily than you can with a normal attack. He also told him that nimble footwork was vital. You had to dance on your feet, side-stepping your opponent's blows and striking him where he least expected it.

He told him that the Northmen always fought in a shield wall. They never fought on horseback like the Normans. In the shield wall, he said, you had to keep your shield in place but otherwise you should use your sword and feet as you would in single combat.

When Theodore was too tired to continue and he sat exhausted on a tree trunk, Ragnar said:

"Don't look so glum, my friend! You're still alive. You still have air in your lungs, and strength in your arms. What more could a man want? You're rich! And when we return to Constantinople we'll have the best women and wine in the city!"

Theodore leaned his head back and smiled for he knew that Ragnar's friendship was a gift as valuable as it was unexpected. He must not squander it as he had Romanus's friendship.

"Why are you so generous to me, Ragnar? What did I do to deserve it?"

"You are a brave man and that's all that matters. I was like you once. My parents were killed by our Carl. He was a tyrant. My mother was a beautiful woman and one day he decided he wanted her. So, he told my father to bring her to his castle. Instead, he brought his axe. But the Carl killed him and then he went to our house. And he slaughtered my family and burned our house down. But he didn't know that I had survived. I was out working in the fields when it happened. And then one night I broke into the castle and split his head open. I was captured and brought to trial. I didn't care whether I lived or died. My family was avenged. It was then that I met Harald. The court said I should hang but Harald, who was still a prince, said that I was a brave man and should live. So, the court made me his serf. When he became King, Harald freed me and made me a Carl."

Theodore didn't reply. He sat there, imagining the wild young man Ragnar must have been in his youth. Then, without thinking, he asked him:

"Do you believe in God?"

"Not your god, that's for sure. My gods, yes. Your god is weak. That's why you're in the shit. Your people don't like courage. They just pray and beat themselves and wear hair-shirts."

Ragnar laughed.

"Your god's made you into a bunch of frightened old women. Odin would send you all to Niflheim for being cowards. He only rewards one thing: valour in battle. That's what I like about you: you're not afraid to die. Indeed, I even think you want to."

Theodore looked up at the clear, blue sky. He decided that he wouldn't pray to God any more. No, he wanted to be greeted by Odin in Valhalla.

XI

At the same time, and beneath that same blue sky, the sun shone on the honey-coloured sandstone walls of Amaseia. The ramparts were manned by the local garrison who looked down on the thronging multitude of people below them. There were thousands of refugees fleeing from the Turks. Townspeople from the Eastern Themes like Chaldia whose cities had been sacked, as well as farmers and villagers abandoning the countryside that was now too dangerous to live in. Amaseia was the most heavily fortified town in central and northern Anatolia, and these frightened and grieving crowds came flocking to it like herds of animals in search of safety from their predators.

Eirene, Zoe and the children were riding the horses and donkeys which they had bought at the bridge over the river Iris. They were still with the farmers who were journeying to Ancyra, further west, and they joined the long line of refugees on the main road into Amaseia in a queue which was not moving under the hot September sky. The garrison had closed the gates and were trying to persuade the people to move on since they had no wish to be flooded with refugees. All around them people were getting more and more irritable. Most of them were farmers and peasants who had loaded their belongings into carts and were in a state of despair having left their homes and lands to the marauding Turks. Arguments and scuffles were breaking out among them as they waited.

Eirene said to Zoe: "We will never find shelter here with all these other people. We can restock our provisions and then we can take the military road to Amorium, where my parents live. It's pretty direct and we might have some protection from the soldiers using it. I know it's a long way, a little over two hundred miles from here, but on these horses we could be there in five days."

And so the next day, having restocked their provisions from the farmers who they bid goodbye to, they headed towards Amorium along the dusty military road. But little could they have known, when they told the farmers of their destination, that this information would soon be in the hands of Afsin.

When Afsin had been told of Eirene's escape, he had struck the bearer of the news to the ground and called his men stupider than dogs, outwitted by a feeble woman. Trebizond was no longer his immediate destination. He wanted to find Eirene again. So, his band of raiders had turned around and ridden to Amaseia which was where Afsin believed Eirene had gone since it was the main Roman stronghold in the area. His men knew nothing of Afsin's real motives and believed that it was simply the next target for pillage and plunder. When they arrived they found the Romans well prepared with the gates closed and the ramparts well manned. The town was too strong to take and Afsin was in despair, believing that Eirene must be behind its walls, when they happened to capture a small group of farmers fleeing on the military road running westwards. There seemed little point in interrogating them but Afsin asked them nevertheless whether they had seen a woman of Eirene's description with her family, fleeing from the east. To his amazement they had told him that a woman by the name of Eirene Gabras was heading towards Amorium.

Afsin needed no more information than this. Although the Roman farmers told him that it was two hundred miles to the west, that day he and his warriors set off west towards Amorium, deep into Roman territory

At the same time, Eirene and her family were halfway between Amaseia and Dorylaeum, travelling to Amorium, and completely unaware of Afsin's raid. They were travelling with horses and pack animals but without any protection other than the few weapons they possessed, when they were suddenly alarmed to see behind them, a long way in the distance down the old military road, a cloud of dust that heralded the approach of a large group of travellers.

At first, they thought they must be refugees like themselves. They had seen so many people fleeing west away from the Turks down the great military highway that there was no surprise in this. However, they became alarmed when this host seemed to be gaining on them rapidly and they saw the sun reflecting off what seemed like armour and weapons. Through the heat haze, they glimpsed what could only be a great force of soldiers. Were they Romans or Turks? They could not see.

"Should we hide?" Zoe asked. "We could leave the road now and head towards those hills."

"No, we would only arouse their suspicion even more," Eirene said. "Let's carry on and with luck they will be our soldiers."

They hurried on as fast as they could, but the strange host moved faster and soon it was in sight. To their enormous relief, they could see that they didn't have the distinctive appearance of the Turks. However, their jubilation was short lived for they immediately began to worry about the treatment that these soldiers, even if they were on their side, might mete out to them. No one trusted soldiers even if they came from the Emperor's regular army in Constantinople, and they were used to seeing civilians roughly treated by the soldiers who escorted tax collectors.

But when the soldiers caught up with them they found that they were a well disciplined group of thematic infantry and cavalry. Then with surprise, Eirene saw the Ducas family's emblem on their shields: a white tower on a black background. An officer asked them for information and when he discovered who Eirene was, he said that he would take them to their leader.

Eirene recognized Andronicus the moment she saw him. They looked at each other in disbelief.

"My lord, Andronicus, we have fled the Turks and are travelling to Amorium. Will you give us your protection?" she asked him boldly, half-smiling, pretending it was like the old days when he had been her suitor.

Andronicus studied her face. Her eyes looked more soulful as a result of her suffering, making them even more beautiful. Yet he felt no longing for her as he had done a few years ago. His wife, Maria, was pregnant with their second child. Instead, he remembered that she had made a fool of him by marrying Theodore.

Would he mention that Theodore was a few hours behind them? Did she have any idea of what had happened to him, he wondered.

He dismounted from his horse as he told the officer to halt the troops.

"How pleased I am to find you," he said courteously. "Tell me what has happened to you."

When she had finished a full account of their capture and escape, including a description of Afsin and the privileged treatment he had given her, Andronicus smiled to himself. The Turk Afsin has fallen for her. It did not surprise him. He said: "There has been another raid across the frontier. We believe it is Afsin again. A large Turkish force was sighted at Amaseia and we are searching for them. You must come with us. We will keep you safe."

And so they travelled together towards Dorylaeum. Andronicus was polite and considerate to Eirene. She was left to travel with her family and Zoe in the same cart that they had journeyed in from Amaseia. Yet he wondered what to do with her. He knew that Theodore was travelling on the same road only a day's journey or so behind them, with Ragnar and his group of Varangians. Theodore's accusation against him still smarted. He had been deeply relieved that the Emperor had not believed it. Now, he savoured the thought of revenge.

As they drew close to Dorylaeum, soldiers from the garrison rode to tell them that a Turkish warband was attacking Amorium. They thought its leader was the famous Afsin.

Andronicus wondered what to do. He knew he had to act quickly. Then a plan came to his mind.

He immediately instructed a messenger to ride to Ragnar to tell him that Afsin was attacking Amorium and that he must ride there immediately with the Varangians to rescue the city. He told the messenger to explain to Ragnar that he would need to attack the Turks alone since his own troops were mainly infantry, and that it would take at least two days before they could reach Amorium, by which time it would probably be too late for them to save the city.

Then he sent soldiers to fetch Eirene. When they arrived, Eirene was with Zoe and the two boys, eating a breakfast of bread and goats' cheese. They looked up, surprised to see the soldiers.

"My lord Andronicus has asked you to come to his tent," a young officer said. There was something too abrupt in his voice. His brown eyes looked guilty. Something was wrong.

She tried to reassure herself with memories of Andronicus when he had courted her before she met Theodore. One day he had appeared unannounced in Amorium, at her parents' mansion, with a beautiful horse as a present for her. She had been overcome with embarrassment. Surely he could not mean any harm to them?

Emboldened by these thoughts she agreed to go with the soldiers. When they entered Andronicus's tent, he looked at them sullenly. Immediately Eirene realised that she had been tricked. But there was no escape. They were surrounded.

"What is it that you want?" she asked him nervously.

Andronicus was silent. He looked at her, his lips tightly shut. Now that she was there before him, he could not speak to her. He looked away from her to the young officer that had brought them in and said:

"Seize these traitors. Bind their hands and put them in the cart. We will go immediately."

"Traitors? What do you mean?" Eirene shouted.

Zoe and the children burst into tears. She turned to put her arms around Gregory and Constantine but the soldiers seized her and bound her hands and gagged her.

As they were led to the cart, Eirene was terrified. They were forced to sit on the floor of the cart as they set off on a bumpy track. The hours passed and Eirene could not imagine where they were going. She did her best to comfort Zoe and her children. She told them over and over again that she was sure that Andronicus meant them no harm.

Beside the cart, Andronicus rode with a hundred heavily-armed men to find the Turks. They travelled in the morning towards Amorium, which was fifty miles from Dorylaeum. When they could see Amorium's citadel, they knew the Turks would be close. They tied white pennants to their spears and a trumpeter blew loud blasts to herald their approach. Their Pecheneg scouts rode ahead, calling out in their native tongue, similar to that of the Turks, that they came in peace. The Turkish lookouts saw them and quickly sent back word to Afsin about the appearance of this force of Romans, apparently intent on a parley.

Afsin rode to meet them outside his camp on the side of a hill. Turkish archers lay concealed behind trees and bushes. He was used to the tricks that a parley normally involved and had used them many times himself. Yet this time he was curious to find out what it was the Romans wanted. If it was not a trick, he imagined it would be an offer of gold to abandon the siege.

The Romans leading the column dismounted from their horses and the standard bearer with the white pennant advanced boldly forward. Afsin sent his bodyguard, Ulan, to speak to him. He returned with the news that the Roman commander wanted to meet Afsin personally and to make him an offer. He wanted to meet him unarmed. He had an interpreter, a Pecheneg scout, who would translate for them.

Afsin was intrigued. What was the Roman plan? Was it to send a common soldier dressed as their leader and then to stab him? He sent Ulan again to ask why he should speak with the Romans. What did they have to offer?

Ulan returned to say that the Romans had Eirene Gabras who they knew Afsin wanted. He could take her if he agreed to their terms but they would not say what these were.

Afsin was deeply perplexed. Why would they want to surrender Eirene if indeed it was her? It must be a trick, he thought. Yet his longing to see Eirene again proved too much for him. He ordered his men to tell the Romans that he was ready to meet them now and unarmed. He unbuckled his sword. He felt under his leather shirt for the small hunting dagger that was strapped beneath his arm. He loosened the strings of his shirt so that he could reach the dagger more easily. It had saved him before.

He and Ulan, both supposedly unarmed, met Andronicus and the Pecheneg scout in the middle of an open piece of ground. Afsin wondered what their trick would be. The Roman commander was very tall and he looked uncomfortable as he spoke to the Pecheneg scout.

"My commander has the woman you want," the Pecheneg said in his own Ohguz dialect which Afsin could understand. "He will give her to you. He will also give you a thousand pieces of gold if you sack Amorium. Half now and half when you have sacked the city."

Afsin laughed, which did not please Andronicus. A Roman feud. He was caught in a feud between these fools of Romans. Immediately, he told the Pecheneg that he would gladly accept the terms. Andronicus did not smile. He looked on grimly as if his treachery was distasteful to him. Something that he had to do in spite of its repugnance to him.

Within minutes Eirene was brought, with her children and Zoe. She looked blankly at Andronicus and Afsin, too stunned to say anything. Gregory and Constantine looked confused, unable to understand what was happening in this strange world of grown-ups. They were all too tired to cry except for Zoe who sobbed uncontrollably.

Then, just as the Turks were taking them, Eirene fell to the ground and begged Andronicus not to leave them.

"Have you no fear of Christ?" she gasped. "How can you do this to us? You are giving Christians to the heathens? Why? What have we done to deserve this?"

Andronicus did not reply for a moment, and then he said slowly: "And Theodore is only a few hours away."

"Theodore is alive?" Eirene asked in a hushed voice.

Andronicus smiled. "But he doesn't know that you are."

Eirene stared at him, unable to say another word, as Ulan took her arm.

XII

Leaving Andronicus behind, Afsin and his men rode back taking their four captives with them, each one sitting astride a horse in front of a Turk and desperately clinging onto its mane with their hands bound together.

Eirene knew it was impossible to escape. She was sitting in front of Ulan, who was careful not to manhandle her too much in case it provoked Afsin's wrath.

When they arrived back at the camp, Afsin took the four of them to his tent. He told Ulan to take the two boys and Zoe away while Eirene stayed alone with him.

Eirene was in such a state of shock that she could only stare at Afsin, unable to think clearly. Andronicus's betrayal, and his complicity with Afsin, had been so unexpected that she was still struggling to believe that such an evil change in her fortune had really happened. In contrast, Afsin was delighted. He couldn't believe his luck. But equally he didn't know what to say to the woman who he had longed to regain.

They stood in silence. Eirene was motionless; her hands had been untied and were at her side. Afsin went to sit in the same bishop's chair that he had used in their first meeting. He wanted to speak to her but the lack of a common language frustrated him and left him looking at her speechless.

Then something happened that caught him completely

by surprise. The horror of the situation, compounded by the injustice of Andronicus's betrayal, overcame Eirene's confused mind, and she darted forward, purely on impulse, and grabbed the nearest weapon hanging from the central tent pole where Afsin always stored his personal weapons.

She unsheathed a dagger and held it at Afsin. He hadn't expected this and stood back. He was in fact unarmed, and his weapons were all hanging from the same tent pole which Eirene was now guarding. He could easily call his guards but that would be too embarrassing.

He motioned at her to drop the weapon. She responded by pointing it firmly at him. He knew it wouldn't be too difficult to disarm her, and he approached her stealthily like a wolf about to pounce on its prey.

She held her ground with the tent pole at her back. Her mind was now starting to think more rationally, which meant that she had started to regret her action. What could she achieve? There was no way out. She knew that she wouldn't be able to kill an experienced warrior like Afsin and escape. And even if she could, how could she rescue her children?

Sensing that Afsin was about to attack at any moment, she suddenly reversed the blade and held it at her own throat. Again the action was done purely on impulse, driven by her confidence that Afsin valued her more alive than dead.

Afsin stepped back. This was completely unexpected. Never in any fight had he seen an opponent threaten to end their own life. He stared at Eirene, his eyes starting to show some sign of panic just as hers showed a new-found authority.

She knew that she had outwitted him. But at what cost? She nodded her head at him as if to say "yes I will kill myself", as she pushed the dagger point into her skin so that she could feel the pressure point.

He knew that he couldn't stop her from driving the blade into her throat. He stepped back so that it was clear he was not going to attack her. He held out his hand for her to give him the dagger. But she shook her head. He wished he could speak her language. He wanted to tell her that he would do anything to prevent her death.

Eirene was desperately thinking how she could escape and also ensure the safety of her children. Like Afsin, she wished she could speak to him. She might be able to make a bargain with him. But then she also knew that such an idea was ridiculous. She had one means of cowing him and it would not last for long.

She took the dagger back from her throat. But it was clear that it was only in order to give her the space to jab it more decisively into her throat. She looked at Afsin with fierce determination. He knew that she meant it.

"No!" he shouted in Turkish, and then he he did something purely on impulse. He held out his own arm, his wrist proffered to her.

She stared at him. Both their eyes were fixed in a deadly serious stare. He nodded his head at her and lifted the open palm of his hand up to her. His meaning was clear. She retracted the blade from her throat. He did not move. His wrist remained extended, hers for the taking. She looked into his eyes. There was no trick to be played.

She took the dagger away and threw it aside. Still looking at her, Afsin bowed his head as if in submission. His lust for her had gone. He could not believe what he had just done. He called for the guard and told him to take her to her family. They must all be treated well, he told him.

XIII

The citadel of Amorium was perched on a great rock of stone, above the town, that looked as if it had been placed there by some giant. Its walls towered above the diminutive town walls beneath it. They were made of massive clean cut blocks of ancient stone that dated back to a time long before Christ lived. And at its highest point, in a tower that commanded a clear view for miles around, John Taronites, Eirene's father and Duke of the Theme of Anatolikon, stared down from its ramparts at the host of Turks in front of the town walls. He had counted more than a thousand of them. A sizeable force to have travelled this far into the Empire. Fortunately for him, they had been spotted the day before, close to Dorylaeum, and its commander had despatched riders to all the towns in the area, alerting them to the approach of invaders that had not been seen for over two hundred years since the time of the Arab invasions.

John Taronites had acted fast. His garrison was small, some two hundred men equipped with old weapons, and he had sent riders out far and wide telling people to seek safety behind Amorium's walls or else to flee to woods and high places well away from where these marauders would be looking. His next command had been for all able-bodied men to report to him at the citadel with whatever weapons they had. That morning he had found assembled some five hundred men armed not with soldiers' weapons but with the accoutrements of farmers and hunters: spears to kill wild boars and bears, hunting knives, long-handled scythes and bows and arrows designed for hunting not warfare. He knew they would be no match for the Turks but at least they could man the walls which were still in a good state of repair apart from one stretch which was only defended by a wooden palisade.

He also had one surprise for the Turks: liquid fire. This lethal substance was still unknown to the barbarians, and had turned countless sieges and naval battles in the Romans' favour.

"Why has God sent these devils to punish us?" he asked aloud but more to himself than those around him. No one around him answered. They stared in disbelief at the Turkish host. He had been distraught ever since he had heard of the Turkish attack on Neoceasarea, so close to where his daughter, Eirene, lived. She had always been his favourite child and now he desperately hoped that she had survived this terrible Turkish invasion that he had long dreaded would happen.

Then as they watched, a large group of Turks ran up to the gate and were met by a volley of arrows, shot by the garrison soldiers from the ramparts. They scattered, holding up their small, wooden shields while others behind them shot back at the defenders with powerful, recurved bows. From the citadel, John saw a second group of Turks dragging a heavy wooden battering ram, with iron cladding at the end. The attack was coming right now. He knew that they had little time left.

He rushed down to the town wall with the city's Logothete.

When they got there arrows hissed over their heads, and smacked into the stone walls, as they watched the battering ram approach.

"Bring the fire now!" he shouted to the Logothete.

Soldiers clambered up the steps to the wall above the gate, holding huge earthenware pots and metal siphons. The battering ram was now beneath the main gate.

"Prepare to light it!"

A soldier ran up the steps, holding a burning torch ready to light arrows. The oily contents of the pots were poured into the metal siphons.

"Discharge the oil!"

A soldier aimed a siphon at the Turks, balancing it on top of the walls. As the soldier took aim, an arrow struck him in the neck and he fell backwards, his hands clawing at the air.

The Turkish battering ram struck the gates. They shuddered under the blow.

"In the name of the saints, I will do this. Cover me with a shield!" John told the Logothete, who took a large round infantry shield and raised it above the parapet, his head lowered safely beneath its rim.

John grasped the siphon and peered down at the Turks below. Arrows thudded off the Logothete's shield. He took aim and told the soldiers to light their arrows. More arrows spun overhead and smashed into the shield. He called for the liquid to be poured into the siphon. As he held the siphon up, the liquid poured through it and sprayed and cascaded over the Turks and the battering ram below.

"Fire!" he shouted.

The archers shot their burning arrows at the Turks who were immediately engulfed in flame. They dropped the battering ram and ran screaming, several of them human torches, the others horribly burned.

John collapsed on the ground, his back against the wall, wiping the sweat from his face. The Logothete smiled at him.

"Good shot, my lord."

"Now, we wait for Romanus," John said. Little did he

know that the Emperor was six hundred miles away, campaigning in northern Syria.

After their first attempt to take the town had failed, the Turks set up camp half a mile away. The Romans looked at the smoke as it drifted into the sky from their camp fires. Then later in the day, a large crowd of Turks gathered near to the main gate just out of bowshot range. They rode their horses round and round, shouting their war-cries to the beat of drums that sounded strange and frightening, and jeering at the Romans. Every so often a few of them would spur their horses at great speed towards the walls and as they turned, they shot burning arrows over the walls. At first the arrows did little damage but then one found its mark in the thatched roof of a great barn which burst into flames. John had to order men from the walls to prevent it from spreading.

But the Turks did not attack. Night came and the two sides watched each other as predator and prey. Then the next morning something unexpected happened. A group of Turks rode to the front gate where they stopped just out of bowshot range. They had roped together a group of peasants on foot who stumbled as they were pulled along by their captors. They were the same farmers who Eirene had found and who Afsin had captured.

John came down from the citadel to the main gate to see what the Turks wanted just as they pushed one of their captives forward towards the main gate. Although they had released him from his shackles, the Turks sat on their ponies with their bows strung ready to shoot him if he tried to escape. One of them was Ulan, Afsin's bodyguard, who sat scowling, looking at the Romans.

"Open the small door in the gate in case he tries to run for it. We can let him in that way," John told the garrison commander.

But he did not try to escape. Instead, he came right up to the front gate and looked up at John and his soldiers on the ramparts. He spoke loudly and clearly:

"The Turks tell you to surrender the city otherwise they will take it and kill everyone."

John replied angrily. "In the name of the saints, tell them we won't surrender, not to barbarians!" Then he added: "Look man, save yourself at least. Run to the door in the gate. It is open."

"I cannot," the man said, "they will kill my brother and my friends if I don't return. Is there nothing more I can tell them?"

"No."

The man turned to go. The Turks looked on.

When John returned to the citadel he found his wife, Theodora, and told her what had happened. She sat with her head in her hands and wept. John tried to comfort her.

"We will be safe in the citadel until help arrives. The Turks cannot scale these walls without siege engines which they don't have."

"What about the rest of the town?" Theodora asked, still sobbing.

"We cannot defend it against that host. The walls are low everywhere and the southeastern section fell in two years ago and still has to be properly repaired. We only have a wooden palisade there and the ground is flat as well. They could break in there."

Theodora continued to sob uncontrollably.

"Let's wait and see what their next move is," he said, putting his arms around her. "The longer we wait the more time there is for help to arrive."

The answer to John's question was provided that very afternoon. The group of Turks that had appeared that morning rode to the front gates again with the same farmer.

But this time Afsin's bodyguard, Ulan, pushed him to his knees and held him there as he took out his sword and with a single blow beheaded him. Then he bellowed with laughter and put the severed head on a spear and planted it in the ground.

XIV

The next day, Andronicus's messenger reached Ragnar and the Varangians, who were encamped some ten miles from Dorylaeum, with news of Afsin's attack and Andronicus's command for them to relieve the town.

"He wants the Turks to kill us," Ragnar said grimly to Theodore. "It's as clear as a wolf stalking a deer. He wants us dead. He's afraid of us. We know of his treachery at the battle."

"My wife's family are at Amorium. I must go there," Theodore said. He had never heard of Afsin and was at a loss to explain why these Turks should be attacking Amorium.

Ragnar shrugged. He liked the way that Theodore was not afraid to fight.

They packed their belongings and rode in the morning sun towards Amorium. They did not send scouts ahead. The few villages they passed were deserted. Their inhabitants had fled to Amorium or to the hills.

Ragnar was glum. He knew that the odds were heavily stacked against them. He only had two hundred men, for Romanus had taken the rest of the Varangian Guard with him to Syria. His men were tense, aware of their leader's misgivings. No one spoke except Ragnar, who said to Theodore: "When we get there, you lead us into the town. You know it. We'll be in your hands, Theodore."

Later that day, in the afternoon, Theodore led Ragnar and the Varangians down through the valley to the town. They galloped through trees and scrubland and, as they got closer to the town, they could see that the Turks had already attacked. Buildings were ablaze within the town walls, and as they approached the gates, they could see the walls were empty.

There were some Turks in front of the town walls who saw them and shouted warnings but it seemed that their comrades were widely scattered and they ran off into the town.

Theodore knew that Eirene's family would have taken refuge in the citadel. With Ragnar, he led the Varangians through the main gate. The few Turks they saw scattered before them rather than offer any resistance. A group of Varangians stayed to hold the gate while the rest rode on into the town along the main street, their horses treading over the dead bodies of the townspeople. The church of St Methodius was the main building in the town apart from the citadel, and Theodore headed straight towards it.

There they met a large crowd of Turks gathered in front of the church. These ones showed no intention of scattering and turned to face the Varangians. There were a few hundred of them on foot and they formed a solid block of men. Some of them strung their bows and shot at the approaching Varangians.

"Form a shield wall!" Ragnar shouted, for they made easy targets on horseback. The Varangians jumped down from their horses, holding their shields high to ward off the Turkish arrows. While some of them led their horses back to the gate, the rest formed a shield wall, nearly ten men deep, and advanced forward towards the Turks. The Turkish arrows flew at them, thudding into their shields. One of the Varangians fell, his neck pierced by an arrow.

Theodore was at Ragnar's side as they charged forward. The two sides crashed into each other in an angry explosion of shouting and clanging of iron. The round iron Varangian shields were larger than the light leather-clad Turkish ones and they easily pushed the Turks back who were used to fighting on horseback, and knew that they were at a disadvantage on foot against these heavily armoured warriors.

Theodore felt his energy surge up inside him. He hated the Turks and he wanted every one of them dead. He pushed his shield upwards into the face of the man in front of him while he lowered his sword and slashed at the blur of bodies before him. There was a scream from the man in front of him who fell to his knees. Lifting his shield up, Theodore lowered his sword and drove it into the man's neck. But before he could pull it back, another Turk on his right raised a heavy iron mace.

Theodore tried to turn away from him but he knew he was too late and, just as he expected the mace to smash into his head, he saw the Turk stagger back. Ragnar had driven a sword into his chest.

"For King Harald!" Ragnar shouted, as his Varangians pressed forward, thrusting their swords and axes forward above their shields. But there was no one to meet them. The Turks were running.

They chased the fleeing Turks towards the church. When they reached the main door Ragnar would not go in. He did not like churches and was afraid that they might bring him bad luck if he entered one. Theodore motioned to him that he would go in. He pushed the door gently open with one hand as he leant against the wall. He tried to peer through the open door to see who was inside. He expected arrows to fly at him but there was silence. Raising his shield he rushed in.

The floor was swimming in blood, the priests and

townsfolk lay dead all around him, slaughtered as they had been praying to God for safety. He strode forward. The Turks had fled.

Calling to the Varangians to secure the exits to the church he rushed back to the main door and led his soldiers through the streets.

Meanwhile messages had reached Afsin of the Roman counterattack. He called his men to retreat outside the town. He had Eirene and half of Andronicus's gold. That was enough.

The Turks began to retreat out of the town through the wooden palisade which they had breached in their original attack. Meanwhile, Theodore led the Varangians towards the citadel to link up with its defenders.

The defenders made a sally on horseback out of the citadel with John Taronites at their head. Theodore found himself at John's side. John could not believe it was him. He barely recognized the grim, haggard soldier that Theodore had become.

"Where is Eirene?" he asked hopefully and his stomach churned when Theodore told him that she and his children had disappeared, almost certainly dead or taken prisoner by the Turks.

The fleeing Turks were now massing outside the town, scowling and furious, still shocked by the ferocity of the Varangian attack and the loss of many of their comrades.

Theodore led the Varangians as they filed through the main gates to face the Turks outside. The Varangians formed a shield wall in front of the main gate. The Turks looked at them in shocked silence, not even shooting their arrows.

"Don't try to attack them," John said to Theodore. "Don't throw your life away now."

Ragnar appeared, his axe covered in blood, and took command. He was enjoying himself but he could see there was no point in attacking the Turks. The Turks jeered at the Varangians and volleys of their arrows thudded into the mass of large round Varangian shields

Then something happened that took both sides by complete surprise. A massive Turk, carrying a white pennant attached to his spear, rode forward to within a hundred yards of the Varangians and bellowed out in surprisingly clear Greek: "Blessed is Allah! Yield or fight me!"

It was Ulan, Afsin's bodyguard.

In a moment of madness, Theodore was seized with hatred for this Turk and forced himself through the Varangian ranks, grabbing a spear as he went, and strode forward towards Ulan, squinting at the Turk through the glare of the sun.

Ulan didn't wait either. The moment Theodore appeared he charged forward, hurling his spear at him. Although Theodore was tired, he saw the spear and brought his shield up just in time to ward it off, the blow jarring his arm. Ulan was quick. No sooner was the spear in Theodore's shield than he was in front of him, about to trample him under his horse's hooves and hack at him with his sword. But Theodore still had his own spear and he crouched down in front of the horse and stabbed it up into the animal's chest. The horse reared up in agony and Ulan fell to the ground.

Ulan was unhurt but furious. He quickly got to his feet and shouted at Theodore. This Roman was more dangerous than he had expected. They circled each other warily. Ulan lunged at him, swiping at him with his sword. Theodore stepped back but remembering Ragnar's lessons, he suddenly knelt down and turned his shield up at the Turk, as he slashed at Ulan's feet. His sword ripped through skin and flesh into the bone of Ulan's left foot. He wasn't seriously injured but he was even angrier. He stared at Theodore and then he said just one word, hissing it as he spoke:

"Eirene!"

The single word caused Theodore to stop in his tracks. Had he heard correctly? How could this Turk know her name? And in that second, Ulan threw himself at him, striking his shield fiercely with his sword, splintering the wood and scoring the metal cover. Ulan forced Theodore back, hammering his shield so that it split and Theodore thought his arm might be broken. Then he lost his footing and fell, dropping his sword. The Turks cheered wildly as Theodore squirmed in the dust, holding his broken shield above him, with his eyes blinded by the bright sun. Ulan stood over him, his sword poised above him, ready to bring it down in one massive blow.

But the blow never came. For Theodore drew his knife and flung it at Ulan. Ragnar had told him to put a knife strapped onto his belt behind his back. It might help you, Ragnar had told him, if you've dropped your sword or you have a chance to stab your enemy. You can throw it at them too, he had said, and he had taught Theodore how to throw a knife straight so that the point struck home, deep and deadly.

The sharp metal point caught the big man in the throat. Ulan dropped his sword, his hands clutching his throat. Blood gushed out. He stared at Theodore with shocked eyes and sank to his knees. Theodore jumped to his feet and grabbed Ulan's shoulders. But his eyes were already glazing over.

"Eirene? Where is she?"

But there was no answer. Ulan slumped forward.

Seeing Ulan's defeat, the Turks looked on in silence. Then commands were shouted and they turned their horses and galloped away across the stony, arid ground.

Ragnar rushed to Theodore.

"Odin saved you. He saves the brave and lets the others die. I have seen it many times."

But Theodore wasn't listening. He could only stare into the distance, into the shimmering dust haze as the Turkish cavalry streamed eastwards. How had the Turk known Eirene's name? And he felt just the smallest whisper of hope.

PART III
THE ROAD TO MANZIKERT

January 1069

Afsin informed the Sultan: "Behold, I invaded the territory of the Romans and have come forth with great loot, and there is not among the Romans anyone who can meet us in battle." Then Afsin continued to penetrate into the territory of the Romans until he encamped on the shore of the sea which flows by the wall of Constantinople; and he raided and looted and departed.

Bar Hebraeus, Chronography

XV

The dank morning mist seemed to float above the open grassland of the valley, like clouds that had sunk to earth. Behind it, with its light stone walls lit by the first rays of the pale winter sun, was the town of Isfahan, one of many such fortified strongholds in Khurasan (northern Persia).

Alp Arslan, the Seljuk Sultan and lord of an Empire that stretched from Syria to India, looked at the damp cold winter scene and wished that he was not there. He was a man of medium height but with a wiry, strong body. He had the same short, pointed beard and long black hair that most Turks wore but he was instantly recognizable by his particularly sharp black eyes that pierced you as you looked at him. His face was handsome and there was a shrewdness and sense of energy in his features, so that you would not be surprised to learn that he had brought together the greatest Muslim Empire that had existed since the times of the great Abbasid Caliph two hundred years ago.

However tedious and uncomfortable this campaign had been, he knew it was important to quell this local rebellion. His rule over so many different races and different local rulers was dependent on one thing: fear of him. Any signs of dissension within his huge realm had to be crushed with the speed and brutality that would teach others not to question Seljuk rule.

The towns of Khurasan had dared to refuse payment of their annual tithe, saying that the Seljuk soldiers were thieves and criminals. Alp Arslan knew that what they said was true but the important thing was to show the world that no one could question Seljuk rule and survive.

His army was spread out all around him. Behind him a myriad of tents stretched into the horizon. He knew the town of Ifsahan had no chance of survival whatsoever, and the sooner it was over the better. He gave the command to begin.

A group of ghulam soldiers – slave soldiers who were the elite of the Seljuk army, normally Turks but with some Kurds and Persians, and equipped with heavier armour and weapons than their Turkish brethren, the Turkomans like Afsin, advanced up to the main gate of the town. The walls were heavily manned, and a flood of arrows met the advancing ghulams, who hid behind large round shields which they held up, overlapping each other, in a tight formation. Meanwhile, hundreds of Turkish foot archers followed behind the ghulams, and when they were close enough to shoot, a murderous storm of arrows cleared the walls of its defenders. Under this hail of arrows, the ghulams went right up to the gates and drenched them with buckets of black oil. When this was done they retreated.

Alp Arslan watched grimly. He nodded to one of his commanders and scores of burning arrows shot into the air and thudded into the gate which burst into flame. Let the gate burn, thought Alp Arslan, and he gestured to the group of ghulams with a battering ram to wait.

He watched the flames looping and arching up over the ramparts, blackening the light-coloured stone. He watched the gates burn furiously as if they too were impatient for the town to be punished for its impudence. Then, when the gates had burned enough to present no obstacle to the ghulams, he raised his hand and was about to shout the command to attack, when suddenly the burning gates shuddered and were swung wide open, leaving the road into the town clear. Through the heat and smoke came figures.

Typical, thought Alp Arslan. The town's kadkhuda and his family were offered as scapegoats in a desperate attempt to prevent a sacking. He took his bow and strung an arrow. His skill as an archer was renowned. His fawning courtiers wrote songs about the terrifying accuracy of his bow, of how his enemies were brought down by darts they could not see until they were buried in their flesh.

I had better not disappoint them, Alp Arslan thought to himself. He focused on the figure in front, the rejected kadkhuda, with his wife and family behind him. Their hands had been tied together and they stumbled forward, their faces bloodied and their eyes looking around them in terror. Now was a perfect opportunity to demonstrate his power over such petty rulers.

His aim needed to be good. He waited for the kadkhuda to come forward until he was comfortably within range. Then his arrow spun forward and struck the man in the chest. He fell to the ground. His wife fell to her knees beside him, his children cowering behind. But no, it was beneath him to kill them. He gestured to his commander to unloose the ghulams.

"Spare no one. Put the whole town to the sword. I want people to remember this," he said.

The ghulams streamed forward and Alp Arslan turned to go back to his tent. He had no wish to hear the screams and witness the carnage.

Back in his tent, he called for his maps and his emirs. He wanted to get away from here as fast as possible. He hated these petty expeditions to the far-flung corners of his Empire. He looked at the map spread out on the table before him. To the west were the Romans. He needed to secure his frontier against them but he had never harboured any dreams of conquering them. Their Empire had existed forever. It had existed for centuries before the Prophet Muhammed had spoken to the world. Instead his ambitions lay to the south, to Egypt and the Shi'ite Fatimid caliphate which still rivalled his power in the Muslim world. Egypt was rich and its armies were powerful, filled with strong black warriors from the Sudan and fast Arab cavalry, not as skilled as his own Turks at archery, but nevertheless a true people of the horse. The Fatimids were his real enemy. The Romans needed to be kept within their boundaries but he had no fear that they would invade his own lands. By all accounts they had become corrupt and lazy. He was actually more worried that the Turkish nomads, who had poured into Armenia from the sea of grass, would provoke a Roman counterattack, so successful were their raids into Roman territory.

Just then one of his emirs came into the tent and bowed low before him.

"Great Sultan, I have news! Afsin has returned!"

"Afsin?" Alp Arslan frowned. Afsin was a dangerous rogue. He had had the audacity to kill Gumushtegin, his most trusted hajib (courtier), before fleeing to attack the Romans.

"How dare he return? Has he forgotten my death sentence on him?"

"He has defeated the Romans and sacked their cities, great Sultan. He asks you to forgive him in exchange for his plunder."

Alp Arslan's frown deepened.

"Forgive him? Who does he think he is? If he believes in Mohammed, he should know what his crime means. And he should be afraid, very afraid."

Afsin's second-in-command, Yakuti, would not forgive him either. They had lost too many men at Amorium and it was clear that Afsin's true purpose had been to recapture Eirene.

But they were still deep in enemy territory and were afraid that the Romans would have time to pursue them and cut off their escape route. So they did not pause to argue but travelled fast, not stopping to loot or attack the villages and towns they passed by.

Afsin had wanted to take his warband to Trebizond but they refused to go. Yakuti had told him that, after their losses at Amorium, they had no stomach for further fighting. Winter was approaching and the hills would soon be cold and desolate; they wanted to return to the warmth and comfort of Syria and come back to raid Trebizond in the spring. Afsin reluctantly agreed. At least he had recaptured Eirene. But now he had to face the wrath of Alp Arslan.

One day, after they had been travelling for a week, Afsin went with Yakuti and his scouts to reconnoitre the territory ahead of them when, in the distance, they saw clouds of dust being raised by what could only be a large number of travellers. Spurring their horses on, they got closer and, concealing themselves behind a hill, they waited until they could spy the advance guard of a large Roman army.

"It must be the Emperor returning from the frontier," Afsin said to Yakuti.

"They're returning to winter quarters. They will have strengthened the frontier garrisons but we can bypass them. These Romans don't like fighting…" he paused "… unless that dog we met in Amorium is there."

The thought of that Roman irked Afsin. How had he managed to kill Ulan? He wondered who he was and, for some reason, he felt that he would meet him again. If he did he would make sure that he killed him.

Afsin and Yakuti returned to the main force and decided to take a different route, trying to get as far away as possible from the Emperor's army. Within a few days they had reached the Taurus mountains in Cilicia but they dared not venture through the only pass, called the Cilician Gates, for it would be too heavily defended. Instead they travelled north towards Caesarea, which Afsin had sacked earlier in the summer, and then they climbed high into the mountains near the Roman frontier fortress of Melitene, as they headed east towards the Turkish stronghold of Amida. As they had expected, the Roman garrison at Melitene did nothing to stop them, although Romanus had reinforced it, and the commander had received news that Afsin's raiding party was heading back towards the East. But with the Emperor probably by now six hundred miles away in Constantinople, the commander felt sure that his cowardice would go unpunished, and the gates of Melitene remained firmly shut and the walls heavily manned, until Afsin's band had passed to the east and escaped back into Turkish territory.

As for Eirene, Afsin went to see her every day to make sure that she was being treated well and guarded securely. He was still worried that she might fall into the same state of despair to which she had succumbed when he had recaptured her. He was keen to show her that he meant no harm and, in order to communicate with her, he took with him a former ghulam from the Sultan's army who spoke some Greek.

Eirene was still astonished by Afsin's behaviour but she didn't trust his courteous manner and was still terrified of what he might do to her and her family. She was close to despair every day but it was the need to cheer up her sons and Zoe that gave her the courage to pretend to see a way out of their troubles. She would tell them that they were well treated because Afsin almost certainly wanted to demand a ransom for them. She reassured them that her family and Theodore's both had enough money to buy their freedom. Although she didn't realise it, this was the same view as most of Afsin's followers. But what she did know was that Afsin wanted something else from her. And yet she couldn't gauge what his true intentions were, and what was equally worrying, she sensed that neither could he.

Since their return to Syria, Afsin's followers had become aware of the death sentence passed on him by Alp Arslan, and were now worried for their own safety. Afsin knew he had to act fast before they deserted him. He formulated a plan as they rode through the arid mountainous landscape towards Amida.

As they approached Amida, he rode ahead of his men, his troubled mind causing him to irritate his horse with a jerky use of stirrup and reins, until he saw a group of Turkish warriors, clearly newcomers from the steppes and new to this strange Arab world, just as he had once been, and he trotted towards them calling out a greeting. They told him that Alp Arslan was at Mosul and for a moment he felt like running away back to the sea of grass. But he was no coward and instead he returned to his men, and they made haste to Amida.

When they had rested at Amida, Afsin set off for Mosul with fifty of his followers and most of the plunder carried on mules. He was nervous. He knew Alp Arslan could kill him on the spot if he wished. But he had a plan and he believed that it would work.

When they reached Mosul, word had already got round of their return, and Alp Arslan's soldiers were guarding the walls. Afsin and his men rode up to the main gate, glittering with brightly-coloured porcelain tiles, where they were challenged by a group of Turkish guards, whose leader called down from the battlements to Afsin.

"Afsin Bey, we have come to take you before our master, the Sultan," he said. "Give us your weapons and your horses and we will take you to him."

Afsin looked their leader in the eye, and recognised him

as one of the Turkish emirs, like himself a nomad from the steppes. He remembered that his name was Nizam and he replied: "Do you remember me Nizam Bey? We rode together with the Sultan against the Romans in Armenia. What mood is our master in? I have come to seek his pardon."

"I know not his mood. He commanded me to bring you to him. But he has not forgotten your disobedience and the cruel murder you meted out to his favourite hajib. Have you said your prayers, Afsin, for Allah will decide your fate?"

Afsin and his men handed over their weapons and horses and proceeded on foot to the citadel towering above the city. Nizam had agreed to let the mules with their booty go with them and the plunder rattled and clinked as they walked.

They were led by Nizam into the dark and cool interior of a great hall in the citadel. The heat and light outside was shut out and silence replaced the noise and commotion of the streets. Afsin's eyes took a few seconds to adjust to the dark. He looked up the length of the great room, past the candles lighting its sides, and below the bright sunlight shining through the rows of small square windows beneath the ceiling on either side of the tall walls, until he saw Alp Arslan seated on a great gilt-inlaid chair at the far end.

Nizam motioned Afsin forward and he walked in silence past the lines of guards towards Alp Arslan. He could see that his hand was on his sword and his heart pounded with fear. When he was ten feet away from him he fell to his knees and prostrated himself on the ground. He looked up at him and pleaded nervously, speaking the words that he had carefully prepared.

"Great Sultan, I have come here to seek your pardon for my crimes. I beg you to forgive me. I was foolish and rash when I refused to join your army but I thought my men would not follow your expedition to fight the Fatimids in Syria. We came from the sea of grass to add new lands to your domains. We have waged war against the Romans and conquered their cities and massacred their soldiers. All our plunder is yours and I have information about the Romans that could help you defeat them. Their lands are undefended and the Emperor has only a handful of soldiers who we easily outwitted. I raided hundreds of miles into their lands. See the gold crosses and sacred relics that we have brought back!"

Nizam gestured to the guards to let Afsin's men carry the rich booty forward and to spread it out on the tiled floor before the Sultan. It was a fine sight: the treasures of three Roman cities: Caesarea, Neocaesarea and Amorium. Golden crosses, goblets and gilt-edged books were spread out together with the bones of saints in golden clasps, and religious vestments in bright colours with golden stitching, and piles of coins and weapons.

Afsin turned to Alp Arslan who had looked on in silence and said: "My lord, all of our riches are yours and I place myself and my men at your command if you will pardon me. I have regretted my actions ever since I left your service. If you want me to I will tell you about the routes we found through the mountains into the Roman Empire; where their fortresses and towns are. I could be of use to you my lord."

Alp Arslan stood up. He was silent. He walked towards Afsin, looking at him impassively. Afsin was still kneeling on the clay floor tiles. Alp Arslan's hand strayed towards the handle of his sword, a curved Arab weapon unlike the straight Turkish swords. Afsin's heart started to pound in his chest. He knew that his crime of killing the Sultan's hajib was a serious one. Maybe he had made a mistake returning here.

Then Alp Arslan spoke softly: "Afsin, you committed a terrible crime indeed. Gumushtegin was one of my most trusted men. He died at your hands and then you fled. Now you have come back begging forgiveness. Do you think I should forgive you?"

"My lord, I can help you against the Romans. I know every fortress they have and the roads through the mountains. I can help your armies conquer their lands. Their forces are weak and I beseech you to strike now," Afsin said, his voice strained and his eyes not daring to look up at Alp Arslan's face.

"Who is your most trusted man?" Alp Arslan asked him, again in a soft tone.

"They are all my most trusted followers," Afsin answered.

Alp Arslan ignored his response. "Call him here," he said.

Afsin thought and then called out Yakuti's name. They had fought together in almost every battle Afsin had been in. He too had been a lowly camp-follower like Afsin and had always been his most loyal follower.

"Yakuti!" He called his name and Yakuti stepped forward.

"Come here," Alp Arslan said. "Kneel beside your master." His right hand was playing with the sword handle. Afsin's heart was still pounding.

Alp Arslan said nothing as his hand tightened over the sword handle and in one motion as fast as a snake would bite its prey, he drew the sword and brought it up into the throat of Yakuti where its razor sharp edge severed half his neck. Blood spurted in a torrent, covering Afsin, and Yakuti's body slumped forward.

Still in a soft voice, although slightly strained from his exertion, Alp Arslan said, "Afsin, it will be you next time if there is any more disobedience. You have been warned. Now I want all of your company to report here in Mosul. You will obey my orders from now on."

Afsin looked up. He was shocked but relief was spreading through his limbs and he felt suddenly light and nimble. He jumped to his feet, still dripping in warm blood.

"Thank you my lord. I will bring them here as soon as we can travel from Amida." And saying these words he bowed and stepped back before turning to walk down the great hall.

Two days later, again he went to see the Sultan in the same great chamber in Mosul where Yakuti had been beheaded. Alp Arslan had summoned him. Inside the great hall within the citadel, he noticed that the blood had vanished from the stone floor. There was no trace left of Yakuti. After kissing the Sultan's feet, he rose and waited for him to speak.

Alp Arslan looked at Afsin carefully. Soon he would be ready for his greatest campaign of all: the defeat of the Fatimids. He would drive them from Syria and invade Egypt. He had told the Caliph of Baghdad, nominally his master but in reality his slave, to proclaim in the great Mosque that the day was approaching when the prayers in Cairo would be those of the true Sunni faith.

In Baghdad, he had been mustering a great army not just of Turks but also of Persians and Arabs. He had been summoning his Persian vassals in the east and demanding soldiers from them. Now, he needed the Turkomans in Armenia to join his army. And Afsin would take the place of Gemushtegin, the hajib he had killed, in summoning them.

Finally, Alp Arslan spoke.

"The Caliph has asked that the Qur'an be read by him in Cairo, not Constantinople." Alp Arslan looked down on Afsin and spoke slowly. "I need your men to join my army in Syria to fight against the Shi'ites. It is a long road to Cairo and we do not want war with the Romans. I want to offer the Roman Emperor peace."

Afsin could not believe these words. He looked at Alp Arslan incredulously. Then he spoke in desperation as his dreams crumbled before his eyes.

"My greatest Sultan, I have told you before of the weaknesses of the Roman defences. Their army is small and they only have a few well-trained regiments. Now is the time to strike them when they are weak. We can push them back to Constantinople!"

Alp Arlsan ignored him.

"I will offer the Roman Emperor a truce in exchange for Hierapolis, the town that he took last autumn. That is all that I ask for. And, in return, I will command the Turkomans to cease raiding his territory."

Afsin listened in terror. His dream was slipping away from him.

"Allah wishes us to wage Jihad on the Romans," he begged. "If you believe in Mohammed you will see that it is written. My destiny lies in battle against the Christians."

Alp Arslan smiled. It was typical of these Turks from the sea of grass to want plunder from the easiest victims.

"Only Allah knows where your destiny is written. Forget Jihad against the Romans," he said. "If you serve me well, when the Caliph reads the Qur'an in Cairo, Allah will smile on you. Now, I want you to take your men and go to Armenia where you will gather the Turkomans who are on the Roman border and bring them here. Tell them that they will find more glory and plunder in Syria and Egypt than in the Roman lands. Tell them that disobedience will be met with death. I want you to set an example with anyone who refuses my order, do you understand? I want you to report back within a month. Send me messengers with news of your progress in the meantime."

He gestured with his hand that Afsin was dismissed.

XVI

It was winter when Romanus's army returned to Constantinople. Light snow covered the red clay tiles of the rooftops and the great dome of Haghia Sophia rose above the city like a snow-capped mountain. Within days of his return, Romanus organised a triumphal procession for his returning army.

But the talk in Constantinople was of Afsin's raid on Amorium. How could the Turks have raided so far inland if Romanus's army was victorious, they said. Stories of the slaughter in the church of St Methodius were told. They found the bishop hanging from the bell rope, his hands cut off and placed in mockery on the Bible at his feet, people said in whispered tones of shock. God has forsaken the Emperor, said the men in wine shops as they played backgammon.

Nevertheless, on the day of the triumphal procession, everyone in the city went out onto the streets. The main road, called the Mese, was thronged with huge crowds that formed a mass of moving colours, for the Romans wore brightly dyed fabrics, mainly blue and red, that were cheap and plentiful.

The army marched into the city through the Golden Gate, the main entrance through the great land walls of Theodosius, built more than six hundred years ago. The walls ran for five miles from one side of the peninsula on which Constantinople stood to the other side, completely blocking the land approach to the city. In front of them was a moat that allowed the sea to join and make an island of the peninsula, and the walls were built as a double set with a smaller outer wall as a first line of defence, behind which, and overshadowing it, stood a gigantic wall with ninety-six mighty towers placed at intervals along its entire length. No enemy had ever breached these extraordinary defences and many armies had perished in the attempt.

Behind the walls was a city that was also unimaginable to those that had not been there. For it was a city perfectly preserved from the times of ancient Rome and Greece. No other city had survived from the ancient world through the dark ages until now. Its great aqueducts, basilicas, churches, palaces and hippodrome had been built of such size and grandeur in another age that they left foreigners speechless with wonder.

The city had many different quarters. Close to the walls were thousands of poorer houses made of brick and with red clay-tiled roofs. Further into the city, following its broad avenues were grand houses and the mansions of the nobility. Along the sides of the peninsula were four harbours filled with boats from every land, not just those of the Empire but from the whole Mediterranean world. Arabs, Moors, Venetians, Franks and Vikings came here and traded, paying the Emperor's customs duties. The sea was filled with a busy maritime traffic, taking goods north into the Euxine Sea and south into the blue waters of the Aegean.

The heart of the ancient city was near the end of the peninsula, and contained the great forums of Theodosius and Constantine, the huge hippodrome which was the principal meeting place of the city, and the Emperor's great palace, as it was called, that spread over a hundred acres. And the very greatest building of all, the centre of the Christian world, was the church of Haghia Sophia, the largest building in the world with a dome that could be seen by travellers and seafarers from many miles around.

Romanus and Andronicus rode at the front of the army with the Scholae. Row upon row of these heavily armoured soldiers could not fail to impress the crowds. Riding big horses, the Scholae looked look like men made of iron, not flesh and blood, their bodies covered from head to toe in chainmail and lamellar armour, with only their eyes visible through holes in their chainmail face masks. They rode behind their tall purple standards, fully armed, with swords, maces and spears at their sides. Behind them marched the Varangians, carrying great axes over their shoulders, and looking like a race of trolls, so tall were most of them and with blond hair and piercing blue eyes. Behind them was a great mass of cavalry and infantry from the Themes.

Romanus led the army down the Mese, from the Golden Gate into the centre of the city, until they reached the Forum of Constantine and then into the hippodrome where a huge crowd was waiting.

Romanus went with Andronicus to sit in the imperial box. He raised his hands for silence and then he spoke, shouting out his words so that they could be heard. He said that he had hunted down and destroyed one of the Turkish war-bands. He had captured Hierapolis from the Arabs. But this was only the beginning, he said. The army would march again in the spring and this time it would be larger and stronger. He would defeat the Turks once and for all and bring peace to the Empire. He did not mention that he had failed to stop the Turks from sacking Neocaesarea and Amorium.

Then a group of ten Turkish and Arab prisoners was led forward by the Varangians into the middle of the hippodrome and beheaded beside the great obelisk. As the Varangian's axe fell on each captive's neck a great cheer went up from the crowd.

Theodore stood on guard at the far end of the hippodrome, having marched with the Varangians in the triumphal procession. His eyes were fixed on the imperial box, where Romanus was addressing the huge crowd of seventy thousand people. His heart pounded angrily in his chest as he thought of the injustice of losing his inheritance because he had dared to tell Romanus the truth. He remembered the words of his father-in-law, John Taronites, after the battle at Amorium.

"I'd like to tell Romanus what I think of his behaviour to you!" he had said angrily. "The Diogenes family have long been our friends. We helped them when Romanus's father was banished. But I fear that you have offended him beyond repair since everyone knows that he's besotted with Andronicus. The reason is that he wants to use him against his father, the Caesar John."

Eirene's father had explained that the Caesar John was Romanus's main political rival. He had been given the title of Caesar by his brother, the last Emperor Constantine, a title that showed he was the second most important man in the Empire after the Emperor. Naturally, because of this, he had expected to be made regent, the de-facto Emperor, when his brother died, since Constantine's own son, Michael, was only a shy, bookish teenager and not strong or experienced enough to be Emperor in this time of war.

He had been furious when his ambitions had been undone by the Empress Eudocia, who had not relished the idea of being told what to do by the Caesar John, who she had never liked. And in any case, opposition to the Ducas family had grown in the last years of Constantine's reign. When Afsin had sacked the city of Caesarea, in the heartland of the Eastern Empire, Eudocia feared that there was about to be a revolt by the Eastern nobles. Then she had met Romanus, who himself had recently been widowed, and she had fallen for his handsome self-confidence. So, when Constantine died, she had sided with the nobles from the Eastern provinces against the Caesar John and made Romanus, the Empire's leading general, her Emperor.

"You are right. Romanus won't change his mind," Theodore said. "I am better to stay with Ragnar."

He had left them, promising that he would never give up his search for Eirene and his children. He didn't tell them of the Turk's utterance of Eirene's name at Amorium but he thought of it continually. He knew it had been a trick to throw him off his guard but the Turk must have known something about Eirene and it gave him a glimmer of hope.

"The army is the best place for me. We will go back to the Eastern frontier, and if Eirene is still alive, that is where I will find her. I will not come back until I find out what has befallen my family."

John had embraced him. His wife, Theodora, was weeping and she put her arms around him.

"We will pray for you every day. May God hear our prayers and show you the way to our daughter and your children. Go, Theodore, before our hearts break."

He forced himself to banish these memories from his mind as he looked more closely at the imperial box, and was intrigued to see that Andronicus's father, the Ceasar John, was not there. What greater insult could he give Romanus than not to attend his triumphal procession when everyone else in the city was there? He wondered how Romanus could trust Andronicus when the Caesar John's defiance was so blatant?

And although he did not know it, that question was about to be answered.

The next day, Theodore was standing guard at the Senate house, an ancient, tall-domed building, where Romanus was discussing his next campaign. There, standing around a great table inlaid with gold and ivory and covered with maps, were on one side, the Ducas family and on the other side, Romanus with his main generals. Seated all around them were members of the Senate, consisting of those who held rank and position within the Empire, from noblemen who commanded the themes to high-ranking government officials and heads of the many different guilds in the city.

The Caesar John had arrived after his conspicuous absence at the triumphal procession. He was tall and thin and he looked at Romanus and his generals with a defiant and challenging stare, his lips curling with a mix of disdain for them and frustration at his own lack of power. A little behind him and to his right, was Andronicus. He stood with a passive expression on his face, as if he was bored with the proceedings.

In between them was the commander of the Italian Themes, the Catepan, as his position was called. He was a dark, squat man who stood aside from Romanus's generals, between them and the Ducas family, his arms folded across his chest and his mouth set in a frown with his eyes fixed on the maps in the centre of the table.

The discussion was of the military situation in Italy, where the Empire's territory had been reduced by the Norman invaders to the great fortress of Bari and a few other towns on the southern seaboard.

The Caesar John spoke haughtily, not concealing his contempt for Romanus:

"We cannot leave Italy to the Normans. We must send reinforcements to Bari otherwise it will fall and we will have lost everything. We will never be able to recover our lands there!"

The Catepan of the Italian Themes nodded vigorously.

Romanus did not seem troubled by this. He raised his hands imploringly.

"We can't attack on two fronts at the same time, and you know that what is happening in the East is many, many times more dangerous to the Empire than the Normans. Once we have victory over the Turks, we can turn our attention to Italy."

"And your estates are in Cappadoccia are they not?" the Caesar John sneered.

"So does the loss of the East not matter to you?" Romanus snapped back.

"The East will not be lost," the Caesar John said. "These Turks are just simple barbarians. They're not a real threat to the Empire. And while you are chasing these Turks around in circles, the Normans will attack us again in Italy. And when we lose Bari, we will have lost Italy forever."

"I will send reinforcements," Romanus said, turning to the Catepan. "I will order the Theme of Epirus to send its soldiers to you. I will pay for their transport using merchant ships, and the Adriatic squadron of the fleet will protect them."

"Then we're finished," the Catepan said. "The Theme of Epirus is not enough. We need more Varangians. Men who can fight."

"That is out of the question," Romanus snapped. "This year I will take all the Varangians, except for the regiment that you already have, on campaign in the East. The army is too weak to be divided between two fronts. That is the position that I have inherited. It will take at least another two years to restore the army to the size and strength that it should be."

The Caesar John suddenly interjected, with a sneer in his voice: "So, we have soldiers and money for a triumphal procession but not to defend Italy."

Romanus's face was reddening, betraying his growing irritation. But the Caesar John seemed oblivious of this and continued: "When my brother was Emperor, we held both Italy and Armenia."

At these words, Romanus exploded into a fit of anger. He banged his fist on the table, making the maps and documents jump.

"Your brother's the cause of our misfortune! He's responsible for the pitiful state of the army today. He knew nothing about war!"

John was taken aback by this public outcry against his brother. Everyone knew that what Romanus said was true, and that was the reason why the Comneni and other nobles had supported him as Emperor, but to say it so openly was unheard of.

"How dare you criticise my brother! Retract your insult about him!" John demanded of Romanus as if he was challenging him to a duel. Romanus stood to his full height, facing John.

"Retract what I said. Don't be ridiculous. He was worse than what I said. He was afraid of the armies of the Themes in case they might object to his profligate life here in Constantinople, spending the treasury's money on his friends instead of soldiers that the empire needs."

John said nothing. Then, turning away from Romanus to face the senators, as if appealing to them, he said: "When you were crowned Emperor, it was only on condition that you would respect my family and my wishes as Caesar. Now that you have insulted my family and failed to listen to my advice, you leave me with no option but to resign my support for you."

The Caesar John looked around him as if he expected the assembled nobles and leaders of the guilds to rise up in support for him. But no one moved or said anything until Romanus spoke in a cool tone: "My lord Caesar, you will take no further part in government."

The Caesar John stood quite still and then, with everyone's eyes fixed on him, he turned to Andronicus, who had said nothing during this whole exchange, with his expression of neutrality unchanged.

"Andronicus," he spoke in hushed tones to his son but just loud enough for everyone to hear. Andronicus looked up.

"The Emperor has insulted the honour of our family. I wish us to leave."

There was a long pause. Everyone waited for his answer, knowing that the empire's fate would be decided by it. Was there to be civil war or not? The Ducas family was still powerful enough to challenge Romanus's authority if Andronicus supported his father. The silence was oppressive like a storm gathering. And then Andronicus spoke.

"No, father. I swore my oath of allegiance to the Emperor and I remain committed to it."

Andronicus stood quite still. Romanus could not suppress a smile of appreciation that came to his lips. The Caesar John turned on his heel and strode out of the senate house without another word. Theodore stood watching Andronicus intently. His face was still expressionless. And then as Theodore watched him, he thought he saw the faintest trace of a smile on his lips.

XVII

In the few months since Eirene and her family had been recaptured, Afsin had allowed them a life of unbelievable luxury. They stayed in the castle at Mosul where Afsin was resting his warriors. Her sons even played the games they had played on their estate in the old days before the Turks had come. Eirene promised them that they would return home one day, although Zoe would sometimes run off and cry at these moments for she knew this was told for the children's sake, and that in private, Eirene would tell her that there was no hope of escape this far into enemy territory. But Eirene's strength and determination carried them all into a world where there was hope, and they did not despair but instead they were grateful for the privileges and luxuries they had, and they were more happy than Theodore, so many miles away, could possibly have dreamed or hoped for.

Yet Eirene knew that their happiness was an artifice as vulnerable as a prayer in the temporal world. She was surprised when they left Mosul after only a week's rest, for Afsin did not tell her that they were heading north to round up the renegade Turkoman raiders, as Alp Arslan had instructed him, and to bring them to Syria for his campaign against the Fatimids. Nevertheless, he made sure that she and her family were well looked after. They travelled in a cart which was well furnished and comfortable.

They travelled for a week, and Eirene's anxiety ebbed away as she watched the sun rising and falling each day and calculated that they were heading directly northwest. For she knew what lay ahead of them. It was the Roman Empire. They had left the Arab lands behind them and she realised they were in Armenia which she knew was partly controlled by the Romans. She remembered that Manzikert was the fortress that served as the bastion of the Empire's defences in this area. She imagined that they must be getting closer to it but escape seemed impossible for they were so closely guarded. There was no way that they could jump from their cart and run away without being caught within minutes. Eirene pondered how they could escape as Afsin's warband wound its way along mud tracks and little used paths, ever closer to the Roman border.

As for Afsin, he went to see Eirene every day, and with the help of a ghulam interpreter, he spoke kindly to her and offered her whatever luxuries they had. But she seemed to use their lack of a common language as a means of distancing herself from him. He felt that he was losing what little intimacy he had ever enjoyed with her. And he felt a growing sense of bitterness. Had he not treated her with extraordinary kindness?

One evening when they had camped near to the stronghold of a Turkish Emir who was still raiding Roman territory, and ignoring the Sultan's orders for peace, Afsin went to see Eirene.

He was already angry for he didn't relish his task of telling this Emir, whose name was Malik Danishmend, that he must come with him to Syria to fight in the Sultan's army. This time he didn't take his translator with him. He didn't know why he wanted to see Eirene but his frustration was directed against her. Had she not been treated better than most of his followers, let alone a captive? And what thanks had she given him? Her manner had become even haughtier and more aloof.

When he found her, she and her family were taking their food from the women who had prepared a great cauldron of steaming porridge, heated on top of a roaring fire, in the centre of the camp. They were eating despondently and he told Eirene to come with him to his tent.

She rose, surprised by the unusual harshness in his manner, and followed him to his tent. He motioned irritably to the guard outside the tent to be gone and then turned to face her.

"Are you grateful to me?" he said to her through gritted teeth.

She had learned enough Turkish in her year of captivity to understand his words, and their bitterness surprised her.

"I don't know what you mean?" she replied in simple Turkish.

"You know what I mean," he said abruptly.

But what did he want from this woman? He suddenly realised that he didn't know the answer himself. Her beauty and bravery had captivated him. Looking at her, he began to feel trapped.

He averted his gaze from her and his head dropped.

Sensing his frustration and afraid of a sudden angry outburst, Eirene was more worried than she had been for a long time. Would this be the end of their favoured treatment? She was just about to hold her hand out to him as a gesture of appeasement when a soldier suddenly put his head through the tent flap.

"Afsin bey, Danishmend has refused your offer! He won't join the Sultan."

Afsin looked at the man blankly. He was still thinking of Eirene and it took a few seconds for the man's words to sink in. Then his anger found a new target.

"Then he will pay for his impudence!" he snapped at the man. "Saddle the horses! We go tonight! Get the men ready. I will have his surrender or his head."

He turned to Eirene.

"Go! Get out!" he said abruptly as he left the tent to summon his men.

Eirene returned to her family. They retreated from the campfire to the safety of their tent as the camp turned into a noisy, tumultuous frenzy of activity. Soldiers ran this way and that, with horses neighing and weapons clanging, as Afsin marshalled his forces. The soldiers' faces were grim. There was to be a night attack to teach Danishmend a lesson.

Finally, there was silence in the camp. Afsin and his men had gone. Eirene looked out from their tent. Only a handful of guards and the camp followers were left. She had been forgotten about.

As she looked at the eerie scene of emptiness around her, suddenly her heart began to pound. This was their chance to escape. Afsin's behaviour worried her. She didn't know what he would do next but she felt more threatened now than for a long time.

She decided that she would wait until the middle of the night when she hoped that everyone, or nearly everyone, would be asleep and then they would try to escape. She didn't tell Zoe or her children this, in case they became too excited, and their plan might be given away.

In the middle of the night, Eirene lay wide awake. Afsin had not returned. She had waited until she was sure that most of the Turks were sleep. Then carefully she stood up. She untied the strap that kept the flaps of their tent shut and peered into the darkness outside. The camp was quiet. They were in the middle of nowhere and the Turks had not bothered with any defences around the encampment. Instead, their tents were pitched randomly around the cooking fires and they had relaxed their guard duties. Nervously she peered around. There was no sign of any guards. The sky was bright with stars. The air was cold. She shivered. She returned to the tent and roused Zoe.

"Now is our chance. Wake the children. But be gentle. No noise. I'll get the pony."

Zoe nodded. She did not ask what the plan was.

Eirene left them and went to where the horses were tethered. Some were tied to posts or railings while others were simply hobbled with a piece of leather tied around their back legs to stop them from moving.

As she approached them, the horses looked up, surprised to see a person coming towards them at this time of the night. One or two of them snorted, their breath smoking in the cold air. She had always been good with horses and she had a relationship of trust with their small brown pony, which was obedient and with a kind eye. She murmured soft words to him as she approached him. Still whispering, she put his bridle on and then untied the strip of leather around his back legs.

She led him to their tent where Zoe and the children were crouching, waiting for her. Then they all crept towards the perimeter of the encampment. The Turkish guards had abandoned their posts for the comfort of their tents, and no-one noticed the four of them and their pony as they gently made their way out of the camp and along the track they had come from. When they were clear of the camp, the two boys sat on the pony, although there was no saddle since he was used to pull their cart.

Eirene decided that they must leave the path that they had taken since this would be the first place that Afsin would search; so they followed a small, rough track into the mountains. She chose it because it seemed inconspicuous, without any obvious clues for Afsin to follow. She knew she was heading west which was at least the right direction for their journey home. But she had no idea who or what they might meet.

XVIII

A week after the army's triumphal procession, Theodore was let off duty. The Varangians had just been paid by the Emperor and given two days' holiday for their bravery in the battle at Tephrice. In their barracks within the great palace, in buildings overlooking the sea of Marmara, they laughed and joked, throwing their gold coins into the air and betting them on games of arm wrestling.

The more elated they became, the more depressed Theodore was. Ragnar came up to him, his face red from wine, and threw his arm around Theodore's shoulders.

"Come on man, cheer up! I'll take you to the best whore house in the city. That'll put a smile on your face!" Ragnar laughed and Theodore shrugged off his embrace.

Ragnar suddenly looked at him with the exaggerated concern of someone who has had too much to drink.

"I know what's worrying you," he said, slurring his speech. "You're still thinking about your wife. She's dead you know. She can't have survived. And even if she has God knows what they've done to her. And you'd never find her anyway. Come on man, find another one. Women are all the same! Or they are when you're between their legs! And you know what is most important? You're still alive. Odin saved you at Amorium. You should show him some respect and enjoy yourself."

Theodore grabbed a cup of wine and drank it in one go.

"I'll drink to you, Ragnar! But forgive me, for tonight I must see friends who might be able to help me recover my birthright."

Ragnar suddenly became enthusiastic about this, and told him that they all thought the Emperor had been hideously unjust to him. But if he was successful, Ragnar insisted that he must still fight with the Varangians for they had decided that he brought them good luck. Theodore smiled and thanked him.

When Theodore had left Ragnar, he stepped into the streets outside the great palace, without any idea as to what he would do. The wine had made him feel slightly light-headed and he walked almost too purposefully past the towering arches of the hippodrome towards the forum of Constantine. The truth was that he knew nobody in the city. He wondered if he could perhaps visit one of the noble families, like the Comneni, to plead his case against the Emperor, but would there really be any hope of persuading Romanus to change his mind? Now that Andronicus had pledged himself publicly to Romanus in defiance of his father, Romanus would be only too pleased to execute him to reward Andronicus. No, there was nothing he could do.

He wondered down towards the sea of Marmara, through the narrow backstreets, past wine shops where men were drinking after a day's work. He walked past them in the cold winter air, trying to avoid inhaling the foul odours from the drains, until he reached the harbour of Julian. Then he stopped and sat on the steps leading down to the moored boats, and looked along the coastline. To his right there was a massive stone-built mansion, probably the city address of one of the major nobility or a very wealthy merchant. He looked at the grand gates, which were firmly shut, and then his heart missed a beat. The family arms above the gates were those of the Ducas family: a white tower on a black background.

He jumped to his feet. He was standing right beside the Ducas's mansion. Andronicus was probably inside. He wondered whether his father, the Caesar John, was there too? Would they be arguing or plotting, he wondered?

He wandered up to the gates. A small door was set into the right-hand gate, and on it there was a large iron ring to lift the latch. He knew that he shouldn't do this but he turned the ring and pushed the door. It opened. He put one foot over the threshold. One foot into Ducas territory. Then he peered into the half light of the courtyard within. He could see no one. He found himself in a large colonnaded courtyard, with a pool of water in its centre and stable blocks on one side, in which several horses glanced up at him curiously.

Then he heard voices. He closed the door in the gates and rushed into the shadows of a colonnade on his right. He crouched behind a wall and the voices passed by him as they moved in the direction of the main gate. He dared not look up over the wall but the voices seemed to belong to two men.

"The master's in a foul mood," Theodore heard one of them say. "He's drinking himself stupid."

The reply was inaudible but Theodore heard the footsteps of one of them recrossing the courtyard, presumably leaving the other one to man the gate. He moved forward, still crouching and concealing himself behind the wall, until he reached the end of the colonnade, and peering round the corner, he just caught sight of the man disappearing into a room off the courtyard.

He stood up and walked briskly into the room which seemed to be a hallway with a number of tall rectangular doorways. He heard voices again, echoing through the doorway on his left, and instinctively darted in the opposite direction, through the one on his right.

He found himself descending a flight of stairs that took him out of the light and into a dark corridor. He wondered where he was going until at the end of the corridor, he saw a turning into a large room that seemed to be used for storage, filled as it was with amphorae and wooden tubs of flour and spices.

He stopped and looked around him, peering through the half light. The voices had disappeared and he could hear nothing. His own footsteps seemed alarmingly loud. What was he doing, he suddenly thought to himself? This was ridiculous. He must go before he was caught. He knew that there was now a guard at the gate, so that way would be difficult. The house almost certainly had other side entrances out onto the streets but how could he get to them? There must be a lot of servants and he decided that his only hope of escape would be to pretend he was one of them. Then he could walk through the house until he found an exit. He picked up a reasonably small amphora of wine so as to appear like a servant, and took it with him back up the stairs.

But no sooner had he taken his first step, than a figure suddenly stood in the doorway above him. It was too late to turn back, and he looked up at the figure, still clutching the amphora. The face peered down at him in the half light. It was a man's face and it did not have the look of a servant.

"Who are you?" the man called out.

Theodore realised that his bluff was about to be called. He placed the amphora down on the ground, and reaching for the dagger that he always carried underneath his shirt strapped to his back, the one he had used to kill Ulan at Amorium, he climbed up the steps to the man without saying a word.

The man froze as he saw Theodore approach. Theodore grabbed his arm with one hand and, drawing out his dagger with the other, pointed it at his chest.

"Do what I tell you otherwise I'll kill you," Theodore whispered to him, holding his arm in a vice-like grip and with the dagger a few inches from his throat.

The man nodded and Theodore pulled him down to the bottom of the steps.

"Tell me how to get out of here," he said urgently.

The man nodded again, and indicated with his eyes that the way out was on the other side of the storage room. Theodore did not trust him and pushed the dagger right up to his throat, which made the man quickly find his tongue.

"There are steps over there. They go down to street level. There's a door onto the street."

Theodore relaxed a fraction. If the man was telling the truth, this was easier than he had thought. His escape route had been under his nose all the time.

"All right," he said. "Let's go there."

He manoeuvred the man so that he was in front of him, and pushed him forward, holding the knife firmly at his back.

The man relaxed a little as well, enough to ask him: "Who are you?"

"No friend of the Ducases, that's for sure," Theodore whispered into his ear.

"Nor am I," the man said. "I hate them. One day I'll get out of here through the same door as you. But I need their money to pay my debts. I've got more enemies outside here than inside."

Theodore realised that this was his chance to find out what Andronicus was really up to. He stopped the man as they reached the steps that took them to a lower level and asked him: "Tell me whether Andronicus is a traitor to the Emperor or not? Is he in league with his father and pretending to be the Emperor's friend? I'll pay you well if you tell me."

"We don't know ourselves," the man said. "I'm one of his bodyguards and even I don't know whose side Andronicus is really on." He paused. "Except his own, of course."

"What do you mean?"

"You never know what he's really up to. His father hates him now and won't talk to him. But I don't know what's really going on. It might be one of his tricks. He's good at those."

"What tricks? What's he done?" Theodore was anxious to find some clue to explain Andronicus's behaviour.

"Well, he gives Christians to the heathen for a start."

"What do you mean by that?"

"You know the Turks attacked Amorium a couple of months ago? Well, Andronicus paid them to do it. And he gave a Roman noblewoman to their warlord."

"I don't believe you," Theodore said. "Not even he would do that. And who was she?"

"Her name was Gabras. I'm pretty sure it was Eirene Gabras. She had two children as well. Andronicus gave them to the Turk called Afsin, the butcher who sacked Neocaesarea."

For a moment, Theodore thought he must be in a dream. He asked the man to repeat the woman's name for he could not believe that it was Eirene. He tried hard to control his shaking voice, as he asked: "Were they unharmed? What condition were they in?"

"They were very well when we handed them over to the Turks. The saints only know what's happened to them since then."

The man sensed the emotion in Theodore's voice and asked: "Do you know them?"

Theodore took the knife away from the man's back.

"I might have heard of them," he said slowly. Then he asked urgently: "Do you know why Andronicus did this? Is there any news of Afsin?"

"We don't understand it. We think he paid the Turks to

attack Amorium to embarrass the Emperor. With the woman, the Turk definitely wanted her but we don't know why Andronicus enjoyed giving her to him. Maybe there was a family feud. But he has no fear of God, that's for sure. His heart is as black as the devil's. And we never know what he's going to do next. Now he seems to want to support the Emperor. Perhaps he'll murder his own father. I know he could do it."

The man led him down a narrow flight of steps to ground level and pointed to the door. The keys were obligingly in the lock.

Theodore offered the man the only gold coin he had, his Varangian's pay.

"No. Keep your money. May God protect you."

"Thank you."

And with that, Theodore opened the door and went out onto the street. As he walked back to the palace, his mind was racing. He thought with dread of Andronicus and Afsin. But his step was light and his heart was about to burst. To burst with hope that one day, one beautiful day, he might see his family again.

XIX

Eirene led her children and Zoe up a steep path into the mountains in the darkness of the night, and when dawn broke, and the sun blinded them with its bright rays beneath the pale blue sky, they were already twenty miles away. They continued all day, stopping only for the pony to drink water from a stream. It was spring and not too hot. But the pony was getting tired and they needed to find pasture for him to graze on. They were also sure that Afsin would be pursuing them.

They climbed into the foothills and, by late afternoon, they were too tired to go further. They found a place which had some shelter from the sun and a patch of dry sparse grass which the pony could eat. It was a good vantage point from which they could look down on the valley for any sign of their pursuers. So far, there were none. Evening came and Eirene decided to stay the night there. They all needed to rest. Greedily, they ate some of the food they had brought with them. Eirene knew they only had food and water for one more day but even so, she poured some of their precious water into a naturally formed basin in the rock from which the pony drank, his tongue rasping against the wet stone. Then Eirene lay down beside a rock over the top of which she could survey the valley. Still there was no one. A few minutes later they were all asleep.

Eirene was awoken by the hot sun on her face and flies crawling around her eyes. She felt heavy with sleep but she staggered quickly to her feet, making herself feel dizzy. She squinted around her, panicking that she might be surrounded by Afsin's men. But there was no one except the pony looking at her quizzically. Zoe and the children were fast asleep. She looked down into the valley. Still there was no sign of life. The sun was very low in the sky. It was still early morning. She sat down to steady her giddiness. She wondered what to do now. Afsin could be close. But he did not know the direction she had taken.

She peered up into the mountains. Desolate hills rose up in the distance before her. Beyond them, great mountains towered into the sky. Although they could lose Afsin in this wilderness, how could they survive? There were some olive trees but not much more to live off. She hoped that they would stumble on some human life, some goatherds or villagers. Anyone but the Turks.

They set off into the hills, the children riding on the pony. They found a stream and they all drank from it. They found a few orange trees and ate the sweet fruit which tasted heavenly. They finished the last of the food they had brought from Afsin's camp.

By evening they had made their way high into the hills. In the distance, the mountains towered above them. The land was deserted and they followed the sun as it set in the west and darkness fell. They felt hungry and Eirene knew that there was no food for tomorrow.

Then just as she thought that they might as well stop for the night she heard the sound of goat bells jingling. She froze. Who could they belong to? Surely not Afsin's men? She told Zoe and the children to hide in a hollow behind some rocks and to wait for her return. Then she tied their pony up and crept forward through the rocks and undergrowth, until in the distance against the fading light in the blue sky, she saw smoke drifting across the valley that dipped away behind the hills. She stopped. What should she do? She had no weapons. Not even a knife. But she knew this was their only hope.

She set off towards the smoke that was still drifting across the sky. When she got to the brow of the hill she looked down and saw camp fires burning a little way down the valley. She felt that her prayers had been answered. She imagined them cooking lamb and her hunger bit into her, making her feel weak. The fact that they had their livestock with them almost certainly meant that they were goatherds or farmers. But it was a gamble whether they would be friend or foe. She decided to take a chance.

When she got closer to their encampment, she stooped down low so they would not see her approach. She knew the dogs would smell her and be the first to raise the alarm. And she was right. When she was a hundred yards away and she could smell their cooking, a dog started to bark. Better to make yourself known, she thought, and she shouted out in Greek: "I come in peace. Who are you?"

There was no reply but more dogs joined in the barking and then she heard human voices calling out. She continued walking forward and called out again, repeating the words.

And then, as she approached, a group of men and dogs came forward to meet her. They were dressed in goatskins and woollen garments. They were dark skinned, burnt by the sun, and had black piercing eyes. But they were not Turks.

"And who are you?" A man asked in Greek but with a thick accent that made it clear it was not his native tongue. He was short and powerfully built, with thick black curly hair and a bushy dark beard. His eyes looked hostile. Across his chest was a necklace of large animal teeth from a bear or a wolf.

Eirene stopped. She realised that she had made a mistake

hoping that these people would be her friends. But it was too late to run away now. So she stood up straight, and looking around at them all, she said as clearly as her pounding heart would allow: "My name is Eirene, daughter of John Taronites, the Count of Anatolikon. I ask for your help."

But she knew it was a forlorn hope that her nobility would impress them. There was a moment's silence and then all the men laughed, the moonlight shining on their yellow teeth. The one who had asked her the question came forward, and in his hand he held a stout wooden club, which he began to beat against his other hand.

"You're a long way from home," the man snarled at her. "And such a pretty face too. I think you'd better tell us what you're doing here."

When she did not answer, he laughed and started to move towards her. Eirene turned and began to run. But he was quick. He sprinted after and grabbed her by the waist so that they both fell to the ground. She tried to kick him but he dodged her blows and grabbed both her hands with one of his in a tight vice.

"Now my beauty," he said, pulling at her clothes. "We'll teach you a little lesson."

She looked up into his piggy black eyes and was nearly overcome by the stench from his foul smelling body and clothes. Holding her down, with his free hand he ripped open her linen clothes, exposing her breasts. But suddenly his clawing hands were held back. Eirene looked up. A powerful brown arm was across the man's throat and she heard someone say:

"That's enough Zarkas, she's not one of your goats."

Eirene jumped to her feet, holding her torn clothing together and backing away. She heard the other men laughing and squinted into the dark to see who her saviour was. In front of her was what seemed to be a giant of a man with curly black hair, holding her attacker by the throat. He held him motionless for a moment and then released him, allowing him to fall to the ground. There was more laughter.

Her attacker looked up at the big man, mumbling obscenities in his own native tongue. He found his wooden club on the ground and picked both it and himself up and approached the big man, snarling like a dog.

Her saviour did nothing. He simply stood there. He had no club or weapons of any description. He merely looked at the piggy-eyed man and said:

"Come on man, we don't need to fight. Come back to the fire."

But her attacker took no notice of this advice and, raising his club, he threw himself at the big man, who side-stepped his attack and, putting a foot deftly forward, tripped him up so that he fell to the ground. But the big man took no joy in his victory.

"Save yourself for the Turks," he said, offering Zarkas his hand. Zarkas ignored him, got up and stumbled away, muttering.

There was silence. Eirene looked up into the big man's eyes. They were strangely calm as if the fight with Zarkas belonged to a different world, a world that had little significance for him.

"Thank you," she muttered.

"Come with us, lady," the big man said, and when Zarkas had returned to the camp fire, he added: "I apologise for Zarkas. He's more of an animal than his goats."

"Who are you?" she asked.

"We are Armenians," he replied. "My name is Ashot. We live here but now we are travelling west away from the Turks."

"Where are you going?" she asked.

"Manzikert, if it's still in Roman hands," Ashot said.

Eirene went and found Zoe and her children, cowering

behind the rocks where she had left them. Their faces, wide-eyed with fear, turned to delight when she told them she had found friends. Ashot came and greeted them in a gentle, friendly manner, patting the children's heads. He took them to the camp fire and fed them on roast lamb which they devoured like wolves. Later, he found them a tent and they fell asleep, exhausted by their adventure.

The next day, they awoke to see Ashot bringing them milk, honey and bread for their breakfast. And after they had eaten, the group of travellers set off. The children rode their pony with Eirene and Zoe walking beside them. Ashot stayed with them. He had a tough little horse but he did not ride it, preferring to walk with them. He surprised Eirene by not asking questions about who they were or why they were there. Instead, he talked about the route ahead of them to Manzikert, telling them of the steep climb into the mountains, the colder atmosphere that they would find there, and then of their descent into the valley which would ultimately lead to Manzikert.

Ashot would come and go during the course of the day. At first, Eirene could not see any social hierarchy or order among the group of goatherds but during the course of the day, she pieced together how they all interacted. There seemed to be three groups. There was Ashot and a small group who spoke Greek and who were the most sympathetic towards her. Although they were Armenians, they were clearly higher born and had some education. The second group included Zarkas and they knew little Greek and spoke always in their own Armenian tongue which Eirene did not understand. They were rougher and they had no liking for Eirene and her family. She guessed that they came from the easternmost parts of Armenia where Rome had the least influence. The third group was a mix of refugees from Armenia as well as some from as far away as Persia. Most of them seemed to be farmers rather than goatherds and they had with them farmyard animals like cows and chickens. Their women knew how to milk the animals, and they had cured their skins to make clothes and sheets for their tents.

There was no clear leader of the whole group but Ashot commanded some grudging respect. Zarkas made the most noise but that seemed to count for little.

One thing that puzzled Eirene was the apparent absence of any family belonging to Ashot. Most though not all of the Armenians had families and there were many women and children. Yet Ashot was alone. She imagined that he had lost his family to the Turks just as she had lost hers. She wanted to ask him but couldn't bring herself to utter the words.

XX

Romanus's hopes for victory in 1069 had come to nothing. He had taken his army back to the east in the spring, shortly after exiling the Caesar John to his estates in Bithynia, but just as he was about to launch a major offensive into Seljuk territory to secure the area around the great fortress of Manzikert, the last Roman stronghold in Armenia, the Turks had broken through the frontier near Melitene. This time the Turks were not led by Afsin, but by another Turkish emir, who was nearly as ruthless and resourceful. They sacked Iconium in the south of Anatolia before retreating back to Syria.

Romanus had no choice but to lead his army all the way back from Manzikert to catch them. But they eluded him, and he returned to Constantinople at the end of the year, frustrated and with nothing to show for the year's campaign. There was no triumphal procession this time.

Instead, shortly afterwards and to Romanus's huge surprise, Alp Arslan's envoy arrived with an offer of peace. War or peace? Romanus wanted war, but when he received Alp Arslan's envoy with the offer of peace, he accepted it because he thought that it would buy him time to help his preparations for war.

With Andronicus, who was more than ever his trusted ally

since his father's exile, he was building the greatest army the empire had seen in living memory. The blacksmiths of Constantinople had to work through the night to keep up with the orders from the Great Palace, for more swords, maces, shields, chainmail coats, even battering rams and siege towers, for Romanus's ambitions went far beyond securing the frontier fortresses; he was dreaming of a campaign that would destroy the Seljuks.

Every day, he and Andronicus would supervise the training of the thematic levies that were pouring into Constantinople. There were so many of them that Romanus was afraid that plague might break out in their flimsy encampment outside the city walls, and he ordered half of them to march two hundred miles to Dorylaeum, the main military base in Anatolia. He was also recruiting more mercenary troops, not just Normans but Germans and Franks, who his emissaries brought back from the West, lured by gold and adventure. For the thematic armies were untried in war, full of farmers who were wielding spears and shields for the first time, and he needed experienced soldiers who would face the enemy and not run.

But the peace did not last long, for in the summer of 1070, one of Alp Arslan's brothers-in-law, an emir called Erisgen, rebelled against him, just as Afsin had done, and fled into the Roman Empire, pillaging and plundering as he went. Romanus dispatched a force against him which was defeated but, to everyone's surprise, Erisgen sent the general back to the Emperor with a proposal to form an alliance against Alp Arslan, saying that the Sultan was his enemy as well.

Romanus accepted. He was not sorry to break the peace. His preparations to lead a great army against the Turks the next year, were progressing well. So, he sent a message to Alp Arslan that Erisgen was welcome in Constantinople. Alp Arslan was irritated by this but not overly concerned, since he knew nothing of Romanus's plans for a major offensive the next year, and thought that he would teach the Emperor a lesson to respect him by sending a raiding party across the frontier.

For this he chose Afsin.

Romanus was at Constantinople when he heard that Afsin had been sighted crossing the Euphrates. He was not too bothered by the news of Afsin's attack for it was small and the fury of his great onslaught was only months away. So, he dispatched a unit of crack troops to find Afsin and destroy his raiding party. Those troops were a unit of the Varangians under Ragnar's command. And among them was Theodore.

They travelled two weeks in the late summer heat, covered with dust and flies, towards Sebasteia which was the main town in the area were Afsin had been sighted.

"We'll have to be clever on this mission," Ragnar told Theodore. "We're too few to fight Afsin without reinforcements. We'd better just find out where he is and then track him while we wait for help. The Emperor doesn't want him to sack another town. We'll be well rewarded if we can stop that, I promise you."

When Theodore heard of this mission from Ragnar, he was elated. Afsin was the man he most wanted to find in the whole world. At last, after more than a year of boredom and frustration, his life had a purpose.

When they reached Sebasteia, they found that the countryside had been laid waste by Afsin's men. They passed villages silent except for the grim chatter of birds as they fed on the rotting corpses of men, women and children who had not fled to the safety of Sebasteia's walls.

"At least they're better dead than prisoners," Ragnar said, and Theodore said nothing as he thought of Eirene and his children.

The governor of Sebasteia, a devious looking man who

Theodore thought would happily betray his town to the Turks if it would save his own skin, said that Afsin had not stayed in the area but had passed by rapidly.

"Let's get out of here," Ragnar said. "We'll lose them completely if we stay here."

Although the men and horses were tired, they left Sebasteia and rode west, following Afsin's route of devastation. Then one day they happened to meet a small Turkish foraging party. They killed some and took the rest prisoner. When they interrogated them, the Varangians cut off the hands of the first one who hesitated to answer their questions. Theodore wondered whether he did not understand the simple, basic Turkish words that Ragnar asked him, or whether he feared Afsin's wrath even more. But the next Turk was quicker to answer. Afsin was heading south to the sea. He thought the cities were less well defended there.

"We'd better get moving. Doesn't look like Afsin thinks he's being pursued, judging by how easily we caught this lot." Ragnar said.

But they didn't catch Afsin. Maybe he realised he was being pursued when the foraging party never came back. The Varangians found villages unharmed. At least we're saving someone, Theodore thought.

Ragnar could not believe how far Afsin had travelled into Roman territory for the Turks were several hundred miles behind the front line. It was just like his raid on Amorium. But Ragnar hoped it would be his undoing since he could trap them on their long journey back to Syria. So, he sent messengers to Dorylaeum and Antioch calling for reinforcements. At least, they should be able to block the passes through the Taurus mountains and stop Afsin returning to Syria.

"We'll have Afsin's head on a spear to celebrate Easter, I wager you Theodore," Ragnar laughed.

But Afsin had not become the Sultan's most feared emir for nothing. Just when Ragnar thought he must be turning back home empty-handed, he struck the wealthy city of Chonae, a hundred miles further west than Ragnar believed him to be.

The city was just what the prisoners had said Afsin was looking for. Rich and poorly defended. Nearly six hundred miles from the Turkish frontier, in the supposed safety of the southeastern corner of Anatolia, its citizens had not even bothered to repair the city walls. The thematic garrison was below strength, and they paid the price. The slaughter was complete. Almost all the citizens were killed. A freak thunderstorm caused even more loss of life when it flooded the ancient underground sewers of the city in which the survivors of the Turkish attack were hiding.

The Varangians were too late. When they arrived, Afsin was long gone and the city was a smoking, desolate scene of destruction. Ragnar and Theodore picked their way through the corpses strewn across the streets and in the ransacked houses. The city had no citadel and almost the entire population had perished, either slaughtered by the Turks or drowned in the sewers.

As they walked up the main street, a child ran out of a house and up to Ragnar and Theodore. A boy of about five years old, he stared up at them, silent and wide-eyed with the horror he had seen.

"What's your name, son?" Theodore knelt down and took the boy's hand.

The boy looked away. Tears welled up in his eyes and he leant against Theodore and then pointed behind him to a house.

"Keep him for a moment, please," Theodore said to Ragnar and he hurried over to the house.

The front door had been smashed in. Inside the hallway,

he nearly tripped up over a body. It was a man's, lying face down in a pool of blood. Theodore didn't turn him over. He didn't want to see his face. He looked around the rest of the room. There was no one. The others had probably fled into the other rooms. Theodore didn't want to look but something made him go into the next room. What he saw there made even his hardened stomach churn. A dead baby lay sprawled on the floor, its head smashed open, blood on the walls against which it had been beaten. A young woman lay on the floor and looked up at him, her glazed eyes staring into space, her clothes torn from her body.

Theodore could look no more. He thought of his own family. His stomach convulsed and he bent over and retched.

"God let me kill you, Afsin," he whispered to himself, wiping the vomit from his lips, and he rushed away from the house, averting his eyes from the bodies, and back to Ragnar.

The boy had steadied himself and hung on to Ragnar who looked bored and angry. He had seen it all before.

"Let me go to find Afsin by myself," Theodore said. "I will kill him. I promise you."

"What, just you? You haven't got a hope. Are you mad?"

"It'll be quicker if I travel alone. Give me two horses. I'll travel by night and day. I'll find him."

"And what will you do if you find him? Ask him to surrender to you?" Ragnar laughed at his own humour. The crows eating the corpses were surprised by the noise and squawked and flapped their wings.

"I'll find a way of killing him. I'll get into their camp at night."

"An assassin." Ragnar looked sombre. "If you kill him, you might save our skins, that's for sure. But you don't stand a chance. Oh well, good luck, my friend." And he held out his arm and gripped Theodore's in an iron grasp, sure that he would not see him again.

And so Theodore left with two strong horses and enough food for a week. He wore the heavy chainmail coat of a Varangian. He knew it would tire him as he rode but it would give him a huge advantage in close combat with the Turks for they seldom wore body armour. He also took an array of weapons: his heavy axe, which all Varangians carried, a long sword and the dagger that had killed Ulan. He promised himself that it would kill Afsin next.

He rode throughout the next day and night towards the east, thinking that Afsin would want to return to Syria as quickly as possible, his mission accomplished.

Then the next day, he found a deserted village. Its inhabitants had fled. The silence of the houses was almost tangible, louder than noise. Their locked doors told him to move on but he dismounted and shouted out that he needed help, he needed to know if they had seen the Turks. No one answered.

He stayed in the village until sunset when the villagers returned under the cover of dark. They found Theodore asleep in one of the houses, exhausted from his travel. At first they thought he might be dead when they shook him, but he jumped to his feet and reached for his sword. The villagers backed away.

"Don't be afraid," he said through bleary eyes. "Tell me: have you seen the Turks?"

"We saw them before they got to the village," the boldest of the villagers spoke up, a big burly, curly-haired man with some of his front teeth missing. "We saw them from the hill. There were thousands of them. They went past the village this morning. They didn't even stop to loot it. They're going east into the mountains."

"Thank you. That's all I need to know."

And with that Theodore left. He rode into the night. He knew the Turks would have to pitch camp to rest their horses.

He followed their trail from the village, which was easy to see, since the ground had been scarred by thousands of hooves. He followed it high into the mountains. They seemed to have no captives, for there were no bodies of stragglers that they had killed. They must be moving fast, he thought.

Under the starlit sky, he rode carefully up the steep slopes of the mountainous terrain. His horses had better night vision than him and trod carefully. Even so, the one Theodore was riding went lame, and he let it free, and rode the other one which was less tired and they made good progress. In the dark, he could barely make out the tracks that the Turks had left, and he was beginning to give up hope when his heart missed a beat. Ahead of him in the distance he saw a faint glimmer of light. He told himself that they were probably just the campfires of goatherds but he clutched his sword handle and hoped that he had found Afsin.

When he had got halfway to the campfires, he dismounted and tied his horse to an olive tree. Then he walked towards the glimmering spots of red, and as he got closer, he could see that there were many campfires and he heard the occasional neighing of horses. It must be Afsin.

He wondered what to do. He knew that it was madness to try to get into the camp. He would certainly be killed. But what else could he do? This was his one chance to find out something about his family's fate.

He needed to be careful not to be seen and he looked for the vantage points where lookouts would be posted. On his right there was a small hill and he guessed that there must be a Turkish lookout there. Perhaps he had already spotted him. He crouched low and tried not to make a noise as he scrambled up the rocky incline, but the dry ground was brittle and stones noisily rolled away from his footsteps. He couldn't see anyone at the top as he approached it, but he felt that someone's eyes were watching him. Suddenly he heard the hiss of an arrow pass within inches of his head. He fell to the ground and rolled to one side, trying to see where his attacker was. He lodged himself behind a bush and looked up towards the top of the black silhouette of the hill, marked out against the starlit sky. He couldn't see anyone. There was complete silence.

He pulled his axe from behind his back and held it in his shield hand. Then he grabbed a stone with his right hand, and threw it as far as he could. The stone clattered over to his right, and the moment it struck ground, he launched himself through the oleander bush and straight up the hill, his shield held in front of him, his axe in his right hand. He felt the thud of an arrow as it embedded itself in the wooden frame of the shield but he kept sprinting straight ahead. The Turk would be restringing his bow. And then as he reached the top of the hill, he saw a dark form moving on his left. Instinctively, he held his shield up. Another arrow screeched off the shield, glancing off its metallic cover. He turned and ran towards his assailant, pulling back his right hand with the axe in it.

The Turk decided to hold his ground and knelt down, perhaps hoping to slice at Theodore's legs with his sword. Sensing this, Theodore crouched low, and protected by his shield, charged into the man, so that they both sprawled on the ground.

Theodore's heavy shield weighed him down but the moment he stood up, he felt the impact of a sword smashing into the shield. It had saved him. In an instant he swung his axe at the Turk. He knew that he had the advantage since the Turks seldom wore body armour. He was right. The Turk grunted as the heavy axe-head shattered his wooden shield and smashed into his face. The man tumbled over and Theodore jumped over him but he was already dead, his face crushed and ripped open in a bloody, unrecognisable mess.

Now, Theodore had to move fast and silently. He knew that the man he had killed would be guarding a corner of the perimeter of the camp. Luckily, he had not had time to scream when Theodore's axe had hit him. To get into the camp he must be as silent as a ghost. He dropped his heavy shield and took off his chainmail coat and laid his axe down. They were too heavy and would slow him down. Stealth would be everything. He ran down the hill towards the campfires. He looked carefully as he ran, for the Turks normally had tripwires with bells attached to them strung out around their camps to warn them of attackers. But this time they had not bothered, or else Theodore stepped over them, for he reached the camp, which had no palisade or fortification, without raising any alarm.

He paused and, crouching low, looked into the dark for any sign of movement in the camp. But it was silent. He had to find Afsin's tent, and he imagined that it would be in the middle of the encampment and presumably the grandest.

Jumping to his feet, but keeping his head down, he moved forward into the camp, treading carefully so as not to trip over the guy ropes. There was a half moon and he could see reasonably well. There was a myriad of tents and some of the Turks were also sleeping in the open. I must be mad, Theodore thought to himself, but he kept on going, further and further into the heart of the camp.

He trod softly so as not to wake anyone. And in the middle of the camp, he saw what he thought must be Afsin's tent. It had poles that raised it to a height well above the other tents, and it had animal skins instead of fabric to keep the rain off. Theodore crept towards it. He decided to go round the back and cut his way into it.

Crouching down, he took his knife out, and pushed the point through the thick goatskin. The noise of tearing made by the knife, as he slid it down through the goatskin, alarmed him. Surely, it would wake whoever was sleeping in a tent? But nobody stirred and Theodore removed a large square of goatskin that he had cut, and putting his arms and head through the hole, he looked into the interior of the tent.

At first he could only see darkness. Then, as his eyes became used to the dark, he could make out the shapes of small pieces of furniture: tables and storage chests. On the sides of the tent hung weapons and armour. There was no sign of life and at first he thought that the tent was empty. Then he saw woollen rugs and cushions in one corner. And someone was lying there asleep. He thought it must be Afsin. Clutching his knife, he tiptoed towards the sleeping body. He planned to pin Afsin down and hold a knife to his throat and ask one question before he killed him: where was Eirene?

Then suddenly the body moved, rolling over, and Theodore rushed forward and put his knees into its back as he felt in the dark for Afsin's neck. The body squirmed underneath him and Theodore was shocked to feel the smooth skin of a naked woman.

He pinned her down and she looked up at him, her eyes wide with fear. Instead of putting his knife to her throat, he put his hand over her mouth to stop her from screaming. Then just as he did that, the flap of the tent opened and a man strode in, bare-chested.

Theodore jumped up and away from the woman, letting her flee into a corner of the tent where she sat cowering. The man saw Theodore and immediately rushed to the side of the tent where his weapons hung and reached for a sword. But Theodore was quicker and he drew his own sword and held it squarely to his chest.

He could barely make the man out in the dark. Like most Turks, he had a moustache and short black beard. He could just see the whites of his eyes. He jabbed the sword at him and forced the man back. The man stumbled over a storage chest and Theodore leapt at him, grabbing his shoulder. The man stayed perfectly still as Theodore held his sword inches from his throat.

"Eirene. Where is she?" Theodore whispered using the little Turkish he knew.

The man looked at him and Theodore knew that he was Afsin. He didn't expect an answer, and he was about to drive his sword home, when the man said in simple Greek:

"Eirene gone." He paused. "I save her."

Stunned by his words, Theodore missed Afsin's kick which hit him hard in the shins, causing him to stagger back. Afsin ran back to the entrance of the tent shouting out loudly, calling for his guards. Theodore knew he had only seconds to escape. He raced back to the hole he had made in the tent and, still clutching his sword, he ducked through it and sprinted towards the side of the encampment where he had killed the guard. If he could get there quickly enough he might escape the guards.

Dodging the guy ropes, he ran as fast as he could, past the tents and out into the open. No one seemed to be following him. He ran up the hill, crouching low, until he reached the dead body of the guard. Then, gasping for breath, he stopped for a second and looked behind him. No-one was pursuing him. The darkness of the night had concealed him well. He knelt down and gathered up his chainmail coat and axe, abandoning his shield since it was too heavy, and turned to run as fast as he could to his horse. He could hear shouts in the distance as he mounted his horse, but they were a long way off, and soon faded away as he rode back towards Chonae.

As he rode through the night, he had only one thought: what had Afsin meant by his words: "I save her."

XXI

Eirene liked her new life. For the first time in more than a year, she was not a prisoner. But she was still deep in enemy territory.

Over the last few days, they had made their way across the steep mountain slopes with their flocks grazing as they went. They felt reasonably safe because they were higher up, where the Turks would find it hard to follow them, and in any case, plundering poor goatherds would be of little attraction to them. They ate well for they had a plentiful supply of milk and cheese and the farmers still had flour to bake bread. As they travelled, they gathered olives and sometimes they found honey, and very occasionally they would slaughter some of the flock and roast them on a great fire.

Sometimes, Ashot would come and walk with Eirene and her family; indeed he seemed to like them more than anyone else in the band of travellers. He even played with Constantine and Gregory. One time, he lifted them on his shoulders and charged this way and that while they screamed with delight. Eirene laughed until she realised that it was the first time that she had laughed since the Turks came. She stopped, and as she watched Ashot, she thought of Theodore and she felt terribly guilty. She was laughing and yet he might be dead. Seeing this, Ashot clearly felt embarrassed, and he put the children down and left them to help herd some goats that were wandering too far afield.

When he had gone, Eirene thought again how strange it was that he enjoyed their company so much without apparently wanting to know anything about them. He seemed satisfied that they were just another family fleeing the Turks. But the next day, her impression proved to be wrong when he joined them and asked her:

"I remember you said you are the daughter of the Count of Anatolikon. Is that right?"

Eirene nodded.

"So, you are a Taronitissa. A great family. I hope you will forgive my asking but is your husband alive?"

Eirene looked away. They were walking along a dusty path in the early morning sun and, as she looked at the hills that stretched into the distance and thought of the Roman frontier on the other side, she suddenly felt desperately worried that she would not find Theodore again. She couldn't bring herself to tell of Andronicus's cruel taunting that he was still alive when he betrayed her to the Turks. She burst into great sobs of tears, and Ashot put his arm around her shoulders as he murmured: "Stop. Please forgive me. I am sorry."

Eirene took a deep breath and stemmed her tears.

"I don't know what's happened to him. He may have been killed by the Turks."

"I am truly sorry. Forgive me for asking."

"No, it's not your fault. If he were alive, he would be so grateful to you. We lived near Neocaesarea," she continued. "The Turks raided our village. My husband was out, mending the watermill, and I don't know what happened to him."

She stopped and then continued, for she felt that she owed this kind man more explanation and gratitude than she had given him.

"We owe you so much. My husband would have been so grateful to you. His name is Theodore. Theodore Gabras."

Ashot's compassionate expression changed to one of surprise when he heard the word Gabras.

"Gabras? The Gabras family of Trebizond?"

Eirene nodded. "The same. He is the third son of the Count."

Ashot let go of Eirene's shoulders suddenly as if he had been stung by a wasp. Eirene felt him recoil, and she looked up at him with bloodshot eyes, surprised and worried that she had offended him in some way. But he was smiling broadly.

"Your husband saved my life once, a long time ago."

When Ashot told Eirene of the story of his escape from Trebizond through the tunnel, she remembered hearing about the incident from Theodore. How strange, she thought, that they should meet all these years later. She thanked God in gratitude.

The days passed and she knew that they were getting closer to Manzikert. Then one evening, as the Armenians were setting up camp high on the mountainside, she asked Ashot:

"What chance do we really have of reaching Manzikert?"

He sat down beside her.

"Manzikert lies that way but to reach it we must come down from the mountains across the plain," he said, suddenly deep in thought, looking ahead into the distance.

"Do the Turks control the plain?"

"Yes, they control the land around Manzikert."

"How do you know?"

"I travelled this way a few years ago. Even then the city was pretty well surrounded. But it is a powerful fortress with high walls and it's resisted many sieges in the past."

"But how can we can get through to Manzikert if the

Turks are besieging it?" Eirene asked hesitantly, and her voice was slightly choked with emotion, for she knew that Manzikert was the only Roman stronghold for hundreds of miles around. If they could not get through to it, they would have to stay in the mountains forever since they could not risk going into the valleys and plains that were controlled by the Turks.

"If we are to get to Manzikert we need to think of a way to get past the Turks. The last time I was there they had a camp guarding the plain. The more I think about it the more I am convinced that a few of us need to distract the Turks in some way while the rest cross the plain with their flocks. We need to find the exact position of the Turkish camp. I think some of us should go ahead and scout out the countryside and find where it is. The others can carry on along the high mountain paths where they are safe."

"I want to come with you," Eirene said.

"It's too dangerous for you."

Ashot turned to look at Eirene. He was struck by how beautiful her eyes were. He felt like seizing her in his arms.

"No," he said, looking away. "I cannot let you. I don't want to be the cause of your death."

Eirene stood up to go. Before she turned, she said quietly to him, almost in a whisper:

"I will come with you. Don't try to stop me. I know the Turks and I can be more useful than Zarkas or the other goatherds."

Eirene felt a strange confidence in Ashot which she could not explain. Although he said he would not fight, she sensed his affection for her and had seen how strong he was when he had saved her from Zarkas's unwelcome attentions.

Over the next few days the Armenians were like a beehive, full of purposeful activity. They happily accepted Ashot's plan, as they normally did with everything that he proposed to them. And they showed Eirene increasing respect. When she approached them they would even talk to her which they never used to do.

As they approached the plain, they travelled more in the evenings and at night time so as not to be seen, and they rested during the day beneath the trees and in the caves. The days were getting a little cooler as summer started its slow metamorphosis into autumn.

Eirene felt more and more nervous. The closer they got the more she felt that they would fail to reach Manzikert. She had insisted on going to scout out the Turkish camp with Ashot. They had ridden to a high point at the top of a steep pinewood-clad hill, where they could look down onto the plain. At one end they could see the walls of Manzikert, small but clear in the distance. At the other end was the Turkish encampment. They were too far away to be able to make out much detail but it seemed to have a wooden palisade surrounding it, and within it there were tents and a large number of horses penned in.

They stayed for several hours watching the Turks' movements. It was within a day's ride from the large Turkish fortress of Khilat and they saw Turks coming and going along the dusty road that disappeared into the mountains towards Khilat. They also saw a Turkish patrol going out into the plain and riding towards Manzikert. The patrol did not get close to the walls and circled in the plain, as it headed back towards the camp. But its intent was clear. The Turks controlled the plain and wanted to stop any traffic from reaching Manzikert. Of the Romans there was no sign. The city of Manzikert might have been inhabited by ghosts for all they knew.

When Eirene looked down on the Turkish camp from under the cover of the pine wood, her heart pounded for she knew that this could be where her journey ended. What if

Ashot died as well as her? Could she really leave her children to the care of the Armenians?

The day of the planned attack approached and served to unite the Armenians. They all thought that Ashot's plan represented their best chance of success. Even Zarkas listened to Ashot as he went through the plan again and again. They would all descend towards the Turkish camp, for there was only one easy way down the hills that came out near to the camp. Then, Ashot and a few of the strongest and most warlike men, as well as Eirene, would venture to the camp with the aim of breaking in and stampeding the Turks' horses. If they were successful, the main group, with all the goats and sheep, would start across the plain as quickly as possible.

They spent a tense evening beneath the stars. And then in the middle of the night, they roused themselves and went down the steep slope of the pine forest, towards the Turkish camp.

Leaving her children and Zoe with promises that she would soon be back, Eirene, Ashot and the others set out for the Turkish camp on foot. When they reached the bottom of the slope, they hid behind the trees and bushes, surveying their best approach route.

The camp had an outer palisade of tree trunks with sharpened ends. There was one entrance which was guarded by a wooden tower in which a lone guard was posted. Ashot told them to go to the side of the palisade furthest away from the tower. They must not be visible to the guard. Ashot went first. He scrambled forward, crouching low and darting behind the rocks and boulders that littered the rocky, sandy ground all around the camp. When he reached the outside of the palisade, he stopped and lay on the ground in semi-darkness, lit only by a ghostly light from the half-moon. Zarkas followed him and then two others. Eirene had been told to wait and watch, ready to rush and tell the main group to get moving if the plan worked.

Ashot and the others busied themselves digging up the wooden palisades so that they could get into the camp unnoticed. The Turks' horses were on the other side of the palisade and they planned to take out several of the wooden stakes and drive the horses out onto the plain. They worked slowly but quietly and Eirene watched the guard in his tower. He was looking out onto the plain, clearly unaware of their presence on the other side of the camp, as he leaned his arms on the sides. Although she could not see his face, she imagined his look of boredom as he contemplated the dark emptiness all around him.

Half an hour passed and Eirene was getting impatient, expecting to see the horses suddenly being herded through the palisade. But there was no sign of any activity and she wondered whether something had gone wrong. She looked up at the guard tower and gasped. The guard had gone. Where was he? She stood up to get a better view. Perhaps he had fallen asleep in the tower. She couldn't see any sign of movement.

Was the guard looking for them? Was that why Ashot was so quiet? She waited for another quarter of an hour but still there was no sign of movement from Ashot or any re-appearance of the guard. Then her impatience got the better of her. She had to see what was happening.

Like the others had done, she crouched down low as she went, treading softly and carefully, moving from one large boulder or bush to another. Suddenly, the silence of the night was shattered by a loud voice calling to her. It was the guard who was standing between her and the palisade. He shouted at her in Turkish, asking who she was and what she was doing. Eirene stood up and faced him. She knew enough Turkish to understand his questions and walked up to him, her hands held up in a gesture of surrender.

His surprise when he saw that she was a woman was quickly surpassed by his amazement when he heard her speak in broken Turkish, and say that she had been sent by the Emir Afsin, to call for help since his men had been attacked by a group of Armenians. The sentry was a short stocky man with bow legs who would have looked better astride a horse. He had dark beady eyes which squinted at Eirene. He had no idea what she was talking about in her broken Turkish but her mention of Afsin impressed him and he had seen enough of life to know that Eirene was too suspicious to be treated lightly. Pointing a spear at her, he motioned to her to come with him. She obeyed and walked in front of him as he pointed to the camp's gate.

Scarcely had he closed the gate behind them, when there was suddenly a sound of horses neighing and screeching with panic. Ashot must have succeeded in breaking into the horses' compound. The guard looked round to see what was happening and Eirene seized her chance and ran straight towards the horses.

About a hundred horses were in the pen, and they were all neighing, rearing and snorting. The wooden rails in front of her, penning them in, suddenly broke under their weight and they spilled out, careering towards her. She stopped and stayed quite still, allowing them to pass her by her on both sides. She knew that horses would try to avoid her if she kept absolutely still. Then, when there was a gap, she rushed forward. Suddenly, behind the fleeing horses, she saw Ashot's tall figure.

"Ashot! It's me!" she called out, overjoyed at the sight of him.

"Here! Come here!" Ashot called back to her, above the din of panicking horses.

She wound her way through the horses to Ashot who, with Zarkas and the others, was still untying them and hitting the animals' flanks so that they reared and charged away.

Ashot reached out and grabbed Eirene.

"Praise the saints you're still alive!"

Pointing to the gap in the palisade which they had made, he grabbed her arm and pushed her towards it.

"Get through there! Quickly!"

The Turks were now emerging from their tents. Initially just one or two looked out to see what was happening, and then as they saw their horses galloping free, they shouted so that in a few minutes scores of them had grabbed their clothes and weapons. When they saw the Armenians, they rushed towards them. Horses were still running in every direction, as the Turks charged them, so that it was only in between the horses rearing and stampeding, that they were able to lunge at the Armenians with swords and spears.

Ashot had a sword which he held up against the Turks while Zarkas hit out at them with his hunting spear. The Turks were angry and would have made short work of the Armenians if the horses had not been in the way.

"Run!" Ashot shouted and they all fled through the gap in the palisade.

They reached the pine trees, with their lungs bursting. The Turks were too shocked to pursue them. They were trying to recapture their horses, half of which had galloped out into the plain.

Eirene and the Armenians ran and ran until they caught up with the main group, making its way hastily across the plain towards Manzikert, a mass of bleating goats, neighing horses and men and women pushing carts as fast as they could.

Within another half hour, exhausted and frightened, they reached the towering walls of Manzikert and stood before the gates of the great fortress. The plan had worked.

Or had it? The gates were firmly closed. In the darkness of the night, they called up to the soldiers manning the walls and begged them to let them enter. They explained who they were again and again. Finally, when Ashot said that the Turks were pursuing them and would soon be within sight, the gates creaked open and they were ushered in, surrounded by Roman soldiers.

The garrison commander came to meet them. He was a young nobleman in his mid-twenties and he looked careworn and tired. His handsome dark eyes stared at them from a thin and pallid face. Eirene wondered who was rescuing who.

"So, tell me who you are," he said. When they told him, he laughed grimly and said: "I regret to tell you that your journey will end here. We've been cut off by the Turks. We haven't received any supplies for five months now. We're starving to death. I hope you're still happy that you've made it here." Looking at the goats and sheep, he added: "But your animals are very welcome here I can assure you. We haven't eaten meat for a month."

Ashot stepped forward and spoke, his great height intimidating the commander who looked up at him apprehensively. Zarkas and the other Armenian men stood behind him, eyeing the Romans viciously.

"The flocks are ours. We've travelled a great distance with them. We might sell them to you but only for a fair price."

"We might pay you something for them if we're feeling generous," the commander said dismissively to Ashot who stood his ground. Sensing that a fight was about to break out, Eirene, who was guarding her children, jumped forward and begged the commander not to rob the Armenians. She told him her name which seemed to impress him.

"They saved my life, please spare theirs," she implored him, her high spoken Greek leaving him in no doubt of her rank. Finally, he relented.

"You can find shelter in some of the empty houses here. There are plenty of them. Half the town fled a year ago. For goatherds, you can live like lords in palaces!" he laughed.

Later that day, Eirene went to see the commander in the fortress. He told her that his name was George Kellinikos, and his family had large estates in Cappadocia.

"The Emperor himself ordered me to command this fortress and promised he would return here with his army. He was on his way here a few months ago but then he turned back and left us to rot. The Turks have taken the hills all around us so that we're surrounded. We haven't heard from the outside world for five months. I doubt the messengers we sent to Melitene have got through, and we have provisions for only another two months at most. Your friends' animals will help us but we need a few more flocks like those to get us through winter." He looked at Eirene sternly before continuing: "You were probably better off where you were than here."

Although he treated her as befitted a noblewoman, and gave her and her children lodgings in the safety of the castle, Eirene felt deeply depressed. In spite of their heroism in getting to Manzikert, there seemed to be as little hope as ever of finding safety. And she felt sad not to see Ashot any more. He and the Armenians lived in a rundown part of the town, mainly abandoned by its inhabitants, which a noblewoman like her dared not venture near.

Winter came and a freezing wind blew through the bleak town and snow swirled around its walls. Its few remaining inhabitants knocked down those houses that had been abandoned and broke their wooden structures up for firewood. George Kellenikos occasionally led his soldiers out into the hills to hunt for food, but they found little and they dared not be away for long in case the Turks attacked.

Then one cold winter afternoon, she met Ashot again. He was walking close by the main gates to the town. She saw his tall form and ran up to him.

"Ashot!" she called to him. He stopped and, seeing who it was, he smiled. He had forced himself to stay away from her. It was less painful for him that way.

"Ashot! We've missed you," she said. "You saved us from the Turks. I've never thanked you properly."

They walked up to the walls above the gates. Eirene had developed a liking for pacing the city walls, and looking at the river that wound its way through the flat open plain, and stretched away into the distance. She felt envious of the river's escape from this place in which she was trapped. Not knowing when she would see Ashot again, her curiosity overcame her.

"What happened to your family?" she asked him suddenly.

Ashot looked at her in silence and then said slowly and quietly:

"They're dead. Murdered. By the Romans."

"Who did it?"

"Andronicus Ducas."

Eirene shuddered.

"I would kill him if I could," she whispered.

XXII

The great army left Constantinople in the spring of 1071. The cherry trees were in blossom and the first insects buzzed noisily as row upon row of cavalry and infantry marched into the city through the Golden Gate from their camps outside. They were on their way to the various harbours where they would take boats across the Bosphorus to Asia and the long march east would begin.

Andronicus Ducas rode beside Romanus. He was not only in charge of his own thematic troops but he was also the deputy commander-in-chief of the army, ready to take over from Romanus, should he fall ill or be wounded. He was still intensely popular, indeed more so than Romanus, who was in the fourth year of his reign, and yet only six months ago had not prevented Afsin from sacking a city that was hundreds of miles behind the front line.

As for Theodore, he rode with Ragnar and the Varangians. He had returned from Afsin's camp with nothing to exonerate Ragnar from Romanus's fury that another city had been sacked. Yet Romanus forgave Ragnar for he knew that he and the Varangians were among his best troops and would fight to the death rather than flee, and he desperately needed what few good troops he had.

The army that Romanus led was the largest that had been

seen in living memory. Numbering some sixty thousand troops, it was many times larger than the armies he had led on campaign in 1068 and 1069. Great siege engines were dragged by horses, and herds of cattle were driven forward to feed the army. And yet there was no sense of cohesion among the troops as they marched, because the army consisted of so many different races and regiments. In addition to Romanus's elite troops of Varangians and heavy Roman cavalry, the Scholae and Excubiti, there were mercenaries drawn from all over the world: several companies of Franks and Germans each under different leaders and each with their own aims and schemes; and a large number of Pechenegs and Oghuz Turks from north of the Danube who were of the same racial descent as the Seljuk Turks, although they had not converted to Islam.

The Roman soldiers from the Themes were also heterogeneous with levies from every Theme in the west and east, soldiers that had never met before let alone fought together, and each unit was commanded by a count with his own designs and allegiances. The Armenian infantry from the Eastern Themes were particularly difficult to control since they did not speak Greek as their native tongue and felt little loyalty to the Emperor.

When they crossed the Bosphorus into Asia, the army's lack of unity became a smouldering source of discontent which found expression in a heightened sense of superstition. Bad omens were seen in every incident. When it was heard that the centre pole of the Emperor's tent had suddenly and inexplicably broken there was widespread conviction that the campaign was doomed to failure.

Theodore was deeply troubled as they marched east. The Emperor had become more and more impetuous and it was said that he would not listen to anyone's advice. It was clear to Theodore that Romanus harboured grand ambitions for a campaign that went far beyond just securing the Eastern frontier. He was hoping to defeat the Sultan decisively in battle and even to recover the Roman lands in Syria and Palestine lost to the Arabs centuries ago.

Theodore was also deeply suspicious of Andronicus. He wanted to spy on him in order to see who he was talking to, to see which nobles were his friends and which were his enemies, but apart from occasionally standing guard outside the Emperor's tent, he had no access to any of the meetings or discussions to which Andronicus was privy. His position was hopeless. There was nothing that he could do to help Romanus.

And then one night, when they were camped on the road to Dorylaeum, he was sent to help guard the Emperor. Romanus had recently taken to pitching his tent and those of his generals away from the main army, something that in itself was seen as another bad omen. On this occasion, however, he had found a large village and nobleman's estate near to the army's encampment, and had decided to stay there. There were enough stables for his horses and rooms for him and his servants.

Theodore was walking alone towards a large stone building in which Romanus was lodged when he saw smoke and flames coming through the windows of the building beside it. He assumed it must be a fire that had got out of control. That sort of thing often happened. But he was more alarmed when he heard horses neighing with fear. Men came rushing out of the dark, shouting. Theodore ran forward trying to see what was happening. The fire was spreading. The Emperor's building was the largest and it stood in the middle of the village. Smoke was coming from its windows. Theodore sprinted towards it. He saw Romanus staggering out of it.

"My lord, are you hurt?" Theodore called out to him.

"What?" Romanus said, staring in anguish at Theodore. "What's happening? How did this fire start? I must save my maps and weapons!" And he turned to go into the building next to his that was on fire.

Theodore grabbed his arm.

"No!" he shouted. "Don't go in! You'll die!"

"Who started this?" Romanus stared at Theodore, shaking off his grip. He had probably forgotten who he was, Theodore thought, since the battle of Tephryce. Then his eyes stared past Theodore and a look of horror came into them.

"My horses!" Romanus cried out. "They're burning my horses!"

And he started to run. Theodore ran with him. Some of the other Varangians who were trying to put the flames out, joined them as they ran to the stables. The Emperor's horses were stabled in an old wooden barn, which was now engulfed with flame. They smashed the doors in, and what they found made even the stomachs of these battle-hardened soldiers churn. The horses were being burned alive. Tied to posts or with their hind legs hobbled together to stop them moving, they could not escape from what had become a cage of fire. Some had collapsed while others reared, beating against the burning stable doors.

It was too late to save Romanus's horse, a handsome grey stallion, sixteen hands high, called Tigris. The rope he was tied to would not break and the horse reared and whinnied as the flames burnt into his flesh. Theodore cut the rope but it was too late. As he pulled the horse away from the flames, the animal collapsed on the ground and lay in agony.

They did what they could to save the animals but they could rescue only a few. Most of them had been so badly burned that the best they could do was to put them out of their misery with a sword.

Away from the stables, the other buildings burned

furiously in the cool air. There was too little water to put the fires out and all they could do was to wait until they had burned themselves out. In the dark they watched the flames die out, leaving the charred and blackened remains of the buildings, furniture and equipment.

Then Andronicus appeared. He looked shocked.

"My lord, how did this happen?"

"I have no idea." Romanus looked thoughtful rather than angry.

"Could it have been arson? Did you see anyone who might have started it?" Andronicus asked, looking at Theodore as if it might have been him.

But Romanus did not take Andronicus's bait. Instead, he fixed his eyes on him and said wearily: "Someone did this. It was not an accident." And then signalling that he considered the matter closed, he turned to Ragnar and asked him to get his men to salvage what they could from the wreckage and to pitch tents with the rest of the army.

"When we get to Dorylaeum, they will have maps to replace those that we have lost. The horses are different. I can never replace Tigris."

Two days later they reached Dorylaeum. More troops were waiting there to join them: domestic levies that looked dishevelled and dispirited. Farmers who had been pressed into military service against their will, and had almost no body armour, only shields and axes. Such men will run, Theodore thought, we are better off without them.

Then in their first evening camped outside Dorylaeum, Ragnar appeared with a command that left Theodore stunned.

"The Emperor wants to see you," he smiled. "Good luck, man. I hope he wants your sword, not your head."

Theodore went to Romanus's quarters in the fortress in Dorylaeum. As he entered a large room in which the sun shone its fading rays through a tall lancet window, he saw

Romanus seated at the far end. He saluted, and the Emperor looked up at him thoughtfully.

"Gabras, do you think I have wronged you?" Romanus spoke gently as if in contemplation of his judgement on Theodore.

Theodore wondered if he should try to placate the Emperor by saying that he might have been mistaken about Andronicus's treachery at Tephryce. Yet he remembered Andronicus's refusal to fight and could not bring himself to tell a lie. He knew the Emperor was short-tempered and he could not forget his anger the last time that they had met. His heart started to pound as he stalled for time.

"My lord, I accept your justice."

"What? So you were lying about Andronicus? You admit it?" Romanus no longer spoke gently. There was irritation rising in his voice.

Theodore felt trapped.

"I did not lie, my lord."

"So, you still say Andronicus is a traitor?" Romanus rose to his feet and went up to Theodore who stood back, unable to look him in the face.

"Who do you think started the fire?" Romanus asked firmly. "Was it you? To get your own back?"

Theodore closed his eyes. So, this was the end. The fire was to be blamed on him.

"No, sir. I came to help you."

"Help me? Why do I need your help, Gabras? And why do you want to help me? I have disinherited you, by the Saints! I have made you a common soldier. You must hate me!"

Romanus stood close to Theodore, who suddenly felt tired, tired of life.

"Do what you will with me, my lord."

Romanus stood in silence for a few seconds as if

pondering Theodore's reply. Then he turned away from him and spoke rapidly.

"No, Gabras, that's not why I asked you here. I want to know if you still believe that Andronicus betrayed me at Tephryce? Tell me the truth!"

"He did."

Romanus started to pace up and down but there was no anger in his voice this time.

"I have so many enemies, and so few friends. And I don't know who started the fire. I do not believe that Andronicus is my enemy but his father may have more influence on him than I had thought. I suspect that it is his father's agents who started the fire and hoped to kill me before we achieve victory over the Turks."

Romanus paused and turned to look at Theodore.

"When I saw you on the night of the fire, Gabras, I knew that you hadn't started it, unless you are a better liar and actor than I imagine. No, I believe you mean well although I suspect that you may have misunderstood Andronicus's actions at Tephryce, although now I don't know myself. You have made me think that I cannot afford to trust him as I have in the past. I will give him command of the rearguard where he can do the least harm to me. And I want you to be my liaison officer with him. You will have a handful of men to serve as messengers between me and him. Do you accept this position?"

Theodore listened as if he was in a dream. He thought of the last time he had spoken with Romanus three years ago, within days of losing his family. He wondered for a second if it had all been a dream.

"Thank you, my lord. I accept."

"I think I've been too harsh with you although I still don't believe Andronicus really wishes to betray me. But it is just possible that Andronicus may not be as innocent as I had hoped. Keep me informed of anything that is suspicious in his behaviour. Anybody that seems to be influencing him against me. And if you're loyal to me, I will reward you. Your title has not been given to another man and I can reinstate you when I want."

XXIII

The winter of 1069/70 passed slowly for Eirene and Ashot. She found solace in his company. They would meet and look out from the city walls and talk of when they might be rescued by the Emperor.

Although he never told her or showed her his feelings, she had come to mean everything to him. Yet he could never be truly happy for he felt that in loving Eirene he was betraying his family a second time.

Their hopes to be rescued were dashed when the Emperor did not mount an expedition to relieve the city that year. Spring turned to summer, and summer turned again to winter.

Then one day, when the spring of 1071 was just beginning, George Kellinikos came galloping back with a company of soldiers through the gates of Manzikert.

His face was pale and his eyes had panic in them. He was shouting orders, beside himself with agitation.

"What has happened?" she called to him. "Tell me what is wrong."

"They're coming!" He shouted at her. "There's a huge Turkish army coming here right now. We're finished. We cannot hold out against a force like that."

"How do you know?" she asked.

"I saw them with my own eyes. Out on patrol just now." He gestured vaguely beyond the city walls. "We were lucky to get away. Some of them saw us and were heading after us. There's a huge force out there. They stretch for miles, as far as the eye can see. A sea of horsemen. The Sultan is probably with them. We're finished. We cannot hold out."

"Do they have siege engines?" Ashot asked. "Horsemen cannot scale walls. Manzikert has held out against the Sultan before. The last Sultan, Tughril, could not take the city even with a massive army when he laid siege to it fifteen years ago. We can hold out if we have the will."

"It's different now. The garrison is at half strength. Most of the city's inhabitants have fled. There simply aren't enough of us to defend the walls. Against an army as big as this we have no hope. No hope at all. We have to escape. We have to leave the city."

George Kellenikos looked from Eirene to Ashot. She stood resolutely. He looked at the courage in her eyes and for a moment he felt embarrassed. Yet, he knew they couldn't hold out for long against such a large army. And he had given up hope that the Emperor would ever rescue them.

"I'm going to take the whole garrison with me. We might just be able to fight our way to Melitene," he said. "You must come with me."

Eirene was shocked. Although the garrison was small, Manzikert was a powerful fortress with tall walls and towers. She looked at George disgustedly: "You'll be tried for cowardice. The Emperor will have you executed."

"Well, you can tell him the truth. We cannot hold out. You can tell him that the only reasonable thing to do was to retreat. My God, haven't we held out long enough? And what has the Emperor done to save us? Nothing! He's left us to die here."

"I think we should defend the city," Eirene said resolutely.

"Winter is coming to an end and the Emperor's army could be with us in the spring. The city defeated the last Sultan, Tughril. It held out against him."

"But it was different then. They must have had a full garrison. The city was fully inhabited. My God, it's just a ghost town now."

"We fought the Turks to get here. We're staying."

"You stay then!" he shouted at her. "You stay and defend the city. I'm going and I'm taking the garrison. You stay here with your Armenians."

And with that George Kellenikos left. He did not speak to her again. Later that day he left with the garrison. They rode northwest, towards Theodosiopolis.

Eirene stood alone with Ashot on the battlements.

"What should we do?" she asked him.

"We cannot resist," he said. "I think we should open the gates. The city is theirs. We can save ourselves by giving the city to them."

When the Turks arrived, the Armenians opened the gates and welcomed them in. Ashot told them that the Romans had fled and that the Armenians had no love for the Romans and were happy to be the Turks' vassals.

Eirene stayed in the background, her face covered with a veil. She saw the Sultan, Alp Arslan, riding triumphantly through the city, looking delighted at the ease with which he had taken this famous Roman stronghold, that had been such a thorn in the flesh of his father, Tughril. And then when she saw who rode beside him her stomach tightened. It was Afsin.

But the Sultan did not stay long. He left a small garrison and then his army marched on westwards to fight the Fatimids in Syria, for he only wanted to secure his border with the Romans. On the same day Eirene heard shouts and commotion at the main gate. She and Ashot went to find out what was going on. A large group of Turks were laughing and shouting. They had planted spears in front of the main gate. On the spears were the severed heads of Romans they had caught and killed. Eirene looked at them and felt sick. She saw several heads she recognized from the garrison. And among them was the head of George Kellenikos.

During the next few months, Eirene was desperately afraid that the Turks would discover who she was, and so she hid herself and her children amongst the Armenians.

"The Turks have better things to do than bother with us," Ashot said to Eirene. "But we must escape the moment we can."

Since the Sultan had left strict instructions that he wanted the city to be left unharmed and able to resist a Roman counterattack, the Turkish garrison did not trouble the few remaining inhabitants of Manzikert, and let them get on with their impoverished lives in peace. This meant that the Armenians were happy enough to stay in the city, especially since they were among their own race, but Eirene and Ashot both longed to escape.

Months passed and summer arrived. Then, when they heard that the Emperor was rumoured to be approaching Armenia with a great army, they decided to take a desperate gamble and flee to Theodosiopolis which was the closest Roman city, about a hundred miles away.

When they had gathered together a few days' food, Ashot, Eirene and her children, and Zoe left the city through its main gate to collect water from the river, as they did every day, but this time they did not return. They travelled by night using the stars as their guide. By day they hid behind rocks and in the highest places they could find, looking out anxiously for signs of life. But the land was deserted and barren. The journey was exhausting. Their food and water were running out. Ashot did not eat anything and carried the boys alternately on his shoulders so that they could keep moving. But on the fourth day even he was beginning to tire and their pace slowed to a shuffle through the desolate, sand-blown rocks.

By the fifth day of their journey, they were still forty miles away from Theodosiopolis. They were desperately hungry and had no more food or water left. They stopped in the shade of a huge boulder and they all fell asleep. When Eirene awoke, she stood up and looked out into the shimmering horizon.

She saw horsemen heading in their direction. Her heart started to pound. Were they Turks? There was nowhere to hide and they were too tired to care any more. She woke Ashot up and they sat and waited for them in the hot sun, praying for a quick death if they were Turks.

The horsemen came into sight. Eirene stared in amazement. They were Romans. A young officer rode up to them, eyeing them carefully. Eirene rushed forward and told him her name. He saluted and told her that they were with the Emperor's army.

"Where is the Emperor?" Eirene's parched throat croaked the question.

The officer replied that he was at the gates of Manzikert.

XXIV

As usual, Andronicus showed no emotion when Romanus told him that he would command the rearguard and that Theodore would be his liaison officer.

"It will be useful to have Theodore. When we advance into battle, it will be vital to have a good supply of messengers to maintain contact with you, my lord." That was all he said, his brown eyes betraying no emotion.

Theodore, who was present at the meeting, saluted Andronicus who nodded without addressing him. Thereafter, Romanus allowed Theodore to attend meetings of his war council.

After the fire, the army's obsessive superstition grew as it marched towards its fate in the east. Symbols of doom and misfortune were seen everywhere. Fights frequently broke out between the mercenaries and the Roman troops. Even the Romans taunted each other as the thematic levies quarrelled with Romanus's tagmatic troops. It was not a proud army imbued with belief in its own victorious destiny that arrived at Theodosiopolis in the August heat, but a nervous and divided collection of men of many different races and many different motives.

The only man in the army who was oblivious to this was Romanus himself. He called a council of war in the citadel of

Theodosiopolis. Theodore was there in his position as Andronicus's liaison officer. Romanus told his generals that he had sent an envoy to Alp Arslan demanding the return of Manzikert as well as a pledge that there would be no further raids into Roman territory. The envoy had returned with the news that Alp Arslan had rejected his demands and had given up his siege of the Fatimid city of Aleppo in Syria, to return to Armenia to meet the Emperor in battle.

Romanus's main supporters, the generals Bryennius and Alyattes, both favoured caution. Andronicus was sullen and said little. The next most important general, Trachaniotes, also said little. Theodore could see furtive glances between him and Andronicus. He wondered if they had a plan to undermine Romanus.

Romanus was determined to fight. Everyone knew that he needed victory to quell the rising dissent about his rule in Constantinople. He had mustered the greatest army the Empire had seen in a hundred years, and he could not just sit behind the walls of Theodosiopolis doing nothing. Fate had presented him with the chance he'd been looking for: a decisive battle with the Sultan himself.

But his generals were less sure than him of their ability to defeat the Turks. Alp Arslan had never been defeated in battle and his armies had been victorious from Persia to Egypt. Engaging him in battle would, they thought, be very different from fighting the Turkoman raiders.

But Romanus would not hear of caution. He told them that the time to save the Empire had come. They should welcome it rather than hide from it. They must fire their troops with enthusiasm and prepare them for battle. After hours of discussion, he decided that the army would strike Manzikert first and then move against the fortress at Khilat which Alp Arslan also held. He thought that both of these strongholds could be taken before Alp Arslan returned from

Syria. Then they could meet the Sultan in battle by the shores of Lake Van just south of Manzikert. The terrain was rough and sparse between Theodosiopolis and Manzikert and Romanus ordered his generals to take provisions with them sufficient for two weeks. He also ordered the Frankish mercenary, Roussel, to move with his troops directly towards Khilat to scout out the territory ahead of the main army.

Theodore listened in silence. He thought of Eirene. If she was still alive she would be in the east. This was his chance to find Afsin again.

In years to come, men would often say that it was fate that caused Romanus, on a hot, dusty day in August, to divide the great army. But Theodore knew it was not fate but a calculated risk to defeat the Sultan and to secure his own glory in as short a time as possible.

At the council of war that day most of Romanus's generals opposed the idea of dividing the army. They said that the Sultan might be closer than they thought. As usual Andronicus said little. Theodore watched him carefully. Occasionally their eyes would meet and Andronicus would look away.

Romanus overruled his generals. He wanted half the army to go to Khilat under the command of his general, Trachaniotes, to take it before the Sultan arrived, while he advanced on Manzikert. That way both Khilat and Manzikert could be captured simultaneously. No one knew for sure where the Sultan was. But Romanus wanted to take risks. If he allowed Alp Arslan to arrive and reinforce Khilat he knew that he could still be besieging it by Christmas. And Theodore was sure that by then Romanus wanted to be deep in Seljuk land, leading his army down the Euphrates just as Heraclius had done to defeat the Persians four hundred years ago.

So, Trachaniotes left to join Roussel and the Frankish

cavalry, who were reconnoitring outside Khilat. He took many of the best troops: most of the Armenian infantry and some of the best Roman heavy cavalry, the Excubiti. But Romanus still had a powerful army as he advanced on Manzikert: most of the Western and Eastern Thematic levies, the Varangian guard, the Scholae and the Pechenegs mercenaries. Andronicus went with him, and so did Theodore.

Theodore was still watching Andronicus's every move, and the night before the army divided he saw something that worried him. He saw Trachaniotes leaving Andronicus's tent. As Trachaniotes left they were deep in earnest conversation. What were they plotting?

They marched through a barren land towards Manzikert. Little did Theodore know how close he was to Eirene. And even less did he realise that just before they reached Manzikert she had left the city, and had passed their encampment in the night when it was only a few miles away. When he awoke that morning his only thought was that today would be the first battle of the campaign.

But there was hardly any fighting. After the army had surrounded Manzikert and the Armenian infantry had attacked its walls, the Turkish garrison quickly surrendered the city in return for their lives. They had never seen such a large Roman army before and they knew that they had little chance of holding out for long.

Romanus was triumphant. He had recaptured the great fortress at no cost. That night there was celebration. The priests chanted paeans thanking God for victory. The Roman soldiers were given extra rations of wine and sang drunken victory songs. Hope rose in their hearts. The Pecheneg mercenaries seemed impressed by the easy victory. Theodore wondered if God had stopped punishing them at long last.

And then the next day they met the Sultan's army.

Messengers arrived at the imperial tent with news that Roman troops foraging for food outside Manzikert had been attacked by some Turks. At first they thought it was just a small unit of Turks that happened to be in the area. Romanus was not bothered. He ordered Bryennius, the commander of the Western thematic troops, to take out a reconnaissance force. They found a larger force of Turkish horsemen than they had expected. And the Turks did not retreat. Instead they fought a running battle with Bryennius's men in the hilly and wooded countryside beyond the city. As his casualties mounted he sent back word for reinforcements.

"Bryennius is a fool and a coward!" Romanus cursed him angrily in the imperial tent in front of his generals. The approach of battle had made him increasingly irritable. "He can't even beat back some Turks from the garrison at Khilat! I won't send him reinforcements until he's proved that he's capable of leading them."

Alyattes, the commander of the Eastern Themes and a loyal supporter of Romanus, was not afraid to speak his mind: "Maybe this is the advance guard of the Sultan's army, my lord, and not just the Khilat garrison. You know Bryennius is no coward."

Romanus looked sternly at Alyattes. Andronicus as usual said nothing.

"All right," Romanus said with a sneer in his voice. "Send reinforcements to support Bryennius. We'll send these Turks running back to Khilat. Basilacius will command them. I know that he's a brave soldier."

And so Basilacius left with a large force of cavalry from the Eastern Themes. He was the count of Theodosiopolis, about twenty-five years old and a fine-looking man, and he saluted Romanus as he left, beaming with excitement and saying the words Romanus wanted to hear: "We'll chase them back to Khilat my lord and we'll send word when we find

Trachaniotes. He's probably taken the fortress by now and we can reunite the army."

And that was the last they saw of him. It was not until much later in the day that messengers arrived at the imperial tent, but they came from Bryennius not from Basilacius. They had grim news. Basilacius's men had fallen into a trap. The Turks had retreated but only to counterattack in huge number, surrounding Basilacius and cutting his cavalry down to the last man. Basilacius himself was either dead or captured. The messenger said Bryennius was retreating in the face of a massed enemy attack and requested large reinforcements. They were also sure that the enemy was not the Khilat garrison but the advance guard of the Sultan's army. To prove this, among the Turks were soldiers only to be found in the Sultan's main field army, such as heavily armoured ghulam cavalry.

When he heard this, for the first time Romanus looked worried. His plan had gone wrong. The Sultan had arrived when the army was divided.

"Mobilise the entire army," he said quickly. And then raising his voice, he cried: "Send reinforcements to Bryennius before he's overrun. The Turks will be here soon!"

Trumpets blew and the army's encampment outside the city fell into a frenzy. Men rushed to get their weapons and fall into line. Horses neighed and reared as they were untied and their riders leapt into the saddle.

But it seemed that this time fate was on the Roman side for the Turks did not press their attack home. Bryennius held his ground and when reinforcements arrived the Turks retreated, and he advanced back into the scrubland, recovering the territory they had lost. They found Basilacius's men lying dead where they had been surrounded and slaughtered. Of Basilacius himself, there was no sign.

Bryennius returned to camp. Arrows were still caught in

his shield. The fight had been fierce and the Turks were not afraid of hand-to-hand combat this time. Romanus was hugely relieved that the Turks had broken off the attack. He laughed and put his arms around Bryennius, praising his courage only hours after he had called him a coward.

But the day's fighting was not over. When darkness fell the Turks attacked again. This time it was the Pecheneg mercenaries who were set upon as they bought food from local traders outside the Roman camp. The Turks rode up and down shooting arrows into the mercenaries who stampeded back into the entrance of the camp. Since they looked similar to the Turks, and as there was no moon that night, the Romans inside the camp thought that there was a Turkish attack on the main gate and panic took hold of everyone as they rushed to find their weapons and look for the enemy. Again the Romans were lucky for the Turks did not mount a full assault but they rode off, leaving the army in chaos.

No one slept that night and the next day Romanus called a council of war. He had more bad news to tell. The messengers he had sent to find Trachaniotes had found no trace of him or the other half of the army. Trachaniotes seemed to have disappeared. Romanus cursed him. Theodore looked at Andronicus. His face seemed glum. Had he persuaded Trachaniotes to abandon them? But why? Andronicus's own life would be in danger if the Turks defeated them.

Romanus also said that Turkish prisoners taken in the previous day's fighting had told them that the Sultan was camped with his full army only a few miles away across the plain. He looked intently at the faces of his generals and commanders and said: "This is our chance. We can force them into a pitched battle at last. I want to advance on the Sultan's camp. Does anyone disagree? Speak now if you do."

Both Bryennius and Alyattes, his most senior generals, advised caution. They said that it made sense to wait a little longer for news from Trachaniotes. He must be somewhere close by. The army had not been put together at huge cost for only half of it to fight the Sultan.

"Even with half the army we can beat the Sultan," Romanus snapped at them. "The Turks can't win a pitched battle against us. They can't win against our heavy cavalry and infantry. I slaughtered the Pechenegs in a pitched battle by the Danube and will do the same with the Turks here, I promise you!"

"But remember my lord, that the Sultan's army contains more than just light Turkish cavalry," said Michael Attaleiates, Romanus's trusted quartermaster who was a logistical genius in charge of the army's supplies. "He has heavily armoured ghulams that are the elite of his army. The ghulams are slave soldiers trained for war as boys and only given their freedom if they show exceptional courage on the battlefield. They will stand and fight us my lord, I promise you."

"You may be right, Michael," Romanus said, his voice softening as he spoke to Attaleiates who was his favourite adviser. "We'll wait another day for Trachaniotes."

But the next day there was still no news from Trachaniotes. During that day the Turks attacked again, trying to gain control of the riverbank on the other side of the army's fortified encampment but the Roman infantry just held them off. More ominously, a large contingent of Oghuz Turkish mercenaries, recruited from across the Danube when they had been weakened by plague a few years earlier, deserted to the enemy, their cousins by ancestry. More of them still remained loyal to the Romans, but for how long?

The next day something totally unexpected happened. A large delegation of Arabs arrived at the army's camp. They said they had been sent by the Caliph of Baghdad, the Sultan's master, to offer a truce. But everyone knew that the Caliph was a mere puppet of the Sultan and that this was Alp Arslan's own attempt to secure peace.

Romanus seemed delighted by the offer and it soon became clear why. He saw it as a sign of Alp Arslan's weakness. He saw it as a sign that he was afraid of battle. He made the Arabs bow down before him and kiss the ground in the formal ritual called proskynesis, which the Roman Emperors had decreed since ancient times was required from barbarians in their presence. Then he told them that he would not even discuss the conditions of a truce until Alp Arslan had abandoned his camp and allowed the Romans to occupy it.

The delegation withdrew. Romanus had insulted them without even consulting his generals about the truce. Instead he convened a council of war later that day.

"Tomorrow, we attack," he said. "Prepare the army. This peace delegation clearly shows that Alp Arslan is afraid of us."

"But we still only have half the army. Why not wait for Trachaniotes to join us?" Bryennius said.

"There are enough of us," Romanus snapped. "We have one chance to crush the Sultan. He's here within our reach. Tomorrow we will defeat him."

"Or die in battle."

Everyone turned around surprised to see that it was Andronicus who had spoken these words, breaking his normal silence. He continued: "I, for one, look forward to battle tomorrow. I think the Emperor is right that we should face the Turks and win a complete victory over them."

Romanus looked at him, surprised but pleased. Theodore looked between the two of them. Tomorrow we will discover the truth, he thought.

XXV

The next day the army advanced in full battle order from the camp. Instead of the old-fashioned battle formation advised by the Roman military manuals, with heavy infantry in the centre and cavalry on the flanks, Romanus decided to put his best heavy cavalry, the Scholae regiment, in the centre with himself at their head, and to lead a frontal attack, like an iron fist, straight towards the Sultan's camp which was about six miles across the plain from Manzikert. Behind the Scholae were the Varangians led by Ragnar, moving on foot but at a fast pace, and with the job of providing a powerful support of heavy infantry to the Scholae.

The rest of the army was deployed to support Romanus's strike force as it marched on the Sultan's camp. His two most trusted generals commanded each wing of the army. Alyattes led the right wing with the Eastern levies. Bryennius led the left wing with the Western levies from Greece, Macedonia and Bulgaria. The troops on both wings were divided into mixed battalions of cavalry and infantry. Romanus knew that his wings would become extended as he advanced on the enemy camp, and he wanted them to be flexible and mobile, able to protect his flanks.

Finally, a powerful rearguard was set up under Andronicus's command consisting of his own troops and other thematic levies. Although it had a corps of heavy cavalry, it mainly contained a large number of inexperienced and poorly-equipped infantry, which Romanus wanted to guard against a possible Turkish attack around the back of his army. Romanus had placed Andronicus in a position where he could do no harm. Or so he thought.

The army assembled as dawn broke, and after the troops had had a hasty breakfast, the priests gave them their blessing and held aloft the great icon of the Lady Blachernitissa Theotokos, which was said to make an army invincible. Then Romanus, sitting astride his horse and wearing full armour, addressed them, his voice booming out over the still morning air.

"Soldiers, listen to me when I tell you that the Sultan has begged for peace! We have him at our mercy! I know that God will grant us victory today and that this day will be remembered forever! We have the most holy icon of the Blachernitissa Theotokos which you know is invincible. We have the strength of Roman arms and Roman discipline. And remember that anyone who flees the field or surrenders to the enemy will not just be punished but will suffer in hell for all eternity. Today there will only be victory for the living or an eternity in paradise for the dead. Amen."

Romanus rode up and down the assembled ranks of the army as loud cheering erupted from the throats of thousands of soldiers, for he now seemed like a man who would bring them victory, since as men told each other, was he not the victor of every battle that he had personally commanded?

Theodore and his squad of five Varangians left Ragnar to join Andronicus.

"My lord, I am at your command." Theodore saluted Andronicus, who nodded at him and gestured to him to ride alongside his cavalry. As usual, Andronicus appeared relaxed.

The army advanced across the plain in the cool of the

morning towards the Sultan's camp. There was no element of surprise. The Turks were waiting for them. But they did not meet them in a pitched battle as Romanus had hoped. Romanus's advance guard, his iron fist of heavy cavalry and Varangians, advanced unopposed, meeting no one. Instead the Turks made sallies up to the Roman flanks, shooting arrows before turning and riding off in their usual fashion. The thematic soldiers were frustrated by their inability to hit back. They had too few archers to shoot effectively at the Turks. And every time a group of Roman cavalry charged after the Turks their horses were shot down, leaving the soldiers to flee back to their lines before the next wave of Turks charged them down.

The army marched forward through the morning and into the afternoon, hastily taking food and water when there was no sign of the Turks. The sun rose in the sky so that the heat started to sap their strength. The soldiers in the wings were becoming exhausted, their nerves frayed by the constant hail of Turkish arrows and their morale sapped by their frustration at never being able to strike back at this enemy that hissed and spat at them like a snake.

Theodore and the rearguard had no idea how far ahead the Emperor's advance guard was but he felt sure that they must have covered the six miles to the Sultan's camp. The army's two flanks had now become extended. Groups of cavalry and infantry were spread out over at least two miles, desperately trying to keep together. Every so often a group of Turkish horsemen would ride forward from out of the shimmering heat haze and charge at the Romans, shooting their arrows before turning and circling back. When this happened the Roman cavalry would cluster together, protecting themselves with raised shields and then canter forward to meet the Turkish attack that never materialised. None of the Romans were skilled enough to shoot arrows on horseback like the Turks and there were only small groups of infantry archers who could rush forward and shoot back at the Turks.

Theodore could see that the army's flanks were becoming dangerously overstretched, with the infantry and cavalry breaking up into little groups in an attempt to cover the two miles that separated Romanus's rapidly moving advance guard from the slow pace of Andronicus's rearguard. He spurred his horse to Andronicus and saluted him.

"My lord, the advance guard is too far ahead. Should we not catch them up?"

"If we do that, we risk being surrounded," Andronicus answered coolly. "Manzikert is nearly five miles behind us. The Turks could ride around us. I want to keep our communication line to Manzikert open. It's Romanus who should stop. He's advanced too far!"

It was true that Romanus was a good mile ahead of them, too far ahead for this time of the day, in the late afternoon, when they would have to march back to Manzikert before dark. Still there was no message or sign from him and no-one knew whether he had even met the Turks in battle. Theodore thought that he must have at least reached the Sultan's camp by now.

Communication was done at its simplest by using each regiment's standard that could be seen from some distance. The signal to advance was to hold the standard forward, and to retreat was to reverse the standard. The standards were immensely tall, over twenty feet, of iron and gold, with bars from which hung long white linen pennants. On the front pennant a great black cross was dyed into the material. On the back pennant there was no cross.

Just then Theodore heard shouts.

"The standards have been reversed. Retreat!"

Looking into the distance where the advance guard was, he could just make out crosses replacing the white standards.

Theodore smiled. Thank the saints, he thought, Romanus had stopped and was turning back. No victory today but no defeat either. Let's try to get back to Manzikert in one piece.

But then he heard Andronicus's officers shouting out:

"Quickly! Get back! The Emperor's been defeated! Get back as quickly as you can!"

Andronicus's rearguard, that had marched so painfully slowly and allowed the flanks to become overexposed, stopped and turned to go straight back towards Manzikert. Andronicus's cavalry regiment turned and cantered back.

"Stop! My lord, stop!" Theodore yelled out and spurred his horse after Andronicus. His men followed him as he galloped to catch up with Andronicus.

"We need to wait for the advance guard to fall back, Sir. We cannot retreat this fast! We need to hold our ground in case the Turks attack."

Andronicus reined in his horse in a cloud of dust. He turned to face Theodore with a look of contempt in his eyes.

"Kill him!" was all he said, and he gestured to his men beside him, who raised their shields and maces and advanced on Theodore, who was too surprised to move.

Then, seeing a heavy iron mace raised against him, he lifted his shield and the impact of the blow shook his whole body, deafening him to the sounds of the horses and men all around him. Andronicus had finally struck.

"Run!" he shouted to his men, and turning his horse away from his attacker, he broke free to gallop to the advance guard – to save Romanus.

All around him was confusion. The flanks had stopped and were watching the rearguard retreat. And then the enemy attacked. The horizon was filled with enemy cavalry. And they were not just Turks. All the soldiers of Islam seemed to be present: Kurdish lancers, heavily armoured Persians and fast-riding Arab warriors.

The Sultan's soldiers smashed into the Roman flanks. On either side of Theodore, a sea of men and horses screamed and fought each other. Thousands of hand-to-hand struggles blended into each other like sea waves crashing one upon the other. Roman cavalry fought with Persians and Kurds, the sun glinting from their curved scimitars. Lightly armed Turks shot arrows as their horses reared, and Roman infantry tried to form shield walls as their archers picked off enemy horsemen. The Sultan's ghulams were there, heavily armoured cavalry like the Romans, wielding long lances and curved swords.

Theodore could not see where he was going. He looked for the Emperor's standard but all around him was a screaming mass of men. Then far in the distance, he saw several standards, and hoping that Romanus was there, he told his men to follow him and rode forward. But his way was blocked by fleeing Roman infantry. The flanks were caving in and the Turks and Arabs were breaking through, splintering and fracturing what defensive lines the Romans had. Romanus's strategy of organising the wings into small mixed units of cavalry and infantry meant that they broke up more easily under the weight of the Turkish attack.

A large group of Roman infantry pushed him and his men aside as they fled, and then they found themselves facing a group of ghulam cavalry, drunk with the excitement of their triumph over the Romans. Theodore raised his shield and charged at their leader, swinging his mace at the man's head. His five Varangians followed beside him, shouting out their pagan war cries.

Theodore's heavy iron mace knocked the ghulam leader's sword from his hand, and turning his horse into the ghulam's, Theodore smashed his shield against him and unhorsed him. The other Varangians were giving as good as they got but they were heavily outnumbered.

Theodore wanted to get to the Emperor rather than be caught in this brawl, but he found his path blocked by a heavily armoured ghulam bearing down at him, levelling a spear at his body.

Theodore turned in his saddle to take the impact of the spear on his shield. He felt the wooden frame crack as the spear was caught on it, and he was nearly knocked sideways. The ghulam dropped his spear and, with unbelievable speed, he took his bow and strung it. Theodore lifted his shield to cover his face as he felt the arrow rip into it. He had to get to the ghulam before he restrung. Tearing the ghulam's spear from his shield, he lifted himself up in his stirrups and flung it at the man, catching him in the face as he was about to raise his bow and shoot again. The spear cut through his cheek, the only part of him that was not protected by armour, and the man screamed and dropped his bow, as Theodore broke free and galloped away.

Now his path was clear. He didn't have time to look behind him to see whether his group of Varangians were dead or alive. Instead, he headed straight towards the Emperor's standard, far away in the distance. He spurred his horse forward, pushing past frightened soldiers, fleeing away towards Manzikert, until he found the Varangians guarding the Emperor.

Ragnar saw him and called out: "Theodore! What's happening? Have the Turks cut off the road back to Manzikert?"

"Andronicus has betrayed us!" Theodore called out. "He has fled the field. We must retreat."

Theodore turned to find himself facing Romanus. His face was grim and he gazed at Theodore guiltily.

"Theodore, you've come back! When we get back to Manzikert, I will restore more than your title to you!"

Just then there was a deafening cry from the enemy as

massed ranks of Turks crashed into the Emperor's troops. The Turks were charging around the back of them, trying to surround them in a furious melee of hand-to-hand fighting.

Ragnar could see that the Roman cavalry had no advantage over the Turks fighting on horseback.

"Form a square. Let the horses loose!" he called out. Trumpets blared out and the survivors of the Scholae regiment dismounted and joined the Varangian shield wall.

Soon they had formed an infantry square which the Turks couldn't breach.

"If we can keep this formation we can make it back to Manzikert," Ragnar said to Romanus who was in the front line with him, his sword and armour dripping with blood.

The square began to move slowly back across the plain after the rest of the retreating army. It made good progress at first as the light Turkish cavalry couldn't block it. But Alp Arslan, who was watching with his generals from a nearby hill, saw that his prey was escaping, and sent all his ghulams to stand between it and Manzikert. These slave soldiers stood many ranks deep, thousands of them, ready to stop the retreating Romans.

The two sides crashed into each other. Ragnar was covered in blood and gore, still grasping his great axe. He'd killed scores of the enemy and his eyes were bright with excitement. He and the other Varangians surrounded Romanus, defending him and shouting out the names of the old Viking gods. Romanus insisted on being in the front line, where he fought furiously, hacking and slashing at the ghulams with his sword.

But the ghulams would not give way. Swords swung against armour, axes smashed shields and spears were driven through chainmail. Seeing Ragnar surrounded by ghulams, as he tried to fend them away from Romanus, Theodore rushed to help him. Ragnar was fighting with his axe, swinging the heavy weapon from side to side so that it scudded off shields and sliced into chainmail. But the effort of this was draining his energy and a ghulam brought a heavy iron sword into the faltering path of the axe, knocking it from Ragnar's hands. Quickly he reached for his sword, but the ghulams were quick and closed in for the kill. Theodore leapt forward but it was too late to save Ragnar. Another ghulam had driven a spear through his body.

The ghulams pushed them back away from Manzikert. Arrows rained down on the Romans, fired by Turkish cavalry over the ghulams' heads.

Theodore was forced back, leaving Ragnar's body as the ghulams' trophy. They cut Ragnar's head off and put it on a spear for the Varangians to see. Then Theodore saw Romanus stagger and fall. He rushed to his side as soldiers from the Scholae regiment kept the ghulams at bay. The back of the Emperor's hand had been gashed open by a sword.

"We must surrender, my lord!" Theodore told him.

"No Emperor has ever surrendered on the battlefield." And he leaned on Theodore, his bloody hand on his shoulder. His exhausted eyes stared blankly in front of him.

Then the ghulams stood back, exhausted by the fierce resistance and with many dead. There was a pause in the fighting as battle fresh warriors replenished their front ranks. Theodore's shield hand was so bruised that it could barely grip his shield. He knew that the end had come.

Suddenly, with a mighty roar, the ghulams charged forward, and the Romans and Varangians, too exhausted to sally forward to meet them, gripped their weapons and shields waiting for their onslaught. Theodore watched them as they ran forward, yelling to Allah, and as they got closer, he saw the look of triumph in their eyes.

XXVI

Alp Arslan looked north, towards Manzikert. To his left, the evening sun shone brilliantly, its bright rays piercing the light blue sky. From a hill overlooking the plain of Manzikert, and shaded from the heat of the sun by linen awnings, he had watched the Roman army disintegrate before his eyes.

This was a greater victory that he had dared to hope for. The next day he would advance against Manzikert and the remains of Romanus's army. He wondered what had happened to Romanus in the battle and assumed that he was back in Manzikert. He gave orders to his soldiers not to celebrate yet for, although it was a great victory, the war was not over and tomorrow there would be more fighting.

Then, early the next morning, Afsin arrived at Alp Arslan's tent. He was smiling with triumph. Gesturing to a group of ghulam soldiers, he told them to bring forward a tall, strong man, wounded in the hand and limping. The man looked defiantly at Alp Arslan. Afsin raised the flat of his sword and brought it down violently against the man's back. He gasped in pain and sank to his knees. Afsin put his boot against his back and forced him to prostrate himself before the Sultan. Then he grabbed his hair tightly and, pulling his head back, he told him to say his name.

"I am Romanus, Emperor of the Romans," the man said.

Both Theodore and Romanus had survived the carnage although they were wounded, Romanus in the hand where a sword had pierced right through his palm, and Theodore with a gash to his thigh. Their bodies were bruised and battered and their heads bowed with shame. With a thousand other survivors they had surrendered to the ghulams.

They had all been herded into a compound used for cattle. The ghulams kicked and spat at them. The badly wounded were killed on the spot. The ghulams were still angry because of the heavy casualties they had suffered.

All night they had lain awake, sitting on the dusty ground, groaning from their wounds and desperate with thirst.

When dawn broke, Romanus could stand it no more and went towards the ghulam guard at the gate.

"Take me to your Sultan." He said the words softly. "I am the Emperor."

Theodore doubted that the guard understood the Greek which Romanus had spoken to him. Whether he did or not, he just laughed and jabbed his spear in Romanus' ribs. Romanus recoiled, furious at this indignity, which made the man laugh even more. At this, Romanus seized his spear with his unwounded left hand and, with what strength he still had, he tore it out of the man's hands. The Turk shouted and more guards came rushing over. An important looking Turk came towards them, shouting out orders, and Theodore suddenly realised that it was Afsin. He pulled the hood of his cloak over his head so that he wouldn't be recognised.

Afsin went up to Romanus, his sword drawn, and pointed to the spear, telling him to give it back. Romanus squared his shoulders and stood to his full height and, looking down at Afsin, for he was noticeably taller, he repeated his words. Afsin's command of Greek was good for a Turk and he understood. He eyed Romanus with a momentary look of awe. Then he gestured to him to give the spear back, which Romanus did. He turned to the other Romans nearby, who were the few surviving officers of the Scholae and Varangians, and asked them two words in Greek:

"The Emperor?"

The men nodded.

Afsin smiled triumphantly. He was now satisfied that Romanus spoke the truth. Straightaway he took him to the Sultan.

Romanus lay on the ground before the Sultan for several minutes. Alp Arslan sat in silence, looking at Romanus, for a long time. He seemed to be deep in thought.

He was thinking of the irony that he had not wanted this battle which had turned into his greatest victory. He had taken Manzikert only as a precaution to strengthen the Armenian frontier, not as a prelude to an assault on Roman territory. Indeed, his armies had been fighting the Fatimids in Syria when he had heard of Romanus's advance with his great army towards Manzikert. At the time, he had cursed the Turkoman emirs, like Afsin, who had provoked this Roman attack.

He was also thinking that the most extraordinary thing was that he had feared this Emperor who lay prostrate before him. For not only was he renowned as a great warrior who always fought in the frontline of battle, but his name had always irked him for it was the same name as that of his people: Romanus, Emperor of the Romans. Rome had stood for eternity. It was spoken of in the ancient legends of the sea of grass that Alp Arslan had heard when he was a boy, and it was written about in the Qur'an. Now he felt no hatred for this man.

He showed no emotion, as at long last, he asked through an interpreter, since he knew no Greek himself:

"Emperor of the Romans, tell me what you would have

done to me if you had won the battle and I was your prisoner?"

Romanus lifted his eyes from the ground to look up at Alp Arslan. He tried to raise himself to stand but Afsin kicked him to the ground.

"Stop! Let him stand up and speak," Alp Arslan commanded Afsin.

Romanus rose slowly to his feet. Now was the time to die like a true Roman. He stood proudly, towering over his Turkish captors, and glowered at the Sultan. The ghulam guards put their hands on their swords, ready in case he tried something foolish, unarmed though he was.

"I would have had you flogged!" Romanus spat the words at the Sultan.

There was a long silence. Alp Arslan again seemed to be deep in contemplation. Then he looked directly at Romanus, and he smiled as he said:

"Is that what your Christian God teaches you to do to the vanquished? I had promised myself to treat you with mercy if you were captured. Know therefore that Allah hears those who plan to do good. I did not want this war. You refused my call for peace. You have brought ruin on yourself. Allah has given us victory because we were in the right."

Romanus was silent. He had expected a sword on his neck and he still expected it.

"But you have spoken the truth and if you had spoken in any other way, I would not have believed you." Alp Arslan paused. "Now, tell me, what do you think I should do with you?" He felt a strange liking for Romanus. He seemed to be an honest man, unlike his wily Turkish and Persian emirs. Also to secure the border with the Romans would be greatly to his advantage in his forthcoming campaign against the Fatimids. He imagined the minarets of Fatimid Cairo and beneath them his army, victorious once again.

There was another long pause. Romanus suddenly felt humble before the clemency of this man, his greatest enemy, or so he had thought. He spoke carefully, without arrogance or aggression.

"There are three things that you could do. First, you could kill me. Second, you could take me in a cage around your Empire, showing your subjects your victory over me and your great power. There is a third choice but I dare not say it." Romanus felt weak.

"Tell me," Alp Arslan asked him gently.

"You could set me free. And our domains could live in peace."

Alp Arslan rose to his feet and placed his hand on Romanus's shoulder.

"I hoped that you would say that. You may go free but before you go, I require you to pledge your loyalty to me. And as a sign of your good faith you will pay tribute and you will give to me the fortresses that you have taken along our border."

Romanus stood in silence. He had expected to die. But he knew the price of his freedom would also be heavy. He said quietly and humbly:

"I accept your conditions."

After that Romanus and Theodore were treated like honoured guests of the Sultan. His soldiers bowed to them whenever they passed and every day they dined with Alp Arslan at his magnificent table. Through an interpreter, a small and bright-eyed Arab called Yusuf, they talked of the battle. Alp Arslan condemned Romanus's betrayers. He asked who had commanded the rearguard that had retreated so disgracefully? Without them, he laughed, their positions could well have been reversed.

He also told them that his advance guard had made contact with another Roman army near Khilat but that it had retreated back to Melitene without fighting. Romanus cursed Trachaniotes. Later that day he came to see Theodore and wept before him, asking his forgiveness for not believing that Andronicus was a traitor. If only he had listened, he sobbed, he would have won the war. He promised to restore Theodore to his rank immediately and more than that, he would make him commander of the Eastern Themes.

But Theodore's mind was elsewhere. He still hadn't been recognised by Afsin but he was tormented by the thought of what Afsin had done to Eirene and his boys.

Then, a couple of days after Alp Arslan had pardoned them, and when they were watching the Sultan display his skill as an archer by shooting birds released from gilded cages, Afsin joined them. He did not recognise Theodore since he had only seen him on that one occasion when he had raided his tent, and in the darkness he hadn't been able to make his features out clearly.

Afsin looked at Theodore with wry curiosity and, as Alp Arslan fired an arrow that arched beautifully through the air and caught a bird of prey flapping in vain to find its way to freedom, Theodore felt sure that Afsin realised who he was. But Afsin said nothing.

At that moment, Alp Arslan turned to Romanus. He wanted to discuss the peace treaty with Romanus alone.

"My lord, we have much to discuss. Please come with me."

He signaled for Theodore and Afsin to leave and they parted without exchanging a word.

The peace came at a heavy price. Half a million gold pieces would be paid now and three hundred and sixty thousand as an annual tribute. Romanus knew that he could not pay this. The treasury had been emptied to pay for the war. He also had to hand over all the fortresses he had taken: Manzikert, Hierapolis and the Sultan also wanted Edessa and Antioch, which Romanus knew would not be accepted by the people of both cities.

The Sultan held them for only a week and then set them free to return to Melitene.

Alp Arslan sent a guard of ghulams to escort them back. When they reached Melitene, their worst fears were confirmed. Andronicus had already reached Constantinople and Michael had been proclaimed Emperor

Even so, Romanus found his two most loyal generals, Theodore Alyattes and Nicephorus Bryennius, the commanders of the left and right wings of the army at Manzikert, waiting for him with the remains of the army that had escaped from Manzikert.

With what was left of his great army, he advanced on Constantinople. Andronicus's brother, Constantine, led out another Roman army consisting mainly of his own men and Trachaniotes's troops. The two armies met at Dokeia, two hundred miles from Constantinople. But Constantine's army was twice the size of Romanus's, for the Ducas family had what was left of the treasury's money in Constantinople to spend on mercenaries. And his forces were greatly strengthened by Crispin's Normans, who had joined him to revenge themselves on Romanus for their exile in disgrace to the Eastern frontier after the battle of Tephryce.

Theodore stood with Romanus surveying the battle. At one moment, it seemed that there was hope of victory when the Roman heavy cavalry from the Eastern Themes, together with the Norman mercenaries, broke Constantine's right wing, forcing his levies from the Western Themes back. But just as victory seemed to be in their grasp, Crispin counter-attacked with his own Norman knights and appealed to the Normans fighting for Romanus to join him. They defected to Crispin and the remainder of Romanus's heavy cavalry retreated in disorder.

Andronicus's brother, Constantine, had another advantage. The Ducases controlled more than a thousand Varangian guardsmen that had stayed in Constantinople and avoided the slaughter of their brothers at Manzikert. He used them as his main attack force and they advanced on Romanus's centre, led by a new leader called Rurik. The Varangians hurled themselves at the infantry from the Eastern Themes, and armed with their great axes and long swords, they smashed through their ranks cutting them down savagely. The centre buckled and broke and the troops fled in chaos from the Varangian axes.

Romanus stayed back from the battle with Theodore. He would not repeat the mistake of Manzikert when he had led the front rank of the army only to be surrounded by his enemy. They watched together in silence as their best soldiers died. Theodore thought it would have been better if this time Romanus and he had died in the heart of the battle. At least the civil war would have ended. When it was clear that Andronicus's brother, Constantine, had won, Romanus sounded the retreat and the survivors of his once proud cavalry regiments streamed back. In the retreat, Romanus's general, Alyattes, was captured. Constantine had him tied to a stake and his eyes were gouged out with tent pegs.

Theodore could not think of this time without revulsion. It was a time of madness. The Romans destroyed each other. Romanus mustered another army and there was another battle, this time with Andronicus himself, at Adana by the shores of the Mediterranean. Again the Ducas family had larger forces and won. Roman fought Roman. Blood flowed into the river they fought beside, turning it red. After the battle, Romanus fled to the fortress of Adana with Theodore and only a few hundred soldiers, all that was left of the great army he had led from Constantinople two years before.

Romanus was a broken man. He stared at Theodore. His eyes were blank.

He surrendered to Andronicus at Adana. At first he was treated with dignity. The day he surrendered Andronicus invited him as a guest to a great banquet. The Emperor Michael, the Patriarch and several Archbishops sent him letters and presents, praising his wish to become a monk and guaranteeing his safety.

But Andronicus was not to be denied his revenge. Within days of Romanus's surrender, and when the emissaries of the Patriarch and his Archbisops had gone, he sent his servants to take him back to Constantinople. They did more than that. They gouged out his eyes and strapped him to a mule facing backwards to ride to Constantinople. He rode back blind with his bloodstained face swollen and festering. Andronicus protested his innocence. He said that his men had taken out their anger against Romanus without his knowledge. He had some of them publicly flogged. In a few days Romanus was dead.

By that time, Theodore was long gone. He had fled to Antioch, which would not accept the Ducases' rule, with fifty of his own cavalrymen, the only survivors left from his Chaldian regiment.

There he heard that Alp Arslan was also dead, killed in a rebellion in Persia. So, little more than a year after the battle of Manzikert, both Romanus and Alp Arslan had perished. The peace treaty between the Seljuks and the Romans was now forgotten. Alp Arslan's sons were already starting to fall out over their father's inheritance and the Seljuk Empire was breaking up.

This was disastrous for the Eastern Themes. Turkoman emirs began to raid Roman territory again. And this time the Eastern frontiers were left defenceless by the new Emperor

Michael who only had a small, battered army in Constantinople and an empty treasury.

Then Theodore heard that Trebizond had fallen. A powerful Turkish force had taken it. And at its head was Afsin.

Theodore imagined the brutal slaughter of the people of Trebizond by Afsin and his men. He could picture the churches swimming in blood as he had seen them in Amorium and Chonae.

The next day he left for Trebizond with his depleted regiment of fifty men. They set off from Antioch to ride across Anatolia back to their homeland, or what was left of it.

Fifty men against a Turkish army of thousands.

PART IV
RETURN TO TREBIZOND

November 1072

So Xenophon mounted his horse and, taking Lycus and the cavalry with him, rode forward and quite soon they heard the soldiers shouting out "The sea! The sea!" and passing the word down the column. Then they all began to run, the rearguard and all, and drove on the baggage animals and horses at full speed; and when they had all got to the top, the soldiers, with tears in their eyes, embraced each other and their generals and captains.

A march from here brought them to Trebizond, an inhabited Greek city.

Xenophon, The Anabasis

XXVII

Theodore's worst fears were realised when he arrived. Afsin's warband had overrun the fortresses at Theodosiopolis and Trebizond, whose garrisons, depleted to fight the civil war, had surrendered to save their lives. It was far worse than in the time before Manzikert. Now there was no frontier, just a barren land full of burnt farmsteads and people that had fled to the woods and mountains to escape Afsin's savage brutality. There were no crops. There were no animals. The towns of Neocaesarea and Trebizond were silent; what people remained in them lived like rats scuttling in fear from the Turks who ruled as brutal tyrants from the fortresses they had captured.

Everywhere that Theodore and his men went, they found worse horrors than those they had seen on the battlefield. Many of the villagers and farmers had formed groups that fought each other for what little food and possessions were left. They behaved towards each other as brutally as the Turks did to them. The bigger groups started to terrorise the countryside, stealing, killing and raping as they wanted. The old and the weak were left to die without food or shelter.

Theodore and his soldiers had one advantage. They had weapons and armour that could not be matched by any group of thugs. But Theodore couldn't bring order to the wretched lives of his people. They ran away from him instead of joining him. He knew he had nothing to offer them anyway except their dignity. And they didn't want that.

And as the food ran out there were stories of cannibalism. A priest led them to a cave inhabited by the wretched survivors of a village burned by the Turks, who it was claimed had resorted to cannibalism.

Theodore rounded them up in the open sunlight and they stood cowering in the rags that remained of their clothes.

"Who is your headman? Stand before me now," he commanded.

A bearded thickset man shuffled forward and stood before Theodore, his eyes looking at the ground.

"We were starving, my lord. The Turks killed many of us and took everything and burned the rest. All we did was to eat a corpse or two – people that the Turks had already killed."

Theodore felt the man was lying. He turned to the crowd and called out:

"Is that true? Does this man speak the truth? Tell me now! You will be judged whatever you say, so tell me the truth now!"

There was silence. And then a middle-aged woman spoke. She trembled as she said:

"He made us do it. And it was not just the dead. He killed anyone who spoke against him and then forced us to eat them." The accused man looked at her with hatred in his eyes and protested his innocence.

Theodore didn't trust either of them. He looked at the crowd sternly. "Does she speak the truth? Tell me now. It is your only chance for redemption."

Then one of the crowd cried out that they were both guilty. The rest started to back him. Theodore had no idea who was telling the truth.

"Wait! You tell me what you think," Theodore said,

pointing to a man who looked as though he might still have some honesty in him. He waited a long time before speaking, looking around him nervously, and then he said:

"She helped him. She's a wily one and she's the first to turn on him but she's as guilty as he is. And others too. The rest of us were forced to go along with it. Some refused and they were killed."

Theodore did not know what to do. The good people had been killed for their principles. The evil ones had triumphed. The rest had been too weak to resist them. So, were they guilty too? There was no answer.

He could have easily put them all to the sword. But in a world where life was so cheap, he wanted to show them that something mattered. So, he told the villagers that they would all be tried one by one by him and his officers. They debated for a long time about who was innocent and who was guilty. In the end, they decided to execute nine of them and to release the rest.

"I am the Count of Chaldia," he told the villagers. "My duty is to bring justice and to punish those that have sinned. For what else do we have but our honour?"

They beheaded the nine and the rest asked if they could join his men. He told them he would protect them until they could return to their village. He found other villagers desperately clinging on to life and soon he had a following of destitute villagers, for whom he could barely find enough food.

How could they survive? They could not dream of challenging the Turks. Theodore felt close to despair and wondered if he should return to Antioch.

Then one day when they were in the mountains, keeping out of the Turks' way and hunting deer in the pine forests, he stumbled across a path that led to the top of a hill. His men were busy pitching camp close by and alone he followed the path. He was surprised to find that it turned into stone steps, long overgrown but still distinct. He followed them up onto a wide plateau, so flat that it seemed to be man-made. Before him the view was staggering. He looked down onto the Chaldian plain and its verdant pastures and out to the deep blue sea. He stood transfixed. He looked to his right, and yes, he could just make out the city of Trebizond, so small that it was barely visible. He peered over the edge of the ground that he was standing on and saw massive clean-cut blocks of stone mostly hidden by vegetation but still just visible. What was this? The base of an ancient temple? If it was, he could understand why the pagans had chosen such a place.

It was summer and he breathed in the warm aroma from the pine trees mixed with the faint smell of herbs. He felt more relaxed and at peace than he had been for as long as he could remember and he knelt on the ground, still staring at the panoramic vision all around him.

Then, looking around him, he noticed to his left in the undergrowth a tall stone slab, half a man's height, with writing on it. It looked like a pagan tombstone, a stele as they were called. He had seen many of them. He stood up and walked over to it and pulled away some of the ivy and vegetation that had spread over it. Beneath he saw that it was cleanly, if simply carved, with finely chiselled words. He unpicked the earth and vegetation that clung to it until his nails were black and he could just make out the words. He read:

So Xenophon mounted his horse and, taking Lycus and the cavalry with him, rode forward and quite soon they heard the soldiers shouting out "The sea! The sea!" and passing the word down the column. Then they all began to run, the rearguard and all, and drove on the baggage animals and horses at full speed; and when they had all got to the top, the soldiers, with tears in their eyes, embraced each other and their generals and captains.

He smiled to himself. So, Xenophon had found him again. This must have been the place where Xenophon and his army of ten thousand had first seen the sea as they made their escape from the Persians. He remembered Eirene's words when they had first met.

"Xenophon came here to Trebizond. You must know that."

And suddenly he knew that he would not leave for Antioch. If Xenophon had managed to reach Trebizond, then so would he. Or die in the attempt.

A few days later, a peasant told them of a large group of Armenians that had settled in the mountains. Theodore wondered whether they would join his growing band of followers and decided to meet them.

They travelled through the desolate countryside and the starving villagers came to beg from them. They passed close by Theodore's old house and lands. He galloped to see what remained of it. His house was hardly visible any more. The burned wreckage had become overgrown. It was returning to nature. He went to the watermill. The wheel was free of the branch that the priest had claimed was God's punishment for their sins but its blades were warped and broken and tiles were falling from the mill's roof. Soon it too would return to nature.

They rode into the hills near to Neo-Caesarea where the Armenians lived. For the first time they saw people who were not starving. They saw goatherds and flocks of goats and sheep. They asked a peasant where their leader lived.

"He don't live anywhere," the man replied in broken Greek with a thick Armenian accent. "He takes his flock to new pastures as they need them."

"Where can we find him?" Theodore asked, as he looked down on the rough-looking peasant.

"He may be in the caves up yonder," the man said dismissively. "He keeps himself to himself apart from when he comes to lead us to a new area where he thinks we can get away from the Turks."

"What is his name?"

"Ashot."

"Take us to him now."

The man eyed Theodore nervously. Normally he would have run away from a group of heavily armed warriors like Theodore and his men but he knew they were what remained of the local thematic army and were not enemies.

"Follow me."

As they followed him, one of Theodore's most senior officers, a man called Onemissus, said:

"It could be a trap, my lord."

"We're all trapped," Theodore said.

The Armenian took them high into the hills. The ground was stony and their horses' hooves slipped and stumbled as they went. As the afternoon wore on, his men told Theodore that they were leaving it too late to return before dusk. Then suddenly they came upon a cave. There was a wide opening into overhanging rock and all around it were goats which ran away, startled as the group of six came into sight. In front of the cave was the blackened remains of a fire.

The peasant called out in the direction of the cave and, after a few minutes, a man emerged. He was tall and he wore the coarse woollen garments of a goatherd. He also had a sword.

The peasant called out to him: "These Romans want to speak with you."

Theodore rode up to him. He looked strangely familiar. His face was grave and had a noble aspect. His long black hair was streaked with grey. He looked at Theodore and said without smiling.

"We meet again. It's been a long time."

"How do you know me?" Theodore was astonished.

"My name is Ashot. Do you remember?"

Theodore looked at him, unable to speak. His men looked at each other, wondering what to do.

Sensing their consternation, Theodore told them that he had met Ashot a long time ago, and that he was a friend.

Then he turned to Ashot:

"You told us the truth. About Andronicus."

Ashot did not smile. He looked at Theodore and all he could see was Eirene. Her beautiful face as he had last seen it. He did not want to be reminded of her as he spoke:

"We meet again and yet nothing has changed. Andronicus rules in Constantinople. His crimes have not been avenged."

"It is true."

"Tie up your horses," Ashot said at long last. "I will light a fire and I will share what food we have with you but then you must leave us."

Later in the evening, while Theodore's men were tending to their horses, Ashot and Theodore talked quietly as the fire cracked and sparked in the cold air. They talked about little of consequence until Theodore suddenly said to him earnestly:

"You said that you have lost your family. I too have lost mine. The Turks took them. I have given up praying for them. God does not listen. I still hope that they are alive but I know that my hopes are foolish."

Ashot sat in silence until he could bear it no more.

"I have something to tell you. About your wife and family."

Theodore was stunned. "How?"

"I have good news for you. Eirene and your two boys were alive and well the last time I saw them, a little over a year ago. They went west to find her parents after the battle."

Ashot told him how he had met Eirene, the story of her escape from Afsin, and their journey to Manzikert, and their subsequent escape. Theodore listened and was overcome with joy that Eirene and his boys were still alive. But what had Afsin done to her? How could she have escaped his lust for her? Ashot told him that Afsin had not mistreated her. He did not believe it.

"When we discovered that the Emperor's army was at Manzikert, Eirene insisted that we go there to see if there was any news of you, for Andronicus had told her that you were still alive. But by the time we got near Manzikert, we heard that the Emperor had been defeated. Soldiers were fleeing in every direction. Some regiments were still in good order while others were like refugees. Then we met a sizeable force, almost an army in itself, commanded by Andronicus Ducas."

"We hid and watched his regiments return to the west. Everyone told us that the Emperor had been killed or captured. But Eirene found her parents' regiment among those that were retreating. She decided to return to her parents. I thought she would be safe and bade her farewell."

Theodore felt like turning his horse and riding west to find his family. But Amorium and Constantinople were five hundred miles to the west, and in-between was a battlefield. He also knew that the new Emperor Michael Ducas would kill him as a traitor if he came anywhere near his lands.

Ashot told him that he had stayed in this area to help the refugees from the Turks, be they Armenian or Roman.

"Do you help them to fight the Turks?"

"No, what's the point of fighting? There's nothing here except God's damnation."

"You cannot help me then." Theodore looked away from Ashot. "For we must fight the Turks. Afsin rules Trebizond. We have to take it back from him."

"That, my friend, will never happen. Trebizond has fallen and only an army from Constantinople could ever recapture it."

The next day, Theodore and his men left Ashot and the Armenians.

"Let us at least be friends if not allies," Theodore saluted Ashot, who said:

"Good luck, Theodore, we will not betray you to the Turks if that's what you're wondering. One day, I hope that you will see your family again. Farewell."

As Theodore left, he wasn't thinking of Ashot but of Eirene and his sons. He hoped that they were happy. They had probably forgotten about him and he told himself that it would be better that way. But he still knew that, more than anything else, he longed to find them again. Just as Xenophon had longed to find the sea.

The knowledge that his family was still alive made Theodore even more determined to give the people of Chaldia something worth living for and he decided that the first thing to do was to hit back against the Turks.

He planned an attack on a Turkish warband that was pillaging what was left of the farms and villages in the countryside. He laid a trap for them. A flock of goats and some peasants seemed an easy target. Then the hunters become the hunted as, out of nowhere, Theodore's fifty heavily armoured cavalrymen charged towards them. Most of the Turks were killed and at night Theodore took their heads and planted them on spears before the main gates of Trebizond.

Soon the Turks would only leave the safety of Trebizond

in large groups. But when they tried to hunt Theodore down they found there was no one to attack. Theodore developed an effective system of lookouts who kept a vigilant eye on the Turks in Trebizond and reported their every movement. When a warband emerged from Trebizond it found the countryside empty. The newly-tilled fields were deserted. The renovated farm buildings were silent. They returned frustrated and fearful of a surprise Roman attack.

And so it continued for two years. Theodore was able to rebuild some of the farming infrastructure. In the more remote areas, far away from Afsin's stronghold in Trebizond, life started to return to a more normal rhythm. Crops were planted. Livestock were reared and even markets were sometimes held, like in the old times, to exchange food and goods. Theodore gathered some blacksmiths and paid them to make weapons with the food and materials that his followers supplied to him in lieu of taxes. Soon he had an army of a few hundred that was modelled on the old thematic army of Chaldia with cavalry and infantry regiments, or banda as they were called.

When his army had grown to more than a thousand, they found a deserted old fortress called Mesochaldia, high in the mountains above the plain that stretched to Trebizond and the sea. There they set up their stronghold.

"These people need something to believe in," Theodore told Onemissus, who was now his second-in-command. "Belief in a better life."

And so Theodore became more than just a warlord. He brought with him justice as well as the sword. He set up a court of law at Mesochaldia where the old laws were implemented. And soon people spoke with approval about him. They said that he brought justice. Stories were told about how he punished one of his own soldiers for stealing food from a poor old woman. The castle at Mesochaldia became well known across the land and people flocked to it for safety and to swear allegiance to Theodore.

For years, Afsin had lived a life of cruelty and debauchery in Trebizond. He drank the fine wines of the merchants and the nobles he had butchered. He had a harem of women: Roman, Armenian and Turkish. He seldom left the city. Instead he and his leaders gave themselves up to a life of carnal pleasure and cruelty.

Afsin had left the Seljuk army after Alp Arslan's death, just over a year after the battle of Manzikert, when the Seljuk Empire started to break up and the Turkish emirs abandoned the peace treaty between the two dead rulers, Romanus and Alp Arslan, and began their raids again. At long last he fulfilled his dream and took a great host of Turkoman warriors to the Euxine Sea, pillaging and killing wherever they went, until they reached Trebizond.

This prosperous city with its great walls, and its port through which passed most of the maritime trade from the sea of grass to Constantinople, had remained untouched by the war. But its garrison had left with the thematic army to fight for Romanus, and its governor knew he had no hope of holding out against Afsin and surrendered the city immediately. Afsin rewarded this by sparing the lives of most of the townsfolk but he still killed the priests and anyone who did not show him the respect he deemed necessary, and he and his men took whichever women they liked the look of.

Then in the spring of 1075, he learned that it was Theodore who was challenging his authority from the fortress at Mesochaldia. Immediately, he set out with a great force to take Mesochaldia. Afsin was certain that they would slaughter the Romans. He would bring Theodore's head back on a spear.

They followed the path that wound into the mountains. Afsin did not even bother to send scouts ahead. Since the Romans had been defeated at Manzikert, they had not dared to face the Turks, and he imagined that Theodore's army would consist of a few hundred desperate peasants, armed with wooden shields and blunt spears.

They did not see the boulders that came crashing down on them as they filed through the steep ravine surrounded by great flanks of rock. They did not see the archers who shot them down from every side. They did not see, until it was too late, the heavily armoured cavalry that smashed into their rearguard. They turned to flee in panic. And their flight turned into a rout as the Romans slaughtered them as they ran. They streamed back to Trebizond, leaving a thousand dead and wounded.

Theodore had led the cavalry charge that broke the Turkish resistance and turned it into a rout. The trap had worked better than he could possibly have imagined. The Turkish forces were shattered. That night, as his army celebrated its victory, he knew that he had been given a chance, a slim chance but one that he must take. He must now attack Trebizond itself.

And far away in Constantinople, news of Theodore's exploits reached Andronicus Ducas and the Emperor Michael, as they ruled fretfully over what was left of the Empire.

XXVIII

Eirene awoke startled. There was a colossal banging on the gates. It was late at night. Who could it be? She was afraid. Her sons were in a different part of the great house in Constantinople that belonged to her parents. She got out of bed and rushed through the empty hallways and corridors to their room. She looked into it and saw that they were both still asleep. The deep sleep of adolescence.

But the banging continued. She walked fast down the corridor that led to her parents' rooms on the other side of the house. She met a servant running, fear on his face. He was one of the grooms and a favourite of her sons.

"Sirius, what's going on?"

"There are men at the gate my lady. We don't know who they are!" he gasped.

"Who can they be?" she asked incredulously. "Go and get my father," she told him.

She rushed to the main door of the house and, as she opened it, the cold night air made her shiver slightly. In front of her there was a courtyard and a wall with gates, heavy structures of wood and iron, that led out on to the Via Egnatia, the street in Constantinople famed for its rich and powerful inhabitants.

Servants were gathered in the courtyard in front of the

gates. They turned to face her as she approached, looking at her questioningly. There was another loud bang on the gates. It sounded like a sword or an axe. A voice called out:

"Open the door! In the name of the Emperor open the door!"

The voice sounded strangely familiar to Eirene. She was frightened.

"Who is it?" she shouted back.

There was a pause. Then the same voice spoke again: "We are your friends. Open the gates!"

"Why are you here?" Eirene spoke firmly. She didn't like the sound of the voice. There was another pause. And then the voice spoke again: "Open the gate and we will tell you."

Just then her father, John Taronites, Count of the Anatolikon Theme, appeared with Sirius, asking what was happening.

"I don't know. They say they are friends," Eirene told her father desperately.

He drew himself up to his full height and called out crossly: "What do you want with us at this hour? Who are you?"

"We want to speak with your daughter, Eirene," the voice said. "It is about her husband, Theodore."

"And what about him?" she called out without hesitating, betraying her surprise. His name was never mentioned publicly because of his association with Romanus, the long dead enemy of the Ducas family.

"We will tell you if you open the gate. We have important news."

Eirene was caught by this offer, just as a fish might rise to a bait. She must know.

"Father, it is best to open it. Please."

John, her father, nodded and two servants lifted the heavy wooden beam that secured the door. The moment the beam was lifted, the great gates were pushed open and the owner of the mysterious voice was revealed. It was Andronicus Ducas.

Eirene flinched. Of course it was his voice she had recognised. Behind him were soldiers, the Varangian guards.

But it was not the Andronicus that she knew from old. He was thin and emaciated, stooping and leaning on a walking stick. She knew that he had been badly wounded a year ago fighting Norman mercenaries who had rebelled against the Emperor.

Her father immediately moved forward to confront Andronicus.

"My lord Andronicus, what is it that you want?"

"To summon your daughter and her sons to the great palace," Andronicus replied "See this: I have the Emperor's command right here."

And he lifted a parchment with a heavy waxen seal. Her father stepped back. He saw the document and was shocked.

"But what on earth has she done?"

"She has done nothing. But her husband, Theodore, is raising a rebellion in Chaldia. He has an army and is trying to seize the province for himself. He was an ally of the traitor, Romanus, and the Emperor has condemned him to death. His family is to be held in case they join him in this conspiracy."

Eirene was stunned. She had been told that Theodore had fought at the battle of Manzikert but after that it was a blank. She prayed every day that somehow, somewhere he was safe. Could this news really be true?

"Don't look so pleased, my lady," Andronicus snarled at her. "He is a traitor. He fought against us and now he has raised an army in Chaldia. We will hold you until he submits to our authority. You will not be mistreated. We will allow you the luxury of the great palace."

Eirene looked around her. Her father looked at Andronicus with a mix of anguish and relief in his eyes. He was relieved that the worst they wanted to do was to hold her in the great palace. He knew how politics worked and he understood that the Ducas family would be worried if Theodore really had re-established Roman authority in Chaldia. They did not want yet another pretender to the throne emerging. He confronted Andronicus and said: "I want to see the Emperor tomorrow about this."

Andronicus looked sullenly at him as he said: "My lord, you may see the Emperor tomorrow or any other day. But tonight I have the order for your daughter and her sons to come with me to the palace. I believe she has two sons? Where are they?"

Eirene backed away. Could she escape? If she hurried to the back of the house she might be able to run into the back streets. But she needed to take her children with her. Sirius, sensing what was in her mind, moved forward to meet the Varangian guardsmen as they advanced to seize her.

"Stop!" Andronicus shouted to her as she started to turn and move back into the house. Sirius stood blocking the way for the Varangians. One of them grabbed him and punched his face so hard that he fell to the ground, spitting out broken teeth with blood pouring down his shirt. Another Varangian put a dagger to his throat. Eirene saw this as she turned into the house. She stopped. She couldn't let them kill Sirius. She ran back and shouted:

"You're a brave man, Andronicus, aren't you? Brave at fighting slaves."

Her father told her to be silent. Andronicus laughed as his soldiers surrounded her, while others pushed past her, and ran into the house to find the boys. They waited for their return. The minutes passed. Then a Varangian, a heavily-built Frank, appeared. His face had blood on cut lips. Eirene gasped.

"What have you done with my boys?"

She broke free of the grip of the Varangians who were holding her and turned to the Frank. He looked embarrassed.

"My lord, they have gone. They have fled the house."

"What!" said Andronicus. "You idiot!"

Eirene looked at her father and burst into tears. Her boys had fled. Anything could happen to them.

She turned to Andronicus.

"One day, God will judge you."

He ignored her. Eirene's father said to him slowly, as if challenging him to a duel:

"You have performed your duties very poorly, my lord. I will see the Emperor tomorrow and tell him. You may take my daughter but I want to see her tomorrow. Do you understand?"

"Of course, you may see her and the Emperor tomorrow, my lord. If the boys return to the house, please let me know. Two of my men will stay here to bring them to the palace."

Eirene's father was silent as he glowered at Andronicus.

"I'm sorry but those are the Emperor's orders. Until tomorrow, my lord."

Eirene was taken to the great palace. With a Varangian on either side of her, she was marched to the hippodrome, and then down into the tunnel that joined it to the great palace.

She was marched past the Senate house, and down a long colonnade, to a building that she knew was the palace's prison, the place where traitors and rebels were kept awaiting their fate.

"Is there any sign of my children?" she asked the Varangian holding her arm but he ignored her, and she was taken down a spiral stone staircase into the basement where the dungeons were. She glimpsed cells that reeked of human excrement, past men that barely looked up through the iron bars of their cells, so hopeless was their position, their bodies destroyed and their minds deranged with pain and fear. But then thoughts of Theodore dispelled her despair. He was alive! If only she could join him. She would do anything, anything to be with him. How she hated Andronicus. If he was in front of her now, she imagined herself grabbing his throat. Yes, she would kill him if she could.

Down they went, deeper into the underworld until they reached the bottom, and there they found a large, unoccupied cell, equipped with furniture and a bed, a veritable paradise compared with the cramped squalor above them. A tall Varangian with long blond hair, pushed Eirene into the cell and closed the bars behind her, locking her in. She went to sit on a chair. The comfort of her surroundings gave her a sudden hope that she might be released. This must be a cell reserved for noble prisoners like herself for whom no real harm was intended, she hoped to herself. They left her and she stood for a long time, looking through the bars. Eventually she lay down on the mattress but could not sleep. She stayed with her eyes open staring at the iron bars of her cell.

The next day, after she had been given some bread and water for breakfast, she heard footsteps clattering on the stone stairs. She looked up, past the tall Varangian guarding her cell, and saw Andronicus appear, limping awkwardly from his wound. He told the Varangian to unlock the cell and walked in, leaning heavily on his walking stick.

He looked at her through eyes that were bloodshot and yellow, so different from those days when he had courted her.

"Your father has seen the Emperor this morning. You are to be held here until your husband submits to our authority."

"I prayed every day that he was still alive," Eirene was dazed by what had happened to her and spoke quietly, without emotion.

"Well, your prayers have been answered," Andronicus said grimly. "He is only too well, as far as we know. He has raised an army and controls much of the land around Trebizond. But not the city itself."

Andronicus smiled wryly.

Eirene looked at the sneer on Andronicus's face. She hated him more than anybody or anything in the whole world. He had betrayed her. He had betrayed Romanus. Now he wanted Theodore, who had somehow survived his treachery and brutality, to submit to his injustice. But she would rather die than help him. She would gladly suffer whatever horrors they had in store for her. She felt like attacking him now that he was alone in the cell with her, kicking him and clawing at him with her nails. But there was one thing that made her control her anger and worried her more than anything else: what had happened to her boys?

"My children, where are they?" she asked.

"That's another problem," Andronicus said. "They've run away. They're not at your parents' house. We've searched it from top to bottom."

"And my parents, are they alright?"

"Of course. They are not implicated. The Emperor respects your father."

"So, what will you do with me?"

"Hold you here. When we find your boys, we'll bring them here."

"So, you won't harm us?"

"Not unless you give us reason to."

So, her children had escaped. She imagined Gregory leading Constantine to some hiding place. She knew that he had enough courage and independence to escape. But then she felt terrified about what might happen to them. She felt an overwhelming urge to run and find them.

She saw Andronicus blocking the way to her children and she was choked by a sob of frustration and anger. She dropped to her knees and tears came to her eyes. She sobbed silently in front of him so that even his hardened heart was momentarily touched and he put his hand out to her. Little did he know that behind her tears was a furious anger welling up inside her.

As he placed his hand on her shoulder, she rose shaking with anger, and drove her fist into his stomach. He doubled up in pain and dropped his walking stick. She kicked him and he sank to the floor. She grabbed the dagger that was in his belt and, as his hands fought hers for it, she dug her knee into his chest and jabbed her elbow hard against his face so that his head cracked back against the stone floor. With both hands she pulled the dagger from its scabbard, and as his hands clawed the air, she stabbed it down into his body. Once, twice, five times the dagger jabbed into his chest. His head rolled back, blood gushing from his mouth. And the yellow eyes were suddenly glazed with death.

XXIX

Afsin still held Trebizond. And better than anyone, Theodore knew that its great walls made it impregnable if they were fully manned by the remains of his army.

"All we can do is to hold the countryside," Onemissus advised Theodore the day after their victory over Afsin as they held a council of war in the castle of Mesochaldia.

"There is the tunnel," Theodore said.

"The Turks probably know about it," Nicephorus, Theodore's other general, added. "There isn't a hope of advancing along it if they're defending it."

"What if they don't know about it? It's just possible they don't. My father kept it as secret as possible. No one was allowed to use it on punishment of death."

"My lord, we have had one victory. God won't grant us another so easily."

Theodore rose from the table and looked out of the window towards Trebizond. He imagined the remains of Afsin's army fleeing into Trebizond, their anger directed at what few inhabitants were left.

"And the city gates? Could we open them from the inside if we sailed by night into the harbour?" he asked, thinking out loud.

"It would be suicide to venture into the city that way, my lord," Onemissus begged.

Theodore turned around to face his generals.

"But it's all that we can do," he said.

The next day, Theodore prepared the army for a night attack. The plan was for two assaults on the city. The first would be a direct attack on the main gate led by Nicephorus. However, before they attacked, Theodore and a small group of men would enter the city by the harbour. They would try to open the gates or cause some diversion to distract the Turks away from the main gates. A little later when the Turks were preoccupied with the first attack, a second attack would be made through the tunnel into the castle, led by Onemissus. Theodore hoped that the Turks hadn't discovered the tunnel but he knew that he couldn't count on that.

They had no siege equipment but they had one surprise to use against the Turks: a large quantity of liquid fire that had been moved to the castle at Mesochaldia when it was clear that Trebizond would fall to the Turks. For centuries, Trebizond had been a major port for the Euxine fleet which was well equipped with liquid fire that was shot at enemy boats through bronze siphons. This had been the main weapon of the Roman fleet for centuries. Although the Roman navy used a furnace to heat the liquid and a pump to fire the ignited liquid onto enemy ships, Theodore's men only had clay grenades full of the liquid that they could throw at the enemy and then ignite with burning arrows. It wasn't much but it was something.

Theodore's army advanced on Trebizond. The Turks were waiting for them. The battlements were crowded with Turkish warriors. The Romans fell silent when they saw the numbers that they still faced.

Theodore's plan was their only hope if they were not to be slaughtered underneath the walls. They reconnoitred the entrance to the tunnel outside the city walls. It was as

Theodore had last seen it. The iron grille was still in place but they could easily remove that.

Later that day, as Theodore was riding around the city's walls, still pondering the best way to attack, one of his guards galloped up to him.

"My lord, there's a man who begs to see you. He won't tell us who he is but he says you know him well."

Theodore returned to his tent perplexed. Then he saw Ashot.

"I heard of your victory!" Ashot called out to him.

Theodore looked at him bemused.

"But you said that you wouldn't help us. Why are you here?"

Ashot ignored his question.

"Are you really going to attack Trebizond?" he asked.

Theodore nodded.

Ashot shook his head.

"You'll die. Leave the city to Afsin. I told you that only an army from Constantinople could take the city."

"An army led by Andronicus?"

Ashot did not answer.

"There is no other way. We have to attack."

Ashot looked at Theodore grimly. Then to Theodore's huge surprise, he said:

"This time I will join you. Have you weapons and armour that I can use?"

Two days later, at midnight, Theodore said goodbye to Onemissus, Nicephorus and Ashot as he and three other men waded into the cold water and clambered aboard a small rowing boat.

Ashot watched Theodore and his men go, the boat bobbing above the surface of the water until it had disappeared into the darkness. He sat on a sandbank above the beach and looked up at the bright stars in the night sky, wondering if he should have stopped Theodore from going into the city.

Barely an hour later, he was startled to see a figure emerging from the darkness of the sea, staggering forward out of the waves. He jumped to his feet. It was one of Theodore's men.

The man was soaked and panting. He looked exhausted and frightened. Ashot saw blood running down his leg.

"They caught us! The Turks caught us in the harbour. We didn't stand a chance. We were surrounded."

"What happened to Theodore?"

"I don't know," he stammered, shamefaced. "They were captured. Maybe killed. I got away."

Ashot rushed to find Theodore's generals, Nicephorus and Onemissus. He had already decided what to do.

"I'll get into the city through the harbour and open the main gates. They won't be expecting more of us through the harbour. Somehow I'll be able to find a way of opening those gates, I promise you."

Nicephorus looked at him in amazement. What did this man know of war?

"But how can you open the gates by yourself? The Turks will be guarding the gates. And you're no soldier. You don't know how to fight."

Ashot spoke softly: "I was once a soldier. I know how to fight. Trust me. I will find a way. Wait by the gates. Give me until daybreak."

He turned to Onemissus.

"Stay by the tunnel. Wait for Nicephorus' attack just as Theodore planned."

Yet Ashot knew that he had already failed them both. He had no plan. But he wanted to get into Trebizond. He felt strangely responsible for Theodore's capture and possible death. He had to do everything he could to save him.

He put on a chainmail coat and took a sword. He waded into the water and heaved himself into a small rowing boat. The water was cold and dark. But his mind was racing. He knew that if Theodore was still alive he wouldn't be alive for long. Everything depended on him now. His heart beat hard as he pulled the oars against the water and the boat eased its way out into the darkness.

XXX

Staring at Andronicus's dead body, Eirene jumped to her feet, panting for breath and shaking all over.

She looked up. The Varangian guard had come into the cell, his sword drawn. She crouched low and held the bloody dagger with both hands at him.

"He deserved to die! He betrayed Romanus at Manzikert! He betrayed me! He betrayed all of us!"

The Varangian looked startled and slightly in awe of this noblewoman who had just brutally murdered the Emperor's cousin.

"Manzikert?" he asked.

"Yes, Manzikert. He betrayed Romanus."

"My father died at Manzikert."

The Varangian spoke Greek slowly in a thick Norse accent.

"Then help me to escape!"

The Varangian pointed his sword down to the ground.

"I will. I came here to avenge my father. And you have done it for me. His name was Ragnar. And he died at Manzikert. My name is Ragnarvald."

Eirene wondered whether this was a trick.

"Keep away from me. You're lying." she said, still pointing the dagger at him.

"Vikings don't lie," Ragnarvald said, his blue eyes looked

affronted. "You insult me and my father. Believe me, I will help you. I would have killed Andronicus if you had not. I knew he was a traitor. But he is not the only one. There are many of them here. Now we must go."

Something about Ragnarvald made Eirene feel she could trust him. Anyway, she had no choice.

"I have to find my children."

"Where are they?"

"They could be anywhere."

"And then what will you do?"

There was a moment's silence. Then she remembered Theodore. He seemed to belong to another world.

"Trebizond. We go to Trebizond."

"Then I come with you."

As he said these words, Eirene's eyes registered some movement on the stairs outside the cell. She looked over and saw another Varangian coming down the stairs. He was a big man, with long dark hair and a black beard, heavily armed with chainmail and a sword at his side. Was he friend or foe? He stopped and looked at them in astonishment.

"Ragnarvald, what has happened?" he snapped at him curtly.

"This woman killed the lord Andronicus," Ragnarvald turned round to face the man.

And then he raised his sword and held it pointed at him.

"And if she had not, I would have done. For he betrayed my father and the true Emperor, Romanus, at Manzikert. Just as you did, Rurik. You supported Michael against Romanus so that you could gain command of the Varangains. Now you will die as well."

Rurik laughed.

"Ragnarvald, you speak bravely for one who has yet to make a killing. You are not your father. Come and try to kill me."

Rurik drew his sword. Ragnarvald motioned to Eirene to stay back. He raised his own sword and threw himself at Rurik who stepped back deftly. He parried Ragnarvald's blow and struck back hard. Ragnarvald was forced back. Neither man had a shield and both knew that a well aimed sword blow would be lethal. They circled each other warily while Eirene stayed motionless. She didn't want to distract Ragnarvald. She still had Andronicus' dagger but what could she do with it against Rurik's sword?

Ragnarvald chanced another attack. He knew that he didn't have much time. This time he tried to slash at Rurik's face but Rurik ducked and nearly caught his legs with his blade. Ragnarvald was able to ward off Rurik's blow just in time. They stood facing each other, breathing hard.

Then Rurik launched himself against Ragnarvald. He moved his blade fast, cutting this way and that, and as Raganarvald's sword met his, their blades glanced off each other, and Rurik just managed to twist his sword, so that it glanced off Ragnarvald's side. He was not wearing chainmail, and his tunic was suddenly stained red.

Eirene gasped in horror. Ragnarvald held his hand over the wound, his eyes fixed on Rurik, as he backed away from him, keeping his sword pointed straight. Rurik stepped forward, closing in for the kill. Just then Ragnarvald stumbled against a chair. He immediately picked it up and threw it at Rurik who had not expected this. It hit him in the face and Rurik stopped for a moment, his hand holding his face. It might have caught his eye for he seemed stunned. Seeing this, Eirene rushed behind Ragnarvald to the door.

"Go!" he said to her. "Go now!"

"No!" she shouted. "Come with me." And she pulled his arm, dragging him with her through the cell door.

"Quickly, the keys!" she said.

The keys were on Ragnarvald's belt. He fumbled with

them as Rurik recovered from the blow with the chair. He watched them rush through the cell door, his eyes blinking as they regained their focus. Then he lunged forward just as Eirene shut the door against him and held it tightly closed, her whitened knuckles gripping the iron. Rurik brought his sword down against the iron bars, and Eirene let go of them just before her fingers were sliced off. She leaned her body against the door to keep it shut as Ragnarvald searched for the right key. But he couldn't find it immediately.

Rurik took his sword back and plunged it through the iron bars. Eirene jumped back, inches from the point of the blade. Ragnarvald kept the door shut with his foot against it, and at last finding the right key, he put it in the lock and turned it just as Rurik jabbed his sword through the bars again, this time the blade aimed at Ragnarvald who twisted sideways to avoid it.

"Up here! Quickly!" Ragnarvald shouted as he took Eirene's arm. But he felt a searing pain in the wound on his side. He looked at his felt tunic and saw it was drenched with blood. He knew he didn't have much time.

Eirene climbed the stairs after him, leaving Rurik shouting from behind the bars. She held Andronicus's dagger in her hand, ready to use it against anyone who stood in her way. Where should they go?

"My children!" she called to Ragnarvald. "I must find them! I can't leave them. I would die first."

"First, we must get out of here," Ragnarvald called back as they made their way up the spiral stone staircase. They rushed past the entrances to each floor, as they made their way to the ground level. A guard called out to Ragnarvald from the interior of a room that they passed, asking if he was alright. He shouted back that everything was fine. The man seemed to believe him. He could only have glimpsed them as they passed and had not seen their wild, desperate appearance.

Finally, they reached the ground floor and they could see sunlight through the door. They had escaped from the dungeons! But Eirene knew they were still trapped. They still had to escape from the palace. And where were her children? She must find them. But how? How in the name of the saints, could she hope to find them in this great city?

XXXI

Gregory opened his eyes. A noise had woken him. He looked across the room to see his brother, Constantine, still asleep. He'd sleep through anything, Gregory thought. What was the noise? Someone was banging on the gates. But at this time of night? Very strange.

He jumped out of bed. The stone floor was cold on his feet. He went past the long pinewood table, where the rudder of his boat was laid out. He had been spent the previous day mending it. His mother would scold him that his boat was the only thing he cared about.

He went to the door and opened it, peering out into the hallway. He saw Sirius rushing round the corner.

"Stay there!" Sirius called as he went. "Don't come out until we tell you it's alright."

Something was wrong. He turned back into the room and went to his brother. He grabbed him and shook him

"Wake up! Wake up!"

"What are you doing? Get off me!" Constantine mumbled, his voice slurred and thick with sleep.

"It's not a joke," Gregory said. "Get up and put your clothes on! Quickly!"

Constantine sat upright in his bed, his feet over the edge. They didn't quite reach the ground. He sat there rubbing his eyes and yawning as Gregory rushed to put his clothes on. He's just a boy, thought Gregory, who was two years older than Constantine but at his age of thirteen, two years seemed like a lifetime of experience. As he buckled his belt on, he felt irritated by his brother's slowness, watching him fumble around, looking for his clothes. But he also felt something else. He was pleased he wasn't alone.

"Come on! Quickly! Let's go and see what's happening," he said.

"All right! Give me a chance! What's the big fuss?"

Gregory grabbed his small hunting dagger. It was the only weapon he possessed. He tied the dagger to his upper arm with a leather strap so that it could not be seen.

They went out into the hallway. Their bedroom was up on the first floor of the great house that belonged to his grandparents. Down below from the direction of the main gates, they could hear voices shouting and the sound of nailed boots clattering on the stone floors. Something was very wrong.

They walked down the broad staircase that led to a cloistered courtyard which was open to the night sky. In the centre was a beautiful mosaic of dolphins and fish swimming around the pagan god Neptune. As he looked at the doors on the far side of the courtyard, they were suddenly thrown open and through them appeared several soldiers. They stopped and one of them, a swarthy thickset Frank, called out to them:

"Boys! Come here! We have orders for your arrest! It's no good resisting!"

The moment Gregory heard the last words, he decided to run. He didn't know what they had done wrong but he knew that the soldiers were the enemy.

"Quickly, run!" he shouted to his brother as he grabbed him by the arm, turning to run back the way they had come. But instead of the stairs, he chose the doors at the opposite end of the courtyard. They sprinted on their sandaled feet. The soldiers broke into a run behind them. As he passed through the doors, Gregory kicked them shut behind him. Two seconds later, the Frank who had called out to them to surrender themselves, punched them open as he chased after them.

Still grasping his brother's arm, Gregory swerved again, this time to the left, into the kitchens. It was too fast for his brother. He collided with a table and was knocked to the ground. Plates fell and smashed. Gregory stopped and heaved his brother to his feet. The Frank was right behind them. He reached forward and grabbed Gregory's arm as he shouted something in his native tongue which Gregory didn't understand. But as he snarled at Gregory in triumph, Gregory's right hand crunched into his face. Gregory knew how to box and the Frank staggered back, his tongue tasting the blood pouring from his cut lips, a look of complete amazement of his face. He let his grip on Gregory's arm go, and as he did so, the boys turned and ran towards the far corner of the big room, towards the door that led onto the streets outside.

More soldiers burst into the room behind the Frank who stopped to feel his bleeding face and then leapt forward, furiously angry. But the kitchen was full of tables and the Frank collided with one of them, turning it over and sending bowls of summer fruits smashing to the ground. Meanwhile, Constantine had already got to the door. The key had been left in the lock. In a flash he turned both it and the handle and pushed the door open onto the street outside. Gregory came crashing into him and the two boys fell into the dusty street. Gregory leapt to his feet first and grabbed his brother.

"Down here!" he gasped, pushing his brother forward. By the time the Frank appeared in the doorway, they had gone. He jumped out and stopped to look in both directions. It was dark and he paused to look to his right and then to his left. He paused too long. Gregory had already raced down the street and swerved left into another street, pulling his brother with him.

Gregory's heart was pounding. He knew the soldiers would be just a few steps behind them. Which way should they go? Holding onto his brother, he darted down another alleyway. Then he turned into another. He was relieved that he knew these side streets so well. He felt that if they could just keep running, they might lose the soldiers.

They ran and ran. His breath was becoming shorter. His legs were getting tired. His brother was slowing him down. He was dragging him along. Now he was getting lost. He didn't recognise these streets any more. They turned again into another street and suddenly ahead of them they saw the sea stretching beyond the sea walls. The houses around them were broken down and derelict. He stopped and they peered into the falling timbers of what had once been a building.

"Let's stop here," Gregory gasped to his brother. "We can hide behind this wall."

And the two boys jumped over the wall and knelt down behind it, breathing hard. Gregory rested his head against the stone as he took great gulps of air.

They sat in silence beneath the wall, staring ahead of them. Then Gregory said:

"I hope mother is all right. What did they want? What have we done wrong?"

"What should we do now?" Constantine looked at his brother, tears starting to come to his eyes.

Gregory put his arm around his brother as great shudders shook him and streams of tears poured down his face. He needed to work out a plan. Why did the soldiers want them? What had they done wrong? He knew that his mother detested the Ducas family and the young man who had been made Emperor a few years ago. He knew that his grandparents said that they must be careful. They still had power and money but most of their lands in the Anatolikon Theme had been lost to the Turks. And they did not talk much about their father. Their mother could hardly ever speak of him without her voice trembling.

Then he had an idea. In the morning, they would go to the market near their house where the servants bought food every day. He would try to ask them what had happened. One of their favourite servants, Vlasov, a Bulgar slave, went there most days and often they would go with him. They enjoyed choosing the food and helping to bring it home. But what if Vlasov wasn't there? Gregory felt fear in his stomach. He thought of the soldiers. They would be expecting him wouldn't they? How could he go there unnoticed? He thought long and hard but nothing came to his mind. Then suddenly he thought of an idea. He jumped to his feet and turned to his brother who had stopped crying and was staring blankly into the distance.

"Now Constantine, listen to this. I have a plan."

Next day, in the morning, Gregory and Constantine wandered into the market square just off the Via Egnatia, where rows of market stalls were selling goods of all kinds. Great amphorae of wine and oil were set by the roadside, fiercely guarded by their owners. Meat was hanging from hooks, fish was laid out on wooden boards and the delicious smell of freshly baked bread permeated the air and made the boys feel hungry, for they had not eaten that morning.

The boys moved cautiously, jumping out of the way of the storekeepers who would lunge at them with sticks and shout at them to be gone. They walked in the gutter in their bare feet and sat on the pavement edge with a bowl which they held up to passers-by. To anyone who knew them, their blackened faces and the rags they wore were as unrecognisable as if they had become galley slaves. For the two boys from one of the most illustrious families in the empire were dressed as beggars.

Gregory told Constantine to stay sitting on the pavement edge if they saw Vlasov.

"We've got to look as inconspicuous as possible," he said.

Constantine nodded in agreement. He still felt like crying. He wished he was back at home, playing with his soldiers.

"He'll be here soon," Gregory said, looking at the position of the sun in the sky. Vlasov was always punctual and went to the market most days at around mid-morning. But perhaps he wouldn't come today, thought Gregory. They waited for half an hour. Constantine was getting restless. He wanted to go back home and see what had happened. Gregory told him that he couldn't do that.

And then Vlasov appeared. He seemed different from usual. He walked more warily, looking around him carefully. Yes, thought Gregory, he's looking for us. Gregory looked around for signs of soldiers. Then, he saw two Varangians standing at the corner of the market. They could be waiting for him or they might simply be on guard duty. He watched them from the corner of his eye, pretending to be looking elsewhere. Yes, he thought, they're waiting for us. The soldiers seemed to be looking at Vlasov as he went to the baker and then to the wine merchant. He had other servants with him and a cart which they were loading with the goods they bought.

How could he get to Vlasov without being noticed, he wondered? His plan was simply to tell him the name of a meeting place and time later that day and then run away. He hoped that Vlasov would understand what was meant, and that either he or, best of all, his grandparents could meet them there.

They waited a little longer. Vlasov was getting closer to them. He was at the butcher's, inspecting cuts of meat.

"Stay here. Wait for me," Gregory said to Constantine, as he rose and slowly started to move towards Vlasov, holding his begging bowl up to people as he passed.

Vlasov seemed more like his normal self, preoccupied with talking to the butcher about the price of the lamb he wanted to buy. He's probably decided we're not going to show up here, Gregory thought. He was worried now that Vlasov might shoo him away, not realising who he was. That would be ironic, he thought.

He walked up to Vlasov. People stepped away as he approached, not wanting to have anything to do with such a filthy looking beggar. Vlasov turned to look at him. Gregory's face broke into a broad smile. Suddenly Vlasov realised who it was and he stood there dumbstruck, staring at Gregory. Gregory went right up to him and started to speak. Vlasov seemed unsure what was happening and stepped back, dropping the basket he was carrying and backing into someone behind him who turned and swore at him.

Gregory had grasped Vlasov's hand and was speaking urgently to him but Vlasov wasn't listening. He was looking around nervously. Then he said very quickly: "Your mother's in the Great Palace. This is a trap to catch you. Quickly go!"

Then Gregory made a mistake. He broke into a run back to Constantine. Seeing this, the two soldiers saw their prey and charged after him.

"Get up!" Gregory shouted to Constantine, as he pulled him to his feet.

"What's happening?" Constantine asked, his frightened face looking startled.

"We've got to run. They're after us." Gregory yelled as he pushed Constantine ahead of him.

The two boys raced round the corner. Behind them came

the soldiers. But the boys had a good head start on them and they sprinted from one street to the next until they had lost them. They stopped in a doorway panting.

"Mother's in the Great Palace," Gregory told Constantine as he gasped for breath. "Vlasov said so. We've got to go there. Now! Come on!"

He was thinking of the best way to the Great Palace. He'd been there many times. He knew that there was a tunnel from the hippodrome into the palace. That would be the only way they might get in. He had no idea what they would do when they were there but already another plan was forming in his mind about how to get into the Great Palace.

Two hours later the two boys were walking down the long, wide road called the Mese from the Forum of Constantine towards the hippodrome. But they were no longer dressed as beggars. They had put their old clothes back on. And they had cleaned their faces thoroughly. Gregory had bought some perfume and oil and they had sleek oiled hair and smelled of expensive fragrances.

As Gregory had expected, the hippodrome was not well guarded. The Emperor was going to hold the summer races in a month's time, and today there were two charioteers who were practising the course, racing round it.

Guarding the main entrance from the Mese to the hippodrome were two bored-looking Varangian guardsmen. The senior of the two was a dark-haired man who looked like a Frank or a Saxon. He looked at the two boys sullenly as they approached him.

Gregory strode up to him. He put on his most confident voice and said rather loudly: "Soldier, we've come to see the Patriarch, Xiphilinos. He wants us to sing in the choir at Haghia Sophia."

"Really?" The soldier half laughed. But then he checked

himself. These two boys were clearly from a noble family and it could be true what they were saying.

"All right," he said. "Come with me." He nodded to the other soldier and said: "You stay here. I'll be back soon. I'll just take these pretty-smelling boys to the church." He held his nose between his thumb and forefinger and snorted a laugh.

They crossed the front of the hippodrome. The charioteers were oblivious of them. They entered the tunnel leading to the Great Palace. As they went from the bright sunlight into the dark of the tunnel, which was lit up by only a few burning torches, their eyes struggled to see and their feet stumbled. Within a few seconds, their eyes had adjusted and Gregory could see the guardsman striding ahead nonchalantly, without even caring to look behind him to see if the two boys were there.

Gregory had no plan, no idea of what he was doing other than desperately searching for his mother. But as he saw the Varangian's sword dangling at his side while he walked nonchalantly, whistling to himself, he acted purely on impulse. He stepped forward and taking the small dagger from its strap on its upper arm, he put it firmly against the Varangian's back as he spoke fiercely to him:

"Stop! Stay still and you won't be hurt. Lift your arms high." The Varangian froze. Then to his brother, he said: "Get his sword."

Constantine did nothing. He was too afraid.

"Get on with it!" Gregory shouted at him. Constantine moved forward and with two hands on the sword handle, he lifted it out of its scabbard and passed it to Gregory.

"Sit down," Gregory commanded the Varangian who looked at him furiously. He held the sword at the man's chest, his dagger in his other hand.

"Take your shoes off," he said to the Varangian and then he told his brother to take the leather straps from his shoes and first tie his hands behind his back and then tie his feet together. They gagged his mouth with some material torn from his tunic. And leaving him there they ran away into the sunlight at the end of the tunnel.

They emerged into a great colonnaded courtyard which was the entrance to the Great Palace that extended over a vast area of more than a hundred acres. Gregory knew they would be discovered very soon and that they had no time at all to find their mother. He remembered that the prisons were on the other side of the Great Palace and he thought that was where his mother was most likely to be. They headed towards them across the courtyard. It was midday and most people were eating or seeking shelter from the hot sun, so the boys passed unnoticed.

Then before they had gone very far, straight ahead of them, Gregory saw his mother. She was walking with a soldier who seemed to be wounded, as he clutched his left side, his grey linen tunic stained bright red. He could not stop himself calling out to her.

She turned and looked at them in amazement.

"How did you get here?"

"We tricked our way in here," Gregory said. "Vlasov told us they'd taken you. What have we done wrong? Why are they doing this?"

"Your father's alive. They want him. They want us as hostages. Quickly! We can go to the palace harbour. There are plenty of boats there." She turned to Ragnarvald, who smiled at the boys but he was clearly in great pain.

"The harbour's on the other side of the palace. We mustn't run. People will notice us."

"Mother, are you all right? What did they do to you?" Gregory asked.

"They didn't touch me. I'm quite all right." She paused. "This man saved me."

Then Ragnarvald said urgently: "I know the way to the harbour. Follow me!"

He led them down a long colonnade. The palace was almost deserted at this time of day and they went unnoticed.

They passed from bright sunlight into the cool of the shaded colonnade. Gregory had never been this way before. They passed the Varangian barracks where there was no sign of anyone. They would probably be eating lunch in the great hall. They walked past the beautiful marble columns that lined the colonnade. Past the lopsided patches of sunlight that shone through the arches. It seemed too easy.

They reached a colonnade. Suddenly, they saw some servants scurrying across it. But the servants turned away before noticing them.

Then as they turned a corner, ahead of them they saw a group of Varangian guardsmen marching towards the Imperial throne room. Luckily they were going in the same direction as them and they didn't look back over their shoulders to see them. But they could see that the way ahead was blocked. Soldiers were everywhere outside the throne room.

Ragnarvald stopped and ushered them into the shadows under the pillars. Then he whispered, pointing away from the colonnade towards the sea: "We'll go down to the sea walls. There'll be fewer people there."

They crossed a deserted courtyard to the sea walls, which stretched down past the lighthouse and to the harbour. Ragnarvald was hoping that they could walk along the top down to the harbour without being noticed. He ran up some steps that led to the top of the sea walls and beckoned to them to follow him.

They found that the wall had a flat top which was just wide enough to walk along but there was a steep drop on either side and there were no sides to hang onto. On the inside, the drop was two storeys down, and on the outer side, there was a sheer drop down to the rocks covered in foam by the sea. At regular intervals along the wall there were great stone buttresses that supported it, forming wide platforms at its top.

"Can you walk to the first platform?" Ragnarvald asked Eirene. "You go first and then the boys. I will go last."

She nodded and set off immediately, walking carefully on the top of the sea wall, crouching down so as to keep her balance. She didn't look down. She didn't want to see the waves crashing on the rocks far below her. Instead, she looked straight ahead of her towards the beckoning safety of the wide platform, and when her shaking legs brought her there, she stopped and turned to look back at them.

Ragnarvald turned to Gregory.

"No! I can't do it," Gregory said. He had always been afraid of heights. "I will fall, I know it."

"I am sorry but you have no choice," Ragnarvald said gently in his thick Norse accent. And, as he said these words, they both looked up and saw that a group of Varangians had appeared through the gateway into the courtyard beneath the steps to the sea walls. And at their head was Rurik.

"Leave this to me. Now, you must go and join your mother. Walk with your head up and don't look to either side of you," Ragnarvald patted his shoulder and turned to walk down the steps, his sword drawn. He called out to the Varangians.

"Brothers! Leave this to me and Rurik. It is a blood feud and Odin will curse you if you try to intervene. Rurik betrayed my father, Ragnar. Respect my blood feud. I have sworn to kill Rurik. Let the Romans leave. They have done you no harm."

The other Varangians looked at Rurik, who just laughed and called out to Ragnarvald:

"Come then, Ragnarvald and meet your death."

The Varangians put their weapons down and backed away from Rurik.

"Go!" Ragnarvald turned and called out to Gregory and Constantine, as he ran down the steps to meet Rurik. But Gregory was transfixed, looking at Rurik, even as Eirene called to him to join her on the platform.

Rurik lost no time in rushing up to Ragnarvald, his sword raised. This time he had the advantage of a shield and chain-mail. Ragnarvald was clutching his bloody side. Gregory could see that he had no hope. Although he parried the first of Rurik's blows, his wound and loss of blood made him slow to meet Rurik's blade as it cut and thrust at him. After holding Rurik back for a few minutes, he turned and ran to the steps.

Rurik raised his sword and shouted out in triumph. But the other Varangians didn't cheer. They looked on in silence. Rurik ran after him. Ragnarvald pointed his sword at Rurik as he backed his way up the stairs towards the top of the sea walls where Gregory stood, holding Constantine's hand.

Ragnarvald glanced up at Gregory. He reached inside his tunic and took out a purse, heavy with coins, and flung it at Gregory.

"Take this and go! Both of you. I will hold him off!"

"Run!" Gregory told his little brother, putting Ragnarvald's purse inside his tunic. Constantine did not have his brother's fear of heights and eagerly darted along the wall to the wider section where Eirene waited. One slip and you would fall. But Constantine made it across.

Still Gregory couldn't run. He looked at the waves churning a hundred feet below him against the bottom of the sea walls. And then he looked at Ragnarvald who was now nearly beside him, still with his sword pointed at Rurik who was climbing the steps after him.

Then Gregory ran. He felt that he was running into open air. The top of the wall was nothing more than a narrow ledge.

He crouched down low as he ran. He wanted to drop to his feet and crawl. He almost closed his eyes he was so keen not to look down. At last, he reached the wide section where Eirene and Constantine were crouching. Eirene grabbed his shaking arm.

They all turned to watch Ragnarvald who had halted at the top of the sea walls, facing Rurik. Ragnarvald retreated a few steps, carefully checking his footing, one arm clutching his bloody side. Rurik followed him to the top of the sea wall and called out, mockingly:

"Ragnarvald, don't back away from me. You can join your father now. In Niflheim, where the traitors and cowards are."

"No, Rurik, that is where you will go. I will live in Valhalla with my father. And you will be our slave."

Then they heard Ragnarvald shout out one word, so loudly that it echoed against the sea walls, and caused the seagulls to jump from their crevices and alcoves scattered among the ancient stones, and flap away, squawking with surprise.

"Odin!"

They saw him drop his sword and throw himself at Rurik. His long, powerful arms grabbed Rurik and they both lost their footing and fell. Their arms grabbed wildly at each other and at the open air, as their feet hit and scraped along the side of the wall. Down and down they went, plunging towards the churning sea. Within a second both of them hit the rocks and their bodies bounced like dolls into the sea.

Gregory watched them fall as if in slow motion. He gazed at their bodies lying in the sea, arms flung out wide, the sea turning red with blood. And as he looked down, he felt giddy. Suddenly his terror of heights returned in a flash and he froze, shaking with fear. He was going to fall.

Then someone grabbed his arm.

"You're alright! You're nearly there! Stay with me!" He

heard the words as if he was in a dream. He didn't know whose words they were. He sank to his knees and looked behind him. It was his mother. Gregory's senses came flooding back to him.

"I'm all right," he said. Eirene told him to follow her and she stood up and ran forward, leading the boys along the walls, which were still terrifyingly high. Eirene led them quickly to the next wide platform and stopped. Gregory was not sure he could carry on. His fear was returning. How much further did they have to go? He looked down along the length of the sea walls. It was too far for him to go.

"I can't go on. I'm sorry," he said.

"Steps. There are steps at the next platform. Just one more to go and we can go down the steps. Do you see them?" Eirene pointed and Gregory saw that there were some steep steps leading down from the next platform.

"Go now. Follow me." Eirene told Gregory. She could see that if he didn't go now, he never would. She pulled his hand. He stood up and followed her, trying not to look at the waves crashing below him or the ground that looked so far away. His heart was pounding as he reached the steps. They were very steep and he held an arm out against the wall to steady him, as he followed his mother. Finally, he jumped with relief down to the ground.

They stopped at the bottom of the steps and looked around. The other Varangians had not followed them. They seemed to have honoured Ragnarvald's blood feud. The harbour looked to be deserted except for the lighthouse behind them, from which wisps of smoke wafted into the blue sky.

Moored within the harbour was a row of fishing boats. Further along were much bigger boats: warships and cargo boats.

They walked along the quay in silence. Ragnarvald's death

and their terrifying escape along the sea walls had left them too stunned to say anything. But Gregory felt safe in this harbour. He knew everything about boats. He had sailed across the Bosphorus to Bithynia many times. He could go there and back in a day. He knew the coastline. He felt a surge of energy flow back into his shaking body. He grabbed Eirene's arm.

"Mother, I can sail one of these boats. We can go to Trebizond, as you said. Please. We can do it."

Eirene nodded at him. She was still too shocked to say much.

"Let us try. God willing," was all she could mutter to him.

They scanned the row of boats. Suddenly they saw they were not alone. Some men were in one of the cargo boats. Tanned faces looked up at them curiously. But they were not threatening. Eirene could see that they were servants stocking one of the boats. She called to them immediately, putting the most authority that she could muster into her voice.

"We want this boat. Has it got provisions in it?"

One of the servants jumped nimbly out of the boat and onto the quay. He could see that she was a noblewoman and bowed deeply to her:

"My lady, the boat has just landed. It has provisions from Bithynia. We have been instructed to bring them to the palace kitchens."

"Get your men out of it and tell them to wait on the quay for the lord Andronicus. Do as I say, otherwise I'll have you punished. Andronicus will be here soon."

When she mentioned Andronicus, the man seemed impressed. He whistled to the two other men in the boat and they jumped out of it onto the land.

Eirene looked at Gregory and said in a hushed tone:

"Can you sail this?"

"Easily! I've sailed to Bithynia hundreds of times. And

you used to tell me off for sailing so far! When it gets dark we can shelter in one of the bays. There are hundreds of them. If they come after us, they'll never find us, I'll make sure of that."

Gregory smiled. He looked at the boat. It was sturdier than a fishing boat but small enough for the three of them to crew. He jumped down onto the deck. It was strewn with great earthenware tubs and amphorae. He looked into one of the amphorae. It was full of cured, salted beef. Another was full of oranges. He laughed. They could feast on these delicacies from Bithynia for weeks!

The servants waited anxiously on the quay as Gregory jumped aboard and pushed the boat away from the quayside with a hook. They knew something was wrong but what could they do? Gregory told his mother and brother to row as he hoisted the two sails with one hand on the rudder. As they reached the harbour mouth he caught a gust of wind in the sails and suddenly the boat sped through the sea. Constantine and Eirene pulled their oars back into the boat and leant back against its sides panting from the exertion of rowing.

"Now leave this to me," Gregory said as he looked at them, smiling broadly. He still felt guilty about his fear of heights and was keen to make up for it.

"Can we really get to Trebizond?" Eirene asked him.

"We've got enough food for a feast! But we'll have to find fresh water. We can come ashore for that and find a stream. It's easy to do."

Gregory pulled the sails to catch the wind. He smiled confidently at his mother and brother. He put his hand over the side of the boat and felt his fingers slice through the water as the boat raced ahead. Already the great buildings of Constantinople were getting smaller in the distance. Another few minutes and they would disappear. He turned his face into the wind and the spray. He thought of his father. He could only remember him in the dim and distant past. What would he be like now? He could not imagine him as a warlord.

They sailed out into the open sea under the brilliant glare of the sun, leaving Constantinople far behind them. They sailed until the sun set and then on into the evening. There was no sign of any pursuers. Eirene wondered if Andronicus was the only one who really wanted to hold them hostage and that the Emperor didn't care. Had it been his last act of spite against her? Well, he had paid for it.

As darkness enveloped them, they found a sheltered bay on the rocky coastline of Bithynia and dropped the boat's copper anchor. Their exuberance at escaping started to fade away and they all felt tired and a little afraid of what lay ahead of them. Eirene said they all should get some sleep now. Gregory said they would be safe here until daybreak.

Gregory stretched himself out in the boat and, as it rocked gently, he thought about Ragnarvald and felt sad that he was dead. He couldn't rid his mind of the image of his body, together with Rurik's, slipping down the side of the sea walls and smashing into the rocks by the sea.

"Who was Ragnarvald?" he asked his mother, taking Ragnarvald's purse from his tunic pocket and opening it. It had five coins in it, two of them gold. He gave it to his mother.

"I don't know," she said flatly, exhausted. "He wanted to avenge his father who died at Manzikert. He saved our lives."

"So, is it true that father's alive?"

"That's what Andronicus said. He has an army. He's the Count of Chaldia."

Gregory remembered his father but it was so long ago that it seemed unreal. He remembered his teaching him to ride. He had been kind and gentle. But since they had returned from their captivity with the Turks he had always been embarrassed about him. The other boys, who he was taught with by the priests in the great palace, taunted him for having a father who was a traitor and an outlaw. Only his mother's noble lineage allowed him to stand up for himself and hit back at them. He was surprised to hear that his father was a count.

"I thought father didn't have a noble title?"

"Only because he was a third son. But his brothers and father were all killed by the Turks."

"So, one day I will have a title?" Gregory felt embarrassed the moment he said this. His face blushed. His mother looked at him slightly disapprovingly, but then she smiled.

"I just hope that we can find him. And that he's alive and well when we do." She was also wondering whether, after all these years, he would be the same man that she had loved.

They said no more and Gregory fell asleep, his head resting on the side of the boat, and he dreamt about his father, imagining a fierce, bearded warlord. He woke up and snuggled up to his sleeping mother and brother for warmth. He fell asleep again, and this time he dreamt that he was Jonah, in the stories he had heard so many times from the priests, sent spinning towards a great storm where the wild sea or a gigantic beast lay waiting to swallow him up.

XXXII

Dark and forbidding, the harbour wall of Trebizond rose into the night sky, its black silhouette blocking out the bright stars as Ashot lifted his head and looked up from the boat. His mind was still racing although the still water calmed him and helped him to make a plan. He had decided to go straight to the main gate. His one hope was that Theodore's capture had distracted the Turks, and indeed the best distraction would be the confession of their original plan. He imagined Theodore being tortured and his heart churned with guilt and pity for him. Surely he or one of his men would have divulged the plan by now? If so, the Turks would be focused on the tunnel, waiting to ambush the Romans as they appeared from it.

He wondered how he could possibly open the gate himself? There were bound to be Turks guarding it even if some of them had been called away to guard the tunnel. He needed to create yet another diversion. Something that would cause the guards at the main gate to leave their posts. But he couldn't think of anything. All he could do was to go to the main gate and see how well-guarded it was.

He rowed to the harbour quay, looking for Turkish guards. But he couldn't see any, so he rowed cautiously right up to the quayside. Standing up in the small boat, he grasped the stone sides. He looked up and around the harbour. It was too dark to be sure but it seemed to be deserted. The Turks must have been so pleased with Theodore's capture that they'd left it unguarded. He hauled himself out of the boat and onto the quayside.

He ran, half crouching so as not to be seen, along the quayside and past the harbour walls. He was in the lower town which was completely walled in and connected to the middle town by a gate. There were warehouses to the left of the quay and a tall, grand customs house that stood proudly in the middle of the square facing the harbour. It seemed to him that he saw them in a dream, devoid of colour in the darkness of the night. This must be what it's like to be dead, he thought.

He ran from house to house, from street to street. Everything was derelict and deserted. Then, through a broken window to his right, he was startled by some movement. A pair of white eyes stared at him, illuminated by the moonlight. And instantly they were gone into the darkness of the house. They weren't the eyes of a Turk, he thought to himself, but probably of a poor starving Roman. One that had not escaped. Or maybe a collaborator. He had better hurry up before the Turks were alerted. Surprise was his only advantage.

The gate to the middle town was open and unguarded. The Turks clearly did not expect any attack from the sea. He went through it and came to the street that led in a straight line to the main city gates.

He continued stealthily along the street until he was close enough to see the crenellations of the city wall. Then he stopped to consider how best to continue without being noticed. Suddenly he heard voices. They were some way off. He rushed through the open doorway of a derelict house. The door had long since disappeared. The inside of the house smelt of decay. It had once been a grand mansion and Ashot found himself in a wide open hall that led onto a courtyard full of the debris of destruction and looting. He glimpsed a long row of amphorae, many of them broken. The occupants of the house seemed to have filled the courtyard with their possessions, probably hoping to save them from the Turks. His foot trod on something and looking down, he jumped back in horror. There was a body on the ground. For a moment he thought it might be alive but then, in the faint light from the moonlit sky, he saw a rigid hand lying outstretched. The skin was tight and withered on the bone.

Ashot knelt by the window, still staring at the corpse. The voices were getting louder. They were Turkish. And it sounded like a large group. Ashot waited. Nervously he drew the dagger from its strap on his leg. When at last they were outside the house he could not resist raising his head to a corner of the window and peering through. He caught a glimpse of a large group of Turks. Presumably they were going to the citadel at the other end of the city. He pushed his back against the stone wall and held his breath. What should he do? He must get to the citadel fast before they killed Theodore. But for now, he knew that all he could do was to continue towards the main gate.

He stepped back onto the street and peered up and down it. It seemed empty. The voices of the Turks were getting fainter in the distance. He moved forward again, darting from one abandoned house to the next until he got a glimpse of the main gate.

He could see that it was hopeless. Half a dozen Turks were standing in front of the gate and many more were on the walls. There was no possibility that he could get to the gate and open it. He squatted behind a wall, looking for inspiration. All he could think of was to throw a stone to divert the Turks' attention but that would clearly not be enough. He had to do something much more spectacular. He could see a herd of Turkish ponies tethered within a fenced enclosure behind the wall and to the right of the gate. If he could stampede them that might be enough to cause the Turks on the ground, if not on the walls, to abandon their posts. But he couldn't see a way of stampeding them. They were obedient and perfectly trained to carry out their riders' commands and used to the ferocity of battle. It would need a fork of lightning from the heavens to frighten them, Ashot thought to himself.

Ashot looked up at the stars hoping for inspiration. But he could think of nothing. Then he remembered Theodore. He would be in the castle now. Every second that he delayed, would be a second of torment for him. A second closer to his death, if indeed he was still alive. Ashot jumped up. He must act quickly. He must make his own lightning. Suddenly he remembered the amphorae in the house with the corpse. What was in them? Was there lamp oil that he could set alight? The Turks had a torch of fire near the gate. He could use that to light something. He ran back to the house.

He ran back through the open doorway. Past the corpse with the outstretched hand and into the courtyard. He looked into the first amphora. There was nothing inside. The next few were smashed. Then he saw that one of them had some liquid inside. Hope welled up inside him, making his heart pound. He put his fingers into the liquid and smelt it. It was olive oil. His hope was crushed. Olive oil wouldn't burn. He checked the other amphorae: they were either broken or had olive oil in them. Ashot cursed and looked around in desperation. The house had other rooms and he went into two more empty ones before he found one that was full of amphorae. He felt sure that they would be full of olive oil. The owner of this house must have been a merchant of the stuff. He felt a strong urge not even to look inside the amphorae. He didn't want to raise his hopes only to have them dashed again.

Yet, when he put his finger into the first of the amphorae, it didn't smell of olive oil. It was lamp oil! There was hope. He looked around the room. Were they all full of it? He checked them one by one, putting his face into the top of each amphora and breathing its odour in deeply. To his delight, he found that all of them were full of lamp oil. The owner of the house must have traded all sorts of oil and stored his supply here hoping to escape the Turks' notice.

Ashot began moving the amphorae which were small enough to be manhandled across the flat floor. As he passed through another room he saw flints to light a fire. He had no need of the Turks' fire now.

He still had to open the gates to the enclosure in which the Turks kept their ponies and he crossed the street carefully and crept towards the wooden palisade. Luck was on his side as he found that the gate was on the side nearest to him and he did not need to risk passing close to the Turks to open it. The ponies looked at him suspiciously. Although they were tethered, he knew that even these war-hardened animals would panic at the sight of fire.

Ashot returned to roll the amphorae out of the house one by one until he had about twenty lined up. Still no one was to be seen. The street had lost its inhabitants years ago and the Turks were all busy in the citadel or manning the walls. He started to pour the oil out of the amphorae, filling the street with a thick liquid, whose smell started to make him feel slightly nauseous. The street sloped down to the main gate and the oil trickled slowly towards it and the horses. He emptied all twenty of the amphorae. He decided that he would need more and rushed back into the house to push the rest of them out onto the street. He worked in a frenzy, worried that the oil would trickle down to the Turks before he could light it. Even in the cold night, sweat poured from him and he gasped for breath. When he had empted another dozen amphorae into the street, he ran back into the house for one of the lighters. He knelt and, with shaking hands, tried to strike a spark onto the sea of oil covering the street. The flint was cold and created only a few sparks at first, before its metal was warmed by the friction, and it produced a sparkling flash. The oil in front of him caught fire with a pale blue flame which spread, like an incoming wave on a beach, down the street.

He could see the ponies starting to rear and try to break free from their tethers. He could see the Turks shouting and starting to run towards the ponies and the strange blue flame that was advancing on them. But he didn't stay looking for long. He knew this was his chance. He crept down the street.

He peered around the corner of a building. The gate was deserted. The Turks had all run to their ponies. He ran forward to the gate. It was secured by two huge wooden beams that ran across both sides of the gate. Normally it would take two men to lift them. Ashot struggled to manhandle the first beam out of its holders. He had nearly done it, when he heard something behind him and turned to see a Turk sprinting towards him.

He reached for his sword and drew it as the Turk drew his own sword and circled him.

But the man was quick. He threw himself at Ashot who realised he'd forgotten how to fight. He retreated back against the gate and the Turk's sword smashed into the wood above his head. Jumping aside, he slashed at the Turk who took the blow on his shield and swung his sword at him again. Ashot had no shield and he had to duck down below the Turk's sword. As he did, the Turk's sword embedded itself in the wooden gate. The Turk jumped back without his sword. With all his strength, Ashot swung his sword against the Turk and it cut through his wooden shield and into his arm. The man screamed and Ashot kicked him and hacked at him as he squirmed on the ground. The screaming stopped.

Ashot rushed back to the gate and lifted the last beam off its holder, and with all his strength, for the gates were huge, he swung them open and shouted into the darkness.

"Nicephorus!"

Ashot looked up to see Nicephorus in full armour on horseback, holding a shield up to protect him, charging towards the gate. He looked behind him. He saw Turks running towards him. He leapt through the gate, as arrows hissed past him, and stood with his back against the stone wall.

The Turks charged towards the gate but the Romans had got through first. Nicephorus lowered his spear and drove it straight through a Turk's chest so that he fell to his knees, his hands clutching the spear. Foot soldiers, following Nicephorus, hacked down the other Turks around him. The gate was theirs.

"Take the walls first!" Ashot shouted at Nicephorus who reined in his horse as hundreds of his soldiers streamed through the gates.

"How did you open the gate?" Nicephorus asked.

"It was a miracle! We need to move fast. We need to get to the castle. Theodore might still be alive. Tell the men to follow me!"

Ashot jumped on a spare horse, and led them up the street where the lamp oil had now burnt itself out. The men shouted their war cry and followed him through the dark, derelict town. The Turks in their confusion had fled to the castle and left the gate to the upper town open.

Ashot rode unopposed into the upper town, where the tall walls of the castle rose before them in defiance of their claim to final victory.

But the Turks were waiting for them. The air was suddenly thick with Turkish arrows. One thudded into Ashot's shield. Several of the horsemen around him fell. Horses and riders sprawled to the ground.

"Get back! Get back under cover!" Ashot shouted, as he jumped from his horse, arrows still flying all around him.

They scrambled to find cover behind the houses and buildings around the square in front of the castle gates.

"Dismount and let the horses loose," Ashot told Nicephorus. "We can't use them here."

They looked up at the tall towers of the castle. Behind them the sky was turning red as dawn began to break. How could they rescue Theodore? Without siege machinery they stood no chance of storming the walls. He leant back against the wall of the house, thinking what to do.

Nicephorus put his head in his hands.

"It's hopeless," he said. "All we can do is to keep the castle surrounded and starve them out."

"No, we must take the castle now," Ashot told him. "Get all of the infantry in front of the main gate with a battering ram. And bring the liquid fire. We'll get the gate burning and then smash it in."

Nicephorus nodded. It would be a fight to the finish – to save Theodore.

Just then one of the infantry officers came running. He was covered in sweat and blood. He gasped for breath as he said: "We've cleared the town. We killed all those bastard Turks. We took no prisoners."

Ashot grasped his shoulder. "I need you to go to Onemissus at the tunnel. Tell him to advance down it. But tell him to be prepared to meet the Turks. Tell him this."

The Roman archers shot volleys of arrows at the Turks above the gate to cover Ashot as he led forward a group of men armed with clay grenades filled with combustible oil.

The Turks ducked behind the battlements as the archers shot at them but the moment the Roman arrows had smacked against the stone walls, the Turks raised their heads and took aim at Ashot and his men. The air was thick with arrows from both sides. A man screamed on Ashot's right. Ashot rushed forward, holding his shield high to ward off the arrows that slammed into it. As he got within reach of the gates, he dropped his shield and hurled his clay grenade. It broke against the wood. Then dozens more smashed against the gate, drenching it with oil.

"Back! Fall back!" Ashot cried out to his men as he retreated and Roman archers shot burning arrows into the gates, which burst into flame. But Ashot knew that they didn't have time to wait for the gates to burn through. He called for the battering ram.

Dozens of men grasped the battering ram, a simple tree trunk with a sharpened end, as they carried it towards the gate while others held shields aloft to ward off the arrows. Arrows sped and hurtled towards it, like a swarm of angry bees, as Ashot urged the men on, holding his shield high to draw the fire of the Turkish archers away from the battering ram.

A deadly duel was fought between the Roman archers behind the battering ram and the Turkish archers above the gate. Men screamed and fell as they were hit. Turks plunged from the wall. Ashot seemed oblivious to the rain of arrows all around him, and miraculously he was unscathed, as he called out to the mass of men around the battering ram, some of whom stumbled and fell with arrows piercing through helmets and chainmail.

The battering ram was getting closer. Ashot reached the gate which was was blackened and burning and called to the men to charge at it. The Turks above them were leaning over the battlements to get a better shot. Ashot looked up and saw a Turk falling from the wall, arrows stuck in his body.

The smouldering gates shook as the battering ram smashed into them. Ashot's voice rang out above the din of battle, shouting commands to pull the battering ram back and then to swing it forward.

The Turks were shooting everything they could at the men who heaved the wooden trunk backwards and forwards into the shuddering gate. The Roman archers were now behind the battering ram, restringing their bows as fast as they could, desperately trying to hit the Turks as they leaned forward to shoot at their attackers.

Then there was a great crack and the gates buckled wide. The men took the battering ram back as Ashot called to them to swing it forward for one last massive push. The gates burst open.

But the Turks were waiting behind. Massed Turkish archers let loose a barrage of arrows. The soldiers at the front of the battering ram fell, covered with arrows. Ashot jumped through the gates, calling his men on.

An arrow screeched past his head. Then, he saw Turks running past their archers towards him. They were heavily armed. He crouched down, ready for them, his shield up. Suddenly, he felt a searing pain in his chest and the wind was knocked out of him. He was shocked to see the shaft of an arrow sticking out of his chest. He tried to grip it but his strength was leaving him. He tasted blood in his mouth and found that he couldn't breathe. Gasping, he looked up from the ground and saw an axe swinging at his head. It moved in slow motion. He wanted to shout but there was no sound.

XXXIII

Eirene looked past her son, Gregory, at the small stone jetty that protruded invitingly out into the calm blue water of the cove. It was a little harbour, whose curved strip of sand should have had fishing boats beached on it. But it was empty except for some wooden planks scattered on the sand, lying there discarded, with blue paint cracked and peeling.

"It looks deserted," she said to Gregory.

"Hard to say," he replied, as he looked beyond the jetty to some stone houses. One of them was clearly missing its door. There was no sign of life at the moment but how could they know who might be lurking hidden inside them?

"Look, there's a well." Eirene pointed at a circular stone wall that rose from the bed of a stream, a few yards from the jetty. The stream was dry now that it was summer.

"It's our best hope," she said.

They had left Constantinople a week ago and still had provisions left from the ample cargo in the boat. Water was their problem. The boat had amphorae of wine but no water.

At first, it had not been too difficult to find enough water. When they had crossed the Bosporus to Bithynia, they were still well within Roman territory and could land in coves and beaches without fear of attack from the Turks. And the Ducas family did not seem to have sent any ships in pursuit of them so that Eirene wondered if it had only been Andronicus who had wanted them arrested.

So far, they had managed to find just enough water in streams and wells but now they were critically short. They had half an amphora of clean water left, and the three of them hadn't drunk a drop so far that morning. They must find water today.

"The Turks could be anywhere," Gregory said. His little brother, Constantine, nodded in agreement as he always did.

"I know," Eirene said. "We still don't know where we're going. All we know is what Andronicus said: that Theodore has an army in Chaldia and that he's trying to recapture Trebizond. But we can't sail into Trebizond until we know that it's in our hands."

Whenever she spoke about Theodore, it lifted their spirits. Just to be talking about him again seemed like a miracle.

"Look, we know that Trebizond must be within a few days' sailing. When we get nearer, let's try to land and find out what's happening. We're certainly better off in this boat than we are on land. It's fast and I can outrun pretty much anything," Gregory said proudly.

"And the Turks can't sail," Eirene said. They had met less and less shipping as they followed the coastline eastwards. Around Bithynia they had seen plenty of cargo boats, fishing boats and the occasional dromon, as the warships were called. But in the last couple of days they hadn't seen any vessels at all. The Turks had laid waste the sea as much as they had the land.

"Come on, let's dock at the jetty and I'll go to the well. We've got to have water or we can't go anywhere," Gregory said. He was excited now. The thought of his father had given him new energy. He put his hand on the dagger at his belt. It made him feel braver.

"All right," Eirene said. "Constantine, I want you to look

out for anyone you can see. Gregory, you go and see if there's water in the well. If there is we'll take the buckets and fill as many amphorae as we can."

They rowed the boat to the far end of the jetty and Gregory jumped ashore. There was still no sign of anyone. He looked at the houses. Surely if anyone was in them they would have come out by now? He walked down the jetty, leaving Eirene and Constantine in the boat. There was no sound. He reached the well and peered into it. It was too dark to see if there was water at the bottom. He turned and ran back.

"Give me a bucket. I can't see if there's any water."

He returned and lowered the bucket into the well. The rope went quite a way down and then he heard a splash. He let the bucket sink and then hauled it back up, his arms feeling the strain of the water's weight.

Eirene watched him and then started to walk down the jetty with an amphora. He motioned to her to stop.

"Let me just check that no one's here," he called to her, pointing at the houses.

He scanned the houses. There were three of them. Stone fishermen's houses with thick walls around a single room. He felt a presence in them but they looked empty. He needed to check.

He went up to the one without a door and peered in. It was pitch black inside and he couldn't see anything at first. He waited for his eyes to adjust to the dark. After a few moments, forms became visible. A smashed table. Bits of wood. Rusting lobster pots. The place had been abandoned. The Turks must have been here a long time ago.

Gregory went to the house opposite it. There was a weather-beaten wooden door, slightly ajar. He pushed it open, more confidently this time.

As he stepped inside, an arm grabbed him around the neck.

"Be quiet or you're dead," a voice growled at him.

He stayed totally still. The man grabbed his hand which was holding his knife.

"Drop it!"

He did. He turned to face the man. Bloodshot eyes set in a bearded face, lined and scored from the weather, glowered fiercely at him. He looked quite old, perhaps in his fifties.

"Come with me," he grunted at Gregory in a rough Greek dialect. He was clearly a Laz, one of the ancient inhabitants of the Pontus who had lived there before the Greeks came, and for centuries had been an under-class.

The man pushed him outside into the light. With his knife against Gregory's throat, he moved him towards the well. Eirene stared at them, frozen on the jetty. Constantine looked up from inside the boat.

The Laz manhandled Gregory past the well and onto the jetty, where he stopped and yelled at Eirene:

"Give me the boat or I'll slit his throat!"

"The boat's yours," Eirene called back. "Don't harm him."

The man pushed past her, still holding Gregory.

"Are you a Christian?" she said to him. "Have you no fear of God? We mean you no harm. You can have our boat but please don't harm him."

The man pushed Gregory ahead of him towards the boat.

"We have money. I can give it to you," Eirene called after them.

The man stopped and looked back at her. He guessed that her offer was a trick.

"Get the other one out of the boat!" he snapped at her.

Eirene called to Constantine who jumped ashore obediently.

The Laz held onto Gregory as he edged closer to the boat. Then the thought of the money made him stop.

"How much money have you got?"

"More than two solidi," she said, knowing that this was the fortune of a lifetime for a peasant like this.

"Show it to me," he said.

"Only if you let us go and leave us with the boat."

She took Ragnarvald's purse from her tunic, opened it, and held out a handful of coins, two of them gold.

The Laz gazed at the money. It was worth more than the boat, and it would be easier to run away with the money than to sail the boat, when the three of them could try to stop him leaving.

"Okay. You keep the boat and I'll take the money."

"I'll throw the purse over there," Eirene pointed to the start of the jetty. "Leave my son and go to pick up the money."

The Laz hesitated for a second.

"No, I'll take him with me."

Then the Laz reeled from a savage push. It was from Gregory who had taken a desperate gamble, sensing that the Laz was distracted by this conversation, and also frightened by the thought that he would not be released even when the man got the money.

It worked or it seemed to. The Laz lurched sideways, lost his footing and fell. His knife flew from his hand into the water.

Eirene ran forward. She had drawn Andronicus' knife, the one she had used to kill him, and pointed it at the man.

"Now, run for your life and don't come back."

The man looked up at her. He was furious and, without saying anything, he started to heave himself to his feet.

Afraid that he might attack his mother, Gregory kicked him as hard as he could but the man grabbed his leg and they both fell to the ground. Gregory punched him and struggled but the man was much stronger and lifted himself up until he sat astride Gregory, pinning him down with his leg across his chest.

Then, just as he was about to punch Gregory's face, Gregory saw him gasp and try to stand up, reaching behind his back.

Gregory shoved him aside and crawled out from underneath him. He looked up and saw his mother behind the Laz. She had planted her knife into his back.

The Laz gazed up in terror as he struggled to reach the knife. Blood was now coming out of his mouth. He started to choke and writhe on the ground. Then his breath came in gurgles, blood pouring from his mouth. He lay back, his hands twitching, his open eyes staring up at them.

All three of them were shaking with shock.

"Quickly, let's get the water," Eirene said.

They didn't want to touch the Laz's body but Eirene retrieved her knife from his back. They filled ten amphorae with water, enough to last several days.

"Where do we go now?" Gregory asked as they pushed the boat off from the jetty.

"There's only one place we can go," she said. "Trebizond. Even if the Turks still have it, it'll be no worse than anywhere else." She felt like saying that their own people were as bad as the Turks.

And she didn't need to say what they all desperately hoped: that Theodore had recaptured Trebizond.

XXXIV

It was over. There was nothing more that he could do.

Theodore's arms were locked in manacles hung from a beam and his feet just touched the ground. His half naked body was bruised and bloodied, and one eye was so swollen that he couldn't see out of it.

They had been caught shortly after they landed. Theodore and the two others had left their boat to swim ashore. At first, their plan had worked because the harbour was large, and since the Turks weren't expecting an attack by sea, there were only a couple of guards who at first didn't spot their heads above the water in the dark. But the guards saw them when they climbed onto the quayside and made a dash for the customs house. More Turks appeared and although they split up and tried to escape, all three of them were captured. One of them was killed on the spot. Theodore and the other survivor were taken to the citadel.

Theodore closed his eyes in despair. When he opened them, he was startled. There, before him, was Afsin. He stood, arms crossed, and with a broad smile on his face. Then Afsin called forward a dark-skinned Arab and spoke a few words to him in Turkish. The Arab turned to Theodore and spoke to him in the accented Greek of the Levant.

His question left him bewildered.

"Where is Eirene?"

"I don't know," Theodore croaked through cracked lips. He was too tired to feel the hatred that normally tormented him when he thought of what Afsin must have done with her. He stared blankly at Afsin.

"Is she alive?" Afsin asked through the voice of the Arab. His own voice was surprisingly calm.

"I think so. I hope so."

Theodore frowned. It was as if Afsin cared for her. The thought digusted him.

"But you'll never see her again." He spat the words at Afsin. "She escaped to the west."

"Who knows whether I will see her again," Afsin said mysteriously. "But there is one thing that Allah has willed my friend, and that is that you will never see her again."

When the Arab had finished speaking these words, Theodore said nothing. He knew that Afsin was right.

Afsin paced the ground in front of him, backwards and forwards.

"What did you come here to do? Was it to open the main gates?"

Theodore did not reply. This was his last chance. He had to think of something that wouldn't give their plan of attack away. But his mind was blank. He couldn't think of a deception that would sound convincing.

Afsin took a spear and put the sharp point against his stomach, ready to rip it open.

"No," Theodore muttered. He couldn't think of anything else to say.

This reply only irritated Afsin. He slammed the length of the spear across Theodore's ribs. The blow winded him and he gasped in pain, panting for breath. He knew that he didn't have long to live. Suddenly, in desperation, an idea sprang to mind. He knew it might give their plan of attack away but it was all he could think of.

"There's a tunnel!" he croaked.

"What tunnel?"

"There's a tunnel beneath us. I can lead you there. I came here to open the tunnel and take the fortune of gold that's buried there. It's my father's fortune. He hid it there. If I take you to it will you let me live?"

Afsin looked pleased. He didn't reply to Theodore but he told his guards to unlock the manacles from his hands. The Turks quickly unshackled Theodore and tied his hands together in front of him. Afsin told him to lead them to the tunnel.

The Turks clearly had no idea that the tunnel existed. And Theodore hadn't been there since that day when he had led Ashot to safety about fifteen years ago.

He led them down the stairwell into the basement of the citadel. He looked around the huge, low-ceilinged chamber which had a rancid smell of damp. He remembered it perfectly but he couldn't see the iron plate which covered the entrance to the tunnel. Had it been sealed up?

He rushed to the corner where he thought he remembered it but there were just slabs of stone there. Of course! He realised that this must have been his father's idea to conceal the entrance. He pushed the stone slabs and they moved. They had not been mortared in. But they were heavy and needed several men to move them. The Turks rushed to help him.

When they had pushed them away, Theodore saw the iron cover underneath, and the Turks lifted it up.

The entrance to the tunnel was just as he remembered it. Wooden steps descended into the pitch black darkness. Afsin told one of the Turks to take a flaming torch and climb down the steps into the tunnel. Theodore moved to follow him but Afsin grabbed his shoulder. He gestured for more Turks to enter ahead of Theodore who realised that he had no chance of making a run for it. Then Afsin gave Theodore a push and he too climbed down the steps into the darkness, following the glow from the Turks' torches.

They walked down the tunnel. The natural fissure through the rock had been beautifully chiselled to make a rectangular passageway. Theodore looked at the ground, and in the half-light, he could just make out a beautiful mosaic floor, with a geometric pattern of black squares and triangles on a white background. The last time he had been in the tunnel with Ashot it had been so dark he had scarcely noticed it.

Afsin gave him a jab in his back.

"Where does this lead?"

Theodore pointed ahead of him. He remembered that Xenophon's porphyry disc was about half way along the tunnel. They would be there soon.

Finally, Theodore saw it. The picture of an ancient warrior with a round shield held up and a spear thrust forward just as he remembered. And next to it was the huge porphyry disc that he had noticed all those years ago, within which large white mosaics had been inserted to spell the word Xenophon.

"My father's fortune is buried beneath this disc," Theodore said wearily. "You must break the mosaics to find it."

Theodore's mind was racing. He knew that Onemissus was probably close but not close enough to rescue him. The entrance to the tunnel was about a quarter of a mile away. When the Turks broke the mosaic and found nothing there, Afsin would probably kill him on the spot. He desperately hoped that Onemissus might hear the noise they were making and advance up the tunnel. But he knew that this was just a hope.

Afsin ordered a pickaxe and spades to be brought. As they waited, Theodore looked around him, wondering whether he could make a run for it. But there were too many Turks ahead of him in the tunnel.

Finally, the equipment arrived, and a Turk raised a pickaxe and brought it down on the beautiful porphyry disc, shattering it into fragments. The Turk kicked the broken pieces away with his foot. Impatiently, Afsin pushed the man aside and bent down to clear away the fragments with his own hands. Theodore knew that his deception was about to be discovered. He was sure that there was nothing beneath the disc and was getting ready to make a desperate run down the tunnel. But then he stopped himself as he stared in disbelief.

For he saw that Afsin had uncovered a large golden ring recessed into a stone slab beneath the porphyry disc. Theodore looked at it, astonished. It was the last thing he had expected. What was it that Xenophon had left in Trebizond? A secret chamber?

Delighted with his find, Afsin jumped up.

He grabbed an axe from one of his men and inserted the shaft through the golden ring as a lever to lift up the stone slab. He was just about to heave the slab up when a Turk ran to them, breathless and shouting:

"Afsin bey, the Romans are here. They've taken the town. They're outside the castle!"

Afsin dropped the axe and stared at the man.

"What! How did they get in?"

"They broke through the main gate of the middle town. Now they're battering against the gates of the citadel."

Afsin spun round to face Theodore.

"We'll take him with us! We'll put him in front of the gates. They can batter him to death first!"

Theodore's mind was too dazed to take it all in. Was it really true that his army had taken the town? But he knew one thing. It was now or never.

He shouted at the top of his voice: "Onemissus!"

With his hands still tied together in front of him, he

delivered a ferocious punch to the Turk beside him. The man keeled over, and pushing the next Turk aside, Theodore ran down the tunnel into the pitch black darkness as fast as he could.

He ran shouting out Onemissus's name until he saw the glow of torches ahead of him and heard the clatter of men in armour running.

Onemissus came into sight.

"My lord, are you hurt? Where are the Turks?"

"Behind me! Cut me free and give me a sword!"

Onemissus cut the rope from Theodore's hands with his sword.

"We must move quickly! The Turks will block the tunnel unless we push them back now."

Onemissus called his men to follow him and they ran forward. Theodore grabbed a sword and shield and ran with the rest of his men. But they met a hail of Turkish arrows. Onemissus, who was leading the charge, fell to the ground with an arrow sticking from his throat.

"In the name of the lord, charge!" Theodore shouted, stepping over Onemissus. He glimpsed blood pouring from his mouth and panic stricken eyes looking up at him but he knew there was no time to help him.

The Romans at the front smashed into the Turks.

Several of the Turks were floored as the Romans pushed them back. Theodore swung his sword at one of them in a brutal blow. The man screamed but not for long. Yet there was a weight of Turkish warriors that slowed the Roman advance. Theodore knew that Afsin would defend the tunnel with as many men as he could. He turned round and called to an officer behind him:

"Where's the liquid fire? We need it now!"

The officer shouted at the mass of soldiers filling the tunnel behind them.

"Fall back! Prepare for the liquid fire!"

The trumpet called the retreat and the soldiers at the front edged back, their shields held high to ward off the Turkish blows. Soldiers carrying the clay grenades squeezed through the mass of men to reach the front.

A hail of clay grenades was thrown at the Turks. The liquid within them was not ignited but when it hit the flaming torches, it exploded into a lethal rain of liquid fire, scalding and burning all those around it. The Turks' wooden shields caught fire and they stumbled backwards as they struggled to release their hands from the straps.

Theodore led his men as they charged into the Turks who fell back and started to break and run for their lives, stampeding back down the tunnel, dropping their torches so that darkness added to their confusion.

Theodore led his men after them, killing those who had fallen, until he saw Afsin.

Afsin had rallied his men around him, striking down those that tried to flee. He turned to face the Romans in a last desperate attempt to force them back down the tunnel. His eyes fell on Theodore.

"Gabras!" he shouted out.

His intention was clear: single combat. The Turks shrank back to make room as Afsin strode forward to meet Theodore. Theodore tensed himself. He had no armour, only his sword and shield. Afsin was quick. His sword smashed across Theodore's shield, and the force of the blow pushed him onto one knee.

Theodore held his shield up as Afsin grasped his sword with both hands and hacked furiously at him. With each blow the shield's metal cover was dented. Theodore held it up desperately to meet Afsin's sword, knowing that it could buckle at any moment.

Crouching down as he met his hammer blows, Theodore

felt his hatred for Afsin well up inside him. He thought of what he had done to his family. He rose to his feet, his legs filled with a desperate surge of energy.

But Afsin still had the advantage. He brought his sword down on Theodore's shield in a lightning blow. Theodore couldn't hold the blow and he staggered back, falling on the ground. Afsin raised his sword to smash it down on his prone body. As Theodore looked up, he saw Afsin's sword coming straight at his head. He squirmed sideways and heard a metallic screech as Afsin's sword hit the hard stone floor within an inch of his face.

The force of Afsin's blow gave Theodore a second in which to hit back at him. As Afsin was lifting his sword, Theodore sprang to his feet and kicked him in his side, sending him staggering sideways. Theodore still had his sword and, in desperation, he swung it wildly at Afsin's shield.

Afsin's shield was the type of small, light shield that the Turks liked to use on horseback and Theodore's blow forced him to stagger back. Theodore was quick. He grasped his sword in both hands and, with all his strength, he brought it down again on Afsin's shield. There was a scream. The shield had buckled and split open. Afsin's furious eyes looked in horror at his arm. Theodore's sword had sliced his hand off. Blood was spurting on the floor. Afsin gazed at Theodore with hatred and raised the sword in his right hand to stab it into Theodore's chest.

But Theodore dodged Afsin's sword. He turned and, with his sword clasped in both his hands, he swung it with all his might against Afsin. It sliced through his left shoulder and into his torso, above the bloody stump of his arm. Theodore saw Afsin's innards exposed, pulsating organs, covered in blood. Afsin's eyes rolled as he tried to focus on Theodore. Then he pitched forward, headlong onto the hard stone floor.

The Romans shouted in triumph and charged forward. The Turks turned and fled.

After that, they made their way out of the tunnel and fought their way room by room towards the citadel gates. Theodore's knowledge of the citadel was essential in leading them by the quickest route. But even so the Roman losses were high. The Turks knew they were trapped and fought savagely. Theodore fought as if in a dream. He was exhausted but he kept on going until they met Nicephorus's men who had battled their way through the main gate.

The last surviving Turks in the citadel's main tower surrendered soon afterwards. They had lost the battle and their leader but they were still alive and they threw their weapons down and filed down from the citadel's tower.

"How did you get in through the main gate?" Theodore asked Nicephorus.

"It was Ashot. He rowed into the harbour and opened the gate for us. Just as you had planned to do."

Theodore stood speechless.

"Ashot? But how did he do it? Where is he?"

"Dead. He died fighting in the gateway to the castle. He brought us victory today."

Theodore could only stare at Nicephorus. There were no words to say.

XXXV

Days later, Theodore stood in a field of grass overlooking the city. They were burying their dead in hundreds of graves that they had dug that morning.

In spite of their victory, he felt weary with life. His men shouted his name in triumph but they were weary too. Victory had come at a high price. Half of his army of two thousand had been killed or severely injured. Ashot was dead, as was his general Onemissus. Trebizond was such a ruin that it seemed almost unimaginable that it could ever be a city again.

When they had buried the dead, Theodore went to the castle. He walked through its rooms, up the stairs to the chamber where he had been held prisoner. Blood still stained the stone floors but the castle was empty now, and the battle that had waged through its labyrinthine passageways seemed to belong to another age. He remembered its bustle and commotion on that evening when he had first seen Romanus, Andronicus and Ashot. Now there was a deathly stillness, as his footsteps echoed under the tall ceilings, that made him unutterably sad. He knew that he still had something to do but he couldn't remember what it was.

Suddenly, it came back to him: it was Xenophon's secret chamber. He wanted to know what was in it.

It was late afternoon already, and his body ached from the battle but he forced himself to go down the stairwell to the basement chamber. He looked around him and took in for the first time its shambolic condition. The Turks had used it for storage and shelter, and he found a chaotic collection of casks of wine and oil, sacks of grain, baskets of rotting fruit, cauldrons for cooking and discarded saddles, handcarts, spears and shields. He had taken a torch with him and he descended down the steps into the tunnel where he saw again the beautiful mosaic floor, with its geometric pattern of black squares and triangles on a white background. Now it was blackened from the battle, with fire-marks from the liquid fire in some places, and everywhere it was covered in dirt and debris.

He went to find the porphyry disc that had been shattered and cracked. There it was: the golden ring recessed into the stone slab which Afsin had tried to lift before he was called away by Ashot's desperate attack. He leant forward and cleared away the debris and put his hand on the ring.

He had brought a thick wooden spear shaft, which he had picked up among the Turkish debris, to lift it up. He put the shaft through the ring and heaved the stone up. It was not mortared in and he could lift it and push it to one side. He peered down into the blackness, expecting to see an array of gold and precious objects beneath him, not that he cared whether there was treasure there or not. But to his surprise, there seemed to be nothing at all. Carefully, he lowered himself into the underground chamber, and taking the torch, he held it in front of him and peered around him.

What he saw was a long chamber, maybe thirty feet long by ten feet wide. It was partly a natural fissure in the rock, as the tunnel itself was, but it had been chiselled out to make a symmetrical room. Hanging on the wall all around him were half a dozen sets of weapons and armour: breastplates, helmets, greaves, shields, swords and spears. They were all of an ancient type utterly unknown to him.

In the centre of the chamber was a huge stone sarcophagus, large and high sided with a lid. On its sides was carved a relief of men in battle fighting strange and frightening creatures.

He put his hands on the sarcophagus. The stone was icy cold. He felt the lid. It was heavy but with two hands he could lift it up. He grasped one side and lifted it gently. But he could only see blackness within. So, he pushed the lid over until there was a gap that he could put the torch to. Within the smooth stone carved hollow, he could see skeletons lying side by side.

He looked around him. There was nothing else in the chamber. No piles of gold coins or precious stones. Then his attention was caught by a gold box hanging in the centre of the far wall, away from the weapons and armour. He reached up and unhooked it. He looked at it. It was a beautiful object, with an intricate design, not of Greek origin but of some oriental-looking craftsmanship with lions and elephants depicted among tall trees. He could open it with ease and inside he saw there were papyrus sheets, perfectly preserved, with beautiful black writing in Greek. In the dim light he could just read them, words that had been written nearly fifteen hundred years ago.

The sea! The sea!

We have come so far to find this place. And now the sea will take us home.

I have no fear of the gods any more. Only fear of what we may do in the name of the gods. When I travelled to Persia, I believed that my fate was to prosper in war. For I had been to consult the oracle at Delphi and the priestess there had told me that the gods would favour me.

But they did not. Eighteen months of warfare. Eighteen months of suffering and death. In this tomb lie my companions. We were betrayed by the Persians. Instead of giving us gold, they tried to make us into prisoners. We escaped and fought our way here to Trebizond, over ten thousand stadions, through forests, mountains and ravines. We fought the iron-clad Persians and the wild mountain barbarians. We defeated them all. The Persian horsemen fell before our spears. Our shield wall was never broken. We outran the wild tribesmen of the mountains and captured their hill-forts. The gods had abandoned us. But we were invincible.

Xenophon

That night, Theodore went to sleep in the castle. He had a fitful, uncomfortable sleep in which he dreamt of the day that Xenophon and the ten thousand had first seen the sea in the place in the mountains that he had stumbled on a few years ago. In his dream, he saw Xenophon embracing his men and saying:

"The sea! The sea!"

He awoke just before dawn, not knowing where he was. Then he remembered his dream and Xenophon's words. Hurriedly he put on his clothes and rushed to the top of the battlements to look at the sea. What made him feel such urgency, he did not know. In the first light of dawn, he looked out. The sea was choppy in the wind. White foam broke on the churning waves. The wind blew coldly.

In the half-light, he ran down to the deserted, derelict harbour and looked out at the sea, its waters growing angrier as the wind rose. He thought of Xenophon's words. But for him there was nothing there.

And then over to his left, in the far distance, he glimpsed a boat. It had a white sail. It looked like a small cargo boat. He squinted at it. Slowly it was coming closer. He saw a few figures on the boat. He wondered if they were lost too. Like him.

He jumped to his feet to get a better view, and rushed down to the end of the pier where the old lighthouse stood derelict and ruined. The boat was getting closer. Someone was sailing it expertly. Its sail caught every gust of wind as it sped towards the harbour. He squinted to see who was in it but the figures were too far away to be more than a blur.

The clouds were heavy and the light was poor but he stayed watching, entranced by this strange apparition, and then as the boat came closer, he thought for a moment that he could see Eirene, looking intently at the shoreline. He cursed himself for having such an absurd thought. He carried on looking. Suddenly he knew that it was her. He looked at the other people in the boat. There seemed to be two boys, one almost a man, standing tall and confident as he held the boat's rudder and scanned the shore. Who were they? Then he realised.

He dropped to his knees and tears fell from his eyes. He was overcome by great sobs that shook his body.

But it was no time to cry. Quickly he jumped to his feet and wiped his tears away. He waved at the boat until they noticed him and waved back. Still waving, he looked for a rope to throw out to these smiling faces.

EPILOGUE

This man, Theodore Gabras, came originally from Chaldia. An aristocrat, he was also a famous soldier, of exceptional intelligence and bravery. Whatever he attempted, he was almost always successful, and he was victorious in all his wars. After capturing Trebizond he regarded the city as his own property and was invincible.

Anna Comnena, the Alexiad

HISTORICAL NOTE

Mark Twain said that 'truth is stranger than fiction'. While I have tried to keep closely to historical 'truth' in this novel, there is a great deal that is simply unknown, where fiction has to take over. One of the greatest difficulties in imagining what really happened in the past is that the truth may be so extraordinary that it is impossible to imagine. In this novel, I hope that my imagination is both extraordinary enough and ordinary enough to seem plausible.

In the sections below, I describe what is true and what is fictitious in this novel.

Theodore and Eirene

Relatively little is known about Theodore Gabras except that he became an important political and military leader after his recapture of Trebizond in 1075. During the next twenty-three years, he ruled Trebizond quasi-independently from Byzantine rule in Constantinople, and recovered further territory from the Turks.

His dealings with the Emperor, Alexius Comnenus, are well documented in the Alexiad (see primary sources below) but almost nothing is known for certain of his early life (the subject of this novel). He died fighting the Turks at Theodosiopolis in 1098. He was succeeded by his son,

Gregory. Eirene is thought to have died in 1091 of unknown causes.

After Theodore's death he became the hero of an epic poem (now lost) that was told for hundreds of years after his death, by both the Byzantines and the Turks. He was made a saint of the Greek Orthodox Church in the fourteenth century and documents dating to that time praise his virtue, courage and religious devotion. According to these sources, he was captured by the Turks as he was besieging Theodosiopolis in 1098 and tortured to death, refusing to renounce Christianity.

Trebizond (modern Trabzon)

Trebizond recovered under Theodore's rule from 1075 to become one of the major cities of the Byzantine world. It prospered for centuries as a transit point on the silk road to China and a maritime centre for the Euxine Sea.

After the sack of Constantinople in 1204 by the Fourth Crusade, the Comneni made it the centre of their so-called 'Empire of Trebizond'. It held out successfully against the Turks even after the fall of Constantinople itself in 1453. It finally fell to the Turks in 1461 as the last bastion of the Byzantine Empire.

Even after Turkish occupation, its population remained mainly Greek until the twentieth century when they were forcibly expatriated to Greece at end of the Turkish-Greek war in 1922. There are many impressive Byzantine remains still visible in the modern Turkish city.

Romanus Diogenes, Andronicus Ducas and the Battle of Manzikert

Probably the most controversial character portrayal in this novel is that of Andronicus Ducas. I regard the Byzantine defeat at the battle of Manzikert, which is widely accepted as one of the great turning points in history, as far from being the foregone conclusion that some historians believe. Indeed it is now argued by some scholars that the Byzantine economy was growing in the eleventh century and that the Byzantine state was not in the irreversible decline that the defeat at Manzikert might seem to imply.

I believe that without Andronicus's betrayal at the battle of Manzikert, it is very likely that the battle would have been a 'draw' between the Byzantines and the Seljuks, probably sufficient to have re-established Byzantine military power in the Middle East. This would have had profound implications for both Byzantine and European history, not the least being the removal of the need for the Crusades. One of the most intriguing questions facing Byzantine historians, in my view, is why Romanus allowed Andronicus to command troops at the battle.

I should mention that there is no record that Andronicus tried to betray Romanus at the battle of Tephryce, although we know that he was present, and nor is there any record that he was killed by Eirene! However, we know that he died in 1075 at the time described in this novel, apparently from wounds sustained fighting the Norman mercenary, Roussel.

Turning to the wider analysis of Romanus Diogenes and his troubled reign, I am surprised that there has not been more scholarly analysis of the complex and volatile political environment of the time. It is clear from contemporary sources that his accession to the throne was a radical event and highly divisive in Byzantine politics. On one side, the Ducas family, which was the most powerful Byzantine family at the time, was bitterly opposed to Romanus's accession to the throne, but on the other side, he had considerable support from many members of the Byzantine senate and nobility.

It seems to me that some historians have been too ready to write-off Romanus as one of history's hopeless causes; a man who was simply not up to the challenging task he faced. I think this is perhaps because some of the major contemporary sources are very biased against him and portray him in exactly this fashion (see primary sources below). In particular, the highly regarded Michael Psellus was vehemently hostile to him and ridicules him in his *Chronography*. However, Psellus's views should be taken with a pinch of salt since he was clearly partisan to the Ducas family with whom he enjoyed a close relationship. While less damning than Psellus, the highly regarded Anna Comnena offers no support for Romanus, which again is hardly surprising given that her mother was Andronicus's daughter. These two writers dominate the Byzantine sources for this period and I think their negative views of Romanus have contributed to a rather indifferent view of him from many historians.

More attention should be paid to Michael Attaleiates, in my opinion, who I think is by far the most accurate and reliable source on Romanus, and who is generally very positive about Romanus's intentions and ability as a general, although not without some criticism of his impetuousness and lack of willingness to listen to others, especially in the crucial Manzikert campaign. Attaleiates provides, I think, the most plausible picture of Romanus. He describes him as a charismatic and popular young general before he became Emperor, although reckless enough to raise a revolt for which he was lucky to avoid execution. During his reign, Attaleiates describes how his impulsiveness and lack of control of the political scene in Constantinople caused him to lose much of his popularity. Nevertheless, the Manzikert campaign was a serious and viable attempt to confront the Seljuk threat and Attaleiates clearly attributes Romanus's defeat and capture to Andronicus's treacherous retreat at the most crucial part of the battle. His subsequent description of Romanus's blinding and death at the hands of the Ducases is one of the most moving passages of medieval literature that I have read, and utterly condemns the Ducases as the cause of both Romanus's and the Empire's misfortunes.

Afsin, Alp Arslan and the Seljuks

Afsin's exploits in this novel are entirely accurate insofar as our sources exist. His raids on Amorium, Chonae and his murder of Alp Arslan's hajib, Gemushtegin, are all recorded by Bar Hebraeus (see primary sources below). However, there is no record that he was the Turkish emir who captured Trebizond or that he died there as portrayed in this novel. Indeed, there is no record of what happened to him after the sack of Chonae, or even whether he participated in the battle of Manzikert. Nevertheless, since there is also no record of which Turks captured Trebizond before it was recaptured by Theodore, I think the choice of Afsin is as good as that of any other Turks unrecorded in history. There is of course no record of his infatuation with Eirene.

Alp Arslan's victory at Manzikert is well recorded in Muslim sources in the centuries after the battle although there is no contemporary Muslim account to match that of Michael Attaleiates (see below for primary sources). However, his clemency towards Romanus after the battle became legendary in medieval Muslim literature.

Historians are mostly agreed that Alp Arslan's main political and military aim was to defeat the Fatimids and that he harboured no designs on Byzantium. Indeed, Arab sources indicate that he offered Romanus a truce after Afsin's horrific raids of 1067/68. Somewhat surprisingly, Attaleiates does not mention this truce but most historians think that it did take place and lasted until Erisgen's raid in 1070.

Ashot and the Armenians

Ashot was the grandson of the last Bagratid King of Armenia, Gagik, who abdicated and allowed the Byzantines to annex

Armenia. Nothing certain is known about his life. In addition, very little is known about what happened to the Armenian nobility in this period other than that they seem to have been stripped of their power. The incident described in this novel, when Andronicus deceives and kills several Armenian noblemen, is fictitious but not unlikely in my view.

Ragnar and the Varangians

Ragnar is the only fictitious character in this novel. However, since we have no record of who commanded the Varangian guard in this period, he seems a plausible invention to me.

The Varangians are well documented in Byzantine and Norse sources as an important military unit in this period and became even more important under the Comnenian Emperors. Harald Hadrade was the most famous commander of the Varangian guard when he led it in the 1050s.

Xenophon

Xenophon's flight to Trebizond is recorded in his Anabasis, which is one of the most readable and exciting military adventures in classical literature (similar to Caesar's Gallic Wars). Xenophon is famous as a soldier, philosopher and historian. Opinions about him vary widely but he is one of our main sources on Socrates who he admired passionately.

His philosophical treatises are much simpler than those of Plato but contain moving accounts of Socrates' views and behaviour which may be closer to the real Socrates than those of Plato.

Use of Proper Names

For ease of reading, throughout this novel I have used the Latin spelling of proper names instead of the Greek. For example, I have used Romanus instead of the Greek spelling Romanos.

SOURCES

Primary sources

Michael Attaleiates' *Histories* is by far the most important historical record for this period, in my view. Attaleiates was part of Romanus's entourage for most of the military campaigns and his detailed account (which has, surprisingly, not yet been officially translated into English) is the base source for subsequent, less reliable accounts written by Nicephorus Bryennius (son of the general of the same name present at the battle of Manzikert) and John Scylitzes.

Michael Psellus's *Chronography* is the next most important contemporary account but is so biased against Romanus and lacking in military detail (Psellus was no soldier) that it provides very limited insight into Romanus's campaigns. However, it does provide a very good insight into the Ducas family and the politics in Constantinople.

Anna Comnena's extraordinary *Alexiad,* which is widely acknowledged as one of the great literary works of the middle ages, concerns the period after the battle of Manzikert and offers little commentary about Romanus's reign (since she was Andronicus Ducas's granddaughter, it is also not surprising that she had limited sympathy for Romanus), although it does provide a compelling picture of the desperate state of the Byzantine Empire in the period after Manzikert.

Bar Hebraeus's *Chronography* is the only source providing an account of Afsin's raids from a non-Byzantine perspective but was written half a century afterwards.

Secondary sources

Romanus and the battle of Manzikert

I am always surprised that Romanus's reign and the battle of Manzikert seem to be somewhat under-researched by modern historians, given their pivotal importance in Byzantine history. Claude Cahen and Speros Vryonis have both written extensive analysis of the period but this was done many decades ago. More recently, John Haldon in particular has greatly developed our understanding of Byzantine military history, including the battle of Manzikert, and Carole Hillenbrand has written an impressive analysis of the battle and its significance in the Muslim world. Otherwise, rather surprisingly since he was not a professional historian, the most comprehensive single account of Manzikert has been written some time ago by the distinguished American journalist, Alfred Friendly.

Theodore and Trebizond

My interest in Theodore and Trebizond owes much to Anthony Bryer who has written extensively on the history of Trebizond and the Pontus and has published the only scholarly work on Theodore that I have been able to access. His work enabled me to form an impression of Trebizond as a vibrant Greek city that was remarkable in its ability to eject the Turks after the defeat of Manzikert, and which was subsequently able to resist Turkish encroachment for many centuries. Indeed, it even remained predominantly Greek speaking for many centuries after Turkish occupation. As such, it is a fascinating example of the longevity and power of Greek culture in the Middle East.

GLOSSARY OF BYZANTINE AND TURKISH WORDS

Bey: medieval Turkish term for lord. It has been considerably devalued in modern Turkish to become an ordinary social term for men, similar to mister in English.

Byzantine: this was not a name recognised by the Byzantines, who always called themselves and thought of themselves as Romans, and who did not view the collapse of the Western Roman Empire as marking the end of Roman imperial power. The term Byzantine was invented by French scholars in the eighteenth century.

Caesar: most senior Byzantine title after that of Emperor. Typically awarded by the Emperor to an important political or dynastic ally.

Dromon: Byzantine warship similar to ancient Roman biremes and triremes.

Euxine Sea: Greek and Roman name for the Black Sea.

Excubiti: elite Byzantine cavalry regiment, stationed in Constantinople, and part of the Tagmatic army (see below).

Heavily armoured and equipped with lance and sword (bows had also been carried in earlier centuries but were abandoned by the time of this novel), they had kite-shaped shields, possibly copied by the Normans.

Emir: Arab and Turkish leader, often in this period quasi-independent from the Seljuk and Fatimid Empires.

Fatimid caliphate: Islamic Shi'a Empire which was the main Muslim rival to the Seljuks, based in Egypt and controlling the North African seaboard as well as much of Syria, Jordan and Israel.

Ghulam: generic term for the regular, professional Muslim soldier in the period, serving both in the Seljuk Sultan's army and also in the private armies of independent Arab emirs. They were slave soldiers, mostly Turkish but also Arab and Persian. They were normally more heavily armoured than the Turkomans.

Hajib: high-ranking Arab and Turkish official.

Kadkhuda: Persian term for head man.

Liquid fire: most commonly known today as 'Greek fire', this was a Byzantine incendiary device mostly used in naval battles but also in sieges. Its exact composition is unknown but it is thought to have been oil-based and was shot through siphons at enemy ships or thrown in grenades by foot soldiers.

Logothete: Byzantine high-ranking official, often in charge of civil administration and tax collection, in Constantinople and the provinces.

Mile: Roman miles were still used as units to measure distance in the Byzantine period in addition to other pre-Roman Greek measurements.

Pecheneg: racially similar to the Turks, they were Asian nomads who invaded southern Russia and the Balkans at the time of this novel. However, they seem to have been less militarily effective than the Turks, and were contained and ultimately destroyed by the Byzantines.

Scholae: similar to the Excubiti, an elite Byzantine cavalry regiment, stationed in Constantinople, and part of the Tagmatic army (see below).

Seljuk Sultanate: Turkish dynasty which established a large Muslim Sunni Empire stretching from India to Syria to rival the Shi'a Fatimids. Alp Arslan was the second Seljuk Sultan.

Stadion: ancient Greek unit of measurement, equalling some 600 feet.

Tagmatic army: central Byzantine field army including regiments like the Excubiti, Scholae and Varangians.

Theme: Byzantine term for province. There were over forty Themes at the time of this novel, divided between east and west.

Thematic army: provincial Byzantine regiments. Families were traditionally exempted from government taxation if they provided a soldier for these regiments, although in the eleventh century this practice was abandoned in some Themes, leading to the decline of the thematic armies.

Turkoman: Turkish tribesman from the Asiatic steppes. Seljuk armies mainly consisted of these nomadic horse archers who tended to be quasi-independent and were responsible for the incessant raiding into the Byzantine Empire in the 1060s onwards.

Varangian Guard: elite Byzantine military unit, consisting mainly of Norsemen at the time of this novel, used for both palace guard duty and also as crack troops in battle.

Vestarch: The most senior Byzantine military rank, equivalent in modern terms to a field-marshall.